Gift Horse

>◆<

A Kat Wilde
U.P. Mystery

TERRI MARTIN

Modern History Press

Ann Arbor, MI

Gift Horse: A Kat Wilde U.P. Mystery (Book #1)
Copyright © 2024 by Terri Martin. All Rights Reserved.

2nd Printing – August 2025

ISBN 978-1-61599-839-5 paperback
ISBN 978-1-61599-840-1 hardcover
ISBN 978-1-61599-841-8 eBook

Published by
Modern History Press   www.ModernHistoryPress.com
5145 Pontiac Trail   info@ModernHistoryPress.com
Ann Arbor, MI 48105   Tollfree 888-761-6268 (USA/CAN)

Distributed by Ingram Book Group (USA/CAN/AU)

To all God's Creatures

Especially Horses

The phrase, "don't look a gift horse in the mouth" originates in St. Jerome's commentary in Paul's letter to the Ephesians.

In Latin, the proverb is:

Noli equi dentes inspicere donati
(never inspect the teeth of a given horse).

From Terri Martin

Adult
Kat Wilde U.P. Mysteries
Gift Horse (book #1)
Straw Horse (book #2)

Full Length Novel
Moose Willow Mystery

Short Stories - Humor
Roadkill Justice

High on the Vine: Featuring Yooper Entrepreneurs Tami &
Evi Maki

Church Lady Chronicles: Devilish Encounters

Children's
The Home Wind (age 9+)
Voodoo Shack (age 8+)

Prologue

"Now who's the *liability*?" the woman snarled, swatting at a cloud of gnats. "That stupid rain flooded this so-called trail. Oh, *we'll make it through*, you said. Know what? You're a loser and we're screwed."

"Just shut up, okay?" he said, gritting his teeth. "We're fine. Lots of time. Highway's just over there."

"Yeah? Great. And I suppose we're going to thumb a ride to Maple—whatever that place is, DAMMIT! My shoe's coming off."

"Maple Auto Sales and Service. I think it's just a few miles up the–"

"A FEW MILES!"

"This is the U.P. We can hitch a ride. People are very helpful up here."

"Well that's just perfect. How about we call? Maybe they'll come get us. You know, send a limo."

"No limo. We have a sedan lined up along with our passports."

"What kind of place is this anyway?" she said. "

"They have unique services."

"So *call* them. I can't walk in these shoes. And the bugs— something's crawling up my neck. What the hell's crawling up my neck?!"

"There is nothing crawling up your neck. And we can't call. No cell service out here."

"Of course there isn't. Christ! I just hate this God-forsaken hellhole. Help me up the bank. I'm slipping. And get the goddam thing off my neck."

* * *

A half mile back, Sergeant Tori Haapala saw that the two were going at it. The woman took a swing at the man. He grabbed her arm and jerked her along. The call had come in as a possible domestic around Maki Corners on US Highway 41. Very strange, walking along there, miles from everything. No disabled car in sight. No nearby houses. Haapala flipped on her overheads and braked, sending the cruiser into a bounce.

"Six-one to dispatch, ten-twenty-six."

On the scene.

"Ten-four," dispatch responded.

Haapala watched the two stumbling along the shoulder. This was trouble. When they heard the crunch of tires, the pair jerked around and spotted the cruiser. Both made a feeble attempt to run, but the woman stumbled and fell. The man kept going. An APB alert had just come in on felony suspects—a man and a woman—thought to be fleeing on a Polaris ORV, likely heading east from Peshekee on trail two, adjacent to Highway 41. The off-road vehicles (ORVs), which looked like the love child of a Jeep and golf cart, were ubiquitous on the two-track roads and backwoods trails of Upper Michigan.

Extreme caution. Considered armed and dangerous.

"Hot damn!" Haapala said and snatched her radio mic off the dashboard.

The horses were long gone. I looked around the derelict grounds, which bore little resemblance to the place I'd visited as a child. Winter-dead weeds bobbed in the biting wind broadcasting that nature was reclaiming its territory. Weather-worn outbuildings begged for a fresh coat of paint, or perhaps just a can of gasoline to end the suffering. Across the rutted parking lot, a decrepit mobile home looked a bit off plumb, as if leaning against the unrelenting wind. A rusty pickup truck sat in a potholed drive next to the place. It appeared to have four flat tires and no tailgate. An equally questionable horse trailer was backed in next to it. The finish was badly oxidized and faded lettering that had likely once said *Wildwood Stables* now said *ild ood ables*, which had been owned and operated by my late Uncle Phil. The grounds were situated at the dead end of Horse Camp Road, a two-mile-long private drive featuring a slew of washouts, overgrown vegetation, and unavoidable ruts. One would think that such a nefarious approach would have discouraged trespassing, but empty beer cans, used condoms, syringes and God knows what else gave evidence that the place was the frequent destination for naughtiness.

"So, what do you think, Kat?" asked my father, breaking into my mental ramblings. *Kat* was short for Kathryn and my last name, Wilde, invited unwelcome name meddling resulting in the annoying high school nickname of Wildcat. I guess it could have been worse, since I was very tall for a girl (5'9") and the mean girls tried to dub me Amazon Woman, but it never stuck. Plus I had been pretty good at volleyball in my day.

Dad looked at me then hoisted one foot up on a rickety corral board. Well, to a cowboy, it was a corral. To an English equestrian, it was a paddock. I fancied myself as the latter.

In order to spare Dad's feelings, I tried to be diplomatic, without being too enthusiastic. "Well, it certainly is a fixer-upper," I said, infusing my voice with false perkiness. *Oh my God, how things have fallen to rack and ruin!* was what the voice in my head was saying.

"We could do it," Dad said. "We'd get some hired help, and of course Clara would need to be convinced. There would be a certain financial investment involved."

Clara was my mother who rarely shared the same visions as my father. However, they seemed to make it work, even though I often felt pressured to "pick sides." Sometimes I longed for a sibling to share the burden of strong-willed parents. I guess when I was born, either my parents felt they couldn't improve on perfection, or believed it best to save the world from too many Wildes. Either way, they never provided me with a brother or sister to loathe and blame things on.

Looking at the substandard accoutrements throughout the compound, it was likely that Mom and I might share a similar opinion of the place. I would have to say that on a scale of one to ten regarding career opportunities, the defunct Wildwood Stables was around a two (with a "one" being either waitressing or prostitution). However, it's not like I had a lot of options glowing brightly on my horizon. But horses?

I had loved riding as a kid. When I was just a tot and we visited Uncle Phil, he plunked me on some dead-broke horse and led me around in a circle. As I got older, he took me on trail rides through the Crystal Lake Wilderness that abutted the Wildwood property. I remembered the sense of freedom, being out there on a horse.

Eventually Uncle Phil hired an international grad student from the college to teach English riding. The girls, including me, all thought he was positively hot, since he had an English accent and said things such as, *Now luv, you were smashing on that first jump but bloody awful after that.* I even won third place in a small schooling horseshow, which was more of a teaching learning experience than a true competition, and only included students from Wildwood Stables. And granted, there were only six kids in the class (to assure everyone got a ribbon), but still...

Basically, though, there was tedium in learning the intricacies of equestrianism, which largely involved riding in endless circles in an enclosed riding ring on a "schooling" horse that likely realized he had few options for escaping the annoying human bouncing around on his back. The metaphor was not lost on me. I mean, when you go in a circle, you never really get anywhere.

"Your Uncle Phil loved this place," Dad said, "but he was not a practical man. He lived and breathed horses but had no head for business, despite my advice. I mean, he was such a softie." Dad sighed. "People took advantage. He hemorrhaged money. But, damn, I sure do miss him. He...well, he was just such a good guy."

My Uncle Phil had passed away that last fall after an agonizing bout with cancer. He had never married and Dad was his only sibling. Uncle Phil's "kids" were his horses. Dad loved tossing aside his plastic pocket protector, briefcase, and horn-rimmed cheaters to do manly things around the stable with his brother. Mom, on the other hand, did not care for the smells and roughness of a stable, and insisted that though women certainly could try to compete in the corporate world, I should learn certain domestic skills if I were to survive in a misogynistic society. So, while Dad and Uncle Phil were busy fixing fences, looking at a new horse, or stacking bales in the barn, I was learning the intricacies of a successful molded gelatin salad.

Eventually impending adulthood found me heading off to college at Michigan Tech, so horses moved far into the rearview mirror. And of course, college segued into a job and the pretense of being a grownup. My mom was of the notion that my job working as a grant writer for U.P. Regional Hospital would lead to my landing a suitable husband with an M.D. after his name. Preferably, I'd hook a specialist, perhaps in cardiology or orthopedics or even plastic surgery, which might come in handy for her down the road. *Youth is gone in the blink of an eye*, Mom would mutter wistfully when she primped in the mirror. To me, mirrors were nothing less than wicked.

Grant writing was a dreary vocation. Dad's a certified public accountant, which he finds rewarding and even exciting. However, he is not your stereotypical CPA. Admittedly, he carries a briefcase and keeps his readers close by, but seldom does he wear khakis or button-down shirts to the office. Physically, Dad is tall and actually quite rugged-looking. Lately he has been dabbling in the rustic appearance of not shaving, which Mom hates. While I have inherited Dad's height, I also received Mom's genetically flawed hair, which springs into brown unruly curls with the least bit of humidity. She says we have Hungarian blood, which is apparently responsible for big hair. While Dad's side of the family offered an Irish/English bloodline, Mom's leaned toward Eastern European. In other words, I was a hodgepodge of genetic disarray, like the pooch at the shelter whose info card says "mixed."

"The horse camp was a great idea," Dad said, waving his arms skyward. "If Phil hadn't gotten sick and had to shut it down, he would still be going strong and the place would be in tip-top shape."

Dad's kudos for his late brother were a bit of a stretch. Uncle Phil faced a mighty headwind by promoting horses in Upper Michigan where the winters are long and horse enthusiasts are scarce. Still, he made a fair go of it by eventually converting from a boarding/ training facility to a destination horse camp geared for tourists who were willing to trailer their equine charges to the great Northwoods for a unique camping and riding experience. Additionally, he maintained a string of horses to use for guided tours that could last a few hours or a few days out in the 17,000 acres of the Crystal Lake Wilderness. With a fair amount of advertising, the stable generated enough business to allow Uncle Phil to eke out a living doing what he loved. Then the two, make that three-pack a day habit caught up with him.

"I think your Uncle Phil would want us to carry on his legacy and the timing is perfect for you to oversee this. After a bit, we can check out the campground. Pretty sure it's gone to seed, though."

Dad. Always looking out for his little girl—now a youngish woman of 25 who had been left flapping in the wind. Perhaps it was Dad who encouraged me to carry on the family tradition of crunching numbers. However, balancing financial spreadsheets, doing tax worksheets, and scrutinizing business plans is much different from writing grants and begging for money. It seemed everyone expected me to magically solve their financial woes, which was not typically the mission of foundations looking for a sexy way to peddle their influence and flaunt their munificence. This irreconcilable difference in revenue expectations earned me a pink slip before I could even land one date with a dashing young doctor, not that I was trying that hard.

Parents in general carry the invisible subtitle of "fixer." My fixer was trying to salvage Uncle Phil's legacy and shove me toward the dubious prospect of making it happen. Since the termination of my grant writing career, I had slid down several rungs of the so-called corporate ladder to land a pity job as part-time file clerk and errand girl at my father's office.

The most humbling aspect of my downfall involved giving up my spiffy little apartment in Marquette, with a view of Lake Superior. My folks' house was a lovely three-bedroom ranch with a somewhat finished-off basement. Mom and Dad of course had the "master suite," which included a spacious bedroom with a private bath and jetted tub, dual sinks, and an enormous walk-in shower. A sliding door on one side of the room led out to a private patio where the parental hot tub was located. The smallest bedroom of the house had served as a catch-all over the years, which included items collected for the annual church bazaar, abandoned craft projects, a couple of dusty exercise machines, and a litter box for the cat. Since my old bedroom had been thoughtlessly converted into a home office once I had left the nest, the only option upon my return was to move into my parents' basement. How pathetic is that?

As our tour of the decrepit Wildwood Stables continued, Dad and I crossed the parking area and entered the stable, which was an enormous pole barn and the only building on the place that didn't need razing.

"Barn's one-twenty by forty," Dad said, looking around. "Seems in pretty decent shape."

Rows of box stalls lined both sides of the barn and an asphalt aisle ran down the middle. The end of the barn had a space where a few bales of moldy hay were stacked. I counted a total of seventeen stalls, each with a sliding door with vertical metal bars at the top. It gave the unsettling appearance of an abandoned prison. I half expected bony hands to be clutching to the bars, begging for freedom. Something swooped overhead, making me duck. I swear it was a bat.

"Owl," Dad said. "Probably after the mice."

I guess a predatory owl was slightly more desirable than a bat.

One corner of the place held a room that featured a door hanging askew on one hinge. Dad and I entered, using the light from our phones since the electricity had been shut off. An anemic patch of light struggled through the small, grimy window at one end of the room. Cobwebs festooned every nook and cranny and dust motes drifted in the beams of our lights.

"What died!" I said, gagging. "Wow, this place needs some air."

"Probably a racoon or skunk. They like to make dens under places like this and sometimes don't make it through the winter. We'll have to search for burrows along the foundation."

I looked around, holding the collar of my coat over my nose and mouth. Forlorn wooden racks that had once held saddles and bridles joined the cobweb festival. Mouse droppings trailed along the racks and likely along the edges of the room into hidey holes where the propagation of the species flourished. A large steel box sat at one end. A mantle of dust covered the lid, which was closed and padlocked.

"That's where the grain was kept," Dad said pointing to the box. "Always locked when not in use just in case some Houdini horse managed to get into the tack room to rummage around. Phil said a horse will eat itself sick or even to death."

Speaking of sick, the dead smell seemed to be growing stronger. Perhaps an entire family of vermin had met its demise in the catacombs lurking beneath the asphalt floor.

Dad pointed his phone flashlight at the padlock. "Guess we need to find a key and see what got left in here."

I squinted at the padlock. "Combination," I said.

"Maybe I should just get some bolt cutters," Dad said. "I hate to think there's rotting oats or corn in here. Maybe that's what we smell. Stuff ferments and mildews. Let me check the tool shed."

When Dad returned with bolt cutters, I had managed to pry open the small window, but the brisk April air had done little to dispel the stench.

"Okay, Kat, stand back in case the padlock shoots off. Don't want any injuries. That's all your mother would need to put the kibosh on everything."

The padlock dropped benignly to the floor. Dad tugged on the lid, which was acting a little stubborn.

"Christ," he said. "Help me lift this thing."

We gave it a big heave-ho. The lid relented with a screech as we flung it back against the wall.

A tsunami of putrid air knocked us back, causing me to stumble and fall on my keester and Dad to grab a saddle rack, which tore out of the wall.

"Holy Mary Mother of God!" Dad bellowed.

Me, I just scrambled outside and retched into a dirty pile of snow alongside the barn.

After expelling my hearty country breakfast, I sat up and tried to clear my head, gasping in the brisk air. What I had just seen certainly wasn't a dead skunk or racoon.

"You okay, honey?" Dad said as he hurried to an open area and pulled out his phone. "No sense in calling 911. Not much we can do for the poor soul in there. I'll just call Ollie. I think I have a couple of bars on my phone."

Everyone called Sheriff Olsen "Ollie" because his real first name, Marion, invited ridicule. Dad and Ollie went to high school together where neither enjoyed a ton of popularity.

"Hello, yeah, this is Gary Wilde. Is Sheriff Olsen in? It's important. Sure, I'll hold. Thanks."

I took a handful of semi-clean snow and washed my face as best I could. Eventually, I wobbled to my feet. I stared off into the woods, taking deep breaths, willing the image in the box to vanish. Eyes, staring up from its feed box coffin and mouth, frozen in a scream, were deeply etched into my mind. Probably for a very long time.

Apparently finding a body is one of the times you *should* dial 911. Unlike, say, finding a spider in your shoe or reporting that the neighbor's dog pooped on your lawn.

"What the hell, Gary!" Sheriff Olsen whined. "You didn't think to mention to Suzanne that there was a damn corpse in that, that—"

Suzanne Williams was the dispatcher at the Peshekee County Sheriff's Department.

"Grain storage box," Dad supplied. "Sorry, I mean he—or she was beyond CPR and I thought—"

"Jesus! I thought maybe you were just calling to set up steelhead fishing," Olsen said.

"I said it was important," Dad said.

"Fishing *is* important. A body is a damn EMERGENCY!"

People always said that Dad and Ollie would never be mistaken as brothers. Whereas Dad was tall and cut from a rugged cloth, Ollie Olsen was designed after a fireplug and likely shy of the 5'7" he claimed to be. Dad said Ollie had lost most of his hair after high school and though he claimed he never ate donuts, something had contributed to the noticeable paunch that strained the brass buttons on his uniform jacket.

Sheriff Olsen was pacing around outside the barn while his deputy, Sergeant Tori Haapala, was working to secure the scene. Tori was the first female to be deputized in Peshekee County and had been on the force for almost ten years.

I wondered what the point was of stringing yellow crime scene tape around since there were no gawkers gathering round, threatening to destroy evidence. In fact, there were no close neighbors to intrude. The disreputable Horse Camp Road ran off Little Mountain Road, which was at least paved but not densely populated and mostly led to seasonal camps. Wildwood Stables was about as remote that a place could be and still be on the grid. *Nobody could hear you scream*, I thought. A shiver ran down my spine, and not from the cold.

"So, what's next?" Dad said.

"We wait for the state police and the medical examiner," Olsen said. "I don't suppose you have any coffee."

"Sorry. I wasn't expecting company," Dad said.

I had to agree with the sheriff that a nice cup of joe would have been welcome. Or maybe a good, stiff drink. I had lost all sensation in my hands and feet, and felt one of my special headaches creeping in. Seeing a corpse—and not a nice fixed-up one lying peacefully in a satin-lined casket—had a way of ruining one's day.

"How long before the troops arrive?" Dad said.

"Well, now, that's the hundred-dollar question," Olsen said. "Maybe another half hour."

I paced and stomped my feet, trying to get some feeling back. Most of all, I was trying to shake that horrid odor, which hung with me like a twenty-four-hour bug.

Dad looked at me. "Kat, if you want to take the truck home, I can catch a ride with Ollie after we're done here. Right, Ollie?"

"Only if I can put you in handcuffs and lock you in the back seat," Sheriff Olsen said. "Maybe see if my Taser works."

"Ha ha," Dad said. "How are your tax returns coming, by the way? Two days left ol' buddy. Ready to hand them over?"

"Shut up, Wilde," said the sheriff. "I just need a few more things, then me and EZee Tax Home Version have a hot date. You CPA dudes will soon go the way of the dodo." He looked down the driveway. "Where the hell are those guys? Maybe I'll go sit in the cruiser and start my report."

"Don't expect me to get you out of the late fees," Dad yelled after him. "I'm not a magician. And also, no cute stuff like saying that your hunting gear is a uniform expense."

I think Sheriff Olsen did the one-finger wave then slammed the door of his police car. Dad and Ollie Olsen had been the nerd duo of high school. The constant bantering started in those early years and had continued well into adulthood. Each had stood up for the other at his wedding. They went to camp every year and bickered about who was the worst cook and the best hunter. Each had saved the other's life and each claimed superior heroism. It went on and on. My mother and Ollie's wife, Frieda, just rolled their eyes heavenward when the four of them were together.

The Olsen's only offspring, Nikko, had been one year ahead of me in high school and was a football jock. Though I had a humungous crush on him, he gave no indication of any mutual feelings. Nikko went to college on a football scholarship while I had to pay my own way, with the help of my parents. Nikko did not exactly follow in his father's footsteps of law enforcement but came close by becoming a conservation officer for the Department of Natural Resources. He was currently assigned to Ontonagon County and, according to his mother, came home when he needed his laundry done or a home-cooked meal.

Sergeant Haapala came over to Dad and me shaking her head. "Don't mind him," she said nodding toward the sheriff's car. "He's in a snit over budget stuff. He's always a bit cranky this time of year."

"He's cranky every time of the year," Dad said. "Even Christmas."

"Especially Christmas," the sergeant said. She looked down the driveway where two vehicles minced their way toward us. "Thank God."

"Okay, well, since I don't want to see my father treated like a common criminal, I'll stick around so we can ride home together," I said.

"You sure?" Dad said. "All that Taser and handcuff stuff was nonsense, you know. At least I think it was."

"Yeah, I'm sure," I said. "I think I will borrow the truck though and take a look at the campground."

"Sounds like a good idea," Dad said handing me the keys.

While the equestrian campground was within walking distance under fair-weather conditions, the winter residue of slush and mush made driving more appealing. The two-track leading to the campground was fraught with the same bone-jarring potholes and washouts that the main drive offered, but at least it was shorter.

At first I wasn't sure I had found the right place, but the tin roof of an outhouse glinting through the overgrowth verified that, indeed, this was the rustic horse camp. The sad remains of a few slapdash corrals stood throughout a cleared area. Splintered picnic tables and dilapidated fire rings marked the individual campsites where equestrians and cowboys could pitch their tents or park their truck campers. Horses likely would have been secured on a picket line or put in one of the corrals. I noted a weed-choked hand pump with no handle. Winter brown ferns and brittle grasses inundated the campground, and sapling trees and brambles taking root sprouted throughout. Dad had been right. It had "gone to seed."

I got out of the truck and wandered through the campground. In spite of its state of disrepair, one could imagine the peace and serenity of sitting around the campfire at night after an exhilarating day on the trail. Tired horses would doze or munch from their hay bags. Perhaps someone would be playing songs on a guitar that folks knew and could sing along. There might be beer and marshmallows. Maybe it would be a family bonding experience or just a group of adults getting away from it all. There would have been no highway noise or other distractions. Cares would fade and melt into the sunset. Uncle Phil did have a grand idea here. But for reasons only God knows, the stars did not align favorably for him. I wondered if they would for me.

There was, of course, the minor inconvenience of a body in the tack room—a well decomposed one at that. I supposed that along with finding a lot of cheap help and begging for discounted materials, getting Mom onboard, and tilting at the ridiculous windmill of hope, we would need to have the crime—how could it not be murder? — solved or at least fully investigated before things could move forward.

I sighed and walked toward the truck and its toasty-warm cab. As I pulled around the circle drive, something caught my eye in the woods—something seemingly out of place. I wondered if I was seeing the results of illegal dumping. That was a common thing in the Northwoods, where idiots saw no problem with throwing their trash out in the brush.

I pulled the truck over, hopped out and trudged through crusty snow to take a closer look. Indeed, there was an assortment of things indicating that this was not an ordinary makeshift dump. The main item was a nylon tent along with a number of human tracks all over the site. The door of the tent was unzipped and flapped in the breeze, making a snapping noise. The area had once been a campsite tucked away in the woods and still held some stones for a campfire ring along with a partially collapsed picnic table. Charred chunks of wood lay scattered in the ring and a tiny thread of smoke rose from the center. A couple of blackened pots and pans and an old-fashioned enamel coffee pot sat on the picnic table and a metal fire grate leaned against a nearby tree.

My heart began to pulse in my ears as I willed myself to bend over and look inside the tent, praying mightily that it would not contain another body. Well, there was no odor, except maybe a lingering smoky smell that clung to the nylon. A jumble of clothes and blankets were strewn about. I noted in one area—perhaps the designated tent "pantry"—that there was a loaf of bread, a bag of potato chips, some Cup-a-Soup packets, a box of crackers, and a jar of peanut butter along with various canned goods. A coffee can sat off in a different area, perhaps serving as either a storage container or a chamber pot. A more chilling discovery was a very large knife—really a sword of some type— propped against a tent pole in the corner. It appeared free of blood residue, but I didn't venture inside to check.

I was trying to convince myself that I had simply stumbled upon a squatter's campsite and not that of a psychotic murderer who stashed bodies in grain storage bins. While the homeless population in big cities slept in doorways and on sidewalks, it wasn't unusual for a person in the U.P. who lacked a roof over their head to simply set up camp somewhere in the thousands of acres of wilderness, or in this case, an abandoned horse camp, complete with rustic amenities.

I hurried toward the truck, hoping to catch Sheriff Olsen and report my discovery. I gave one last glance toward the squatter's compound and damned if I didn't see something move in the woods. In light of the day's disturbing discoveries, I fairly leapt into the truck and hit the lock button, then tried to focus on the movement in the woods. Perhaps it was the homeless guy—or gal—returning to their humble abode to sharpen his/her machete.

But it clearly wasn't human. It looked toward me and tossed its head, as if impatient, gossamer mane fluttering. A horse. What was a horse doing roaming the woods? Could it possibly belong to whomever had set up the camp? Unlikely. I squeezed my eyes shut then opened them slowly, wanting to believe that my overactive imagination was playing with me. Maybe it was just a deer, but it wasn't. Out of the corner of my eye I caught a movement and watched the horse's hindquarters disappear into the woods. And there was no sound. No sound at all.

≈ 3 ≈

His name was Jupiter and he was sitting on my face. Hard to tell what time it was since I was immersed in inky darkness. The more pressing concern, however, involved the difficulty of breathing with a 16-pound cat blocking my air intake in order to make a point. It took me a minute to orientate myself. Okay, I was in my temporary quarters in my parents' basement sleeping off the delightful experience of the previous day: exploring Wildwood Stables. The remnants of my headache lingered along with tingling cold in my extremities. In all the excitement—if finding a decomposing body is considered exciting—I think I had forgotten to feed Jupiter, an intolerable transgression.

Dad and I had hung around Wildwood until the remains of the unknown dead person were removed (a job that ranks below everything, including waitressing and prostitution) and the potential crime scene was processed. Since the "victim"—who upon initial examination was identified as female— had been not of this world for a very long time, likely months, collecting physical evidence had challenges. While clearly decomposing as evidenced by the stench, the "remains" had been somewhat preserved during its feed bin slumber due to the well-below-freezing temps of the U.P. winter months.

And, to their credit, the crime scene investigators did due diligence with photos, lifting fingerprints (likely Dad's and mine), inspecting tire tracks, recording footprints in the mud, searching all the buildings, the mobile home, decrepit truck and horse trailer, weeds, corrals, and moldy hay bales. They took into custody a large number of empty beer cans (assorted), used condoms, hypodermic needles, and miscellaneous trash. Actually, this was good and saved me the trouble later on when we started the massive cleanup of the place.

Sheriff Olsen had sighed dramatically when I told him about the squatter's campsite but agreed to ask the staties to include it in their investigation. The consensus was that it was likely unrelated to the body in the feed bin, but no stone would go unturned. Unfortunately, the resident of the campsite did not return during the police canvassing of the area, so one of them put his card in a plastic storage bag and attached it to the tent zipper with a note to call or come to head-quarters. Everyone knew that wasn't going to happen. It was recommended we post no trespassing signs and eventually tear down the camp ourselves.

Another thing: the police found no hoofprints indicating that a horse had been wandering through the woods. This earned me a few furtive glances and shoulder shrugs. "Lots of deer tracks, though," one officer had said. "The cold can play tricks." Yeah? Since when does the cold transform a deer into a horse? They all thought I was a bit off tilt. After all, I was living a life of shame in my parents' basement.

I none too gently removed Jupiter from my face and plunked him (also none too gently) on the floor and swiped at the cat hairs stuck to my face. Jupiter vocalized his opinion of my rudeness and strutted toward the stairs. When he got a few steps up, he looked over his shoulder and let out a banshee-like scream that made the roots of my hair levitate.

"Okay, okay! Fancy Feast for his highness coming up!"

Jupiter had been a stray that Mom took in on a cold morning in January during a nasty polar vortex weather event. I had been assigned as his caretaker to help earn my keep during my temporary return to the parental nest. For all the perks he enjoyed, (neutering notwithstanding) Jupiter never showed one iota of gratitude. His surly attitude might explain his homeless situation to begin with. Jupiter was mostly black with a white paw, a white tip on one ear, and about half of the other ear completely missing. One can only imagine what the "other guy" looked like. He had spooky yellow eyes and, most notably, his tail was like a giant bottle brush weirdly marked with spiraling silver rings flowing from beginning to end in a kind of Fibonacci sequence. The silver rings were why he was named Jupiter because Mom thought Jupiter was the planet with the rings. When I told her it was actually Saturn with the mysterious rings, she shrugged and said that he just didn't seem like a Saturn, so we stuck with Jupiter, spiral tail rings and all. My opinion, the rings indicated he was part racoon or ocelot, or maybe space alien, which explained his despicable personality.

"Kat!" Mother bleated from the top of the stairs. "I'm headed to (sound of cat yowling)—oh for heaven's sake, Jupiter, she'll feed you in a minute—anyway, I'm headed to— (sound of cat yowling)—and I'll pick up—(yowling). Good Lord, Kathryn, will you please feed this cat?"

With that, Mom clacked away in her heels and slammed the door. It was Sunday morning, so I suspected she was headed to church—a place whose doors I hadn't darkened since Christmas Eve. I'd managed to avoid the Lenten and Easter services earlier in the month due to various conflicts, real and fabricated. I'd settle up with God later for my transgressions.

I trudged up the steps with Jupiter trying to entangle himself around my ankles, perhaps warning me that he could cause an unfortunate accident resulting in an unscheduled trip down the stairway. I snapped open a can of savory salmon "With Real Flakes!" and plopped it in Jupiter's food dish, then changed his water. He casually sauntered over to the food and gave it a critical sniff. Apparently, it passed inspection and he dove in, making annoying humming noises as he ate. After I scooped out his litter box, I considered my feline duties complete. Ironic that my nickname "Kat" was a play on words for the creature that I was mandated to serve.

I opened the fridge to look for dinner options. We always ate dinner at lunchtime on Sundays, then snacked on junk in the evening. It was a Wilde tradition, except for Mom, who limited her snacking to unbuttered popcorn and perhaps some fruit. And while I could cook— Mom had seen to that—I was limited to culinary basics. My go-to standby was meatloaf featuring my secret ingredients: salsa and Worcestershire sauce. These added zip to the mundane basic ingredients of seasoned breadcrumbs, an egg, onion, ketchup, and salt and pepper. Sides generally included mashed potatoes (pre-made available little tubs at the store), gravy (from a jar), and green beans (from a can). Sometimes I'd add dinner rolls (from the bakery) or a pie (also from the bakery). However, I had to have the materials and very few were inhouse. While I had given up my cozy little apartment, I still had my aging Subaru with over 200K on it. I grabbed the keys and headed to Manninen's Market, which everyone called Manny's, since Manninen had an overload of "n's" to deal with.

I made a mad dash through Manny's and the express self-checkout, which took my bank account balance dangerously close to overdraft status. However, this week was payday at Wilde Accounting, so if I could make it until Friday when my paltry three-day-a week income would auto-deposit into my bank account, I would remain solvent. Of course tomorrow was only Monday, and I needed gas and *really* needed to see my stylist. But no rent was due for my basement abode at the Wilde homestead, nor utilities, so there was that.

When I got home, Mom still had not returned and Dad was apparently at the office, even though it was Sunday. Being less than a week from the dreaded April 15 tax filing deadline, things were furiously busy at the office. Sunday was also Dad's gym workout day (no crowds) and I think Sheriff Olsen said something about meeting up there.

I got the meatloaf thrown together and molded into a pan then popped it in the oven. I put the pre-made potatoes in a bowl ready to nuke and the gravy heating in a saucepan. I plopped the green beans in a serving dish, blobbed on some butter and salt and pepper and readied it for the microwave. I put the rolls in a basket and the pie displayed on the counter. Cherry, Dad's favorite. Mom likely would pass on the pie, always being mindful of her waistline.

Jupiter, apparently attracted by the smell of cooking, emerged, and positioned himself next to his empty food dish.

"You just ate!" I said as I set the table. "The vet says you are too fat," I added.

This revelation did not seem to alter Jupiter's position on things. After all, if humans were eating, so should the cat. He drove the point home by blocking my path wherever I went and became more aggressive in his position by jumping on the table and sniffing the butter.

"Get down!" I yelled.

He blinked at me then sat on one of the plates. When a car pulled up, which I swear he recognized as Mom's Buick, Jupiter jumped down and vanished, leaving a deposit of cat hair on the vacated plate.

"Hello Kat!" Mom chirped as she stepped into the kitchen. "Oh. You're cooking," she said with an obvious lack of enthusiasm. "I brought home some take-out, but I see we have a breakdown of communication. I think the cat was yowling when I was talking."

"We can stick the stuff you got in the fridge—"

"Well, it's Chinese and I'm not sure how...oh, no matter. Of course, we will very much more enjoy your meatloaf. Again," she said, stuffing sacks in the fridge and shedding her coat. She eyed the table. "The fork goes on the left, dear—with the napkin, and the knife and spoon on the right, with the sharp edge of the knife pointing toward the plate." She busied herself rearranging my table settings then picked up one of the plates. "Oh my, cat hair. And why has the butter got this strange indentation in the middle?"

Dad saved the day. He parked his truck in the driveway then hustled into the kitchen. "Wow!" he said. "Smells great in here. I never get tired of your meatloaf. I'm starved!"

That was more like it.

Jupiter reappeared and sat by his dish. *He* liked my meatloaf. One big happy family.

* * *

"We are cordially invited to appear at the police station tomorrow to give our statements," Dad said, as he buttered a roll. He scowled at it for a moment and picked off a couple of Jupiter hairs. "Ollie and I checked out the Silver River to see if the steelhead had started—which they haven't—and anyway, he wants us in tomorrow. I figure we can take a long lunch from the office, do our sworn statements, and grab a burger." He paused and picked off another cat hair. "My treat, of course," he added.

Typically, Dad tries very hard not to show favoritism to me in the office setting, and that generally included my chipping in for the office coffee, lunchtime pizza and so on. Being the boss's daughter had challenges, with people being afraid that I'd blab about workplace goings-on to him. More than once I walked into a room and had everyone abruptly stop talking. It was a bit unsettling.

"Ollie's boy, Nikko, came along too—to the Silver," Dad said. "He's a good kid. I think he's up for a promotion with the state—specifically the Department of Natural Resources, or DNR as he calls it."

"You could do worse, Kathryn," Mom said. Apparently, Mom had downgraded her son-in-law expectation from wealthy surgeon to woods cop. After all, I was in the middle arc of my 20s.

"Whaaa?" I said, dropping my fork with a clank. "Nikko is a jock who never gave me a second look."

"Well, he asked about you," Dad said. "Anyway, he's hoping to get some kind of supervisory job and spend less time slogging through the marsh. I invited him over to watch the game later today. Also, he's real interested in the horse camp."

"He is?" I said.

"Yup," Dad said with a smile.

It seemed that my parents were so desperate to be rid of their deadbeat tenant (yours truly) that they are trying to fix me up with a guy who has never given me a second look—or even a first look. Plus, excuse me, but I could find my own dates. If I wanted to.

I arrived at the office exactly three minutes early, hung up my coat, and threw my purse on the circa 1950s desk located in my tiny cubbyhole. Wilde Accounting occupied a storefront on River Street in downtown Peshekee (pronounced pah-sheek-ee), the Peshekee County seat. The upstairs had once been an apartment that the storeowner of days past had occupied. Originally the store had been a leather goods shop, which went into obscurity with the passage of time and death of the owner. Wilde Accounting purchased the space after it sat vacant and neglected for years and converted the living/kitchen area into a combo storage/breakroom. Dad's office occupied the former bedroom, which has a spectacular view of Crystal Lake.

"Good morning," I said to the office secretary and overlord, Rose Gustafson.

Rose glanced at the wall clock, which I suspect she set according to the nuclear clock.

"Morning," she clipped back. "Sounds like you had quite a weekend at your uncle's place," she added, as if she were talking about attending a backyard barbecue.

"I'm quite surprised that you are here today," she added. "After all, it's not every day that someone is murdered in Peshekee County."

Rose was baiting me. I had no idea how she knew about Dad's and my weekend discovery, and even more curious was that she called it murder. But my lips were sealed.

"Well, it is tax time, and the police seem to have things well in hand," I said, booting up my computer. "It's best we don't discuss it."

Rose sniffed, clearly annoyed that she couldn't extract any gory details out of me. And to top it off, I was punctual, which gave her less overall leverage in our sparring relationship. I was quite certain—actually positive because I snooped—that Rose kept a log inside her right-hand top desk drawer to notate any office transgressions, including tardiness, swearing, not replacing the toilet paper roll, or—God forbid—improper handling of a client file. Each employee's name had two columns: one for the date and time and another for the offense. We called it her Nasty List. *Watch it (whomever), you better not leave that empty pop can just sitting there or you'll get on Rose's*

Nasty List! While I wasn't exactly sure how Rose's Nasty List could be used against me and the others, it was intimidating. Dad likely didn't take much stock in such nonsense, but I was always edgy when called into his office, fearing I'd been tattled on and that he'd sternly remind me that even though or actually *because* I am family, I am not only expected to pull my weight but actually exceed minimum expectations. The fact that I let the paper tray in the copier run out, again, did not go unnoticed nor that I'd left my coffee cup (they know it's mine because it has a deranged cat on it) soaking in the bathroom sink. I suspected that I was not alone in my Nasty List anxiety and truthfully, I had to hand it to Rose in her subtle "control by fear" tactics.

But two could play the game. I always made it a point to arrive early at the office, or at least on time. I also tried to be the last one to leave and lock the place up. I loved to dilly dally, just to annoy Rose. Clearly to her, there was to be only one brown-noser go-getter in the office, and that was she and by association, her son, Gerald, whose status was a few notches above me. While Gerald—or "Gussy," which is a nickname derived from Gustafson—did not have an actual office, he was assigned a reasonably roomy cubicle located near a back window that overlooked a small parking lot. Gussy poked his head up over his partition and gave me a lopsided smile then muttered something indecipherable, which I surmised to be the normal morning platitudes, or maybe he was trying to grill me about the body in the grain box. Gussy could best be described as a geek on steroids. He had an oversized Adam's apple, which tended to bob vigorously when he was stressed. He was pale, balding, painfully skinny, had tape holding his glasses together, and had the demeanor of an abused house pet. Plus, at age thirty-ish, he lived with his mom. Not that I could really judge.

"I think it's warming up out there," I said, attempting to get things back to a neutral topic.

"Hmmm," Rose said, not bothering to look up from her computer screen. She had to tilt her chin up, though, to look through the lenses of her half-rim glasses. Everyone in the office wore half-rim cheaters except me. I suspect that those who didn't need glasses still wore them, just to look the part. Rebellious badass that I was, I refused to bow to the social pressure, especially since I still had excellent eyesight. Plus, who was I kidding? As a lowly file clerk, I had no delusions of number-crunching grandeur.

I walked past Rose's desk to the coffee station located within her invisible domain. Should anyone take the last cup and either forget to make more or turn off the warmer, out came the Nasty List. The plastic name plaque on Rose's desk said: *Ms. Gustafson, Administrative Assistant.* Rose did not endorse the title secretary, which, according to her, was outdated and referred to servitude rather than her role as feudal lord of the office minions. Dad said that Rose was "invaluable," but truth be told, I think he was just a little bit— well maybe more than a little—afraid of her. While Dad was largely a straight-shooter, he was not entirely sinless. Nothing so dire as being unfaithful to Mom or orchestrating a Ponzi scheme, but he was known to sneak off for a couple of brews with the guys when he was supposed to be working late, or tossing a line in the river when he was sup- posedly attending a meeting, or flying cross-country to a convention that happened to be at a hunting lodge off the grid someplace in Montana. While I knew Dad may have drifted off the rails of propriety on occasion, Rose likely documented each incident in great detail. So long as she was given free rein in her fiefdom, his secrets were safe with her.

And while Rose's hostility toward me likely was due to my being the boss's daughter, nepotism did not stop with me since she finagled a job for Gussy as an "in-training" accountant. Gussy was taking online classes to become a certified public accountant. I was certain that Rose helped him with his homework. But until he completed the course- work, Gussy was merely a bookkeeper for some of our clients as well as for the office. Clearly, to Rose, I was some kind of interloper likely lusting after her boy. She assumed all females were after her Gerald, which was a total delusion. In any event, she obviously felt that the sooner I found my way to other gainful employment, the better. That reflected my opinion as well.

"Damn school buses!" spewed a coworker and Dad's right-hand- person, Char Houle, as she thundered through the client waiting area into the office. "I mean, do they have to stop at every fluffin' house?"

Char always looked as if she had just stepped out of *Vogue*. She was blessed with perfect auburn hair, which she kept smartly styled in a chin-length bob. Her makeup was always expertly applied, and she rotated a closet full of classy business suits, tasteful dresses, and strappy shoes. Char was single and a known maneater.

"Char! Such language!" Rose said, pulling open her top right-hand drawer to access the Nasty List.

Char slapped her hand over her mouth and cringed. "Oh, shit, do we have clients?"

"No," Rose said. "But we could. And I for one do not appreciate such foul language."

Char poked her head around my cubicle partition. "Hey girl, what the fu—, er heck is going on out at your uncle's place?"

"Wildwood," I said.

"She can't discuss it," Rose snapped.

"Rose is right," I said. "I'm to keep my mouth shut for now."

Rose snorted.

"Allergies?" I said. This earned me a scathing look.

Gerald's head popped over his partition. "Hey Char," he said, Adam's apple bobbing furiously. "You look nice."

"Hey Gussy," she said absently, ignoring the compliment as she strode past to her private office. She turned and snarled, "Now I'm out of hearing range, *Rose*," then slammed her door.

Rose huffed dramatically and sent a couple of papers fluttering off her desk. "Such a potty mouth."

Personally, I thought Char livened the place up, though perhaps she was tightly wound.

Dad arrived next, accompanied by Raymond Leblanc, who was Anishinaabe, or Ojibwa. Raymond not only added diversity to the otherwise homogenous office population, but also was our freelance tech guru who kept Wilde Accounting from falling into the abyss of technological malfunction. This was very important when submitting tax returns to those persnickety agents of the Internal Revenue Service. Raymond came when he was needed and didn't hang around when he wasn't. He did not embrace the notion of having a cubicle at Wilde Accounting, or with any of his other clients. Raymond always wore jeans and a tee shirt with such catchy phrases as *Time to Reboot!* or *It's International Geek Appreciation Day,* or sometimes shirts that featured Native American themes such as a soaring eagle or a dreamcatcher. He had long gleaming black hair that I would kill for. Today it was pulled back in a loose ponytail at the nape of his neck. He was wearing a faded black tee that morning with a vivid red-winged creature on it, which I had learned was called a thunderbird.

"Good morning everyone," Dad said. "Busy day coming up. Rose, any messages from the Swartz account? I need those spreadsheets *yesterday!*"

"I'm afraid not," Rose said, pointing to a stack of pink message slips in dad's inbox. "But there are several others including that new cannabis place Reed's Weeds wondering about some deductions."

Rose plucked the Reed's Weeds message from the pile and held it at arm's length as if it contained a deadly virus. Her opinion of handling the account of a cannabis store had been very clear from the start. While we were all skeptical of the proclaimed benefits of such products or their derivatives, Reed's Weeds was a bona fide business that paid their bills on time. Unfortunately, there may have been inventory issues involving employee benefits and extraordinary merchandise shrinkage. One simply cannot write off the disappearance of products as "charitable donations."

"Kat, after we meet with Sheriff Olsen, I'll need you to go to his house and pick up some paperwork from Frieda. Seems Ollie tried to use one of those do-it-yourself online tax returns and apparently didn't get too far."

"Well, can we just help him finish up his online return and not start over?" I said.

"Not really," Dad said. "He apparently crashed the computer."

"Maybe I can help," Raymond said.

"No, not even you can help," Dad said. "When I say crashed, I mean he literally physically destroyed the computer. Apparently, the do-it-yourself tax prep program didn't work out, and kept giving him dire warnings about audit risk, and asking about retirement funds, and so on, then the so-called 'circle of death' gizmo spun endlessly according to Ollie, and I quote, 'Until I thought I was being hypnotized by Satan.' The computer wouldn't shut off, reboot, or otherwise quit. So Ollie declared it possessed by the devil and destroyed it."

"I wonder if he tried holding down the control-alt-delete buttons simultaneously," Raymond said.

"Probably not," Dad said.

"How badly was it damaged? Sometimes we can salvage the data."

"Maybe," Dad said, "except he poured gasoline on it and, then apparently burned it in his firepit. I'm not sure that is even legal."

"Dude has some anger issues," Raymond said.

"Computers will do that," Dad said.

Rose cleared her throat and said, "Shouldn't Gerald perhaps go visit Mrs. Olsen? After all, he is nearing completion of his degree and could answer any questions."

"Well, I'll tell you what, Rose. Since Kat here is our runner, she can get the paperwork from Frieda, but turn it over to Gussy and we'll see if he can perform a miracle and get the Olsen's tax return filed by the deadline. He does, I'll give him a bonus."

Rose gave a satisfied little smirk. "And perhaps a nicer office, since he will soon be meeting with clients."

Rose had her eye on my mother's small office located at the end of a narrow hall. While Mom didn't come in every day, she handled the office payroll and health insurance—things that were confidential and required a private office that could be locked. A cubicle did not offer such an option. In that she was only in a few hours a month, Rose made it clear that the space would certainly be put to better use by moving Gussy there and buying Mom a locking file cabinet.

"Perhaps," Dad said. "We'll see." He strode past Rose and hollered, "Char! Emergency meeting about the Koskimaki return."

Char whipped her door open and stuck her head out. "You're kidding. *Again?*"

"Yes, again," Dad said. "They *sort of* forgot about the ten grand they made when they sold timber off their property. We have to file an amended return before they get all kinds of penalties."

"Well, crap on a cookie," Char muttered quietly under her breath.

But not quietly enough. Rose smirked again and pulled open her top right-hand drawer.

I mean, why can't we have a swear jar like a normal office, and save up for pizza? Or Char could just buy us pizza once a month and call it square. And is "crap" really a swear word or just slang?

"Kat," Dad said, "we go to the police station at 11:00. Meet me there," he added, and he and Char stomped up the stairs to Dad's office and slammed the door.

"Police?" Rose said.

"Yeah," I said. "I got caught again, you know. Well, don't tell anybody, but I've been selling knockoff Victoria's Secret underthings around the schoolyard. Mostly to young boys."

Rose huffed and gave me a withering look. Then, of course, that iconic smirk returned to her face and she said, "There are seven liberty boxes to go up in the attic for storage. Please remember *this time* to actually *mark the boxes*. And saying 'misc. paperwork' is not adequate. Then, of course, there are the five or so boxes for you to bring down and we will send those to the shredder. It's a good thing you wore old clothes."

"Hey, these are my best jeans and sweater!" I said.

Rose sniffed and turned her attention to her computer screen.

Rose always wore dresses. But not stylish dresses. More like anyone's great-grandmother wore around the house to do the dusting and knead the bread dough. Additionally, Rose's hair never varied. It was an unlikely shade of honey blonde (certainly Rose was born gray-haired), with a cinnamon bun type swirl over each ear. It poofed aggressively upward from the crown of her head, then dashed forward melding into spray-stiff bangs draped rigidly over her forehead. Beneath, we caught glimpses of eyebrows, which appeared to have been drawn on with a Sharpie pen. Indeed, Rose dwelled in some retro-era fashion time warp from which there was no escape. But I elected not to get into any kind of fashion discussion with Rose. Such a battle would only result in more righteous entries in my column of the Nasty List. And I had a feeling my column was filling up.

⇗ 5 ⇗

Dad and I were crammed in Sheriff Olsen's office, which had nary a square inch of empty space. Every surface was covered with piles of paperwork. We had to move things off the "guest chairs" in order to sit. File cabinet drawers were partially open with the edges of paperwork jammed in the rims, appearing to stage an attempted breakout from their file folders. Various wadded-up paper balls were scattered in the vicinity of an overflowing wastebasket. The sheriff's computer had so many sticky notes attached around the screen, it was a wonder he could see his Microsoft tool bar. The Sheriff's Department building had been constructed in the 1960s when, apparently, cinderblock was cheap. Not only was the exterior basically made of blocks, so were the interior walls. While the outside was painted poop brown with black trim, the interior walls featured a bilious shade of green that seemed popular for use in institutions during the wonder years of the 60s. Apparently, there was the theory that somehow green had a calming effect.

Sheriff Olsen had many things taped to his ugly green walls, including an outdated laminated poster about labor law, a map of Peshekee County with pins stuck here and there, a very large calendar displaying the month of December from several years ago, and various strips of dried and curled tape that perhaps had once held something important. His row of file cabinets displayed yellowing cartoons and newspaper articles taped randomly on the side. One was a piece on "First Female Officer Hits Her Beat," featuring Tori Haapala when she was hired ten years previous. Another was the sheriff getting an award. He had more hair and less belly, so it was old.

"You'll have to excuse the mess," Sheriff Olsen said. "Budget time."

"Odd time of year for budget," Dad said. "What happened to your eyebrows?"

I thought something looked off with the sheriff. Upon closer inspection, it appeared he was missing a good deal of his eyebrows.

"Okay, let's say budget *revision* time. Anyway, who asked you, Wilde? Butt out."

Dad just smiled. "Gas has a way of exploding when you throw a match on it," he said. "You were damn lucky you didn't set yourself completely on fire."

"Who says I didn't?" said the sheriff rubbing his forehead where the eyebrows had been.

"Seriously?" Dad said.

"Maybe."

"And you the sheriff."

"Bite me."

A day wasn't complete without Dad and Ollie going at it. Likely they both felt better and now could move on.

"Well, anyway," the sheriff said. "We have a tentative ID on the dearly departed."

Dad and I were all ears.

"Sergeant Haapala was busy yesterday and dug up some helpful information. Your brother ever mention a gal named Sasha Saari?"

"Sasha!" Dad said. "After Phil got very sick, we looked into hospice and they sent a caregiver named Sasha. But her last name wasn't Saari. The invoice from the hospice service said her name was Sasha Summers. Seemed a nice enough gal."

"One and the same," Ollie said. "Also goes by the hyphenated version, Sasha Saari-Summers. As you know, the outfit she worked for goes by Yarrow Hospice and Home Healthcare."

"How did you find her so quickly?" I asked.

"Well, when we have an unclaimed body, we start by looking at missing persons matching description, timelines, and where last seen. Seems Sasha Saari, aka Summers, never reported back to Yarrow after Phil passed away. You know, to get a new patient assignment. Well, they prefer to call them *friends,* not patients."

"So they reported Sasha missing then?" I said.

"No. Yarrow said there is a lot of turnover, especially with their caregivers for terminal *friends.* Generally they just call it job abandonment. Though they did think it odd that she never came into the office to pick up her personal items. Her pay was auto deposited. We're trying to see if the account was closed. It was her brother who reported her missing. Well, half-brother, Scott Summers. Talked to him bright and early this morning."

"She had a brother?" Dad said. "I saw her from time to time, but I guess we always talked about Phil, not her family. Kind of rude of me now that I think of it."

"And so the brother reported her missing, when?" I said.

"Well, not right away after Phil passed away," said the Sheriff. "I guess he thought maybe she went out of touch for a while. He said she was very fond of Phil and maybe she had to think about things. But after a couple of months he got concerned and filed a missing person report, which basically got filed away since there was no evidence at the time of foul play. While Mr. Summers hasn't yet viewed the remains of Miss Saari-Summers, he mentioned a tattoo of a unicorn on her upper left arm. Bingo! Preliminary report mentions gender, which is female, white, early to mid-twenties, a single bullet hole in the back of the head. After the autopsy, we'll get the bullet and know more about the type of gun and any other distinctions with the remains. There was moderately advanced deterioration of the remains, but the unicorn tattoo on her upper left arm was still identifiable. No other obvious distinguishing marks. They are checking for sexual assault or signs of a struggle, but I don't have anything back on that. Of course her hands were bagged for nail scrapings and the clothes have been sent to the lab." He looked down at a paper on his desk. "She had been wearing jeans, a sweatshirt, *one* tennis shoe on left foot, no socks, and the usual underthings that ladies wear. Sure would be nice to know where the other shoe might be. And we are looking to see if there are dental records anywhere that we can use to confirm."

"Wow," Dad said. "You guys work fast." He frowned for a moment. "I don't remember a tattoo."

"Probably her sleeve covered it," the sheriff said.

"So now what?" Dad asked.

"But wait, there's more."

"More?" I asked.

"Oh, yes," Olsen said. "Scott Summers said he is Sasha's only kin and that he's here to claim her estate."

"So?" I said. "I assume a caregiver doesn't have much of an estate."

Sheriff Olsen shifted uneasily in his chair and cleared his throat. He looked down at some papers he had in front of him. "Well, according to Mr. Summers, his half-sister was, shall we say, related to your brother."

"Huh?" Dad said. "Phil didn't have anyone except me. Never married, never had—uh, oh."

"Yup. According to Scott Summers, Sasha was Phil's—for lack of a better term—love child. Now of course, this is normally not a matter for law enforcement except when said person ends up dead."

"Phil, you dog," Dad said. "I didn't know. I mean, maybe he didn't know. Regardless, he never talked about anything like this. But there were those years when I was off to college and he was in the Army. It's little known, but they still have horses in the cavalry and that's where Phil ended up. The horses are mainly used for exhibition purposes, but also sometimes actual military duty. He was involved with training wild mustangs to become cavalry mounts and somewhere along the line, Phil found a special bond with horses. Once he came back home here and started up the horse camp, we kind of picked up where we left off as kids. I got married but he remained single, which surprised me, since he was the good looking one. Anyway, I guess everyone has their secrets."

"According to Scott, their mother, Mary Saari-Summers, has passed away," Sheriff Olsen said. "It sounds as if she was a nurse in the Army then after she mustered out was a nurse at a hospital in Green Bay. Somewhere along the line she and Phil apparently met and, well, according to Scott, Sasha was the result of that relationship. So why the two last names?"

"Scott claims Summers was his father's last name. His parents split up and divorced when dear old dad went to prison. I'm trying to look into that. Apparently Saari was Mary Summers' maiden name, or previous married name. Not sure. And I suppose when she and her husband, Summers, split up, she may have reverted to the hyphenated last name of Saari-Summers, then passed that on to alleged child, Sasha. Of course, just speculation at this point. But I know that Sasha simply just used Summers as her last name for Yarrow Hospice."

"I wonder if Phil made the connection," Dad said.

"I would think so," Sheriff Olsen said.

"Why didn't he tell us then?" I said. "I mean, I had a cousin, or half cousin, and Mom and Dad a niece. We would have welcomed her into the family."

"Her half-brother, who by the way I wouldn't trust to clean up after my dog, says she was shy and reluctant to make waves. And of course, so far we only have his story. No hard proof that she was Phil's offspring."

"Hmmm," I said. "I mean, what's the deal with this Scott person? And what are the chances that Sasha would just by coincidence move to this remote rural neck of the woods and apply at an agency for hospice care, then just by further coincidence get assigned to her biological father?"

"I'm trying to figure that out," said the sheriff. "I'll admit it's a can of worms. The assignment had to be planned or even contrived."

We all sat quietly for a spell, digesting the weightiness of the situation. If Scott Summer's claim was true, I had a cousin I never knew and now a half-cousin, or maybe a cousin once or twice removed, or maybe just a gold digger sniffing around looking to cash in.

* * *

After leaving the sheriff's department, Dad and I had a burger and fries at a place with the uninspired name of "Bill's Burgers." While the name was unimaginative, the burgers were made from a generous portion of fresh ground beef (never frozen!), hand smashed onto a sizzling grill, and topped with a variety of options, including my favorite, the Yooper Classic. It not only had the juicy beef patty, but also fried onion rings, melted cheddar cheese, sliced black olives, spicy brown mustard, and tangy dill pickles. Eating a Yooper Classic required a minimum of six napkins. It came in a plastic basket lined with a parchment paper and heaped with thick, crispy, homemade fries made inhouse that were first dipped in cold water then deep fried with the skins on. Lastly, Bill's made its own coleslaw, which was served in generous portions, with the rough-chopped cabbage oozing their "secret recipe" slaw dressing that you could buy in pint jars for a tidy sum and take home to enjoy.

If you had any room left, Bill's always had an assortment of homemade pies, slices warmed when appropriate, and served with either ice cream or real whipped cream. Additionally, they baked enormous cookies, with my favorite being macadamia nut cheesecake. And the coffee was known to make one's eyes pop open even after a night of carousing. Other than a variety of soft drinks and something from the milkshake machine, there was nothing else on the menu, which was actually just a chalkboard that Bill's wife wrote the special on each day. The special, of course, was a variation of the hamburger, all with U.P./Northwoodsy-themed names, such as the Miner, the Whitetail, and the Smokey Bear, which is what Dad had because it had a smoky barbeque sauce, smoked gouda cheese, secret smoky sauce, and grilled onions.

I passed on dessert, but still felt like a slug ready to burst as Dad and I went to the parking lot.

"I'm going to give Dewey Bilkinen a call," Dad said. "Go over this mess with him. I'll let you know when we can meet with him."

Dewey Bilkinen was the attorney who handled our legal affairs and had taken care of Uncle Phil's estate. Even though he was known to be a very conscientious attorney, Dewey was subject to ridicule by having his name morphed into *Do We Bilk 'em!*

* * *

When I pulled into the Olsens' drive, I noticed a very muddy truck bearing the seal of the State of Michigan Department of Natural Resources parked in the driveway. Stenciled beneath the seal was *Conservation Officer*. Nikko was there. I pushed the doorbell and a dog started frantically barking. There were footsteps and Frieda Olsen opened the door, wiping her hands on an apron.

"Tobey! Hush," she said to a bulky tan dog that poked his jughead around her legs to check me out. It gave a couple of woofs, then quieted. Mrs. Olsen smiled broadly and said, "Kathryn! How lovely to see you. Nikko was just finishing his lunch. Can I fix you anything?"

"No thank you, Mrs. Olsen," I said. "I've been to Bill's and should probably skip meals for a while."

The dog seemed to be sizing me up. I hoped he—yes it was a he—had had his lunch. The creature was buff colored with a white paw and a white patch on his face. He had a neck the size of a rain barrel attached to a thin but muscular body. He yawned extravagantly, giving me a good view of a substantial set of fangs. I didn't know much about dog breeds but this K-9 appeared to have some pit bull in the mix.

"First off, call me Frieda, for heaven's sake. Oh, and this is Tobey. Nikko found him wandering in the woods, totally emaciated and terrified. No luck finding the owner. I think some horrid person dumped the poor thing. He was probably used for fighting or worse yet, a bait dog. You can see the scars. It's appalling. We're nursing him back to health and trying to gain his trust. He's very sweet but traumatized. How about a nice chocolate chip cookie?" she added. "Just fresh from the oven."

"Ma! Let the poor girl in the door and quit trying to feed everyone!" came a voice.

"She's in the door, Nikko," she yelled. "And if you were any kind of a gentleman, you'd come out and say hello and get ahold of this dog. Come on in, dear," she said sweetly, "and let me take your coat. Will spring ever arrive? I have Ollie's paperwork for your father somewhere in the computer room. Of course, there is *no* computer anymore since Ollie set it on fire. What a fool."

Frieda took my coat and went off to look for the papers. Tobey remained in the entryway, essentially blocking me. Nikko walked in, wearing a pair of pajama pants and a DNR sweatshirt with the sleeves cut off. Only guys with some muscle to flex cut the sleeves off a perfectly good sweatshirt. Nikko was tall, especially considering that his parents were not. His hair stuck up in blond spikes, which seemed to further add to his height. I suspect he had not shaved for a day or two judging by the stubble. Clearly his morning did not involve personal grooming but somehow it worked for him.

"You'll have to excuse my appearance," Nikko said as he munched on a cookie. "Wash day."

I thought his appearance was fine, just fine.

"Tobey, let the girl pass," Nikko said. "Come on into the kitchen and have some coffee and a cookie."

"Well, I really should just get the papers and get back to the office," I said. "I had a big lunch." I patted my belly. "Don't want to get any fatter!"

Really smooth, Kat. Way to go.

"Fat?" Nikko said looking me over. "Hardly."

I decided to take that as a compliment.

We sat at the kitchen table. Tobey plunked down at Nikko's feet and closed his eyes, apparently satisfied that I was no threat. Nikko got a mug down from a kitchen cupboard and filled it with steaming coffee. "Cream or sugar?"

"Huh?" I said. "Oh, no black."

Somehow a cookie appeared in my hand and I took a bite.

"Great cookie," I said. A small piece dropped to the floor, and Tobey sprang to life to vacuum it up.

"My favorite," Nikko said. "Ma spoils me."

I nodded and took another bite then sipped my coffee. "Mmmm," I said. "Nice and strong." Tobey was now staring up at me, tail sweeping gently back and forth. I snuck him another bit of cookie, making sure there were no chocolate chips in it. I had heard dogs couldn't have chocolate. Strings of drool hung from Tobey's fleshy lips, which I swear were smiling.

"Do you like things strong?" Nikko said.

I stopped chewing and looked up. Was he flirting? "Depends," I said.

"On what?" he said, grinning broadly.

The inuendo couldn't have been any more obvious. Or was he just messing with me?

"Well, I like a, er—"

"Here we are!" chirped Frieda Olsen as she entered the kitchen. "I think everything is in this file folder that your dad needs." She placed a manilla folder next to me on the table. "Oh good. I see my harebrained son at least got you some coffee."

"Strong," I said. "Good!" I added.

Nikko grinned and ran his hand through his hair, making it stick out even more. How could that look, well sexy? But it did.

"Nikko! Your dog is drooling all over my clean floor!"

"It's my fault, Mrs.—er, Frieda," I dropped some cookie crumbs and—"

"No big deal," Frieda said. "And thank your dad for rescuing us. I have to scoot. Nikko, make sure Kathryn takes some cookies back to the office to share."

"Okay, Ma," he said.

We heard the door shut and a car drive off.

"Well, I should be going," I said, rising from the table. "Thanks again for the coffee and cookie."

"Wait, let put some in a zip bag for you to take to the office," Nikko said. "If you don't, I'll catch hell."

"Okay, thanks," I said.

"But before you go, hey, I'm dying to know what's going on out there at your uncle's place. I mean, a murder?"

"Well, I'm not supposed to talk about it," I said.

"Okay, so I heard you were going to fix the place up and get it operating again," he said.

"Yup, that's the plan. Truth is, the place creeps me out."

"Understandable, given the circumstances." He handed me the bag of cookies.

"And there is the tent and stuff all set up in the old campground," I said. "Somebody's living there, I think, even though they have to be freezing their butt off."

"Yeah, same thing happens a lot in the state forest campgrounds the DNR manages. In that technically the rustic campgrounds don't close in the winter, it's really just a failure to pay for camping. Impossible to enforce with the resources on hand. We have homeless folks up here in the U.P. Instead of living on the streets, they take to the woods. But some guy squatting on private property is a different story. It would be wise to get rid of this person so he doesn't somehow claim squatter's rights on a so-called abandoned property."

"Or gal," I said. "I never saw the person, whether male or female. And yeah, the state police said I could remove the person's stuff and should probably post no trespassing signs. Thing is, I took a peek in the tent and there's a very large machete type knife in there and I'm not real eager to confront whoever this squatter might be."

"Could be harmless, could be mental. Staties won't help? I mean there was a murder there, right? Seems like they'd want to chat with this person."

"They left a card on the tent asking him—or her—to contact them," I said.

"Tell you what," Nikko said. "I'm on a few days leave and maybe you and I could go on out to the horse camp and check things out. I can always wear my DNR jacket with the patches and badge, even though I have absolutely no jurisdiction, that is unless this guy—or gal—is poaching."

"Well I have Tuesdays and Fridays off," I said. "And most weekends."

"How about tomorrow afternoon, then?" Nikko said. "And we can take Tobey. He scares the shit out of people, even though he's a big ol' teddy bear."

Tobey perked up at the sound of his name and wagged his tail.

"Sounds great," I said. I reached down and let Tobey sniff the back of my hand. It seemed to pass muster, so I ventured a tentative pat on the head, then a scratch behind his ears. This triggered a full butt wiggle with tail whirling around in a circle.

"I think someone's in love," Nikko said.

6

"Phil's Last Will and Testament clearly stated that you, Gary Wilde, were the primary beneficiary of his estate, per stirpes," said Attorney Dewey Bilkinen. "There was a modest bequest to Miss Sasha Summers as his 'faithful and devoted caregiver,' along with another modest sum of money and tack and other accruements going to some English fellow who was a riding instructor—"

"Justin Wright," I said. "I remember him from way back when I took lessons as a kid. We were required to call him Mr. Wright to show respect, which was a hoot. And then of course, that kind of morphed into *Just Right,* to us girls."

"Yeah, he stayed with Wildwood even when things were going downhill," Dad said. "Once Phil was gone and the last few horses were placed in good situations, Wright disappeared. Not sure what happened to the tack he inherited. Probably sold it on eBay or Craig's List to raise a little cash, maybe for a plane ticket back to England."

"As you know, there weren't many liquid assets," Bilkinen said.

"Believe me, I know," Dad said. "We had to sell off the tractor, conveyor, generator, and some other equipment just to pay the outstanding debts. Truthfully, I used some of my own funds to square the delinquent taxes."

"Anyway, in my professional opinion, this Summers fellow has no legal claim, other than perhaps Miss Summer's personal assets, though I suppose he can try to find counsel to attempt to milk something out of it. Now, if Phil's *issue* were living, she might. But her half-brother? Well, we'll see if he brings suit. And, of course, it's only Scott Summer's word. I'm assuming if there had been a paternity test, Mr. Summers would have brought that up."

"Could he get a court order for a paternity test?" Dad said. "I mean Phil was cremated and buried in the family plot. Can they even get DNA from the ashes?"

"Possibly from the bones and teeth," Dewey said. "But as far as a court order, I think unlikely unless it involves information needed to investigate Miss Summer's murder. I can't see how proving the paternity of a man who died before the alleged offspring died would warrant an exhumation."

"And Phil was bedridden and on heavy painkillers for months before he passed," Dad said. "He couldn't even lift a damn glass of water." Dad seemed to be drifting into a funk, recalling the awful suffering his brother went through.

"Sheriff Olsen was right," I said. "This is a can of worms. Do you think Scott Summers will push this?"

"Hard to say," Bilkinen said. "He'd likely need to find counsel to take the case. And most attorneys expect to be paid either hourly or by a percentage of the award. Phil's will was clear that he believed you to be his only living relative and that everything, except as I already mentioned, went to you."

"Mostly he left me with a big, fat headache," Dad said, seeming to snap out of his dark mood. "Of course, now that Kat has agreed to bring the place back to life..." He looked at me, grinning.

"I get to inherit the big, fat headache," I said.

"Exactly!" Dad said, reaching out and fist bumping my shoulder. "Tag! You're it."

Attorney Bilkinen sighed. "Kathryn," I suggest you consider getting your affairs in order."

"Hey, I'm just being coerced into taking on a defunct business, not undergoing open heart surgery," I said.

"I mean a will and a trust," he said. "Wildwood Stables may have, shall we say, declined in value, but the land alone is worth a lot. Especially abutting the Crystal Lake Wilderness and the footage on the Peshekee River that runs through the property."

"Good idea, Kat," Dad said. "I'll pay to have things drawn up. Be sure to leave everything to your mother. Of course that's just until you get married and have kids of your own." He gave me a look and grinned. "I hear you're meeting up with Nikko Olsen later today. If you have a chance, ask him about a good place to hunt turkey."

"Dad! How did you know—"

"Well, I heard you mention it to Char after you came back from picking up the Olsen's tax stuff. Anyway I got the voucher for a turkey license and for sure Nikko knows where the gobblers are hanging out."

I gave an ever-suffering sigh. When would I learn that the office gossip mill never stopped grinding away?

Dewey Bilkinen laughed. "Gary, you never change. All you think about is hunting and fishing."

"Well, one can't totally be buried in his work," Dad said. "Got to have something to make it all worthwhile."

"Agreed," Dewey said. "I prefer a luxury resort with tropical drinks sporting little umbrellas and of course, lots of ladies in bikinis basking by the pool."

"What does Mrs. Bilkinen think of your, shall we say, wandering eye?" Dad said.

"Hell, she likes to ogle the studs in their speedos."

"Such a letch," Dad said.

"I beg your pardon!" Dewey said. "That's my wife you're talking about."

"I wasn't referring to Alice. She's obviously a saint," Dad said.

"Ahem," I said.

"Yes, well, anyway," Dad said, "when April 15th is in the rearview mirror, we're shutting down the office for a week to celebrate."

"We are?" I asked.

"Yup," he said. "Paid vacation," he added.

Wow! Paid time off. Then I frowned when I looked out the window at the snow flurries. "Maybe we can go to Florida? Have a cocktail with a little paper umbrella in it. Check out the *wildlife.*"

"Nope," Dad said. "We're going to start working on Wildwood."

"Oh, crap," I said.

"Good thing Rose isn't here," Dad said.

Bilkinen looked from Dad to me and shrugged. "Anyway, I'll get your estate planning in order, Kathryn."

"Yippee," I said.

* * *

"Man, what's with this road!" Nikko said as we bounced and lurched down Horse Camp Road. "I've driven old logging two-tracks with less ruts. Good thing I borrowed the Tahoe from Dad."

"Why not take the DNR truck?"

"Oh, that's a no no," Nikko said. "Can only use it for official business or to drive to and from work under some circumstances. I'm hoping that the baling wire Dad used to repair this bucket of bolts doesn't give out." He swerved around a large rock protruding from a rut.

"Horse Camp Road is on the list of a million things that need fixing," I said as I braced myself for a washout I knew was coming. "I appreciate your driving. I'm not sure that my Subaru's exhaust system will survive many more trips."

Nikko's dog, Tobey, had his paws on the back of my seat and his muzzle mashed against my ear. The message was clear: some interloper, namely me, had usurped his rightful place of riding shotgun and he was making a point.

We finally pulled into the weedy parking lot of Wildwood Stables and piled out of the SUV. It was still blustery, and Nikko had exchanged his pajama pants for a lined pair of overalls and true to his promise was wearing his DNR jacket replete with patches and badge. He wore a Stormy Kromer hat, the preferred headgear for men and some women of the U.P. Tobey dashed around, overwhelmed by powerful and unfamiliar scents. I wondered if the smell of death still lingered. Seemed unlikely after all the time, but I knew dogs had a phenomenal sense of smell.

"Well, as soon as the weight restrictions are off, you should have a grader run down that road," Nikko said. He surveyed the premises and added, "And maybe this parking area, too. Well, the main barn looks in good shape, but the winter snow did a number on that mobile home."

"I know, where to start, eh?" I said. "The squatter's tent is back a ways in the old campground. There's a road of sorts going back if you want to drive."

"Here's the deal," Nikko said. "Dad—in official capacity as sheriff—thinks that they'd very much like to talk to this guy—"

"Or gal," I said.

"Right. Or gal. So I've brought along my trail cam—"

"Trail cam?"

"Yeah, a camera mainly used to watch wildlife around the bait pile for hunting purposes or to prove that the neighbor's dog is pooping on your lawn or just to confirm that things like cougars and lynx still roam these woods."

"Cougars?" I said, glancing around as if one were lurking just out of sight.

"But it will work great for, shall we say, spying on your squatter. So we'll head back to the campsite—kind of sneaky—and if he or she is there, that's great and we'll have a chat. If not, we can mount the camera and give it a few days, then maybe get a good shot of our person of interest."

"Why isn't the sheriff's department doing this?" I said, feeling more than a bit apprehensive.

"Why should they when they can push it off on a CO? Plus, you own the property, so you have every right to put up a trail cam or any other means to monitor your property. Whereas the sheriff's department can't just spy on people without jumping through some hoops."

"So we try to sneak up?"

"Yup. I'm going to snap a leash on Tobey, just in case," Nikko said.

"How does this trail camera work?" I said.

"Your dad doesn't use one?"

"Not that I know of."

"Well, there are different options. You can even connect some to a cell phone, but this unit is not that sophisticated. It's battery powered and uses infrared to detect a lifeform. Once triggered, the camera snaps photos, or in some cases can record a video. I'm hoping whatever we get is in the daylight, which will provide us with better detail."

"So, is there like a flash drive stick or something in there?" I asked.

"Sort of. It's called an SD card. We can download the info onto a laptop or other device and pull up the photos."

As planned, we skulked up to the squatter's campsite. The faded blue tent, listing heavily to one side, was still there.

"I don't see any sign of life," Nikko whispered.

"Me neither," I said. "But I think someone's still living here," I said pointing to a blackened coffee pot sitting on a grill over the fire pit.

Tobey gave serious attention to the fire pit, which contained an array of charred garbage. His next order of business was to lift his leg on everything and anything.

"Probably letting any coyotes in the area know not to mess around," Nikko said. "Hey Tobey, enough already."

"Looks like our guy or gal is out and about," I said, looking off into the woods. I didn't see any sign of the ghost horse. I wasn't sure if I was relieved or disappointed. If it were there and Nikko saw it too, then I was not bat-crap crazy. If he didn't see it and I did, however, then I was ready for some serious psychotherapy.

We poked our heads inside the tent. Empty food containers, rumpled clothing, a couple of grungy blankets, garbage bags, and a small backpack like kids would use for schoolbooks were haphazardly strewn about.

"Okay, it's definitely a guy," I said looking around. "What a disaster. The giant knife was propped against the tent wall. I don't see it. I also don't see much food," I said picking up an empty potato chip bag. "Maybe our person of interest went out to get some provisions. But I don't think he has a vehicle."

"Right, and we didn't see anyone on Horse Camp Road or the highway," Nikko said.

"Of course, there are a bunch of trails and two-tracks winding through the woods and maybe an old road connecting at U.S. 41. If you come out that way, there's a truck stop up the road that has a few groceries and you can buy a shower."

"Wow, a long walk to get a Slim Jim," Nikko said.

"True, but people still pick up hitchhikers, so maybe he thumbed a ride. Hell, Dad gives lifts to hitchhikers all the time along Big Lake Road."

"I know the truck stop you're talking about—"

"King's Crossroads," I said.

"Maybe I'll stop by sometime and have a chat with the help there," Nikko said.

Tobey took great interest in a coffee can sitting in the corner. He made a garbling noise.

"Whatcha got there boy?" Nikko said as he picked up the can and pulled off the plastic lid. "Maybe used this to collect snow to melt for drinking water."

"I saw that can last time I was here," I said. "I thought maybe it was the chamber pot."

"Ug," Nikko said, snapping the lid back on and putting the can back in the corner. "Might be. Usually guys just find a tree."

"Or use the outhouse that's still standing over there," I said. "Though God knows what it's like inside."

Tobey stared up at Nikko and wagged his tail. Nikko pulled a doggie biscuit out of his pocket and gave it to the dog.

"He expects a reward," Nikko said.

"Even when he finds something disgusting?" I said.

"*Especially* if he finds something disgusting."

"This tent smells awful," I said. "I'm outta here."

"Okay, I'm going to look for a good place to mount the trail cam," Nikko said. "Keep a lookout for anyone coming."

"Sure," I said. It was all so cloak and dagger, what with me keeping a lookout.

"That should be hard to spot," Nikko said, pointing to a tree trunk where the camouflaged camera blended to near invisibility. "Let's hope our pal comes back and smiles for a full-face shot."

We headed back to theTahoe. Nikko took Tobey off the leash and let him continue his sniffing and territorial peeing.

"Really would have been nice to talk with him," Nikko said. "I'm assuming we can now safely presume this is a guy—and hope that he doesn't spook and skedaddle. Sometimes people see things, but don't want to get involved. Especially when they're breaking the law themselves, such as trespassing."

We climbed into the SUV and Nikko started the engine. I cranked the heat up full blast.

"I guess we come back in a couple of days to pull the card." Nikko said. He looked at his watch. "Do you have to get home?"

"Not really," I said. "Dad is working late wrapping up some tax returns and Mom said she has a meeting at the church. There won't be a family dinner tonight. The only caveat is Jupiter."

"Jupiter?"

"Yeah, the family cat," I said. "Or actually, he's not our cat, more like we're his people. If he doesn't get fed by 5:00, he's known to perform an indiscretion in an inappropriate place, such as on my pillow."

"Ah, well, best get you home to feed the critter," Nikko said. "But after you take care of Jumper—"

"Jupiter."

"Jupiter, we could maybe go to the drive-in for a chili dog."

"The drive-in?" I said. "It's only like 40 degrees out."

"So?" Nikko said. "It opened April 1st as it does every year, even in a blizzard. No worries. We'll turn the heat up." He gave me an interesting look.

"With a nice frosty mug of root beer?"

"You bet! Anyway, I promised Tobey if he was a good boy, I'd buy him a hot dog, hold the onions. Dogs can't have onions."

"And he's been a good boy?"

"Far as I know," Nikko said. "And so have I. And I'm willing to hold the onions on my hot dog too."

I glanced at him. He smiled and said, "I've been *very* good."

"Well, in that case, and because I appreciate your going with me to squatter's paradise, this will be my treat."

Tobey perked up at the word "treat."

"You've got a deal," Nikko said, slipping the dog a biscuit. "We love treats, don't we Tobey?"

Maybe I'd hold the onions too.

7

"Going, going, gone!" Dad said as we watched the derelict mobile home collapse into itself.

A swarm of workers began the further dismantling of Uncle Phil's former residence. It amazed me how easily the thing disintegrated into a pile of rubble. Some items were being salvaged for repurposing, but the rest I surmised was destined for the great trailer park in the sky. We had pulled out most of Uncle Phil's furnishings and personal belongings and donated them to charity. He had boxes and drawers of papers, photos, manuals, and miscellaneous memorabilia, which we sorted through, purged, and reduced to a single box that was temporarily put in my storage unit.

"Once all the crap is out of here," Dad said, "we'll bring in a manufactured home, which is more suitable than a mobile home."

I stood mute. It was assumed that I'd be the person residing in said new home about which I had, thus far, not been consulted. The state police had officially concluded combing every square inch of the Wildwood Stables property for murder clues and had released the premises for our use and pleasure. Dad wasted no time jumping into renovation plans. I had to admit that I was getting a little caught up in it, though simultaneously feeling as if I were being excluded.

"Believe it or not, with a new battery and some air in the tires, Phil's truck is more or less road-worthy," Dad said.

Uncle Phil's truck had been rendered so-called "road worthy" and pulled away from the demolition site, with the horse trailer attached and creaking along behind.

"Of course the plates are expired. You need to get the old registration and head down to the Secretary of State."

"Sure," I said, wondering if the cost of plates would exceed the value of the twenty-year-old truck.

"Got someone coming for the moldy hay in the barn who's going to use it for garden mulch," Dad said. "New crop won't be available for a while, but Kat, you can check around and see if there's any of last year's hay in good shape to tide you over."

I suspected that Google or even good ol' fashioned yellow pages wouldn't be helpful, but Pete's General Store outside of town might give me a lead. Pete's had everything from garden seeds to farm-fresh eggs to tractor sparkplugs to doggie chewies to fashionable muck boots. We got Jupiter's special hairball gel there, along with kitty litter that was way cheaper than the grocery store. I had a feeling that I'd be spending a lot of time at Pete's.

The resurrection of Wildwood Stables had thus far been largely handled by Dad. He had a tendency to do that—just take over. It wasn't a bad thing in the case of a client who couldn't handle an Excel spreadsheet or FICA deductions. However, as Gary Wilde's only offspring, it had been a bit of a struggle all my life to break out of the parental shelter and have a thought or two of my own. Really, when I thought of it, what was I thinking in becoming a grant writer when in truth, my interest had been in outdoor recreation.

"You can of course do that if that's what you want," Dad had said when I expressed this desire when applying to colleges. "But I don't believe that you'll have much luck making a living by climbing rock walls or whitewater rafting through the Grand Canyon."

"And you won't be young forever," Mom had added. To her, it was all about youth. Once that is over, a gal better have some security built into the plan.

I took a deep breath as I watched the pile of mobile home rubble being worked on by a large steel dinosaur. It even had an eye on a clawed bucket-like affair. Of course the eye was really some kind of major bolt; it seemed to be watching me.

"I'd like to think about what type of house to put here," I said.

"I've already picked one out, Kat," Dad said. "It's perfect."

"Still," I said. "I'd like to have some input."

Dad stopped watching the bolt-eyed monster and looked at me. "Oh. But I've made a down payment."

"See, here's the thing," I said. "I'm thinking I should have a little more say so about this venture and probably—no definitely should have a little bit to say about this prefab house. That is, unless you are thinking of someone else living there."

I now had Dad's full attention. He frowned, then smiled. "You know, you're absolutely right. I'm always overstepping—"

"And I appreciate you and Mom always propping me up," I said. "But I could start standing on my own two feet by figuring out this house, how I'll pay for it—"

"Oh, don't worry about—"

"As I was saying, how I'll pay for it. At some point this joint needs to turn a buck or two and I should be able to draw a salary."

"Absolutely!" Dad said.

"In the meantime, I'll keep working at the office, and perhaps if the bank won't lend me money for a mortgage, you will, and I'll pay you back."

"But—"

"I'll pay you back. It will be a business deal, or no deal, Dad."

There was what you might call an awkward silence. I knew what he and Mom were thinking—that they'd be stuck supporting me until I got married and some nice fellow would take over the burden. Not gonna happen. This wasn't the 1800s. Still, I felt like an ungrateful brat and was just getting ready to cave and tell Dad that I was sorry, but he blinked first. In fact, he blinked several times, then grinned ear to ear.

"Well, I guess you are a Wilde through and through," he said. "It's a deal, then. I have put some money down with Lake and Land Homes, which you can call an early birthday present. I do hope you'll go along with the house I've ordered, which by the way is called a modular home, not prefab. It's too costly to change now. It's really more of a bungalow, with two bedrooms, a bath and a half, and—"

"Okay," I said, grinning. "You know my birthday isn't until August, right?"

"How could I forget? Your mother carried you through the hottest summer on—"

"So, whatever you give me for my birthday—even a down payment—is a gift and of course it will be perfect!"

"Perfect it is!" Dad said. "I'll carry the paper on the place and I'll give you a break on the interest. But it will be a business deal. There will be other money up front needed as well. Maybe we can wrap it all into the same loan. But since Phil was my brother and since I'm the fool that wants to bring this place back to life, I expect to have some skin in the game too. We'll form a partnership."

I started to cry. What the...

Then we hugged.

"Someone's coming," Dad said.

We turned our attention to an SUV slowly working its way down Horse Camp Road toward us. As it drew closer, I recognized it as the Olsen beater-mobile. It pulled around next to Uncle Phil's truck and stopped. The driver's door creaked open and Nikko got out then turned and lifted Tobey out, set him on the ground, and snapped on a leash. Tobey made a dash to the nearest tree. Nikko looked around and nodded, then came over to Dad and me.

"Mornin'." Dad said.

"Hello Mr. Wilde," Nikko said. "Looks busy around here."

"Yup! I—er Kat and I are just talking about what to do next."

Nikko smiled at me. "Hi."

"Hi," I said back.

"Well, I'm going to go see about getting the new foundation poured ASAP," Dad said. "Nikko, if you think of it, tell your dad that his damn taxes were filed with seconds to spare."

Nikko laughed. "I will, Mr. Wilde. And Dad asks that you give him a bump at the sheriff's office. Something about meeting with the state police for some questions"

"Will do," Dad said, turning on his heel and walking away.

"So..." Nikko said looking at me.

"So..." I said.

To say we were standing in awkward silence would be the understatement of the century. Likely we were both thinking of our little trip to the drive-in for a hot dog. Or rather what happened when Nikko took me home. Just as I fumbled for the door handle to get out of the car, he reached over and pulled me toward him and, in spite of the gearshift console interference, we engaged in a rather passionate, lingering kiss. Totally unexpected, but not unwelcome. Once we pulled apart, Nikko grinned at me and said something about wanting to do that since high school. But there was no talk of any follow up. Maybe now that he'd kissed me, he could check that off his to-do list.

Yet, here he was, unexpectedly.

"So," he repeated, "I thought we could check out the trail cam. See if there's any action. Maybe reload and change the batteries, if needed."

"Sure," I said.

"I think it's important we both go to check it out. You know, to make sure things are on the up and up."

"Okay," I said. "Walk or ride?"

"I wouldn't mind walking. I'm still recovering from the ride over that damn road coming in."

"Yeah, well after they get the old mobile home hauled off, I'll get a road grader to fix it."

"Good, I guess," Nikko said. "But I kind of like the adventure. I'll keep Tobey on the leash for a bit."

We fell silent as we approached the squatter encampment, likely both thinking we needed to be a bit cautious. After all, there *had* been a murder at Wildwood Stables, and we did have a person living in the old horse campground who was yet to be questioned. I had to admit that my heart had picked up speed, and I noticed Nikko had his hand inside his coat. I suspected he was armed, even though not in uniform.

As we drew closer, I could make out the image of the blue tent, which appeared even more lopsided than last time. Nikko and I looked at each other.

"What the hell," he said, shrugging. "Might as well let him know we're here."

"Sure," I said. "If *he's* here."

"So..." Nikko said.

"Um, go ahead," I said.

"HELLO! ANYBODY AROUND?" Nikko's voice bounced around in the trees.

We waited a couple of beats for a response. It reminded me of that show on TV where the Bigfoot hunters give spine-tingling "vocals" into the inky darkness of alleged Bigfoot territory, hoping for a return screech from something "squatchy."

"CONSERVATION OFFICER!" Nikko boomed, sending a couple of noisy crows into flight.

We again waited but heard only the sound of a stiff breeze rushing through the pine boughs.

"Okay, then. I guess your guest is out and about, perhaps hunting for nuts and berries," Nikko said.

We approached the encampment, which looked pretty much the same as in the past—lived in, but far from homey. Tobey strained at his leash trying to reach a cast iron skillet that appeared charred beyond hope.

"Leave it!" Nikko said, giving Tobey a tug. "Christ, why do dogs like the most disgusting things?"

"Unlike Jupiter," I said, "who is disgusted *with* everything."

We peeked into the tent and found things in the basic disorder that we have seen in the past. The giant knife was back, leaning against a tent pole.

"Yikes!" Nikko said.

"I know," I said.

"Well, not the murder weapon, but a formidable object nonetheless."

We backed out of the tent and went over to the trail camera.

Nikko dropped Tobey's leash. "Be a good boy, and go find something disgusting, then Daddy will give you a yum yum."

"Daddy? Yum yum?" I said.

Nikko gave a sheepish smile and started to fiddle with the trail camera.

"Okay. I've pulled the card and put a new one in. Maybe we can check it out on your computer since Dad has destroyed ours. I left my laptop in my apartment in Ontonagon."

"Sure," I said. "Let's just head into the office and use my dinosaur of a computer. I don't have a computer at home right now. Dad schlepps his laptop back and forth and I always used the one from the hospital when I worked there, but of course that's no longer an option. All I have is my phone for tech stuff."

Nikko looked at me and smiled. "Hey, I'm sorry you've had a tough time. But I've always kind of believed that things happen for a reason."

"Did I mention that my Subaru broke down two days after the career bomb?"

"Ouch," Nikko said looking around at the defunct equine campground. "So, you really are going to try and get this place going? I'm sure you could find a job grant writing somewhere. Maybe even the DNR."

"You know," I said, "I'm kind of glad to be done with that chapter in my life. Thank God I have my parents as a safety net, or I might be the one living in this crappy nylon tent cooking beans over a campfire."

"There but for the grace of God…"

"I guess so."

We were quiet for a moment. Tobey was sniffing around a pile of junk along the edge of the woods—presumably Mr. Squatter's household refuse pile.

"Tobey, come!" Nikko said.

We watched the dog's hind end wiggle with enthusiasm, his head buried in the garbage.

"I said *come!*"

Reluctantly, Tobey waddled toward us, carrying some sort of treasure he had found.

"Drop it!" Nikko said.

A somewhat subdued Tobey slunk toward us, still carrying his find of the day.

"I SAID DROP!"

That did it. Tobey dropped the object at Nikko's feet and lowered his head submissively.

"Good boy!"

Butt wiggle.

"What the hell?" Nikko said, bending over the object.

"Please don't tell me that it's a butchered critter that Mr. Squatter cooked up for din din," I said.

"Nope," Nikko said. "Just an old tennis shoe."

8

"So, you got this at that squatter's garbage pile in the old camp-ground?" Sheriff Olsen said when I dangled the grungy tennis shoe in front of him. It had a combined moldy/fermented smell and I held it by its shoelace. Tobey looked distressed, as if sensing that he was losing claim to his find.

"Yup," I said.

"Tobey found it," Nikko said.

"Good dog," Sheriff Olsen said. "I think this is the vic's missing shoe. We're pretty sure she was killed somewhere other than where the body was found, but probably close by."

"Yeah," I said. "Then put in the grain bin until, ah, she could be, I don't know, buried or something."

"I—and likely the state police—will want to talk to this person who is living there in that campground," Sheriff Olsen said. "You say you have some video from a trail camera?"

"Yeah," Nikko said. "I've been, ah, helping Kat out to try to get a handle on who's squatting there and truthfully, the last advice she was given was to clear the guy's stuff out and put up some signage about trespassing. But we haven't been able to find the guy—"

"Or gal?" Sheriff Olsen said.

"No, it's definitely a guy," I said. "At least the clothes strewn about appear to be men's and even the most agile woman would not be able to finagle using the makeshift commode involving a coffee can."

"I bet a woman could use a coffee can, if she was afraid to go out after dark." Nikko said.

I gave him a hard look. "It's a guy."

Sheriff Olsen cleared his throat. "*Anyway*, I'd like to take a gander at what you've got recorded. Maybe we can ID this *guy* and I'll see if the staties want to go out and process things in the tent and so on. Maybe get some prints, hair, whatever. Now that there seems to be a connection with the victim it would be great to have a chat with this potential witness."

"Is he a suspect then?" I said.

"A dumb one," Nikko said, "if he hangs around after shooting someone."

Sheriff Olsen said, "A person of interest."

"Kat and I were going to her dad's office to look at the video, since, you know, our computer seems to have been destroyed."

"It deserved it," Sheriff Olsen said. "Anyway, I can't really go there with you because it will cause too much of a stir. I've got a new laptop coming from Amazon—I paid extra to have it expedited. Meanwhile, you two watch the thing and whatever you do, don't lose that little gizmo you used to record—"

"SD card," Nikko said.

"Whatever," Sheriff Olsen said. "Let me know *immediately* of anything helpful. I'll be getting ahold of Lieutenant Spiller from the State Police and don't be surprised if they swoop down on Wildwood."

* * *

Rose studied Nikko and me over the top of her half glasses as we walked into the office.

"Good afternoon, Mrs. Gustafson," Nikko said.

"Nikko," Rose said. "How nice to see you. Kathryn, I'm surprised you're here on your day off."

"We need to use my computer," I said. "Nikko has to write up a report about, er, some poaching and the Olsen computer is..."

"I'm very aware of what happened to the Olsen computer." Rose sniffed.

"I know, isn't my father a klutz?" Nikko said. "I mean, he tripped and accidentally dropped it into the campfire."

"Indeed?" Rose said.

"So, anyway," I said, "we'll just slip into my cubicle and—"

"Hi Kat! Hi Nikko!"

Gussy poked his head over his partition and grinned idiotically at us. It was no secret that Gussy thought Nikko was "totally awesome." Perhaps deep down, Gussy longed to wear a snappy uniform and tote a gun rather than don a plastic pocket protector and carry a briefcase. Such a transformation would only occur over his mother's cold, dead body.

"We need to get that report in the mail today, Gerald," Rose snapped.

Gussy's grin vanished and his head quickly disappeared behind his partition.

I wasn't able to close the door to my cubicle, mainly because there was no door, so Nikko and I had to be clever in viewing the so-called "gizmo" from the trail cam. We moved my computer off to the side of my desk so the screen would not be visible to curious onlookers. At least not easily visible.

"SO, ANYWAY KAT," Nikko loudly articulated, "I really appreciate your help on this report I need to turn in on POACHING STATISTICS for the past year in my county."

"HAPPY TO HELP," I bleated.

We booted up my computer and Nikko inserted an SD card reader into a port, then slid the SD card into the reader. The screen came to life and, albeit grainy and blurry, some sort of life form had triggered the camera.

"What the...?"

"Maybe a deer?" Nikko whispered. "The camera should only activate when something triggers it." Then he added, "THIS HERE IS YOUR WHITETAIL INFO."

"JUST LET ME LOOK AT THE NUMBERS," I said.

"I CAN HELP WITH NUMBERS!" Gussy yelled from behind his partition. "I'LL BE RIGHT THERE."

"Shit," I whispered. "This isn't going to work."

Nikko pulled the SD card out and slipped it in his pocket. "WELL DARN IT ALL, WHAT HAPPENED TO MY REPORT?"

"I THINK THE COMPUTER IS HAVING ISSUES," I said.

"Oh shoot," said Gussy as he stood in my pseudo doorway. "Maybe Raymond can help."

"Gerald, you need to work on that report," Rose said. She had also made her way over to my cubicle and was peering over Gussy's shoulder at my computer, which now had switched to screen saver.

"Problem here?"

Raymond. I hadn't even heard him come in.

"No, no," I said. "It's not anything. Just maybe a corrugated file."

"You mean corrupt—"

"Yeah, corrupt. Anyway, we'll figure something out later," I said, standing up.

"Sure, hey Kat," Nikko said. "I think it might be my card reader."

"What's going on?"

Char.

"Corruption of some sort," Rose said.

"Why are you here on your day off, Kat?" Char said. "Though I must say, I like the company you keep." She cast a sex-oozing smile at Nikko.

Annoyingly, he smiled back.

"Char Houle," she said, holding out her hand. "Have we met?"

"Nikko Olsen," he said, taking her hand for a moment. "I don't believe so, Ms. Houle. I certainly would remember if we had."

I was waiting for him to kiss the large, pretentious ring she was wearing.

"Okay, then," I said, glancing at my watch.

Char and Nikko broke their hand holding, but Char managed to position herself so that Nikko would need to brush against her to squeeze past.

"So, Nikko, do you off-road?" Char said.

"Off road?" I butted in.

"He knows what I mean," she said, "don't you?"

"Sure," Nikko said. "DNR has a couple of ORVs for getting around in the toolies."

"Toolies?" I said.

"The sticks," Nikko said.

I was starting to feel a bit out of the loop.

"Well," Char purred, "we should get a little mud on the tires sometime, Nikko. I have an awesome Polaris."

I heard the office phone ring and Rose give her clipped greeting.

"That so?" Nikko said, inching around Char.

"Uh huh," she said, sticking an ample breast in his way.

"Char," Rose said. "If you can tear yourself away from—from whatever you're doing, you have a call."

"Oh, pooh," Char said, pulling her boob back out of Nikko territory, "duty calls." She gave Nikko one last sultry glance and strutted away, butt twitching.

"Whew!" Nikko said. "Is it hot in here?"

"Not for long," I said. "C'mon. We can maybe go to the library and use their computer to look at this thing and if we're lucky, get a gander at your unwanted guest."

Turned out that our efforts were semi-productive. Something did appear on the screen—clearly an animal, presumably a deer, though it didn't seem quite right. Phantom horse? I wasn't even going to suggest it. The next shot was a little more of what we were hoping for. Clearly a person wearing a sweatshirt hoodie or jacket with a hood. You couldn't see his face, tell how tall he was, how old, or much of anything, but it was extremely likely it was Mr. Squatter. We kept going through the photos and other than the hooded mystery person, the only other thing that had tripped the camera was a fox, a squirrel, and a plastic bag that had probably blown from the squatter's compound.

"Well, maybe better luck next time," Nikko said. "If we could get a shot of his face, it would be great."

I felt my cell phone buzz, but by the time I could wrestle the thing out of my pocket and swipe to answer—or try to swipe—the call went to voice mail. While Nikko was driving me home, I cued up the message on speaker.

"Kat. It's Dad. Meet me at the Michigan State Police Post at 4:00. We have an interview with a Lieutenant Spiller about the, er, dead gal."

"Cripes," I said looking at my watch. "It's almost 4:00. Why do they want to talk to me?"

"You're a witness," Nikko said. "I can drop you."

"That would be great," I said.

Things were generally quiet for a while, except for Tobey's panting. As far as I could tell, Tobey panted 24/7, except perhaps when eating or sleeping. When he panted, he made a monotonous clicking noise that sounded like a leaky faucet.

"I've got to head back to Ontonagon in the morning," Nikko said.

"Uh huh," I said. "I appreciate your help. You know, with the trail cam and all."

"Sure," he said. "I'll be back in a few days and we can pull the next card. Maybe get better ID."

"Should I turn the one we have over to the state police?" I said.

"Hmm," Nikko said. "Good question. I guess I wouldn't unless they specifically ask. It doesn't seem to be of much help anyway."

"Okay," I said.

Tobey clicked, sucked in some stringy drool, then resumed clicking.

"Here we are," Nikko said unnecessarily, as the state police headquarters bore an enormous sign proclaiming its existence.

"Hey, thanks for the—"

Nikko put his hand on my shoulder and pulled me to him. Our faces were a couple of inches apart.

"Hey," he said.

"Hey," I said.

Our second kiss I'm thinking wasn't something to check off his bucket list. It involved some tongue and if it weren't for that damn console...

Tobey's panting, or maybe it was ours, was interrupted by loud pounding on the window.

"Hey you kids! You're steaming up the windows."

Nikko and I nearly dove for the floorboards. Tobey let out a startled bark, then resumed panting.

It was Dad. He was laughing at us and shaking his finger. "I'll tell Mother!" he said, then walked off toward the police headquarters.

"Well, that was quite a start," Nikko said.

Yeah, I thought. Good thing the console had kept things under control. I guess.

* * *

After a brief wait in the small lobby of the state police headquarters, a uniformed officer escorted us to Lieutenant Spiller's office. His quarters were a far cry from Sheriff Olsen's. Everything was spit spot, ship shape—almost painfully so. Spiller looked up from a laptop on his tidy desk and stood to shake Dad's and my hands.

"Lieutenant Spiller," he said unnecessarily, in that we had figured that out by the name on the door, the name on a desk sign, and his nametag pinned, or perhaps magnetically attached to the upper flap of his pocket. He wore a shiny gold bar on his collar and a couple of pins proclaiming various accomplishments on a breast pocket. His hair appeared to have been recently buzzed. On the corner of his desk perched a blue, rather tall cowboyish-looking hat, with a large badge gleaming above the brim.

"Gary Wilde," Dad said. "And this is—"

"Kathryn Wilde," I said.

"—my daughter."

"Thank you for coming," Spiller said. "Please have a seat."

Dad and I sat in the requisite molded plastic chairs while the Lieutenant sat back down behind his glowing desk.

"So, as you know," Spiller said, "we are assisting Sheriff Olsen in the investigation of a likely homicide on your premises."

Dad and I nodded.

"Sheriff Olsen has turned over a shoe that we believe to be the victim's. As I understand it, you found this shoe on your property."

I explained the chain of events, and that actually a rescued pit bull named Tobey was responsible for the find.

"And I also understand that you have been recording activity via a trail camera around the area."

"That's right," I said marveling at the speed in which information zipped around. I had a feeling that I was being scrutinized for some misdeed, so added, "One of your troopers did look at the campsite when we first found the, er, body. Of course it was before the shoe was found and nobody thought the squatter likely had any connection to the, um, death. They left a card on the tent asking for whoever was squatting there to get in contact."

"Hmm," Spiller said. "Of course they didn't. In any event, we'd very much appreciate your turning over any recording you have of activity around the compound. We'll have some people from the crime lab back out there to go over the place."

With that, I was forced to turn the SD card over to the Lieutenant. However, he hadn't *specifically* mentioned wanting the replacement Nikko and I switched out.

≈ 9 ≈

When I ascended the stairway from my basement lair the next morning, Mom and Dad were having what I'd define as an *anxious* discussion.

"So when's your sister coming?" Dad said.

Aunt Lindsey was coming? I loved Aunt Lin, as I called her. Aunt Lin was fifteen years younger than Mom, and only seven years older than me—or maybe eight. Anyway, she was more like a sister than an aunt to me.

"A week from Monday," Mom said. "I have to pick her up at the airport—that is if her flight actually arrives—at 1:30."

"And how long…"

"Who knows?" Mom said. "You know Lindsey."

"I suspect she's out of money," Dad said with a sigh.

"In between jobs," she said.

"And probably friends to sponge off of," he said.

"GARY! Truth be told, she's never really found her niche. She does all the Far East hocus pocus stuff and I guess some, I don't know, yoga, but not much of a career path in that. Last I knew Lindsey was working as a waitress at Denny's. I think she got fired when some fresh guy patted her bottom and she smacked him and her ring cut his face. I think he needed stitches."

Dad let out a yelp of laughter. "That sounds like Lindsey. You Galambos women are not to be messed with."

Galambos was Mom's maiden name and of course Aunt Lin's regular last name since she'd never been married. At least that any of us knew about.

I stepped into the bright kitchen lights and shaded my eyes. Jupiter came over to me and gave my ankle a bump.

"Well, of course she's welcome," Dad said giving me an appraising look. Perhaps I was not looking my best. "Good morning sunshine!"

"Don't let that cat trick you," Mom said. "I already gave him his breakfast."

"Aunt Lin is coming?" I said.

"Yup," Dad said. "She doesn't *ask*, just announces."

"She can be a bit, well, spontaneous," Mom said.

"That's nice," I said. "She's fun to have around."

"Uh huh," Dad said. "Fun."

"Gary…"

"So, do we put her in the home office?" I asked.

"Good suggestion," Dad said. "We can buy a cheap blow-up mattress."

"We'll do no such thing," Mom said. "She can bunk with Kat."

"Huh?" I said. "But—"

"Or…" Dad said.

"Or what," Mom said.

"The modular house at Wildwood Stables will be arriving early next week on two flatbed trailers, along with a crane to put it on the new foundation, which is curing as we speak. It should only take a few days for the crew to put on the finishing touches—you know, the mechanics and some drywall, and a bit of shingling. Maybe we can get it inspected and cleared for habitation quickly. Really all we need is electricity, which is already there and ready to hook up, and a flushing toilet. The septic system has passed muster. Kat could move into the house and Lindsey could sleep in our basement."

"Yow!" Jupiter proclaimed.

"I will not have Kathryn living alone out at that—that *place*. At least not right now. There was a murder for God's sake, and the killer could be lurking anywhere."

"Yow!" Jupiter repeated.

Not to mention that some derelict was living in a tent a half mile or so from where I'd be sleeping and then there were my phantom horse sightings, which just added a nice supernatural twist to the place. All in all, I had to side with Mom on this one.

"Hmmm," Dad said. "Lindsey does have a formidable, ah, presence."

"So what's that got to do with my daughter being all alone out in the middle of nowhere?" Mom said.

"How about Kat *and* Lindsey move into the place at Wildwood. Plus we can install some security. I was planning to anyway," Dad said.

I cleared my throat.

"That is, if Kat is agreeable. After all, it's her new, er, venture."

"Yow!"

Mom looked at me, forehead furrowed. I knew that look. She was not entirely onboard to have me living in the "toolies" as Nikko described them, formidable aunt or not. Yow, indeed.

* * *

The state police, or "staties" as Nikko called them did indeed swoop down on Wildwood stables first thing Monday morning, specifically the horse camp where our mysterious squatter was once again nowhere to be found. They left the camp more or less intact but did take photos, supposedly dusted for prints, gathered fibers and whatnot. It was fascinating to watch. Also fascinating that they never spotted the trail camera. Nikko had done an excellent job of blending it in with the environment.

Good to his word, Dad gave everyone a week's paid time off after tax season was officially in the rearview mirror. However, it was not a vacation by any means. Once the state police collected their evidence, they told us to let them know if we actually saw the squatter, but under no circumstances should we attempt an apprehension. No worries there.

Dad and I watched the police mobile crime lab leave, mincing its way down our rutted road.

"Hope they figure something out," Dad said.

"Yeah," I said, wondering if the police took the giant machete. I had a feeling they took some of the clothes and that Mr. Squatter might be kind of pissed when he returned to his digs.

"Good job getting hay in the barn," Dad said, abruptly changing the subject.

"I actually got it for a buck a bale from Pete's on Saturday," I said, "and he delivered it for free. I think he was glad to get rid of it and make room for the new stuff this spring. The wood chip bedding cost more than the hay, though. I just got a few bags, since who knows when there will be any horses in this place."

What I didn't mention was that I had to start a tab at Pete's since I didn't have sufficient funds in my account to swipe a debit card. Pete was used to running accounts for folks. For the most part, he got paid. Eventually.

"Well, that's what I was going to mention," Dad said, looking a bit contrite. "I have a client who couldn't pay his bill, so we kind of bartered."

"Bartered?" I said. "Which client?"

"Jonas Dubba," Dad said.

I vaguely remembered Mr. Dubba. He was a crusty old reprobate that I heard owed money to everybody in the county. Rose showed high contempt for Jonas Dubba.

"Deadbeat Dubba?"

"Yeah. His daughter has a horse, but she just got married and moved out. She can't take the horse with her and Dubba wants it gone. He said he's going to take it to an auction or something and dump it."

"What! That's horrible," I said. I hated people that thought animals were disposable. Tobey was an example of a critter just kicked to the curb, and except for the incessant panting, he was a very good boy.

"So, I agreed to forgive the client's outstanding bill, which I'll never collect anyway, in exchange for this horse. Sorry I didn't consult with you, but it just kind of happened."

"What breed?" I had to admit, I was starting to get excited. My first horse! Maybe an Arabian or a Quarter Horse. Or maybe one of the trendy new warmbloods. And I didn't even have a roof over my head yet. I wondered if my old riding jodhpurs would still fit. Was there still some usable tack around? I didn't have a clue what had happened to my black leather riding boots. I think I wore them as fashion boots and vaguely remember them being in a box somewhere.

"I've got no idea what breed. It sounds like it's older, so probably nice and quiet. Since I'm not sure Phil's old horse trailer is up to snuff yet, I got the farmer up the street to bring it over in his stock trailer, in exchange for some free tax advice. It should be here tomorrow, so maybe you want to get a stall set up, get a couple of buckets out. Buy some oats."

I thought about the feed bin that the late Sasha Summers had occupied. It was gone, of course as evidence, but nothing much had yet been done to get the tack and feed room up and running. But still. A horse! I felt like a kid at Christmas.

"What color is it—and is it a gelding or a mare?" I asked.

"I think Jonas called it a 'he' and mentioned his name was Rusty, to match his color."

"When is, er, Rusty going to be delivered?"

"Well, the farmer said he could do it tomorrow morning,"

Rusty. Not the most promising name, but better than Diablo or Brutus. Rusty conjured up a kind of "well used" image.

And well used he was.

* * *

"Most cantankerous animal I've ever dealt with," snarled Will Maki as he walked around to the back of his stock trailer. "And I've raised bulls that just as soon tramp you into the mud as look at ya. Only got this pain in the, er, butt in the trailer with some molasses corn and my three boys pushing for all they's worth."

I heard a lot of stomping and snorting from within.

"Stand back, girlie. I think the dang thing broke his tie and got hisself turned around."

When Maki unlatched the back door and lowered the ramp, Rusty stuck his head out and took a look around. True to Maki's prediction, Rust launched out of the trailer and Maki barely got hold of the broken lead tie that the horse had apparently either snapped or chewed through.

Rusty snorted and took in his surroundings while I took a look at him. I'd never seen a more neglected, pathetic horse in my life. His rust-colored coat was dull and chunks of matted hair hung from his belly. His mane and tail were snarled and probably full of burrs. Clearly there were scars where perhaps an ill-fitting saddle had sat and maybe the horse had had a run-in with barbed wire. The halter he wore had rubbed his nose raw. His hooves were overgrown and cracked to the point that it had to make walking awkward and maybe painful. But most distressing of all was that the horse was beyond thin. He was emaciated. I couldn't decide whether to be angry or to burst into sobs for the poor creature's condition.

"Well, here yous go, miss," Maki said holding out the frayed lead rope. "Tell yer pa we're even now. And good luck with this rascal. That bum Dubba should be thrown in jail for neglecting an animal like this."

I tentatively took the frayed lead rope and reached to stroke Rusty's neck. He instantly jerked away, nearly pulling the rope out of my grasp. Maki hopped in his truck and sped off.

"Smacked you around, didn't they," I said in a low voice. I remembered Uncle Phil telling me that horses responded better if we kept our voice down and soft. Rusty eyed me, waiting to see what this human was going to do to him. His eyes were dull and anxious at the same time. His ears were not exactly flat, but slightly pinned back. He twitched his ratty tail impatiently.

"Well, your days of being smacked around are over," I said, tentatively extending my hand. Rusty ignored it but dropped his head a bit.

I looked him over again: the emaciation, cracked hooves, matted dirty coat, and most disturbing, the lackluster expression. He needed a lot of attention—expensive attention—to give him a chance, such as from a vet, farrier, and maybe a horse shrink. So far I owed Pete's for the hay and the bedding and a bag of Happy Horse sweet feed. I was still making payments to the mechanic who had fixed my Subaru. The landlord had let me out of my lease on my apartment when I had lost my grant writer job at the hospital, but I lost my security deposit in the deal. I wondered how much credit the town would give me before they cut me off. Then, of course, there was the massive debt to Dad, which in a fit of pride I had insisted on incurring. I may have been a bit hasty in doing that.

Speaking of Dad, what was he thinking, bringing this broken-down horse to Wildwood, without running it past me? Not like Dad at all to do something slap dash. I suspected he was hoping I'd feel sorry for something other than myself. Well played, Dad.

Rusty and I headed to the barn where I had cleaned up a stall, put down some fresh bedding, and set up a water bucket and hay net. Rusty allowed himself to be led into the barn but made it clear in no uncertain terms that he would not enter the stall. When I urged him along, he balked, snorted, and flung his head side to side, nearly jerking the lead rope out of my hand.

"But there's food and water inside, fella," I said, trying to keep my voice low and soothing. Rusty backed away, pulling me along. For a horse nearly starved to death, he had mustered an amazing amount of strength.

"Okay, okay," I said. I wondered what horrors the horse had endured in the confines of a stall—a place he obviously viewed with great apprehension if not outright terror. "We'll figure something else out."

Once back outside, Rusty seemed to relax and actually pricked his ears forward a bit and we both looked the place over. He likely wondered where the heck he was and I wondered what in hell I was doing at Wildwood alone, the site of an unsolved murder, holding the frayed end of a lead rope attached to a deranged horse. While I'm not sure what Rusty was looking at, I was eyeing a paddock that was more or less in decent shape.

I led Rusty toward the paddock gate and chatted him up, shamelessly promising him this and that. Much to my relief he allowed himself to be led into the paddock. Somewhat against my better judgment, I removed the halter that had rubbed his nose raw. I mentally added *new halter with padded noseband* to my ever-growing list of equine needs. Next I transported the hay net and water bucket to the paddock. Rusty continued to stare off into the horizon, nickered then whinnied loudly, lips flapping around his yellow teeth. He gave a little snort then finally came over and took a long drink, emptying the bucket. I went back to the hydrant in the barn and refilled the bucket and returned. In my brief absence, Rusty had begun pulling hay from the hay net. His expression may have softened a bit. Praise God, he was settling in.

I wasn't keen on leaving Rusty alone at Wildwood, but my new modular house wasn't supposed to arrive until the next day, and then Aunt Lin on Monday. Officially, I wasn't to take residence at Wildwood until such time as those two items were in place, not to mention some kind of security system. Well, I had the whole week off work, so could spend days working to try to bring Wildwood into some kind of shape so that maybe, just maybe, we could attract some potential customers by summer. I figured I'd start with boarding horses. Then maybe teach beginning riding lessons to little kids. Of course I'd need a string of schooling horses for that. Details, details. Maybe someday we could outfit trail rides and get the horse camp going again. It was all so overwhelming. I looked over at Rusty in his paddock. He had gone over to the fence and was staring off at the horizon. I wondered what was going on in his little horsey brain. Surely he wasn't longing for his crappy life at Dubba's rundown homestead. Then I heard the growl of a big engine and saw what looked like an aircraft carrier approaching slowly down Horse Camp Road. Rusty snorted and tossed his head around. He even managed to prance a bit, albeit a bit jerky.

My modular home had arrived a day early.

10

I was the first one up the next morning, an anomaly for certain in the Wilde household. That is with the exception of Jupiter, who stood haughtily next to his feed dish when I staggered upstairs. My shoulders, back, arms, neck, legs, and other parts of my body yet to be identified screamed in pain. I had spent the better part of the previous day cleaning, shoveling, hauling, lifting, bending, and dragging things around at Wildwood. I also spent over an hour with currycomb, brush, hoof pick, and mane and tail detangler on Rusty, trying to bring some life back into his ratty, neglected coat. I had rigged a set of crossties in the barn and hooked Rusty up, waiting to see how he felt about things. He pawed a bit, tossed his head, but didn't freak out. Once I got into the grooming regime, he twitched a bit, then went into a kind of relaxed readiness, suspicious of any kindness or pleasure. Rusty still refused to enter his stall, so I was forced to return him to his paddock. It worried me. There were wolves and coyotes around, though I was pretty sure Rusty would clean their clocks if need be. Nonetheless, I had anxiously watched his image in my rearview mirror as I left Wildwood and headed toward home.

It was my concern for Rusty that got me up and at 'em so bright and early, although I'm sure Jupiter stridently believes that it is he that the Wilde family dynamics rotate around. After I got the coffee going, I provided the cat with a blob of gourmet cat food proclaiming to be liver pâté. Jupiter circled it twice and dove in, making his usual humming noise.

Horse Camp Road was a bit worse for wear from all the machinery and truck traffic that had come and gone. Word was that the finishers, electrician, and a plumber would all be fighting for space over the next couple of days. I beat them all to Wildwood that morning.

I wondered how Rusty had fared alone and standing out in a paddock overnight. I suspected he was used to hardships, but still...

Then a shot of adrenaline set my heart into overdrive as I bumped my way down the road and the paddock came into view. No Rusty. Maybe he was lying down and hard to see. I pushed the Subaru to the limit, exhaust system clanging ominously as I tore into the potholed parking lot, jammed the car into park and jumped out.

The paddock gate hung open and the horse was gone. I did a quick 360 assessment, calling his name, but saw nothing. The stable doors were shut as I had left them. But I slid one open and flipped on the lights. Other than a mouse scurrying for cover, nothing else moved. I exited the other end of the building and scanned the landscape, then looked down. Hoofprints. They were leading toward the horse camp. I called his name again, even though it was fruitless. I stumbled along the rutted two-track toward the horse camp, following the meandering trail of hoofprints. The divots were not deep or spread out, which led me to believe that he wasn't panicked and galloping to flee something, more like a morning stroll through the woods. I spotted the tin roof of the horse camp outhouse and the listing nylon tent. So far, no horse, but the tracks led on. I felt a prickle run up the back of my neck. I wasn't crazy about visiting the squatter's paradise without some backup. But clearly that was where Rusty was headed.

I tried to move quietly, though the opportunity for stealth went out the door from my screaming myself hoarse calling Rusty. I did the only sensible thing and that was to announce myself.

"HELLO! Anybody home?" I called as if I were on the stoop of somebody's house holding a plate of brownies and politely knocking on the door.

As the encampment came into view, I noted that the hoofprints veered off the road and headed into the brush. I bent over to study the broken weeds and disturbed underbrush, trying to decide if I should follow the damn trail, which had a healthy batch of last fall's stickers and burrs.

"YOU!"

I jerked up and spun around in time to spot a figure lurching out of the tent, madly waving something at me.

I heard a scream. I think it was mine.

* * *

At last the squatter and I met. I wasn't crazy about the timing, being nobody else around for miles. We stared at each other. He continued to jut something out in front of him. I was relieved to note it wasn't the previously observed machete, which I suspect the police had confiscated. In fact, it looked like a stick. Rather innocuous. Not that I'd want to be bludgeoned by it, but better than swift decapitation.

"They took all my stuff!" he said. "They had no right. I live here."

"Um, about that. See, you're trespassing, and so—"

"Hah!" he said. "YOU'RE the one trespassing. In fact, get the hell out of my, ah, area."

Okay, now I was getting more pissed than scared.

"This camp is part of Wildwood Stables, which I own," I said. "Therefore, buddy, it's *you* who don't belong here. In fact, I'm officially telling you to get the hell off my land."

"They had no right! That machete had value! I use it to cut up stuff."

"Uh huh," I said. "Well, you might just want to speak to the police about your so-called stuff. In fact the police would love to talk to *you!*"

"That so?"

"Yup. See, there was an, er, suspicious death here and—"

"No shit, lady. You think I don't know that? It was my *sister* who was killed. They haven't done crap about it, either. And I *have* talked to the police, for your information."

Took me a minute to process this latest tidbit of info. Okay, this was the brother of Sasha Saari-Summers. I poked around in my brain, trying to remember his name.

"So, you're, um..."

"Scott Summers. And by all rights you are on my land."

I finally took a minute to take him in. He had lowered the stick, which wasn't much of a threat anyway. And as one might expect of a person living in a crummy tent with no indoor plumbing and only a campfire to keep warm, Scott Summers looked a tad worse for wear. Greasy long hair, possibly blond, hung from under a scruffy knit hat. He had a badly neglected crusty beard. His clothes were filthy and he wore only tennis shoes, even though the weather suggested boots would be the footgear of choice. Summers had no gloves, and I could see that his hands were raw and possibly bleeding from exposure. While I estimated him to be somewhere approaching middle age, he had a wizened look of the aged that reminded me of a cross between Yoda and Merlin the wizard. Most noticeable, just below the edge of his ratty knit hat and smack-dab in the middle of his forehead, was a purplish/red mark. Likely he was the proud owner of a birthmark, which did nothing to improve his appearance. All in all, Scott Summers gave the impression of a disreputable vagabond. The only thing missing was a purloined shopping cart overflowing with his personal effects. Whatever his beef and no matter his appearance I was *not* I going to start feeling sorry for the guy.

I stretched to my full and hopefully intimidating height. "I beg to differ," I said, emulating Rose Gustafson's haughty tone. "This is part of Wildwood Stables, and I own it."

"Your Uncle Phil owned it!" he said.

"Yes, well, Uncle Phil passed away last fall and my father inherited—"

"Bullcrap!" he spat. "My sister was his kid. She should have gotten this shithole. But someone made sure she couldn't make a claim."

He eyed me, converting his demeanor from anger to arrogance. "Seems to me you hoity toity Wildes had a pretty good motive to shut my sister up."

"Hey! We never knew who she was—or claimed to be—until after she was, er, died."

"So you say."

"Anyway, what makes you think my Uncle Phil would have left you so much as a—"

"It doesn't matter what your fuckin' Uncle Phil would have done. It was my sister's inheritance as his kid. And I'm her brother and she would have left it to me, if she had a chance to make a will or whatever. I'm her closest living relative. In fact, her only living relative. Ma's dead."

"I'm sorry for your loss," I said. Okay maybe a lame platitude, but...

"Bite me," he said.

So much for decorum. "Why wouldn't I maybe think that *you* killed your half-sister to get her estate? Pretty good motive."

Maybe I pushed the envelope a bit far with that one, because Summers reengaged his stick and plunged at me. I felt his weight plow into my chest and went down on my back, knocking the wind out of me.

"It's MINE!" he shrieked, flailing the stick around.

I struggled under his weight. He wasn't a great fighter, but then neither was I. I imagined our floundering looked like a couple of beached whales.

"LIKE HELL!" I screamed back. "Get. OFF. ME!"

He pressed his face close to mine and hissed through his teeth fogging the air with really bad breath. "And you, bitch, can bet that when I get this place, I'll sell it to the highest bidder. Maybe they put up condos or something. Maybe a garbage dump."

I felt him let up a bit and managed to maneuver around enough to give him an anemic knee to the groin. It wasn't a fatal blow, but nonetheless effective.

"What th'," he bellowed and rolled into the fetal position. "Fuckin' bitch."

I staggered to my feet and bent over resting my hands on my knees, panting. "Yeah, I'm a badass bitch, and don't you forget it, *Scott.*"

I pulled out my phone; it had one bar. I punched in 911.

The dispatcher gave the usual clipped greeting: *911, what's your emergency?*

I told her. She assured me help was on the way.

I stood and looked down at Summers. He was still distracted by his man parts. Kat Wilde: warrior!

"You'll pay, Wilde," he muttered. "Big time. And I know something about your precious Uncle Phil. And it ain't about my sister!"

I heard some branches snap and the rustling of brush. I looked beyond the camp and spotted Rusty plodding back. With an unlikely friend.

* * *

Summers managed to sit up, knees bent and looked from Rusty to me. I looked at Rusty and his friend, a lovely whitetail doe, that hung back a bit, obviously shy around humans who were known to shoot at her species.

Rusty looked at me then the man sitting in a mudhole. Perhaps the horse and I had bonded a little, because Rusty approached Scott in a less than friendly manner. In fact, the horse's ears were pinned back quite determinedly and he tossed his head up and down. If I didn't know better, I would say Rusty was protecting me. Or, maybe, the deer he had brought home with him. I felt as if I were living in a fairy tale or perhaps a nightmare. It was all so—odd.

"Get that damn horse away from me," Summers said, as he struggled to his feet.

"I don't really have much say in what Rusty does," I said.

The doe continued to watch. I noticed she had one ear that flopped over.

I heard a siren approaching.

I also heard the distant whine of an engine somewhere off in the woods, the sound bouncing in and out. The police siren cut off. Probably they'd turned onto Horse Camp Road. The mysterious engine noise in the woods continued, fading in and out. I was familiar with the sound of an ORV, engine revving, grinding, growling, screaming, and sputtering. This one was a ways off and I suspected they were tearing things up either on the Wildwood property or adjoining Crystal Lake Wilderness. Both scenarios were violations, but not worthy of my immediate attention.

"I'm the fuck outta here!" Scott said.

I refocused on my wrestling partner. "Stay put, Summers," I said. "Actually, Rusty is a trained attack horse, waiting for my signal." *I wish*. I swear Rusty gave me a dubious look.

"Yeah, right," Scott said as he stumbled off toward the woods.

What the hell! The cops *must* be close, maybe making their way back to the horse camp. But Summers would have a head start. However, as fate would have it, his mistake was not fleeing me but rather approaching the floppy-eared doe, albeit coincidentally. Rusty plunged after him, knocked him to the ground and pinned him with a substantial hoof on the shin. Floppy Ear flitted off into the woods. Summers managed to manipulate his stick and give Rusty a whack. When the horse jerked away, Summers freed his leg and scrambled to his feet. Limping noticeably, he plunged off through the thicket.

"Hey! COME BACK HERE YOU, YOU..." I shouted. "Nobody hits my horse!"

The distant whine of an ORV engine continued, but not moving. Idling maybe. Drinking a beer, smoking some weed, planning their next violation.

"POLICE! FREEZE!"

I froze. Summers had fled and Rusty and the deer vanished.

"He went that way!" I yelled at the trooper who dove out of his cruiser. "There, in the woods!" I said, pointing frantically to the spot where I'd last seen Summers. Another state police vehicle arrived and skidded to a stop, overheads strobing crazily.

The original trooper took off into the woods. The other dashed out of the cruiser and hurried to me. It was a woman trooper and she asked if I was okay and mentioned that I was bleeding. Her name badge said "Witz." She had sergeant stripes on her uniform jacket. I lifted my hand to my face and noted that indeed I was bleeding, and also now that the adrenaline had tapered off, my left knee hurt when I put weight on it. And my ribs were killing me. I was having a little trouble breathing. A lot of trouble, actually. Asshole better not have cracked any of my ribs.

"Do you need medical attention, miss?" she asked.

"I—I don't know," I said.

Next Dad's truck bumped down the road to the horse camp. His truck bucked with a sudden stop, still bouncing when Dad jumped out.

"KAT! What happened?" he shouted as he ran over. "Honey, are you okay?"

And another police car arrived adding to the collection of blinding overhead lights. This time it was the sheriff, Ollie Olsen, who came to join the party. He extracted himself from his cruiser, put his hat on and strode over.

"There's a damn horse running loose down the road, there. And I almost hit a deer that darted out in front of me," he said.

"That would be Rusty and his friend, Floppy Ear," I wheezed.

"Huh?" Ollie said.

"It's a long story," I mumbled.

"Hey, forget the horse," Dad said. "What in the hell is going on, Kat? Why are you out here at this—this vagrant's compound all alone?"

"A very long story," I said with a sigh.

"Ambulance on the way," said Sergeant Witz.

"Um, I don't think I need..."

Next thing I knew, a couple of paramedics were crouched next to me, likely checking my vitals and whatnot. I had never passed out before. But then, I had never been attacked by a lunatic and possibly saved by a horse smitten with a floppy-eared deer. I sat up, feeling ridiculous.

"We put a butterfly bandage on that cut," one of the paramedics said. "We recommend that you have your other injuries checked out at the emergency department."

"I'm fine, I just—"

"I'll take her," Dad said.

"But wait," I said. "It was Scott Summers! He's the dude living here at the horse camp. Said a bunch of crap about owning the place."

"Summers, eh?" Sheriff Olsen said.

"Kat, you can talk to the police late—" Dad said.

"Rusty! We have to catch him and get him back in the paddock," I said, trying to stand.

I looked toward the woods and saw the trooper who'd pursued Summers come out empty-handed. He shrugged. "Lost him," he said. "But he can't get far on foot. We'll get him."

During the mayhem, the ORV engine noise had faded away into silence. I stared off into the woods where my apparent nemesis had escaped. And, okay, maybe it was from the earlier adrenaline rush, but I saw it again. And it wasn't Rusty, or the doe. It was the apparition I had seen some weeks ago. Not quite all there, but a horse nonetheless, which cast a greenish-brown image that seemed to undulate like a mist. It tossed its head and pawed the ground.

"There! In the woods," I shouted and pointed.

Everyone turned to look.

And Rusty came sauntering out of the woods, mane and tail chock full of burrs, legs splattered with mud, new halter askew. We watched him stride past us and stroll on down the two-track leading back toward the stable and my unfinished modular house.

"So, that's the new horse?" Sheriff Olsen said. "Kind of rough looking."

I nodded and watched Rusty's butt disappear around the bend. I turned my attention back to the woods, squinting at the place where the diaphanous mystery horse had appeared. Either I was going bat-crap crazy, or something or someone was gaslighting me.

Or both.

11

Eventually all the police cars left. We put Rusty in his paddock with hay and water and Dad took me to the walk-in clinic to have my war wounds evaluated. I was x-rayed and given a little white pill for the pain and possibly to shut me up. Nothing broken or even cracked, just bruised. I may have a slightly torn thing in my knee. Something unpronounceable that sounded like a foreign dish cleverly named to disguise its unpalatability.

Meniscus, Dad told Mom, who fluttered in, bringing all my insurance info with her. I thanked God that Wilde accounting provided me with medical, even though I had no idea how I'd pay the substantial deductible, copay, and whatnot. I giggled when I thought about my ridiculous amount of debt. My parents gave me a concerned look.

"Pain med," the doctor said as he walked into my curtain cubicle. His name badge bore a multi-syllable and totally unpronounceable name. I suspected he was Middle Eastern. Maybe India Indian, Pakistani or some such exotic place. A handsome dude. He smiled warmly and said, "Some people, well, get a little silly."

Then I started to cry.

"And there can be a manic/depressant kind of reaction," he added. "Wouldn't hurt to see an ortho for that knee. Get an MRI. My opinion is that it's minor and will resolve, but we can't really tell without further imaging.

"Ride?" I said.

The doctor looked at me quizzically. "You mean can you drive?"

"She has a horse," Dad explained. "Although he's not really ridable at the moment."

"Oh, I see. Sure, eventually," the doctor said. "What kind of horse do you have?"

"Um, a cross of some kind, I think," I said.

"How nice. My wife raises Arabians. Beautiful animals."

I was glad he was married lest Mom give one last-ditch effort to hook me up with a doctor. I was doing just fine on my own. Yessir! What was another thousand or so of debt?

"The nurse will be in with the discharge instructions and a pair of crutches," Dr. Whatsit said. "Nice meeting you all. I suggest you follow up with your regular doctor, Miss Wilde. He or she can order an MRI and then refer you to an orthopedic doctor."

If I had a *regular* doctor, which I didn't. Crutches? I had walked into the hospital just fine. Okay, I limped a little, well hopped, and maybe Dad held on to me. I'd humor everyone for the moment and wrangle the things but would ditch them once I got home. I mean, I lived in a basement. I snorted unbecomingly and somehow choked on the snot. Was that even physically possible? Kat Wilde: woman of untold talent.

Dad cleared his throat, as if trying to teach me the proper way to deal with phlegm. "I'm heading in to meet with Sheriff Olsen, then out to the stable to see if the workers are there. Mom will take you home." He bent over and gave me a peck on the forehead, then raised his eyebrows at Mom in some sort of secret message.

"So, anyway," Mom said as she helped me out of that ridiculous hospital gown back into my civvies, "we have a little surprise at home." She tried to inflict some chirpiness into her voice, but it came out flat. "Aren't you going to use the crutches?"

"Yeah, sure. I guess. Surprise?" I said. "Good or bad?"

"Well, good, of course," she said. "I guess."

* * *

Mom and I went into the house via the kitchen door. I dumped the crutches on the stoop and grabbed my hiking stick that I kept leaning against the door jamb. I thumped my way in and spotted a figure sitting at the kitchen table—female—with her back to us. Bright purple hair flowed down her back. She wore a serape kind of cape thing, and a knit hat that defied all logic—perhaps made from "repurposed" tube socks. Jupiter peeked over her shoulder and gave us a haughty look.

"Um, hello?" I said.

The woman jumped up, unceremoniously dumping the cat on the floor. "Kat! Darling. Ohmygod, are you all right?"

"Aunt Lin!" I squealed and hobbled to her.

She pulled me in and gave me a big hug. I let out a yelp. "Ribs," I gasped.

"Oh, shoot, so sorry," Aunt Lin said, holding me out at arm's length. "Clara said that you were *attacked!* What the hell?"

"I didn't say *attacked*," Mom said. "I said assaulted."

"Same thing," Aunt Lin muttered. "Clara, dear sister, you haven't changed."

"It's a long story," I said before the two got into a wordsmith squabble. I absently rubbed my bruised side. "I thought you were coming next Monday. Um, your hair is, *interesting.*"

"Yes, me too," Mom said as she removed her coat and hung it in the entry closet. "You could have called, Lindsey. We would certainly have been happy to pick you up at the airport." Mom's voice had a tinge of annoyance.

"Well, see, my plans unexpectedly changed and I didn't have a chance to call. Yeah, and my hair is supposed to be *raven* but it turned out puke purple. I haven't had a chance…anyway, I thought I'd just surprise everyone. You know, get an Uber. Turns out the people at the airport never heard of Ubers or Lyft or even regular taxi service. They suggested I either rent a car—apparently they had a choice of two rentals available—or call a guy named Bob who ran a kind of under-the-table shuttle service. He gives rides for a *donation,*" she said, making quote marks with her fingers. "So, since renting the car was not in the budget, I called Bob and, well, here I am. I gave the dude $25 and he seemed thrilled. And speaking of hair, darling niece, yours looks like it was combed in a woodchipper."

Good ol' Aunt Lin. She never pulled any punches. "Well, in my hair's defense," I said, "I just got out of the hospital emergency department."

"What, they don't have mirrors there? Hey, just kidding sweetie, you look fantastic. Other than you appear to be crippled—temporary, I hope. Have you lost weight? Not that you really needed to, but you look, I don't know, fit. Maybe even *taller.*"

"Well, I've been working at the stable and—"

"Yow!"

Jupiter emerged from under the table where he had been licking his wounded pride and began to wind around Aunt Lin's legs.

"Oh, dear. I'm so sorry *sir,*" she said, picking up the cat and giving him a scratch under the chin. Jupiter stoically tolerated the attention. If anyone else tried to scratch him under the chin or, God forbid, at the base of his tail, they would likely be eviscerated with a multitude of razor-sharp claws.

"Well, we're glad you're here," Mom said flatly. "Have you eaten?"

"I did have a Snickers bar at O'Hare. Cost me five bucks. Actually, I'm starved."

I managed to make my way down to my basement quarters, favoring my good leg and keeping a firm grip on the banister. I flicked on the light and was greeted with a collection of Aunt Lin's suitcases. This was cause for concern since there was only one bed in my cellar suite: mine. While I loved my auntie, I wasn't keen on sharing a bed. At least not with a family member. This thought made my mind wander a bit into the realm of CO Nikko Olsen. He promised to come around to check the trail camera the coming weekend. Of course, now that the mystery of the squatter was solved, the cam could be taken down. Or maybe not. Who knows if the guy would be stupid enough to come back. This sent a chill down the back of my neck. I wondered if it recorded any of the sloppy fight between Summers and me. I also wondered what Nikko would have to say about that. Would he get all chivalrous and protective? Maybe he'd want to look at my bruises. My thoughts were turning a little steamy—maybe from the pain meds? How long had it been anyway? Two years? Five? College? Who remembers what one did at college? Nothing since? How pathetic. And big deal. I mean, Nikko and I had, what, kissed twice? Granted, there *was* some promise in the last one.

"Yoo hoo!" Mom chirped from the top of the stairs. "We're having a late lunch. And we have a special guest!"

Saved by the bell. And just like that, my thoughts turned from lust to lunch.

Turns out the subject of my lusty meanderings was the special guest, Nikko. Good thing I had changed into fresh jeans and a sweater and scraped my gnarly hair into a ponytail before emerging from the bowels of the house.

"Hey, Kat!" he said, rushing over to me and gently grasping both my arms, pulling me toward him. "Are you okay? Dad said you were *assaulted*! Are you limping?"

"Yeah, had a bit of a tussle with our squatter. Messed up my knee, I guess. I imagine your dad told you who it is." Nikko's face was six inches from mine. I could smell his minty mouthwash breath. My exhale probably was not so refreshing. "Hey, I thought you weren't coming until the weekend." I noticed Mom watching, so I carefully pulled away and was released back into the neutral zone.

"Well, I have to get back tonight. I had a meeting, and Dad told me that the dude squatting in your place is the brother of the, er, deceased and that the ass—er jerk attacked you with a stick and that your horse somehow got involved—you have a horse? Anyway. Wow, a lot has happened since last time I saw you. You are not a dull girlfriend."

Girlfriend? This made Mom arch one eyebrow—never knew how she could do that.

"Wow is right," Aunt Lin said. "This is juicy as hell. And I thought things would be dullsville here. Hey, you're Kat's fella, eh?"

"Um," I said. "He means we're friends and I'm a girl. So, girlfriend in that sense." I looked at Nikko.

He smiled and winked. "Whatever you say, Wilde."

Mom set a platter of sandwiches on the table with a thud. "Sit," she commanded. "Time to eat here at dullsville."

We obeyed.

* * *

Somehow the week of great accomplishment had slipped away, with much at Wildwood Stables' resurrection left *unaccomplished*. My knee had improved but I knew it would be stupid to press my luck with strenuous activity, but there was plenty of light duty available. I did have an appointment with Mom's doctor, but it was going to be a couple of weeks. On the bright side, the modular was coming along. We were waiting for some kind of Certificate of Occupancy, which allowed humans to reside legally within the dwelling. There had been serious discussion at the Wilde household about my taking up residence, even with Aunt Lin, at a remote place that had been not only the location of a dustup between Scott Summers (still on the lam) and me, but the scene of a yet unsolved murder. Not a great neighborhood by Mom's estimate. On the other hand, basement bunking with my retro-hippie aunt had been less than ideal. She burned incense and played very strange music—on a lyre—into the wee hours. I had learned to be an early riser, which did not appeal to her. Plus, I gave her my bed (she had a bad back—supposedly), which shifted my sleeping arrangements to an air mattress that slowly deflated during the night. We both very quickly became sleep-deprived and moderately cranky.

"Kat and I can kick ass of anybody who dares to do something that requires ass-kicking," Aunt Lin said. "Plus I can shoot. But I need a gun, of course."

"Oh God," Mom said. "Please, no gun!"

Aunt Lin tossed her head, sending her purple hair into a psychedelic wave.

We heard a knock on the door and Nikko poked his head into the kitchen where our heated debate was taking place. "Hi all," he said. "Did I hear something about a gun?"

* * *

As promised, Nikko had come for the weekend and pulled the SD card out of the trail camera and replaced it with a new one. We hoped that the bum would return to the so-called scene of the crime. But with police departments being chronically short-staffed in the U.P., surveillance was not likely, so the camera could verify that he had returned, but to actually catch the guy would be challenging.

Police had canvassed the area. They checked with local residents who may have seen a man on foot. Zip. They also randomly checked out vacant camps in case Summers was lying low in one of them. Nada. The convenience store where Summers had stocked up from time to time had not seen him since the day of his "alleged" assault on me. We had left the tent and miscellaneous items at the squatter compound just in case Summers returned, which was doubtful. Only an idiot would, right?

After Nikko and I got the trail cam squared away, we climbed into his dad's Tahoe and headed back to the stable.

"So where's Tobey?" I said.

"Home recovering from his surgery," Nikko said.

"Surgery! Is he okay?"

"Depends on what you mean by okay. Well, yeah, he's fine, but he won't be happy when he realizes what they've done to him. Plus he has to wear a plastic cone over his head so he doesn't try to, er, mess with his stiches." Nikko gave a little shudder.

"Ah, I think I have an inkling of what you are talking about," I said.

"Yeah. Seems Tobey got a little amorous with the pedigree female poodle next door and everyone involved, except Tobey, felt it best to get him what the vet referred to as 'the kindest cut.'"

"I see," I said. "We had to do a similar thing to Jupiter. They put the Cone of Shame on him afterwards too."

"Cone of Shame?"

"Right. Animals, at least dogs think they're being punished and have no idea why. Cats, however, more likely think they're being tormented by their humans and have no forgiveness in their hearts. I think cats build grudges over the years. Jupiter managed to get his cone off and hid it somewhere. We've never been able to find it."

"Can't say I blame them—the pets, you know," Nikko said. "I mean, boys will be boys."

"Uh huh," I said giving him a sideways look. "And girls?"

"Well, who the hell can figure out what *they* want? But we guys keep trying."

"Maybe you boys will figure it out some day if you get your head outta...um, the clouds."

"I doubt it," Nikko said. "My dad's advice is to smile and nod."

"Good advice."

Nikko looked at me then dramatically smiled and nodded. We burst out laughing.

We pulled up near the paddock and climbed out. Rusty stood staring off into the distance. At least now I knew he was looking for his friend, the doe, that I decided to call Floppy due to her mangled, bent-over ear. I tried to imagine how a horse and a deer had become pals. I could only surmise that the friendship had formed at his previous home. Who knows how or why Floppy found her way to Rusty's new home.

"So this is your new horse, eh? So do they, er, *neuter* horses too?" Nikko said, approaching the paddock and looking over the bedraggled animal. Rusty had a penchant for rolling in the mud. I had gotten most of the burrs out of his mane and tail, but his ratty coat was pathetic.

"Only the boy horses," I said. "That is unless they are of high quality and fit for stud use. Rusty here is a gelding, which is horse lingo for 'fixed.'"

"Sounds like discrimination to me," Nikko said. "Isn't that right, Rusty?"

Rusty ignored Nikko's comment and continued to stare off into the horizon.

"Yup," I said. "For once it's the male of the species that must step up to the plate. Anyway, Rusty here is not exactly breeding material. And he has a lot of issues from past neglect. The vet's coming today to look him over and then next comes the farrier."

"Farrier?" Nikko said.

"Uh huh. They take care of horses' hooves. Used to be the blacksmith, but now hoof care is the name of the game. Horses have specialists just like people. Dental, orthopedic, massage therapy, psychotherapy, you name it."

"Sounds expensive," Nikko said turning to look at me.

"You got that right. Horses are money pits. That's why Uncle Phil was in the red most of the time. Plus, according to Dad, he didn't manage what assets he had very well. Then he got sick..." I felt a little catch in my throat.

"You were close?" Nikko said.

I nodded. "Yeah, I loved him and loved coming here."

Damn it. I started to cry. What the hell? "Sorry," I said. Guess I'm not quite over it. He went from, from ah, ah vibrant, robust guy to a skeletal shadow. It was, was..."

Now I was sobbing. I felt like a fool, losing control like that. My outburst caused Rusty to quit staring off in the distance and come over to check out what his human was blubbering about.

"Hey, hey," Nikko said, pulling me into a hug. (I hardly noticed the resurrected pain in my ribs.) "I didn't mean to set you off."

I buried my face in Nikko's jacket, likely getting it soggy from my sniveling. Probably smeared a little mascara on it to boot.

"It's...okay. I guess I just..."

Nikko continued to hold me and then things sort of went from being comforted to something else. I felt a tingle that had been dormant for a very long time. I looked up at him and swiped at my eyes. I was sure there was mascara running down my cheeks. Why did I even try with the makeup? He pulled me closer and we had our third kiss, which was even more promising than the second one. I'm pretty sure he would have tried to get even more physical if we weren't both wearing heavy coats with several layers beneath.

Then Nikko let out a yelp and jumped away. "What the hell?"

"What?"

"Damn horse blew snot all over the back of my neck," he said swiping ineffectively at his collar.

I laughed. "I guess I have a chaperone horse that decided to break things up."

Nikko turned to Rusty who had the look of complete innocence. The horse wiggled his lips a bit and shook his head. If I didn't know better, I would say he was chuckling at his victim and telling him to watch it.

"You and me need to talk," Nikko said, grasping the horse's halter.

Rusty grunted then lifted his tail and farted.

12

I admit it was three minutes past eight when I limped into the office. I had borrowed Uncle Phil's cane, which Dad had dug out for me. It made an impressive clumping noise as I entered. Rose looked at the wall clock, then her wristwatch, then me. She pulled her Nasty List drawer open, glanced at my cane and slid the drawer back shut.

"Glad you could make it," Rose said. "Perhaps you'll have to build in a little extra time to get to work until you can get around better."

Rose just oozed with sympathy. But I expected nothing less than her priority boiling down to efficiency. The truth of the matter was that with Rusty now in residence at Wildwood, I had to swing out there to feed and water him before coming into the office, and also make sure he had not again escaped. In spite of allowing nearly an extra hour for this and significantly exceeding the speed limit, I rolled into the office parking lot a minute or two late. It would be easier once I actually lived out at Wildwood Stables—hopefully soon if Mom capitulated.

"Nice to see you, too Rose," I said. "Did you have a nice vacation?"

"Well, I suppose," she said. "I did manage to get a lot of the file cabinets updated and cleaned out here at the office. There are more boxes to go up into the attic." She looked critically at my cane.

I had thought about bringing my crutches to put her into a tailspin, but with my luck I'd get tangled up in them and *really* hurt myself.

"You were supposed to take the week off, Rose," I said, thudding my way over to my work area. I threw my purse on the desk and shrugged out of my coat.

Gussy popped his head over his cubicle partition. "Hey Kat. What happened to you?"

"Hey Gussy," I said. "Had an encounter of the difficult kind."

"Wow! What does the other guy look like? Ha ha. And I told Ma to maybe go visit her sister or go to Branson or something and not hang at the office, but well, she—"

"That'll do, Gerald," Rose said. She looked at me and sniffed. "Gerald went off with Raymond for the week."

"Yup!" Gussy said. "It was totally cool. Ray has a place out on the reservation—it's not all that far from Wildwood, but ya gotta take seasonal roads. It's totally cool. It's got electricity but only a hand pump out back and an outhouse. Even in the winter! He said sometimes he has to snowshoe in when it gets really deep. Anyway, he said it needed some spring cleaning—you know, get rid of mouse turds and stuff—and that he'd buy me dinner if I helped—"

Rose snorted. "Spring, hah! If it ever comes. May is just around the corner and my crocuses are barely poking through."

It was true, spring was taking its sweet time arriving.

"—him set up some new computer stuff. Like the whole place looks like the command center in NASA. I asked where we'd go to dinner and Raymond said *right here* and we went out hunting and he shot a turkey. It was a big one and I—"

"Have you heard the forecast?" Char said as she flounced into the office, slamming the door behind her.

"Nice you could make it Charleen," Rose said pointedly looking at the wall clock, then her wristwatch. I suspected there was no more room on Char's Nasty List column. In Rose's book, Char Houle was beyond redemption.

"Charlotte," Char corrected. "Charleen sounds like a country singer with big hair, saggy boobs, and a twangy voice."

"If you say so," Rose said. "I'll try to remember your name *du jour*."

"So *anyway*," Char said taking her coat off and throwing it into her office, "snow. They are predicting snow overnight and tomorrow."

"Cra ..., er, dang," I said. "Just what the road at Wildwood needs. The frost isn't even out completely yet. And Rusty's paddock is a sea of mud."

Rose gave me a look. Perhaps I'd get a half demerit for half a bad word. Was *crap* such a big deal anyway?

Char peeled off her hat and fluffed her hair, which fell perfectly into place. If I fluffed my hair, I might not fit through the doorway.

"Kat, honey," Char said, "Who's Rusty and what's a paddock? Never mind, what I really want to know is what happened to you. I heard you were beaten up by some—some tramp."

"Well, not exactly beaten up," I said. "I think it was a draw."

"So, out at Phil's place?"

"Uh huh," I said. "The squatter." I decided not to volunteer anything else. I wasn't sure how Char knew about the incident. Rose, well she knew *everything*.

"Any idea who the guy—it was a guy, right—was? I mean, just some vagrant, right?"

"Um, the police are working on it." Char and everyone else would find out soon enough.

"I should hope so," Rose said. "How many crimes can a place have before they *do* something?"

"So, did you know the guy? I mean can you ID him?" Char said.

"Probably," I said. We had been in a death grip rolling around in the slush. I could ID him from his greasy hair to his tattered tennies. Not to mention the scar. I was hoping a police lineup would not be in my future. I mean, the guy *told* me who he was, but I thought it prudent not to share with my coworkers. Especially since he had apparently disappeared.

"And, um, did he, you know, say anything?" Char said.

Char was on a poorly veiled fishing expedition. She was known to be nosy and often used inside information to her advantage, though not sure how Scott Summers could be of any use to her.

I decided to continue the duck and dodge act. "Yeah," I said. "He called me some bad names and said he had a right to be there. You know, like squatters' rights, I guess."

"Hmmm," Char said. "Well, let's hope the asshole hit the road."

Rose sighed. She knew cleaning up Char's verbal malfeasance was impossible and didn't even bother to pull open the Nasty List drawer.

"Anyway," I said, "I guess I have some boxes to sort through. Hey, Gussy, mind giving me a hand getting them up in the attic?"

Gussy's head popped over his partition and he grinned. "You betcha," he said and scurried over to where several bankers boxes were piled next to the very steep attic stairs.

The front door whooshed open and Dad strode in. "Good morning one and all! I trust we are all ready to get rolling again!"

We all muttered various unenthusiastic assenting responses. Dad could do perky like nobody else. Very annoying.

"Char," he said. "Where do we stand with the Koskimaki account?"

The two disappeared upstairs into Dad's office and Gussy and I turned our attention to the boxes. Had I not been favoring a bum knee and sore ribs, I probably had more overall body strength than Gussy, not to mention a couple of inches in height. But he'd been raised by a draconian mother who instilled in him a sense of do or die. Between the two of us, the boxes were successfully transferred to the attic where

I would do some sorting then store them away until such time as they could be dragged *back* down to have the contents shredded and recycled. The attic did have a couple of heat registers and decent lighting. The walls were bare studs with blown-in insulation. The rafters were low and slanted and not tall enough to accommodate my five-foot nine height. Mice were known to take up residence in the attic, and occasionally made a nest out of anything available. So far, cleaning out mouse nests had not been assigned to me. There was a small desk—older than mine downstairs—and a discarded roll-around chair that I would use to go through files and get things properly organized.

Rose had gone through the current file cabinets downstairs and pulled the files that needed to be archived. She had an uncanny ability to know what was what, without even perusing inside the manilla folders. Those no longer worthy of first-class accommodations were unceremoniously stuffed into boxes and turned over to the lowliest of low (yours truly) to make sense of it all. Upon occasion, an employee had to climb up into the attic and dig around for an old file, and having at least some sense of order made the task a little less bothersome.

There were four boxes in all. Two had office records, which contained profit/loss spreadsheets, legal documents, property tax statements, paid bills, miscellaneous receipts, old billing records, expansion plans for the office, and a plethora of other miscellany. We had to save this stuff for seven years in case the IRS decided to make our lives a living hell. I took a large, black permanent marker and scribbled the year and a vague description of what was within, prudently avoiding the use of the word "miscellaneous."

The other two boxes had inactive client files. They were almost but not quite in alphabetical order. I could only surmise that someone as finicky as Rose intentionally shuffled them just enough to make my life at the office even more demeaning. But I'd been through this before and I had a system. The first order of business was to assemble *new* banker boxes, which started out flat and ideally would become reinforced rectangle units after the various flaps, notches, lids, and wire contraptions were correctly arranged in the correct order. This was an activity in which had become quite adept. If persistence is a form of adeptness. The first rule was to ignore the totally confusing instructions and just go for it. Then, when that failed, the second rule was to try to make sense of the instructions, which never worked. The final step was to go on YouTube and, believe it or not, bring up a video on "How to Assemble Bankers Boxes." After about twenty minutes I was sweating like a racehorse (pigs don't sweat) but I had two boxes properly assembled and awaiting my next move, which was to pull files out of the full boxes and begin putting them in the newly assembled boxes. One would hold A-M, and the other N-Z.

To make room for the newbies, I dragged two old boxes that had reached their eighth birthday off the wall-mounted shelving unit and shoved them toward the stairs. These babies were headed to the recycler. As I dragged one box toward the attic door, the string closure on one side of the top popped open and a few papers slipped out and fluttered to the floor. Muttering under my breath, I chased the papers to their resting place and scooped them up. Obviously spreadsheets from days past, I looked at the heading and my heart gave a lurch. It boldly stated WILDWOOD STABLES FY22/23, which was the last fiscal year that Uncle Phil was of this earth. The papers were misfiled and certainly not old enough for shredding. I unwound the string that held the other flap closed and flipped it open. On top was a manilla folder labeled Wildwood Stables. I opened it and found a mishmash of spreadsheets, receipts, invoices, and other paperwork. I wondered why Wildwood's recently deactivated business file would be in a box destined to be shredded. That simply was not kosher by Wilde Accounting standards.

It all seemed so callous, having the file purged like a toxic substance. Dad had settled what needed to be settled, and Uncle Phil's hopes and dreams were filed away, discarded, and *eventually* would be recycled. Okay, it was only a bunch of papers. One's life wasn't reduced to paperwork, was it? I absently thumbed through the papers. The file innards were upside down, creased, folded, bent, crumpled, and in no semblance of order. I couldn't imagine anyone accidentally putting the file, which looked to have been rifled through—in a shred box by "accident." Of course everyone at Wilde Accounting had access to the boxes up in the attic, and I supposed someone could have just been careless. Rose would have an aneurysm if she found out and I sure wasn't going to mention it to her. Perhaps it was even Dad who had rummaged through and jammed the thing in the wrong box. Mom always said he couldn't hit the hamper on a bet.

As I looked at the jumble of papers, the irony of the disarray was not lost on me. After scrounging around, I found a small empty box to put the Wildwood papers in. I would do my best to smuggle the file contents out with me and go through everything when I had more time and a little privacy. It wouldn't hurt to check out the "books" for Wildwood Stables. It might be a learning experience for me to figure out what *not* to do. I didn't expect any epiphanies or blatant evidence of inappropriate spending on prostitutes, gambling, or white powdery substances. But maybe he gave too much to charity, or got double billed here and there, paid too much for too little. Things to think about. People take advantage of those who don't mind the store.

Instead of heading to the Wilde suburban abode after work, my routine involved a detour to Wildwood Stables to tend to Rusty's needs. Because a snowstorm was predicted, I hoped to lure him into a warm, dry stall for the night. I had a bag of apples I'd cut up before leaving the office stashed on the passenger side floor. The plan was to create a trail of apple parts for Rusty to follow and consume. Once he would get near the stall, I would feign indifference and hope he would go inside for more apples and I could slide the door shut. A similar tactic had worked—albeit only once—with Jupiter when we lured him into his carrier to go to the vet.

The days were getting longer and it was still daylight when I bumped down Horse Camp Road headed to Wildwood. The sun stood high and bright on the horizon. A few wispy clouds floated across a bright blue sky. Snow coming? I was hoping the meteorologists were wrong, which they often were. But the local TV weatherman, Hal Hope, seemed cocksure of his prediction of a "white monster" coming. People, sarcastic skeptics that we were, called him "All Hope," implying his predictions were based on whimsy rather than science. He always did a cheerful "silver lining" phrase to his forecasts, such as "we need the rain," or "the snowmobilers will be happy," or "good news for the deer hunters," blah blah bah. This time he assured us that, "It won't stick around long as temps will tease the 50s by next weekend! Break out the beach umbrellas!"

When I pulled into the parking area, several workers were loading up their vans and trucks and heading out. If all went well, there was a good chance that I now had the so-called mechanics in place in the modular, namely, electricity, propane tank, running water, a furnace, a water heater, and central air (part of the package). Being a supposedly ready-made house, the appliances had been included and hopefully those were hooked up as well. And if I were truly blessed, the final drywall and flooring would be in place. I decided I'd check it out after taking care of Rusty. The final step would be to move my bedroom furniture out of the parental basement, which would be a colossal chore. The rest of my furniture was in storage, which would be easier to load—if I had something to load it in. Maybe the slightly decrepit horse trailer would work.

If Aunt Lin were to move in with me, we'd have to find her some bedroom stuff. As far as I could tell, she only brought some clothes and that weird lyre musical instrument with her. I think she was either shacked up or couch surfing before she pulled up stakes and joined the Wilde household. There was a discount mattress outlet in Marquette where we could find her a bed, and they delivered. Another option was a place called Second Chance, which was a repurpose place that took old junk and made it useable again. They hired people that were in one way or the other in "rehab," whether it be from criminal activity, mental illness, or basically unemployable. Thus, the play on words in the name of the place. Second Chance tended to overcharge for things but cited that they were a charitable nonprofit and that "All our profits go to helping those in need!" So, one left feeling a mixture of righteousness while being slightly ripped off at the same time.

Rusty nickered at me as I approached the paddock. I left my cane in the car, as it was just as easy to walk without it. Mainly I needed it as a sympathy prop to keep people off my back.

"So, hi there fella," I said. "Where's your girlfriend, Floppy?"

I had not seen the deer since the day of the great squatter wrestling match. Yet Rusty did seem to always be looking for her.

"Hey old man," I said, "wanna apple?"

I held out an apple quarter and Rusty's rubbery lips reached out and snapped it up. White foam trickled out the sides of his mouth as he chewed.

"Ah hah!" I said, "there's more where that came from."

Well, the trail of apples did not work as planned. I had a nice line of them going from the paddock to the stable, placed about every four or five feet. I led Rusty out of his paddock and pointed to the apple trail. Horses do not understand the concept of pointing. Or if Rusty did, he ignored it. His ears swiveled to and fro and he looked everywhere except at the apple piece a few inches from his hooves. I reached down and picked it up and held it out to him. He happily snapped it up, chewed and swallowed. We moved on to the next piece and repeated the action. And again. And again. I was beginning to wonder who was training whom. Eventually, we reached the large, sliding double doors of the stable, which I pushed open. I had not put any apples inside and to save a lot of bending and stooping, I reached into the bag of remaining apple pieces that I had stuffed into my coat pocket and continued the bribery until we reached the stall door. And, as predicted, we reached an impasse.

Neither apples, promises, tugging on the lead rope, whispering, pleading, nor threatening would get the horse into the stall. In that Rusty weighed approximately seven or eight hundred pounds more than I, there was no likelihood that the beast could be forced to do anything he didn't want to do.

"Fine," I said. "You win." I looked around the stable. At one end was the tack and feed room, which was closed with the door locked. Across from the room were about twenty bales of hay. Otherwise, there was the line of stalls on each side of the aisle, a wash rack, and some assorted items such as shovels, rakes, buckets and so on scattered around.

"I'll make you a deal," I said. "I'm gonna horse proof the place and you can just hang out in the barn. But no stall."

The barn had a long swinging metal gate that could be shut if I left the big sliding doors open, hopefully eliminating any claustrophobia with the horse. It wasn't really a farm gate, but more of a "road closed" style, but unless Rusty could crawl out on his knees and hocks, it would serve its purpose. I picked up all the tools and miscellaneous items and put them in the tack/feed room. The hay was another matter. I did the best I could with several lengths of rope to cordon off the hay. If Rusty—Houdini that he was—found his way to the hay, he might make a mess, but I wasn't concerned about him engorging himself, as he rarely finished his hay between feedings.

I put water and hay in his stall, along with some sweet feed.

"Okay, old man," I said, "if you get hungry or thirsty, you have to go into the stall. Nobody will shut you in. Of course, if you are going to be stubborn, then I guess you skip dinner."

Rusty ignored me and went over to the gate across the doorway. He hung his head over and pawed the ground.

"Nope, you gotta stay inside. It's for your own good."

I was beginning to sound like my parents from when I was a kid. "Eat your broccoli, Kathryn," Mom would say. "It's good for you. It will make you grow tall and strong."

I blame broccoli for my excessive height.

Reluctantly, I slid under the gate and headed for my car. Now it was getting dark, and it had started to snow big, wet flakes. I guess

Hal Hope was on the mark. I decided to postpone my modular house inspection. I hustled to my car and took off down Horse Camp Road wondering if I'd be late for dinner. I had to skip lunch due to lack of funds, and I was starved.

And then there was a funny noise coming from the engine, right before several idiot lights came on. And then it just quit.

⚡ **13** ⚡

The Subaru had conked out approximately halfway down Horse Camp Road, or equal distance from Little Mountain Road and Wildwood. When I turned the key, I got nothing. Not even a click or a whine. *Wilde,* I thought to myself, *you are so totally and completely fucked!*

I stepped out of the car and pulled my cell phone out of my pocket. No bars. Figures. I knew I could get a couple of bars back at the stable, so opted to head in that direction rather than the main road where a car might not come by for hours. I grabbed my cane and work satchel, which contained my billfold, checkbook (with a near zero balance), tissues, pens, breath mints, a tube of dried out lipstick, hairbrush, lint balls, and probably a few cough drops with the paper stuck to them. In other words, nothing useful. Nonetheless, where I went, it went. As an afterthought, I grabbed the assorted papers from Uncle Phil's file and stuffed them in the satchel.

The snow became incredibly heavy and wet, like wallpaper paste being swirled about. A steady east wind had picked up, sending a slurry of snow into my face and down my neck. I hadn't dressed for a winter outdoor adventure, but being a true-blooded Yooper, I never ventured out even in April without a sturdy coat, gloves, and hat. However, my jeans immediately became soaked, and though I was wearing boots, they were more for fashion than function and my feet soon became numb. And my bum knee hurt like a sonofabitch.

Periodically during my trudge, I stopped and checked my phone for bars. I had about a half bar for a nanosecond, then lost it. I increasingly leaned on my cane as I slogged on through the falling darkness. Occasionally it slipped out from under me and almost sent me sprawling. Swirling snow cut visibility to near zero, but I could just see my faint car tracks leading out and used the flashlight on my phone to follow them. Eventually the sodium light mounted on the peak of the barn provided a haloed glow of radiance in the distance. I honed in on it and finally staggered into the parking lot. At least four inches of snow had fallen in less than an hour. I stooped under the metal gate at the barn door and entered. After fumbling around, I found the switch and turned on one bank of lights. At least there was power. I tossed my satchel and cane aside and went in. A substantial amount of snow had drifted into the barn, but being inside was a far sight more pleasant than being outside.

"Rusty?" I said. "Hey fella, where are you?"

My heart did the mumbo jumbo for a minute. Did that crazy horse somehow escape and go out into the storm? I could see that he had been active. As predicted, the ropes cordoning off the hay lay limply on the asphalt and obviously did not prevent him from helping himself. A couple of bales were strewn about. The stall door that I had left open hoping Rusty would capitulate and go in, still stood wide open. I poked my head in.

"Rusty? Hey boy," I said. The horse was lying down, legs tucked beneath him. He had settled comfortably on the thick layer of wood shavings. He looked at me and gathered his feet beneath him, then rose. After a good shake to remove the debris that clung to his coat, he stuck his head out the door and gave it a few up and down nods. I reached out and scratched his velvety muzzle. Then I spotted something moving in the corner.

"What the..."

Floppy turned to face me, placing her body between me and a newborn fawn. The little thing still had the umbilical cord attached to the sack. It tried to stand, fell, then finally scrambled to its feet, trembling slightly. The cord broke and the little guy or gal made its way over to its mom.

"Well, I'll be damned," I said.

It appeared that Floppy must have found her way to the barn, ducked under the metal gate, and sought a good spot to have her baby. I shuddered to think what would have happened to the little one if the doe had given birth out in the storm.

Rusty nickered and stuck his nose over toward the fawn then began to lick it. It was all getting very strange—a horse—a male horse at that, playing mommy to a deer. And the real mom *allowing* it. "Nobody's gonna believe this," I muttered and got my phone out and began recording. After a few minutes, the fawn began to nurse and stopped shivering.

"Hey Rusty, you old softie, is this what it takes for you to use the stall?"

Floppy began nosing the afterbirth and appeared to be eating it. I suppressed a gag. I knew in the wild that afterbirth was an attraction to predators looking for a helpless newborn. Instinctively the mother tries to eat it, move away from it, or otherwise dispose of it. I went over to the storage area and grabbed a bucket then carefully slid into the stall, petting Rusty and speaking the low tones. Moving slowly and under the watchful gaze of Floppy, I managed to push the slimy mess into the bucket. If there had been any food in my stomach I surely would have upchucked. But being basically running on empty, I gagged violently as I hustled the bucket outside and set it next to the barn. I'd have to wait for better weather to dispose of it.

I pulled out my phone again and *glory be* had two bars. I punched in the home landline preset button and Mom picked up on the first ring.

"Kathryn! Where are you? We're so worried. We tried calling you but got a strange beeping noise."

I heard Dad yelling something in the background and a couple of other voices.

"Hi Mom. Yeah, I'm at Wildwood. Car died on me, but I'm fine. I'm in the barn and you'll never guess what—"

"In the BARN! You'll freeze. Just a sec."

I heard some mumbling in the background. Loud voices.

"Okay darling, Nikko is here—he stopped by to drop off one of Frieda's divine apple pies—and he said the car he has can make it out there and he'll come get you. He has chains or something. But I don't know, they are telling people that there's at least six more inches coming and—hey!"

"Hi. Nikko here. Sorry, Mrs. Wilde. Didn't mean to snatch the phone away. Hey, how ya doin'?"

"Um, fine if being stuck out here with a broken-down car and a snowstorm is doing fine. But forget all that, that deer that Rusty adores is here in the barn and she's *had a fawn!*"

"What deer?"

"Rusty's friend."

"But how—"

"Don't ask me. But she came here and got in the barn and had a fawn."

"Seriously?" Nikko said. "In April? Way early. And that mean horse and you are there and she's okay with that?"

"I guess. She hasn't tried to leave and the stall door is open. I took the afterbirth away. It made me forget how hungry I was."

"So, anyway, I think this band of snow is going to slack off in a while, and I'm sure I can make it out in the four by four. So hang tight. I'll be there as soon as I can."

"Are you sure? I mean, I'm fine, really. I even have some apples—"

"I'm sure."

"Well, thanks, Nikko. And since you're coming, could you please bring some of your mom's apple pie?"

"Yup, your ma is packing a bag of food right now."

"And maybe a bottle of wine."

"I'll see what I can do. Later."

I tapped the off button and looked at my battery storage symbol. It showed about a quarter power remaining. I decided I better save what juice I had left and forego using the flashlight or video. I looked over at the "peaceable kingdom" and saw that Floppy was munching hay and the little one was settling down for a nap. Rusty came out of the stall and nosed through the hay he had scattered in the aisle.

I guess now I just wait for my knight in shining armor, I thought. I grabbed my work satchel and cane and headed toward the house, hoping against hope that there would be heat. I had not felt any life in my feet for a long time.

There was good and not so good in the not-quite-ready-for-occupancy house. The good was that the lights worked, water came out of the faucet, it appeared that the drywall was done and I could smell fresh paint. The bad news was that the place was freezing. I found the thermostat on a wall in the tiny bedroom hallway. I turned it on but heard no comforting whoosh of the furnace burners lighting. I went into the utility room where the furnace was located and looked at the unit. It seemed up and ready to go, but what did I know? The house did have a fireplace, but of course I had no firewood. I poked around some more and found that carpeting had been laid in the two bedrooms and the flooring was installed in the full bath. However, the rest of the house—living room, kitchen, dining area, and the half bath still had bare underlayment. Boxes of plank flooring stood along the wall awaiting attention. Well, we were getting there.

I went into what would eventually be my bedroom (the larger one with a nice view of the Peshekee River) and settled down on the floor. I was instantly bored, not to mention cold, and feeling more than a little sorry for myself. I thought about playing some tunes on my phone but didn't want to drain the battery. I thought maybe I had a charger in my work satchel and went back into the kitchen where I'd left it on the counter and rummaged through. No charger. I did, however, find a bedraggled candy bar, which I tore into and inhaled. I pulled out a bunch of Uncle Phil's papers and decided that this was as good a time as any to try to put them in order, and maybe be enlightened about the rise and fall of Wildwood Stables.

I went back to my bedroom and slid down onto the floor. One page of the Excel workbook was dedicated to staff expenses. It contained info on employees, which included a couple of ranch hands/trail guides and the English riding instructor, Justin Wright.

I moved on to the business detail pages. Things seemed to be in order, as one would expect from Wilde Accounting, with expenses and revenue neatly itemized. Unfortunately, the expenses exceeded the revenue. No surprise there. Well, how did he generate income, I wondered. It was a bit general, but appeared to be what one would expect at a horse facility: boarding, lessons, trail rides, camping fees, horse show income, etc. even though specifics tended to be missing. The debit side of the ledger listed other obvious things such as hay, feed, bedding, equipment, vet and farrier bills, utilities, maintenance, and so on. Included was payment to Yarrow Hospice and Home Healthcare where Sasha Saari-Summers had come from as caregiver to Uncle Phil when he was reaching the end of the trail.

What caught my eye and started bells clanging in my head was a column dedicated to something called "Equine Rescue Foundation." While it wasn't a surprise that Uncle Phil gave money to a horse welfare charity, what really stood out was the *amount* he gave. The spreadsheet, which only represented a year, listed multiple large entries totaling in the neighborhood of ten grand. What the fluff? Why didn't Dad question Uncle Phil about this? Did Dad even know? If this was a charity, it would have been a tax deduction for Wildwood Stables. Most of Uncle Phil's bookkeeping was handled by Gussy and probably he or Char did the actual tax return. I'd have some questions for Gussy and Char. What was this outfit anyway? Was it a bona fide 501(c) (3) or something shady?

I saw the reflection of headlights flicker in the window. Nikko! The cavalry had arrived—or at least a functioning vehicle. I stuffed the papers back into my satchel and headed to the front door.

Snow swirled in as I held the door for Nikko.

"Thanks so much for coming. That stupid car chose a terrible time to conk out on me," I said.

"Is there a good time?" Nikko said. "Here, take this. Your ma packed an entire meal. She said we should wait to go back into town until things let up. If they ever do."

"Really? Mom told you and me to stay put out here, just the two of us. Alone?"

"Well, there was discussion of your aunt coming along, but I mentioned we may be holed up without heat or any normal comforts, so she declined. Your mother gave me a very strong look that would make even the most macho fellow shrivel up and whimper."

I took the package Nikko had handed me and hustled into the kitchen. Of course I hadn't yet outfitted my kitchen with plates, utensils, or other kitcheny amenities. I would eat the stuff with my bare hands if necessary. When I unpacked Mom's care package, the delicious smell of still-warm fried chicken, cheesy potatoes, and corn casserole filled the air. Mom, always the perfect hostess, had also packed the promised apple pie along with paper plates, napkins, plastic silverware, and a couple bottles of soda.

"Ohmygod this smells wonderful! How did you keep it warm?"

"I have my ways," Nikko said, waggling his eyebrows.

"I bet you do," I said.

"Oh. I almost forgot." He reached into his jacket pocket and pulled out a bottle. "El cheapo wine!" he said. "Voilà ! Gas station vintage. A very good month."

"And a handy twist-off cap," I said, taking the bottle from him and giving it a twist.

"It's freezing in here," Nikko said. "No heat?"

"Well, I turned it on, but nothing happened. No matter, though, let's eat." I was salivating more than a pack of hungry wolves.

Nikko and I sat cross-legged on the carpeted floor of my future bedroom. We wolfed down the food and drank the wine straight from the bottle. After eating every last crumb of Frieda Olsen's apple pie, I leaned back and groaned.

"Perhaps I'll live after all," I said. "At least I feel like I have a reason to live now."

"Good!" Nikko said. He stood and started collecting the trash from our demolished meal. "I want to keep you alive and plucky."

"Plucky?"

He smiled and held out his hand. I grasped it and he pulled me up a bit forcefully, causing me to lose my balance. I fell into his chest and felt his arms steady me.

"Bum knee gives out on me," I muttered. "Sorry I'm not *pluckier*."

Somehow our faces ended up inches from each other. I was pretty sure he could smell my wino/chicken/apple pie breath. At least no onions had been involved. His breath came out in misty puffs from the cold. There was a momentary pause, with the contemplation of kissing versus awkwardly disengaging.

"Better not," Nikko said. "Your ma…"

"And don't forget Dad," I said. "He's pretty handy with a firearm."

"Yikes!" Nikko said, releasing me completely. "So, let's take a look at the furnace. You're going to get frozen pipes if we don't get some heat. And then I want to visit the critters. A deer *voluntarily* giving birth in a barn. Not normal! Anyway, did you get propane?"

"Um, I don't know. I was at work all day, so maybe. The workers were leaving when I came."

Nikko went outside and made his way through the drifting snow. I watched him plow through a couple of drifts to the large, white cylinder that presumably held the propane. He swept snow off the unit then flipped up a cover. He reached under and did something, then closed the cover. I watched him trudge back to the house. He came in and stomped the snow off his boots.

"Okay, propane is at 80%, which is what they fill it to. But the valve was turned off. I turned it on, so you should get some gas to the house now."

I followed him into the utility room and looked over his shoulder. He opened a panel on the furnace and flipped a switch from off to on (duh). The furnace hummed. We heard some clicking.

"It's the igniter trying to get things going," he said. "Might take a while to get some gas to it."

He kept the panel off and we watched the burners. Eventually a tiny blue flame grew into a robust double row of flames, and we were in business.

"Yay!" I said. Without thinking—or maybe I was thinking—I gave him a peck on the cheek.

He looked at me and moved a bit closer.

"Just being perky," I said.

"Plucky," he said.

"Same difference." I cleared my throat and tried to squeeze past him. "So, wanna see the strange menagerie residing in the stable?"

"Sure," he said, moving aside to let me out of the tiny utility room. "But only if that horse Rustoleum doesn't attack me again."

"I can't make any promises," I said. "And his name is Rusty."

I flicked on the lights and Nikko and I went into the barn. Rusty was still grazing on the hay he had strewn about and I assumed Floppy and her newborn fawn had not yet ventured out and remained snuggled in the stall.

"Watch your step," I said, skirting around a manure pile. "Horses can be very indiscreet with their bodily functions."

"So I see," Nikko said. "But, hey, the place looks pretty good, except of course the mess the horse made. Do they always cause this much trouble?"

"Well, in my experience—which is not extensive—I think horses are like any living, breathing thing. Some are angels, and some are, well, a pain in the ass."

"And ol' Rusty here?" Nikko said.

"He's somewhere in between," I said as I pulled out my manure bucket, rake, and shovel. "I mean, when Summers and I were, er, *occupied* in mortal combat, Rusty intervened and I don't think it was an accident that he planted his hoof on Summers' leg. I can only imagine the bruise." I raked the poop into the shovel and deposited it into the bucket and dragged it toward the door. "And what can you say about a horse that is guardian to a deer and her tiny baby?"

We peeked into the open stall and found Floppy and fawn both lying down; a sign of feeling safe.

"I can't believe it," Nikko said looking at the two. "Wish I had my phone to take a couple of pictures. I left the stupid thing plugged in to charge at my folks' house. Of course, technically you can't keep a wild animal without special credentials, but since this one chose to come of its own accord, I don't think I need to throw the cuffs on you."

"Yeah, just try. My horse will stomp you into a pulp."

"I dunno," Nikko said. "He looks pretty disinterested in things."

"Oh, he's keeping an eye on us."

Nikko tentatively went over to Rusty and reached out. Rusty stepped away.

"Here, do this," I said, grabbing a handful of hay and giving it to Nikko. "Offer him this."

"But there's hay everywhere. Why would he take a crummy handful from me?"

"Just try it."

Nikko approached Rusty again, holding the fistful of hay at arm's length. Rusty eyed him for a moment, then extended his neck and stretched his lips trying to reach the offering.

"My arm's getting tired," he said.

"Don't wimp out."

Rusty took a step closer, latched onto the hay and began to munch.

"Well, I'll be damned," Nikko said. "Hey there fella, are we buds now?"

"The way to every living creature's heart is essentially food. Sometimes it's a friendship-seeking gesture to bond and sometimes it's a bait pile to lure game animals into one's sights."

Nikko picked up another handful of hay and fed it to Rusty, who had moved even closer.

"Or," Nikko said, "sometimes it's dinner and a bottle of wine to—"

"Yeah, another kind of bait pile, I guess," I said. "I admit that I'm much happier when well fed and slightly tipsy."

Nikko turned away from Rusty and looked at me. "Oh yeah?"

"Uh huh."

"So, I might have you—at least metaphorically speaking—eating out of *my* hand just 'cause I brought dinner and cheap wine?"

I smiled. "Of course, Rusty may take exception if one were to—"

Nikko dropped the handful of hay, grasped my arms, and pulled me in. "If we were to what?"

"You know, get, um…"

"Quit talking," Nikko said, sounding a bit husky.

"Okmmm." I was cut off with an exploratory kiss. A little tongue, but not full bore. This was the moment that I could either pull away, righteously declaring we shouldn't be doing this, or I could go with the flow. It really was no contest. I moved in and gave a "green light" kiss. We pressed closer, communicating quite well in spite of our heavy winter clothing. Nikko pushed me gently back against a stall partition and initiated a hip move. He found a small bare spot on my neck and did a combo kiss/nibble that caused quite a stir and some return hip action. Somehow he managed to get his gloves off and his rather icy hands pushed my coat open and snuck under my sweater and up toward my back, making me shiver. He unhooked my bra, then a hand reached around the front and found my breast. I may have moaned a little and could feel some heavy breathing on his part. My knees were starting to buckle.

Before I knew it, we had maneuvered into an empty stall where a deep pile of wood shavings used for stall bedding was stored. Were we really going to do *it* in a barn in the cold? All I could think about was his hand—now warm—exploring things further "south." I had lost my gloves and moved my hands to his warmer regions as well. Now he was moaning. But so many clothes, and the cold. We were still standing, but barely. I looked over Nikko's shoulder and spotted a horse blanket I had recently bought (on credit) hanging on a bar attached to the stall.

"Hold on," I said, breaking free. I grabbed the blanket, hurried back, and tossed it on the ground. When I looked up, Nikko was stripped down to his briefs and a tee shirt. I may have stared a little. He looked at me and grinned as he threw his coat over the shavings.

"You're shivering," I said. "But I guess the cold hasn't affected, um..."

"Uh-uh," he said. "C'mere."

I complied and he pulled my coat off and added it to his on top of the shavings. I got my sweater, boots, and jeans off and of course the bra, being unhooked fell off on its own. I was so glad that I had put on a nice pair of panties that morning. Mom always said to be prepared in case of, well, something unexpected. Thanks, Mom, for the good advice!

We went down on the coats and pulled the horse blanket over us. I think the lights might have flickered a time or two. Maybe because of the weather, maybe not.

Rusty did not come to the rescue.

* * *

I had my eyes closed but could hear a faint buzzing. Maybe the wine was still making me a bit off kilter. Nikko gently caressed my arm and both our eyes opened and we looked at each other.

"So," I said, "was that something you've been wanting to do since high school?"

"Oh yeah," he said, "and after high school too." He reached over and smoothed my hair, which likely resembled a neglected shrub. "Love your hair," he said. "Wildly sexy. Hmm, I think you must have a bad light fixture. I hear a buzzing."

"I hear it too."

The buzzing became louder.

"Snowmobile," Nikko said, sitting up. "Or maybe an ORV. Hard to get a snowmo through soft drifts." He started rounding up his clothes.

"Crap," I said. "Someone coming to rescue us?"

"Or just some idiots out in the snowstorm. Happens all the time."

"Well, they aren't supposed to be on my property," I said, grabbing my sweater and jeans. "Have you, um, seem my things?"

"Things?"

"Yeah, you know, my—never mind," I said scooping up my panties. I gave them a shake to knock off the wood shavings.

More or less reclothed, we emerged from our unconventional love nest and I peeked into the birthing stall. Rusty, apparently having had his fill of purloined hay and apparently uninterested in his mistress' activities, had rejoined his deer family. All three were lying down.

The motor noise came and went as if the driver were following a winding path.

"Makes me mad that people think they can just tear all over the place," I said.

"Well, let's take the Tahoe and go find the jerks," Nikko said as he dumped shavings out of his boots. "Sounds like back by the squatter's camp."

"Yeah, I would have checked on things back there today, but the weather went bad so quickly and, well, I was here alone. I might be plucky, but I'm not stupid."

Nikko grinned at me. "Plucky on steroids."

"Yeah?" I said grinning back. "You weren't so bad yourself."

"Good to not be so bad," he said, stomping each foot into his boots.

We stepped out of the barn into the pool of the outside flood light. I picked up my cane that I'd dropped near the door.

"How's your knee?" Nikko said.

"Funny, but it seems a lot better. Ribs are still a little sore."

Nikko smiled. "Dr. Olsen to the rescue!"

"Oh please," I said. "It was doing better before, well..."

"Whatever you say," Nikko said, looking up. "Stopped snowing. I think I see stars."

"Wind's let up, too. Okay, maybe our, *event* did increase some circulation and seem to help, you know, with a distraction."

"Distraction?"

"Hey, look at the mess!"

We looked around at the snowscape. A lot of trees were bowed nearly to the ground. A couple of big limbs had snapped off and lay about.

"Can't believe we didn't lose power with all that heavy snow," I said. "Hope the drive out is open. There's a lot of trees lining it."

"I have a chainsaw in the Tahoe, if we need it."

We walked into the parking lot toward the SUV.

"What's that?" Nikko said, pointing to a large hump of snow.

"Uncle Phil's truck," I said.

"Does it run?"

"I'm told it should. I think Dad got a new battery, but I haven't really paid much attention. I think he said the keys were under the mat if I needed it. So far I've been able to get things delivered and haven't had to try it out."

"Well, if we can get her started, maybe you will have some wheels after all."

"Yeah, good plan," I said, though I would be heartbroken to give up my Subaru, in spite of its betrayal.

The engine noise roared back to life.

"Come on," Nikko said, "let's go see if we can catch them."

Nikko and I hopped into the Tahoe and headed toward the horse camp. The SUV bucked and swerved but made its way through the deep snow. The headlights picked up a mound of snow ahead, presumably the squatter's tent, nearly flattened. Nikko shut off the engine and we got out and listened. The wind had completely stilled surrounding us in an eerie silence. I grabbed Nikko's arm as we sloughed through the snow, only the sounds of our breathing breaking the quiet.

"There," Nikko said. "Tracks."

We made our way into the derelict camp now reduced to a variety of snow mounds and spotted some tire tracks.

"An ORV, then," he said, looking around. "And some footprints that look fresh. Well, obviously fresh since it just quit snowing."

I turned on my phone flashlight and shined it on the footprints. "Actually, multiple sets."

Nikko bent over and looked. "You're right. Good going, Sherlock."

"Elementary, my dear Watson," I said with a terrible fake British accent.

"Shall we follow them my dear?" Nikko said, with an even worse German accent.

"Indeed, yes," I said. "What better way to spend an evening than trudging through the snow following footprints."

"I can think of a better way to spend an evening, but then we've already explored that option," he said.

"Explored?"

"I could say more, but feel I should quit while I'm ahead."

We followed the footprints, which went off into the thick brush then veered toward the woods. Once or twice, we crossed the ORV tracks as well.

"This is crazy," Nikko said. "What in hell were these idiots doing out here?"

"Look," I said, shining my flashlight down. "Looks like somebody fell down here. There's a big imprint in the snow."

"Maybe a little nookie in the snow?" Nikko said.

"Just stop," I said.

"Well, I bet they weren't making snow angels."

"While I don't have my deerstalker hat on, my conclusion is that there was a tussle here."

"Or maybe someone fell off the ORV. Could've been drunk or high," Nikko said.

We kept following the footprints through the woods. The snow wasn't as deep as in the open and the going was easier.

"I imagine they're long gone," I said, shining my phone flashlight around. "I think I'm about out of juice in this thing."

"Yeah," Nikko said. "I guess we can head back and see about getting ol' Uncle Phil's truck going and I can follow you home."

I shined my light on my watch. "Wow, it's after midnight. Oops, I guess I have a few missed calls. Probably from my parents."

"You'll have some 'splainin' to do," Nikko said.

I felt my cheeks burning a bit. Living with one's parents had its drawbacks. Just as I went to turn off my phone light, a patch of color was caught in the beam.

"Hmm, I wonder if our ORVers dumped some trash," I said, heading toward the object.

"Guess we better check it out," Nikko said.

We moved closer, me keeping my light on the object. Nikko froze and put his arm out to stop me.

"Not trash," he said.

"What the hell?" I said. "A jacket?"

"Yeah, and more."

"Hat?" I said, trying to shine my light.

"And someone wearing it," Nikko said, hurrying to the spot and kneeling down.

I was right behind him.

"Oh God!" I said. "Is he...dead?"

Nikko felt for a pulse in the person's neck then looked up at me and nodded. He tore open the person's jacket and began chest compressions, alternating with two quick mouth-to-mouth breaths.

"We have a situation here," Nikko gasped. "Got enough juice in that phone to call 911?"

⇙ 15 ⇙

"So you recognized Scott Summers—the deceased?"

This question was posed to me by Lieutenant Spiller of the state police who was handling the investigation, along with a Sergeant Witz who was interviewing Nikko. We had been separated for questioning in case our stories didn't match up. In spite of Nikko's valiant attempt at CPR, the "deceased" could not be resurrected. By the time the paramedics arrived, Nikko had given it all he had, with me trying to help. As the Munchkin said in the *Wizard of Oz*, Scott Summers was most sincerely dead.

I was told that I was not under arrest or anything of the sort but was entitled to a lawyer, which the court would appoint if I couldn't afford one. (I couldn't.) The mention of lawyering up makes the hair on the back of one's neck bristle. However, I figured I could handle a one-on-one interview. After all, I had nothing to hide—or nothing relevant. If I decided to invite either parent, I was certain it would not end well. Dad would just get angry and Mom would root around looking for an unattached trooper with a healthy bank balance that she could fix me up with. As far as getting a lawyer, our attorney wasn't into criminal defense, though he'd have been happy to make a referral to someone who was. Typically they charge a zillion dollars an hour, so that was not an option. Especially since I had nothing to worry about, being totally innocent and all.

"Yes," I said. "I recognized him once I saw his face."

Spiller didn't question how I knew Summers' face or I would have mentioned the birthmark. Obviously the earlier altercation between Summers and me satisfied the identification process.

"Tell me again how you and your boyfriend, Nikko Olsen—"

"Nikko's not really my boyfriend," I said, "he—"

"Okay, friend who's a biological male, found the need to explore the campground in the middle of a major snowstorm. For that matter, why were you out at..." he frowned, and shuffled a couple of papers around.

"Wildwood Stables," I provided.

"Yes. Why there in the first place?"

I explained about it being almost my new home. And also about Rusty, Floppy and the fawn, my car breaking down, Nikko coming to my rescue, us waiting out the storm (obviously I didn't go into detail), and our hearing the motor noise, thus exploring the cause. *Yadda yadda yadda.*

"And you were out in your barn when you heard the engine noise?"

"Uh huh," I said.

"Instead of the house. Where, presumably, there was heat?"

"Well, we had been in the house—and Nikko did get the heat going—but we went to the barn to check on the horse and the deer."

"The horse and a deer?"

"Right, like I told you before," I said.

"Ah yes. And you heard the noise then?"

"After a while."

"Lots of stuff to do, I suppose, in a nice drafty barn."

"A few things," I said, feeling my cheeks blush. Spiller was good. He *knew*.

"And as I recall, you and Scott Summers had an altercation a few days ago. He claimed ownership of the horse place."

"Correct," I said. "It should all be in my statement in your report."

"Of course," Spiller said. "Just clarifying. And Summers, Scott that is, believed he had rights to the place because?"

I knew what was going on. Spiller was getting me to verbalize what he already knew.

"I don't really know what he believed," I said. Two could play the game. I didn't watch TV courtroom drama without learning something.

"Well, something about his sister." Spiller looked down at the papers again on his desk and shuffled them around. All for show. "Ah, yes, his sister, Sasha Saari-Summers."

"Half-sister," I corrected.

"Right, but only relative, apparently. Anyway, possible offspring of your uncle, Phillip Wilde. And of course we know her passing is currently under investigation."

"So the story goes," I said. "Actually, Scott Summers has or at least had a father in prison."

Spiller gave me a steady look. "Interesting you know about that."

"Well, Summers did talk to the sheriff a while back, and it came out when Sheriff Olsen interviewed my father and me. I get the impression that father and son were not close. I believe his father is deceased."

"Thank you, Miss Wilde, for the analysis."

"How's that coming?" I asked. "The investigation, I mean for Sasha?"

Spiller gave me a frosty look. "Can't comment," he said. "But back to Scott Summers and his role in all this. He allegedly set up an illegal encampment at Wilde Stables—"

"Wildwood Stables," I said. Of course correcting Lieutenant Spiller may have been provocative, but I've never been known for my diplomacy. I'm told I'm a lot like my father, always poking at the hornet's nest.

"I beg your pardon," Spiller said with a touch of sarcasm. "I would assume you had issue with Mr. Summers setting up camp at the place. Obviously, at some point, there needed to be a resolution."

"Yes," I said. "We were holding off disassembling the encampment because of your investigation. The guy was never around when we tried to catch him, until after your police officers—"

"Troopers. We state police call ourselves troopers or officers of the state, but not *police officers*," Spiller said. "That would be your city police," he added.

"*My* apologies," I said. "Anyway, I was trying to round up my horse that had wandered back by the squatter's camp and Summers and I came face to face. Like I said, it's all in my statement after he and I—"

"There was an altercation, if I understand correctly," Spiller said. "Didn't he threaten you? Say he was going to gain ownership of the premises? Maybe threaten you with bodily harm?"

"He did. He *caused* bodily harm. I have—or had— a messed-up knee, and my ribs are bruised."

"And now he's dead," Spiller pointed out.

I nodded and tried to stifle a yawn. I had been up all night and was totally wasted. I really needed a shower and about twenty hours of sleep. As the British would say, I was knackered.

"Well, needless to say, we'll be checking some things out: footprints, tire tracks, and other evidence to be analyzed. We're going to want to get some impressions of your and Nikko Olsen's footwear you were wearing, so we can determine if there was anyone else there besides you two and the deceased."

"We saw lots of footprints besides our own," I said. "But they were all jumbled up. And the ORV tracks were all over the place."

"Oh yes, and about the ORV, did you ever get a look at it?"

"No, it was long gone by the time we found the, um, Mr. Summers."

"And Mr. Olsen doesn't own one?" Spiller said.

"You mean Sheriff Olsen?"

"No, I mean *Nikko* Olsen."

"Not that I know of," I said. "He's never mentioned—well he did mention to a coworker of mine that the DNR had one he used sometimes for, you know, chasing down poachers and search and rescue. That kind of thing."

"And perhaps he brought it out to Wildwood Stables?"

"No! He came in his dad's Tahoe. Not an ORV." The implication was clear and somehow my protest seemed a little too defensive. Well, the guy was unnerving me.

He gave me a hard look. I felt totally guilty, when clearly the so-called evidence pointed to anyone but me or Nikko. We didn't have an ORV with us. There would be footprints from Summers and whoever else was there. Someone chasing him? And my Subaru had to be towed in, so that confirmed the reason for Nikko coming out. Since neither of us were married, we weren't even having illegal barn sex.

"Well," I said. "At least Summers is no longer missing." A bit flippant on my part, but Lieutenant Spiller was ticking me off. I wanted to point out that maybe if the police had found the guy, he'd still be alive. Of course I wasn't stupid, so I kept that thought to myself.

"Okay, thanks for coming in," Spiller said, rising from his cushy executive chair and coming from behind his gleaming desk. "We'll be in touch."

"Okay," I said. "Oh—do we know how, you know, how he died?"

"Not prepared to share anything at this time."

"Right, of course," I said. "But, I mean, we didn't hear any gunshots or anything."

"Good to know," Spiller said.

"Come to think of it, there wasn't any blood spilled that I remember. And it sure would have been noticeable," I said.

Kat Wilde, plucky investigator.

Spiller smiled, a rather condescending smile.

"Blunt instrument?" I said.

Now the Lieutenant was gesturing for me to head towards the door. His smile was gone.

Aha! I thought. Then mentally retracted the thought. Summers might have been riding an ORV and either hit a tree or rock or flipped it. But his machine wasn't around. Plus Summers likely didn't have a machine. He didn't have anything but a collapsed tent with a coffee can to pee in.

* * *

After sleeping until midafternoon and missing work, I emerged from my basement hovel into the family kitchen and was greeting by blinding sunlight and my aunt standing at the stove stirring something—perhaps a potion of some kind involving eye of newt. I noted that her hair was no longer purple but instead emitted a harsh orangish glow.

"Hey Kat, girl," Aunt Lin said. "Glad you're finally up. Time to pack. We're moving out to Wildwood tomorrow morning!"

"Huh?" I said.

"Yow!"

Jupiter inserted himself into the conversation with his signature command.

"I assume the cat wants to be fed, but I didn't think I should do it," Aunt Lin said. "I made some lentil soup. It's vegan. Are you hungry? Anyway, it's like almost fifty degrees out there! Snow's melting like crazy. A couple of guys with a big truck are coming around nine tomorrow to get your stuff out of the basement and storage place and take it on out to your new digs at the horse place. I've got an air mattress I'll put on the floor for now and plan to get some more stuff once I, er, get some funds besides my paltry unemployment."

"Huh?" I said.

"Funds," she said. "You know, income."

"Move? Really? You and me?"

"YOW!"

I stumbled over to the cupboard and pulled out a can of cat food that "has the flavor that cats love!" After plopping it into Jupiter's bowl and changing his water, I went in search of coffee.

"When was all of this decided?" I asked. "I mean, moving with like one day's notice. My parents *are* aware that there have been two deaths out at the stable, right?"

"It was decided this morning after you all got home and you went to bed. I guess your folks think that so long as I'm out there with you, it will be better than your venturing out after dark on your own. Of course you weren't on your own completely, as it turns out."

"Well, yeah, Nikko came 'cause my car took a dump, but—"

"You had quite a night, eh?" Aunt Lin said. She turned from her cauldron and gave me a wry look. "You look—different."

I picked up the coffee carafe and poured the bottom sludge into a cup and stuck it in the microwave.

"Different, how?" I muttered. "You mean like totally haggard because my car died in the middle of a major snowstorm as darkness was closing in, and I walked a mile in a blizzard using a cane? And of course there was that dead guy, you know, the *second* body at the stable in less than two weeks. And maybe I'm a little worse for wear because I had no sleep all night and was interrogated by a puffed-up Lieutenant at the state police headquarters this morning?"

"Nuh uh. Something else." She grinned broadly. "You guys serious?"

"Huh?"

"Oh come on. You know I have special powers. Spill it kiddo. That Nikko dude is a hottie."

"I have nothing to say." I couldn't help the grin that spread across my face. "Well, there was one redeeming situation in an otherwise tragic night at Wildwood Stables. It seems that my bum knee was miraculously cured." I bent my knee back and forth and it did feel pretty good. I smiled again. "And my ribs seem all better, too." I wondered if a metaphorical roll in the hay had anything to do with it.

Aunt Lin put a bowl of her vegan concoction in front of me. It did smell good.

"Eat! This soup is incredibly healthy. I mean, what was with the fried chicken last night? And cheese potatoes, corn, AND pie. Sodium, fat, and carbs. Not to mention animal flesh. Anyway, we'll get things packed up spiffy jiffy."

Due to a careless youth, Aunt Lin, now only in her thirties, was diabetic. She was convinced, however, that she could reverse the situation and control her blood sugar through "lifestyle," rather than insulin or pills. Thus, the vegan, low-carb, whatever diet. Plus she did some sort of meditation, apparently dyed her hair colors not found in nature, and played a lyre at strange hours, usually when everyone was trying to sleep. According to her, this regime was supposed to align her psyche with her mortal husk. An ambitious goal for certain and it was shaving months if not years off everyone else's lives.

Though I had apparently slept through the discussion, I was starting to understand why Mom and Dad had capitulated to the idea of me moving out, despite the nefarious destination of Wildwood Stables. It was the only way to get my Aunt Lin, purveyor of bizarre diets and nonconformity, out from under the Wilde rooftop. What kind of parent is willing to sacrifice their only child to the uncertainty of a multi-death scene, not to mention the influence of a misplaced hippie who would likely have me sitting in the lotus position intoning a Gregorian chant? A desperate parent indeed.

"Oh, and your mom said we have to take the cat."

16

The flooring still hadn't been installed, which was going to create a logistical issue, since we had random boxes piled everywhere on the underlayment. To add to the problem, mud had been tracked everywhere. But true to their promise, the two guys and a truck, along with Dad and Nikko, managed to get my paltry collection of furniture inside while Aunt Lin, Mom, and I hauled in my lighter worldly goods. The shiny new appliances that came with the house had all been put in place and we turned on the fridge. Mom immediately started putting my kitchen in order, without consulting me. Aunt Lin had brought along her potions and brews to start the pantry-stocking process. I contributed a box of toaster pastries, partial jar of peanut butter, a crushed box of crackers, half a package of Oreo cookies, and a six pack of Dr. Pepper. These were the items that had been stashed in my basement lair. We'd also brought along a half case of canned cat food, a bag of kibble, kitty treats, and a large bag of product for the feline commode called "Magic Kitty Krystals." Obviously a trip to Manny's would be in order unless I wanted to live on Aunt Lin's kale, bulgar, and herbal tea, or Jupiter's stinky cat food.

After Mom had my hodgepodge of kitchen items properly stored in cupboards and drawers, she sighed and looked at me then at Dad. Nikko and Dad were finishing up the installation of industrial-strength deadbolt locks on both doors.

"Well, at least nobody will get in the doors," Mom said. "That is if you remember to lock them." She gave me a pointed look.

"Don't worry Clara," Aunt Lin said. "We'll lock 'er up tight."

Mom looked around. "I'm glad the place came with blinds. Put those down after dark too. And we'll see about getting some decent curtains." She looked around again. "Among other things."

"Like food," I mumbled.

"Oh, that reminds me," Mom said. "I have some basic provisions in your dad's truck. A few things to get you by."

"Thanks Mom," I said.

"Where's the cat?" she said.

"Hiding," I said.

I had brought Jupiter to our new home ensconced in his carrying case with a towel over it. It had taken over half an hour to capture him and shove him into the crate back at my parents'. He howled pitifully the entire drive to his new home. Once all the stuff had been brought in and the door was shut, I let him out of his carrier and showed him his litter box in the utility room along with his water and food dish that I'd placed in a nook in the kitchen. I even put some special "cats can't resist them" treats in the bowl, which he ignored. As far as I could tell, the cat took up residence deep into the underworld of my bed. When I peeked under there, I could see his two satanic eyes glaring at me.

"You'll be in for work tomorrow, right Kat?" Dad said. "I have a meeting in Marquette, so won't be in."

"Yup, I'll be there. I need to make up some hours."

"See you later, then," Dad said. "Ready, Clara?"

"I guess. Kathryn, do you think you could show your face in church this Sunday? People are asking about you. I can't go on making excuses forever. It's been months—since Christmas, I think."

Mom was determined to save me from eternal damnation. Truth was, I wouldn't mind darkening the doors of the Peshekee Methodist Church again, now that things were looking a tad up for me. "Sure, I'll be there," I said. I looked at Nikko and he smiled noncommittally.

"I will probably be back late Saturday, depending..." Nikko said.

I'd love to swagger in with a hunky guy on my arm. But then, that would just be prideful, and God had a way of humbling me when I got cocky.

"Wonderful," Mom said. "Service starts at ten. Now darling, just call if you need anything. Gary, are you sure Phil's truck is safe for our daughter?"

"Safe enough," Dad said. "It runs and the lights, brakes, heater, and radio work."

"Thanks Dad," I said.

"We'll be fine," Aunt Lin said. She looked at Nikko. "We can always call Officer Olsen to the rescue."

"Oh, stop," I said. "Nikko has to head back to work tomorrow, too."

I watched Dad hand a wad of cash over to the two guys and a truck. They had large grins on their faces as they hopped into their beater-mobiles and headed out to navigate the muddy ruts of the road.

"Well, it's time for me to meditate," Aunt Lin said. "I'll be in my bedroom."

Aunt Lin's bedroom consisted of her on-the-floor mattress, a bean bag chair, a cardboard dresser, and some sort of exercise mat. It made my thrift store décor seem luxurious.

"Well, I'm going to check on the horse," I said. "Wanna come along?"

"Sure," Nikko said.

I had kept Rusty in the barn the previous night, with his stall open and available, but the metal gate still closed across the main door going outside. When we got in the barn, Rusty was standing at said metal gate, staring off into the distance. I checked the stall and Floppy and her fawn were gone. Since the day had turned warm and the snow was going fast, I figured the deer had returned to their natural habitat where they belonged. We moved Rusty out to his paddock where he could roll in the mud. Next I grabbed my trusty manure bucket, shovel, rake, and manure fork and began cleaning the stall and the barn aisle. Nikko held the shovel while I pushed stuff into it. Next I dragged the bucket outside and dumped it into a newly created manure pile.

"Next thing I get is a wheelbarrow," I said as I headed back to the barn. I spotted the bucket with the deer afterbirth and hauled that away too. Nikko watched, hands shoved in his pockets.

"Major yuck," I said. "Flies are laying maggots."

"I'll say one thing for you, Kathryn Wilde," Nikko said. "You aren't afraid to get your hands dirty."

I put all the implements away and went over to Nikko who was looking out at the grounds of Wildwood.

"You can only say *one* thing for me?" I said.

He grinned. "Well, maybe a couple other things too."

We faced each other. He took my shoulders and pulled me in for a lingering kiss. We pulled apart and I looked across the parking area at the modular house, which I decided to call "the mod" for short. It would take time to call it home.

"Aunt Lin is in there," I said.

"Yes," he said.

"She's already onto us."

"The lady is scary."

"Weird, but harmless," I said. "Likely strategically put here by my folks as a chaperone and to scare off serial killers."

We both sighed. While a follow-up to the blizzard barn night was on our minds, the logistics would be tricky.

"Hey, now that the squatter no longer walks this earth, have you thought about dismantling the camp?" Nikko said. "That is assuming the cops are done with it."

"They didn't string any crime scene tape around it, so I guess they got what they wanted after their last trip out here," I said. "Anyway, I haven't had a chance to think about it, you know, with the murder, interrogation, move to the mod, and, um..."

"An evening of unbridled passion," Nikko provided.

"Cute. Nice double entendre."

"Wow. Fancy language for a gal who wallows in horse poop."

"I am a woman of many facets."

"Another word I don't fully understand, but I am pretty fond of your facets, whatever they are."

I smiled. "Google it."

"So—the horse camp...?"

"No time like the present."

We took Uncle Phil's—now my—truck back to the campground. Summers' tent was completely flat. Most of the snow had melted and his paltry possessions that had at one time been organized around the fire ring now lay in the mud and slush, as if fusing with the surroundings.

"Depressing," I said.

Nikko and I loaded the stuff into the back of the truck. We'd add it to the "dump" pile that was hidden behind a storage shed. Nikko went over to the trail camera, which was still mounted on the tree.

"Amazing the police didn't think to take this," he said. "Guess now that the squatter has been identified, not to mention dead, I might as well take this thing down. We can check out the SD card and if there's anything that might help the police, we'll let them know, I guess. I think our pal Summers was offed way out of the cam's range, though."

"Okay," I said. "Ready?"

"Yeah, in a minute. I, ah, gotta see a man about a horse," Nikko said as he headed off toward the ramshackle privy.

I wondered where that expression came from. I looked off into the woods and shuddered. What should have been a lovely woodsy site was the scene of a suspicious death. I wondered if the campground would creep me out to the point where I would not be able to deal with it. On the other hand, Wildwood Stables being the scene of an alleged murder or murders, might actually serve as a marketing tool at some point. People just naturally had morbid curiosity.

I gave one last look at the woods. Buds were starting on the trees, apparently undeterred by the spring snowstorm. Birds were chirping and the sun poked out for a moment, creating an ethereal movement off in the woods. And there it was again, the horse. Its image, reddish-brown this time, flashed through the trees, as if a ghost that could walk through solid objects. It seemed to stop and look at me. I stood, paralyzed, and watched as the specter horse evaporated into the forest.

"That was quite an experience," Nikko said as he walked over to me from his trip to the outhouse.

"Huh, what?" I said.

"Hey, didn't mean to startle you," he said. "I think every beast of the forest has taken up residence in that little crapper."

"Yeah, I, um—."

"Well, now that Scott Summers is no longer hanging out here, maybe—hey, you okay?"

"Yeah, sure," I said. "Just kinda spooked and all." I was still staring off to where the image had appeared. Now, of course, it was gone. I wished that just once someone else would see it so that I could confirm my sanity.

"Sure," Nikko said.

We got in the truck and after unloading at the dump pile, headed back to the mod. We could hear the lyre's plinking tune coming from within.

"I guess I better head home," Nikko said, giving me a chaste peck on the cheek.

"Yeah, and I got some unpacking to do."

"I'm going back to Ontonagon for a stretch, then will be back for a couple of days."

"I'll likely be here," I said. "Or at the office."

"How about an actual date?"

"You mean like dinner and dancing and stuff?"

"Actually, I was thinking of something more adventurous. It will be a surprise," he said. "Say goodbye to your auntie and her guitar for me."

"It's a lyre," I muttered.

I watched Nikko climb into the Tahoe and drive off, then headed back to the mod wondering what kind of adventure he had in mind. The prospect brought a smile to my face.

17

"So, Gussy, what's this Equine Rescue invoicing all about?" I asked.

I confronted him first thing Friday morning, before he had even booted up his computer.

"Huh?" Gussy said.

"Sorry," I said. "Here's the deal. I was sorting files and came across Uncle Phil's paperwork and there was a whole lot of money spent on some place—presumably a foundation—called Equine Rescue. I figured that since you handled Uncle Phil's bookkeeping, you could shed some light."

"Well, um, I don't really—"

"Good morning, Kathryn," Rose said as she emerged from the ladies' room. "Nice to finally see you."

"You too," I said, matching Rose's insincere tone.

"Just wondering if Mr. Wilde was aware," I said. "You know, about that kind of exceptionally large donation." I was required to call Dad Mr. Wilde while at work, if I remembered.

"Um, I'm not sure. I just went ahead and processed—but I don't recall. What was the name again?"

By this time Rose had become interested in our conversation and made herself busy making coffee nearby and tsk tsking the dirty coffee mugs left on the counter.

"Equine Rescue," I said.

"Is—what's ah, um equine?" Either Gussy was stonewalling me or was dumber than a rock.

"It has to do with horses."

"Oh for heaven's sake," Rose said. "Gussy just paid the bills, he didn't question your uncle's life choices."

The door opened and Char came waltzing in. She didn't look her usual spiffy self, though. Maybe a bit of a hangover.

"Life choices?" I said.

"Whose life choices?" Char asked.

"Uncle Phil," I said.

"Hm," Char said.

"You're only wearing one earring," Rose said.

Char reached up and felt her earlobes. "Oh, well, must have lost it."

That wasn't the only thing askew with Char. Once she shed her coat, I noticed her sweater was inside out and had the tag showing at the front of her neck.

Rose gave her a scrutinizing look. "I'm assuming you were in a hurry this morning."

Expecting any kindness from Rose was like waiting for a unicorn to magically appear in the backyard. If one were in intensive care after a tragic car accident, Rose would chide them for not wearing a seatbelt.

Char went into her office and shut the door. Uncharacteristic of her not to get the last word in with Rose.

"So, anyway Gussy, about this expenditure—should I ask Dad, er, Mr. Wilde?"

"I guess."

I sighed and went to my office nook. I was getting nowhere with Gussy. I'd have to get him alone and put the thumbscrews to him. I would like to have the USB flash drive gizmo from *all* of Uncle Phil's business dealings. While there were of course hard copies of some things, not everything was deemed worthy of using up the pricey laser printer cartridges and space in the file cabinet. And even though things went to the shredder's after so many years, once the floppy disk went to the tech graveyard, we did electronic backup on flash drive sticks and saved the data indefinitely. Raymond periodically worked his magic and upgraded the data to whatever the latest software version happened to be.

Of course the Wildwood flash stick was not easily accessible to me since Rose was keeper of these things, which she secured in the office safe that had a combination only she and Dad supposedly knew. I happened to know where Dad kept his note with the combination hidden, but I couldn't just waltz over to the safe and open it up in front of everyone. I had no idea *who* to trust at that point. Even though Uncle Phil was a nice guy and had trouble saying no to people, I suspected that money for this so-called foundation was extracted from him under duress.

I booted up my computer and googled Equine Rescue. As you'd expect, I got about 2,000 hits. I added "foundation," which didn't help narrow it down one bit. Practically every state had an equine rescue foundation, and there were also national and international ones. Not to mention articles and sponsored ads up the wazoo. I pulled one of Equine Rescue's invoices out of my office satchel. The address was a P.O. Box in San Bernadino, California. There was a phone number, which I suspected was a throw-away cell. I gave it a shot and dialed. I got a message that the party had not yet set up a mailbox. This whole thing stunk to high heaven. Yeah, I'd have to consult with Mr. Wilde on this one. Unfortunately, it would have to wait because he was at his CPA meeting in Marquette. Could anything be duller? I envisioned endless PowerPoint presentations along with esoteric networking and an exchange of dreary publications. Though I do believe there generally was alcohol involved after the wrap-up session.

I doubted that Uncle Phil would have the bank balance for such exorbitant donations. If it were me, my checks would bounce and the bank would inflict a hefty penalty. However, I was pretty sure that Gussy or Char handled paying Uncle Phil's bills, especially toward the end. And if things were getting tight, I knew that Dad periodically brought Uncle Phil's account out of the red with supplementations. I wondered if Dad just figured the constant cash flow issues were simply because Wildwood Stables was a money pit. A money pit that I had inherited. However, I would not be making obscene donations to this so-called Equine Rescue place anytime soon.

Rose interrupted my reverie, "How's the client newsletter coming?"

I gave a start. The woman wore crepe-soled shoes so she could sneak up on unsuspecting prey.

"Um, just doing a little research," I said, "then I can wrap it up."

"Good," Rose said. "It should go out May first."

May first was Monday. And Rose knew I was fibbing. Truth be told, I hadn't started the newsletter, other than to stick a few articles in a computer file labeled "News Stuff." The semi-completed newsletter would be reviewed by Rose before it was sent electronically to our client base. It included scintillating articles on tax breaks, tax pitfalls, tax investments, tax liabilities, tax forms, how to succeed in business, why businesses fail, and a cheerful letter by Dad, who whipped it out at the last minute and electronically signed it "Gary."

Then two good things happened. The first was that it was payday and I'd had a deposit in my checking account. This would enable me to make token payments at various places, put gas in the truck, buy food, and perhaps get my hair cut. Obviously there would not be adequate funds to repair my Subaru, which was being scrutinized that day. A glum preliminary report mentioned something about a pump, or timing belt, or rods, or all of the above.

The second good thing was that my cell rang. Not that a ringing cell phone is good news, per se, but it's not always bad either. Initially, I had hoped maybe it was Nikko, you know, just checking in. But it wasn't Nikko or Mom or any familiar number.

"Hello?" I said.

"Um, hi," said a youngish-sounding female.

"Hi."

"Is this the owner of Wildwood Stables?" the person said.

"Yes." Now what, I thought. Did Rusty get out and terrorize the neighborhood?

"Hi," she repeated. "Um, I was wondering what you charge to board horses."

"I—board horses?"

"Uh huh. I seen your ad at the feed store. See, me and my sister have got two horses and I'm gonna be a counselor at a youth health camp downstate. I'm going to go into therapy—I mean, not me—I'm not getting therapy, but I'm going to take some classes next fall about horses and therapy for kids. Plus I want to become an animal technician. I'm real good at math and science and I love animals. Anyways, my sister's getting married. We want to keep our horses until she can get a place, you know, to have them. So, I got your number off your poster at Pete's and, you know, thought I'd call and check it out."

"Well, Miss..."

"Susie—Susie Koskinen," she said. "My sister's name is Sharon and when she's married, she'll be Anderson, or maybe Koskinen-Anderson. She hasn't decided."

"Well, Susie, glad to meet you," I said. "Yes, I could handle a couple of boarders. I have lots of stalls, but right now the pasture fence needs fixing before I can turn horses out. We do have a couple of paddocks, though. Well, one paddock and a riding ring, which could be a paddock. We'd need to do a little fixing."

"Uh huh. So, um, how much? See, Daddy says he'll pay for a while, but he's pretty cheap. He don't wanna take care of our horses though. He and Ma are gonna do some traveling when me and Sharon leave."

"Cheap huh?

I ran a figure past her and she said she'd get back to me but was pretty sure "Daddy" would go for it. We hung up with the plan to meet out at Wildwood Saturday afternoon to hopefully seal the deal.

"Hot damn!" I said.

I heard the low rumble of Rose's Nasty List desk drawer being pulled open. But I didn't care because I had the prospect of some actual income at Wildwood Stables.

"Hot *diggity* damn!" I said, even louder.

* * *

Susie and her dad showed up promptly at 9:00 a.m. I was outside with my dad and Aunt Lin doing some makeshift repairs to the riding ring, which would serve as a turn-out paddock until we could make the pasture fence serviceable. I still hadn't gotten Dad alone to ask him about the overly generous donations to the so-called Equine Rescue charity.

Mr. Koskinen and Susie got out of a big, shiny truck with nubby tires and generous sprays of mud, probably from their trip down our road. He put his hand on Susie's shoulder and looked around, then spotted Dad, Aunt Lin, and me replacing a broken board on the ring fence.

"Hello!" I said. "Give us a minute."

After the board was in place, we all walked over to the Koskinens. Dad wiped his hand on his pants and reached out to Mr. Koskinen, who returned the gesture. Nobody shook my hand, but Susie and I smiled at each other then she looked at Aunt Lin.

"I love your hair," Susie said.

"Thanks," Aunt Lin said, reaching up to her now rainbow-streaked hair. It was almost painful to look at it.

"My Susie here says yous might take care of the girls' horses, eh?" Mr. Koskinen said. "By the way, name's Al."

"Nice to meet you, Al," Dad said. "Call me Gary. This is my daughter, Kat, and my sister-in-law, Lindsey."

Everyone made the usual perfunctory greetings.

"Just so you know," Dad said, "I'm just the free hired hand. Kat here is the owner and operator of Wildwood. She's just getting it up and running."

"That so," Al said. "Well, isn't that somethin'?"

"I'd love to start out by boarding your daughters' horses," I said. I looked at Susie. "What kind of horses do you and your sister have?"

"Oh, just kinda mixtures, I guess. I call mine Shadow, because he's dappled gray, maybe some Arabian in him. Sharon's horse is named Misty. She's a roan mare and kind of snotty. We think she is part Arab too. We don't have papers or anything."

Susie looked over at Rusty, who had temporarily abandoned his staring off into the horizon to observe the human activity. He had had his usual roll in the paddock and clumps of mud hung from his mane, tail, and belly hair.

"That's Rusty," I said. "He is impossible to keep clean."

Susie laughed. "Yeah! Don't they love to always get muddy and lie in their poop!"

"Let me show you the barn," I said.

We all went in and I flicked on the lights. In anticipation of the Koskinens' arrival, I had spent some time sweeping, knocking down cobwebs, and neatly organizing things the night before. I had two stalls bedded with shavings and appointed with scrubbed-clean rubber buckets for the anticipated new arrivals.

"This is real nice," Susie said. "Ain't it Daddy?"

"*Isn't* it, honey," Al Koskinen said.

"Yes, Daddy," she said.

"So, I guess Susie and you discussed the cost?" I said.

"Yup," Al said. "I'm pretty good with the cost but I'm wondering about the things going on out here."

Damn.

"Any idea what that fella died from?" Al asked.

"Boy, things get around Peshekee quickly," I said.

"All the talk at Pete's General Store," Al said. "I just want my girls to be safe if they come to visit and ride their horses."

"Totally understandable," I said. "I can assure you that we'll make sure the girls aren't alone when they come out."

"Won't be too much," Susie said. "I'll be gone and come home a couple of times. Sharon and Brian—that's her fiancé—are moving to Escanaba where he's got a job."

"And I'll be here with Kat," said Aunt Lin.

Al looked at her dubiously.

"Be a hired hand soon, too," Dad said.

"I'm planning on applying for the job," Aunt Lin said.

This was news to me, but whatever. "And more boarders and riding lessons, too—once I get more horses."

"Well, it ain't—er isn't like there's a lot of places we can go without payin' an arm and a leg. And I knew your brother," Al said to Dad. "Me and him had some good chats."

"Him and me," Susie corrected. "Or is it him and I?"

"He and I," Aunt Lin said.

"Well, he or him was a good guy. And I've been proud of my girls, too. They both took jobs in high school to have money for their horses.

Won some ribbons at the fair. We don't just want to put the horses anywhere. You seem like you know your stuff."

"Thank you," I said.

"And Brian—that's who my sister's marrying—says he's gonna look for some land to build a place for the horses someday," Susie said.

Al gave a snort. "We'll see. He'll have his hands full just takin' care of your sister."

"So, when would you be bringing them over? I have some questions before you do, you know, about vaccinations and stuff."

"I'll go make tea," Aunt Lin said. "Everyone can come in and we can talk about arrangements."

"Tea?" Dad said. "You got any coffee, Kat?"

"Sure, I'll put a fresh pot on when we get inside," I said. I was familiar with Aunt Lin's ghastly tea and did not want to inflict it on anyone. "Probably Susie would like a soft drink? Do you like Dr. Pepper?"

"Sure," she said.

We all traipsed into the mod. I measured coffee and water into the machine and pushed start. I popped open a can of Dr. Pepper and handed it to Susie. We crammed around my tiny kitchen table. Dad had to get the clothes hamper from the bathroom to sit on. Dad and Al chit-chatted about work. (Al was a plant manager at the area manufacturing plant.) They also blabbed about fishing, hunting, off-roading, and their wives. Susie yawned then pulled out her phone and began fiddling with it. I got out coffee mugs while waiting for the machine to wheeze out its last drop. I put a few of my Oreo cookies on a plate and put them on my table. Aunt Lin brewed a pot of tea and having no takers, excused herself to attend to some personal business. I prayed to God it didn't involve an annoying plink-plunking on her lyre. Her exit freed up a chair and Dad moved off the clothes hamper.

"Cream or sugar, Al?" I said.

"Black please."

Sight unseen, the horses that would be coming into my care sounded as if they had been well cared for. They were up to date on recommended vaccinations and they used the same farrier that I had used for Rusty's mangled hooves. I was cautioned that the mare was a brat sometimes. We had a bit of discussion about the gender mix of two geldings and a mare—a recipe for trouble. Likely Rusty would have to be separate from the two, or the mare separate from the geldings. It was not insurmountable, but we needed to get the pasture fence replaced and horse-worthy.

"So I can write yous a check today, Kat, if we're all squared away."

"That sounds—"

"Hey!" Al said. "I got something to barter with."

Uh oh.

"Them—the two horses have a loafing shed that I bought pre-made. Come on a flatbed. It was meant as a storage shed but worked great for the critters. We never had a proper barn, so we set up the shed for them. I wonder about maybe throwing it into the bargain."

"Are you thinking of me waiving the board money, because—"

"Oh heck no. I mean just as a kind of, you know, security deposit, in case one of our horses breaks something."

"Breaks something?" I said.

"Daddy!" Susie said. "You're going to mess everything up. Shadow and Misty are good horses. The only thing they broke was that stupid hitching post Brian built. Horses gotta be trained to be tied to a hitching post. Don't listen to him, Kat."

"Horses are big animals," I said. "Stuff happens. I think a loafing shed would be ideal."

Eventually I was the recipient of a check that represented not one but two months' board for two horses. This would be sufficient to stock up on feed and bedding and start saving for hay when it would be cut in a month or two. The Koskinens got in their truck and headed out.

I was feeling pretty good about things until I saw Sheriff Olsen's police car coming in.

 **18**

"This can't be good," Dad said as he squinted into the sun.

The cruiser pulled into the parking lot and Sheriff Olsen got out and put on his hat. Aunt Lin came out of the mod and joined our little cluster.

"What's shakin'?" she said.

I shrugged.

"Morning' Ollie," Dad said.

The sheriff nodded at Dad and me and did a double take of Aunt Lin. She had changed from her jeans and flannel shirt to a poison green, flowing caftan, with an equally blinding orange drape around her shoulders. She'd also put on a pair of earrings big enough to serve as basketball hoops.

"You remember Clara's sister," Dad said.

"This is Lindsey?" the sheriff asked.

"Yup," Aunt Lin said. "The one and only."

"What brings you way out here, Ollie?" Dad asked.

"Just wanted to give you folks a heads up. Probably shouldn't but I think that the staties are—well to use an old expression, barking up the wrong tree."

"How so," Dad said.

"Getting a search warrant for Wildwood."

"What!" I said. "They've been over the place a million times. They never got a search warrant for before."

"Sounds like a fishing expedition," Dad said.

"I know," Sheriff Olsen said. "But I guess they have some new info and want to make sure they can keep what they find."

I made a quick mental inventory of things I would not want people to keep if found, or even find for that matter, such as birth control pills, acne cream, and a hemorrhoid product "specially formulated for women." I could only imagine what Aunt Lin had tucked away. She could be accused of *death by lyre*. I started thinking that would be a good title for a poem or even a novel.

"I see," said Dad. "Well, let them look. They are welcome to keep all the manure they dig up."

"Good one," Aunt Lin said.

"So, they still don't know how Summers died?" I asked. "I mean, Nikko probably told you that we didn't hear any gunshots or see any blood around the, er, body."

"Thing is," the sheriff said, "Nikko was with you when Mr. Summers' body was found. They've talked to both of you—"

"Lieutenant Spiller," I said, "he could make Mother Teresa confess to war crimes."

"Yeah, and he won't talk to me because of a so-called conflict of interest. But I have a good friend at the state police and he won't tell me everything—getting ready to retire—but gave me some info. Besides, I did the initial investigation on Sasha Saari-Summers, and truthfully, I don't see Spiller or any of his crack investigative team making much progress on her case."

"I asked him about that," I said. "I think it kinda pissed him off."

Dad looked at me and frowned.

"I'm a lot like you," I said.

That made Sheriff Olsen laugh.

"You could do worse," Dad said.

"Yes," Aunt Lin said. "She could be more like me."

We didn't know what to say about that.

"You got any coffee?" the sheriff asked.

"Come on in," Aunt Lin said. "I make great herbal tea."

Eventually I hoped Aunt Lin would give up on her attempts to convert us to her tea concoctions, which frankly tasted like a cross between pond scum and pee. Not that I had tasted either, but I could imagine.

We all trundled into the mod. I went over to the coffee maker and started a fresh pot. We once again crammed around my tiny kitchen table. It was really the only place to sit since the floor in the living room was yet to be completed and my scant living room furniture was still pushed off into a corner along with a so-called entertainment center, which consisted of a "dumb" TV that was currently not operational. Raymond promised to get me squared away with some gizmo that hooked onto it and streamed shows. There wasn't any cable out here in the middle of nowhere.

"Yow!"

Jupiter had finally come out of hiding that morning—likely due to hunger.

"Well, there's a good kitty," Aunt Lin said, reaching down and picking him up. He positioned himself so he could look across the table. He flattened his one functioning ear and fixed a beady glare on Sheriff Olsen.

"Good God, what in hell is *that?*" Sheriff Olsen said.

"It's a cat, obviously," Aunt Lin said. "And one with very special powers."

That was news to me.

"So, psychic cat aside," Dad said, "what's going on that the state police believe they need a search warrant? And for that matter, when are they gracing us with their presence?"

"Again," I added.

"They like to surprise people. So if you have any other bodies to hide, best get to it," the sheriff said.

"Such short notice," Aunt Lin said. "Well, we'll just have to drag our victims into the river and hope the current sweeps them away."

"Hilarious," Sheriff Olsen said.

"I repeat: what are they looking for?" Dad said.

"Best I could tell from my *source* is that the only thing they found with the autopsy was a tiny mark that could have been an injection site for a drug."

"What kind of drug?" I said.

"Good question. Takes a while to run a tox. I'm hoping to find out at some point. I think mainly they want to search the woods more thoroughly to see if they can find evidence of a drug being used, such as a syringe or empty vial."

"Wouldn't that be pretty stupid to leave evidence lying around?" I said. "Besides, for all we know, Summers could have been taking drugs all along. He sure looked the part."

"Well," the sheriff said, "apparently the injection site was some-where on the back of Summers' neck, which would be difficult if not impossible for him to reach. We all know that you and Nikko had nothing to do with it, but of course there is the little issue of a motive."

"Like Scott Summers having a claim to the place," I said. "Not to mention attacking me."

"Yow!"

Jupiter jumped down from Aunt Lin's lap and went over to the cupboard where we kept his food, toys, and grooming tools. Aunt Lin got up and took out something.

"Catnip," she said. "He loves it."

She gave Jupiter a little burlap pouch presumably chock full of catnip. We all watched him snatch it up and haul it away. We heard some guttural yowling from the living room area and all looked at Aunt Lin.

"What?" she said. "Catnip's not even available as an injection. It's all in the aroma and perfectly harmless to cats."

"What else have you got up your sleeve?" the sheriff said. "Wait, never mind. I don't want to know."

"Nothing illegal, I assure you," she said. "I do believe in natural medicine, but it's all perfectly safe. Usually."

"Well, with that I'll—wait, one more thing," Sheriff Olsen said.

We all looked at him.

"Our department did get some of Sasha Saari-Summers' bank records. Her account downstate is closed, but we checked out the activity on it. First off, she and another person were on the account. Someone named Melinda Smith. Secondly, and most important, there was a hell of a lot of money going in and out. Way more than they pay caregivers. Plus she had a regular account locally, also closed, where her pay from Yarrow Hospice was auto deposited and the balance was always running near empty. She was overdrawn. A lot."

"I can relate to that," I muttered.

"So this other account from downstate. You say a lot of money—like how much?" Dad asked.

"Thousands over a period of time."

We all looked at each other.

Olsen took the last swig of his coffee and stood. "If I were to give my opinion, I'd say someone was selling drugs, taking drugs, or being blackmailed. Or all of the above."

Things were getting very tangled up in the Wildwood saga.

We followed Sheriff Olsen out to his cruiser. He took off his hat and threw it on the passenger seat then got in. He started the engine and slid down his window. "Good luck with the search warrant."

He started to slide his window up, then put it back down. "Oh, I almost forgot. Frieda wants everyone over for Sunday dinner tomorrow at two. Glad I remembered to tell you that or there'd been hell to pay. Speaking of paying, I'm not thrilled to owe the feds a bundle on my tax return."

"It could have been worse," Dad said. "You are lucky you don't have any underpayment penalties. You don't have many deductions, Ollie. You might think about having extra taken out of each paycheck."

"Hah!" the sheriff said. "What I need is more creativity in my return."

"That can result in a lot of trouble," Dad said. "Including jail time."

Sheriff Olsen snorted at Dad then looked at me. "Oh, and one more thing. Nikko's coming home tonight. He'll be there tomorrow."

The sheriff was smirking.

* * *

I felt something cold and wet bump into my ankle, then lick it. "What in heck are you doing down there, Tobey?" I said.

Tobey, the recently adopted Olsen pit bull, did not answer, and his tongue moved up under my pant leg and continued to lick. I tried to gently push him away, but he was not deterred.

"Tobey!" Frieda Olsen snapped. "Get away from her. Go lie down."

The licking ceased and Tobey slunk away.

After attending church, the Wilde clan headed out to the Olsens', where we gathered around the dining room table, gorging ourselves on fall-off-the-bone barbeque ribs along with about ten side dishes. Mom had brought a bright green molded gelatin salad embedded with assorted crunchy things, which everyone raved over—except me. I brought my charm and good looks and apparently an irresistible ankle/leg combo that would trigger Tobey's licking frenzy.

"I'm so sorry about Tobey," Frieda said. "Ever since we had him, er, *fixed*, he's been obsessed with licking everything and anything."

"He used to have a cone around his neck so he couldn't lick or chew his stitches," Nikko said. "He came in from the backyard yesterday and the thing was gone."

"We looked everywhere," Frieda said.

"I still say it was the neighbor kids," Sheriff Olsen said.

"Well, anyway, he still leaves his stiches alone, but licks everything else," Frieda said.

Mom and Dad just looked from Frieda to Ollie and didn't say a word. Nikko was trying hard not to burst out laughing. He looked at me a waggled his eyebrows. I rolled my eyes. There was nothing sexy about a slimy dog tongue exploring my leg. But I had to smile a little. Things were awkward for a couple of beats. What could anyone say? I mean, how do you gracefully enter into a conversation about a pooch who had his boy-parts removed and is now obsessed with licking?

Frieda cleared her throat. "I am so sorry that Lindsey didn't come. I would love to see her again. I realize she only eats certain things, but we could have worked it out."

"Well, my sister is quirky," Mom said. "I do apologize for her declining your invitation."

"Doesn't know what she's missing!" Dad said licking his fingers. "Pork ribs are about my favorite." He wiped some barbeque sauce off his face and said, "So, the state police haven't shown up yet at the stable."

"Yeah?" Ollie said. "Bet they couldn't get a judge to sign a search warrant on the weekend. Hah! Serves Spiller right. Pompous—"

"Now Ollie," Frieda said.

Waiting for the state police to come with their officious search warrant had been like waiting for the test results at the doctor's office. You know, sitting in the little cubicle with nothing to look at except a couple of laminated posters and a selection of examination gloves. Then the doctor comes in carrying a laptop, brow furrowed. Turns out the only problem you seem to have is that your blood pressure and heart rate are up, which of course could be contributed to you anxiously waiting...

"They'll get there," Ollie said.

"Good thing we hid all the other bodies," I said, chuckling. Nobody else laughed.

"So, who wants some bundt cake?" Frieda said.

We all did.

Nikko and I eventually excused ourselves to go for a walk. He snapped the leash on Tobey and the three of us went off toward a pond not too far from the Olsen's. The weather was pleasantly warm, the sun was out, and the birds chirped joyfully.

"This doesn't count as our so-called adventurous date, does it?" I said.

"Nope," Nikko said. "I have to make some arrangements and I'll let you know. What days do you have off this week?"

We stopped for a minute while Tobey sniffed something interesting off in the dead grass.

"None, really," I said. "I work at the office on Monday and Tuesday this week because I have two new boarders coming on Wednesday. Then office again on Thursday, then I guess just work at Wildwood the rest of the week."

"Well, can you squeeze me in, say, next Saturday?" Nikko said.

"I'll pencil you in," I said turning to him.

"Ink me in."

"Is this a metaphor for our—relationship?" I said.

"There you go, talking all fancy again," he said.

"You went to college. You know what a meta—"

He pulled me in and we kissed. I could taste just a tiny bit of sweetness on his lips. Probably the bundt cake. It wasn't a bad thing.

When we pulled apart, Tobey was no longer exploring the patch of dead grass.

"Tobey!" Nikko yelled. "Hey pup, where are you?"

We hurried down the path toward the pond.

"Damn," Nikko said rushing forward. "Too late."

Tobey was at the edge of the pond, rolling gleefully in the mud.

Nikko sighed. "Now I have to try to give him a bath. Ma won't be happy."

"What's that?" I said, pointing to something poking above the surface of the pond. Most of the ice was gone; just a few small pieces bobbed around an object that looked like plastic or trash.

"I have no idea," Nikko said.

"It better not be a body," I said. "If there is one more dead body in my life, I'll just, just…"

Nikko grabbed a branch off the ground and reached out to the object, snagged it and pulled it in.

"Trash?" I said. "I hate people that throw—"

"I think we found Tobey's Cone of Shame," Nikko said. "How it got here, I haven't a clue."

"Damn kids," I said.

I remembered Grandpa Wilde always blaming *those damn kids* for any mischief that took place in his neighborhood. Of course I was one of the kids.

Tobey came over and shook, spraying us with mud.

"Bad dog," Nikko said, reaching down and picking up the leash that Tobey had been dragging around. It, too, was crusted with mud.

Nikko looked at me then reached out and brushed something off my cheek. "Mud," he said. "I think there is some in your hair, too."

"Oh my," I said feigning a southern accent, "whatever will people think?" I reached out and touched just above his lips. "Barbeque sauce," I said. "Such a sloppy eater."

"Wanna lick it off?" Nikko said.

"Just stop."

We returned to the Olsen abode where it appeared that the party was breaking up and everyone was standing in the driveway. Dad carried a paper sack with handles that presumably contained leftovers. When Nikko, Tobey, and I approached, Frieda gasped.

"Sorry Ma," Nikko said. "Tobey rolled in the mud. Again."

"Why weren't you watching him?" she said.

"Ah, I was…"

"We found his plastic cone," I said, deflecting any thoughts of the obvious.

"Here, this is for you," Dad said handing me the bag. I could see a grease stain spreading out one side. "You and Aunt Lin, if she will eat any of it."

"Hey, thanks."

Everyone thanked each other, hugged, kissed, and we headed to our cars. Nikko followed me and opened the door to Uncle Phil's truck. I turned to climb in and felt a push from behind.

"Copping a feel, eh?" I said.

"I have no idea what you're talking about," he said. "But if I did, just so you know, there's more where that came from."

I settled into the seat and pulled the door closed then hand-cranked down the window. Uncle Phil's truck was a no-frills model.

"So, I'll text you about Saturday," he said. "And let me know what the state police are looking for, or if they find it."

"Sure."

"And Kat?"

"Yeah?"

"You still have mud on your face."

19

I actually beat Rose in on Monday morning. I had become quite the early riser, now that I had my one-horse operation to tend to, not to mention a longer commute. I had hoped to beat Rose in to give me a few minutes to get things organized with Uncle Phil's so-called horse charity expenditures before approaching Dad. But first things first. I did what every office dweller does when he or she enters their nook at the start of a business day: I booted up my computer and checked out social media.

"Wow!" I said when I started scrolling through Facebook posts. I had about two dozen entries about horse rescues, showing heart-wrenching photos of neglected animals. Horses going to auction with broken legs and newborn foals being separated from their mothers to be sold for meat. Draft animals forced to work with open wounds and racehorses reduced to a per pound value. I wanted to throw up. Obviously, my random googling of Equine Rescue got my algorithms fired up and made me a target for every horse-related charity under the sun. As a former grant writer, I knew the tactic of optics in getting people to open their wallets. I also knew that before you give, you need to do your homework because there were a lot of sketchy charities out there. Some were downright scams.

I abandoned Facebook and opened up my email. Since I didn't have any clients assigned to me, most of my messages were junk mail. I did get one from Rose, reminding me that the newsletter deadline was that day. Of course she would also remind me in person. Repeatedly. I had a few junk emails trying to get me to pay bills online, start a retirement account, send money to an exiled prince in Nigeria, and another touting their new, innovative hearing aid.

Then there was one more. The address was 4HR at Gmail dot com.

Dear Horse Lover, We note that you care about those who cannot speak for themselves. We are not asking for money, but your help. We are looking for...

Whatever. I almost deleted the email, but decided to hold off until I could at least read the whole thing on the outside chance it related to Uncle Phil's philanthropy. I heard the door open and Rose bustled in. She looked at me, then at the clock. I smiled and also looked at the clock. Rose was actually two minutes late. I wondered if she would make an entry about herself on the Nasty List. I quickly opened up my newsletter file in the editor and pretended to look at it.

"I couldn't find a parking place," she huffed. "You parked your truck and managed to take up three spots."

"Sorry," I said. "I'll try to do better."

"See that you do. You didn't start the coffee."

"Nope," I said. "I figured it wouldn't be as good as yours."

What I was really saying was that since Rose criticized everyone else's coffee-making skills, nobody made the effort to step up to the pot, so to speak.

"Mornin' all," Dad said as he breezed in. "Or should I say, Rose and Kat. Where's the rest of the crew?"

"Well," Rose said, "Gerald's not feeling well this morning. As for Charlene—"

"Charlotte," I corrected.

"—I have no idea, but I haven't listened to the messages yet."

"She usually texts me if something comes up," Dad said, pulling out his phone. "Oh, guess I should turn it on…"

"Dad—er, Mr. Wilde, may I have a moment?" I said.

Dad looked at me. "Sure, Kat. Come on in."

I discreetly scooped up the file that held Uncle Phil's philanthropy info and followed Dad up to his office. Rose eyed us, obviously her radar beeping off the charts.

"So, what's this all about?" Dad said.

I explained how I had come across Uncle Phil's file and the questionable expenditure to the so-called Equine Rescue charity.

"Holy Moley, "he said, staring at the papers I had laid out.

"So, you didn't know? You weren't the one to stash these papers in the to-be-shredded box?"

"No, I never saw them before, I'm sure. I mean, I knew Phil gave a *certain* amount to help out some horse charity, but—wow."

"Almost ten thou, in just a year," I said.

"Well, that explains some things," Dad said. "But then opens up a lot of questions."

"So, checks were cut to this Equine Rescue place—probably about fifteen or twenty from Uncle Phil's business account. Only a P.O. box for mailing, which is in California no less. Cell phone number and no way to leave a message."

"California! What does Gussy say? Did he cut the checks?"

"He hedged, either totally ignorant or feigning ignorance."

Dad turned his chair and stared out the window for a couple of minutes.

"Do you think Uncle Phil knew what was going on?" I said.

"I don't know. Maybe he just wasn't paying attention. Same as me. I assumed Char had it covered."

"I'm sure she'd explain, if she were here."

"Hell," Dad said. "This stinks to high heaven. Okay honey, thanks for catching this. We'll talk some more. I need to think about things."

"Sure. Hey, I'm wondering about getting Uncle Phil's USB flash drive from the safe."

"Good idea."

"But, well, not that you don't trust Rose and all, but maybe get it when nobody's around. You know, in case, well…"

"God. Not Rose," Dad said. "Gussy?"

"Somehow I don't think Gussy has the guts or, frankly, the smarts to embezzle let alone blackmail," I said. "He lives with his mom, for God's sake and drives an old beater car. Where's the money? Drugs? Gambling? I'd bet my, well something of value, that Gussy has never taken any drug stronger than a multivitamin or even gambled with a scratch-off lottery ticket."

"Okay," Dad said. "I'll get the flash drive and we'll check it out. Rose usually leaves to go to lunch and apparently Gussy won't be in and Char texted me that she thinks she's got a bug and wants to work from home. So, that gives me an idea. Since I really don't want to raise any eyebrows, maybe you should take the laptop home that Raymond got set up for you."

"Laptop? Great!" I said. "Where?"

"On my credenza. He transferred everything, I think. If not, let him know. He said the old clunker you've been using was likely to crash any time. Anyway, work from home and consider it on the clock. Check out the data and see if there is anything else that gives us a clue."

"Great idea," I said. "But Rose will hate it."

"Yeah, but I'm still the boss," Dad said. "I think."

"And Dad?"

"Yes, honey?"

"I'm sorry."

"Yeah, me too."

I went back to my nook and started getting serious with the newsletter when my cell rang. I had found an app that sounded like a horse whinny for the ringtone. The noise made Rose sit up and look around with a confused expression.

I answered. The call was from the auto repair place where my Subaru was undergoing evaluation.

"Yeah, Miss Wilde?"

"That's me," I said.

"This is Mike at the shop. Uh, we can fix up the Subaru, but wanted you to know we are looking at about two K."

"Two thousand!"

"Right. First off, you should have had the timing belt changed about a hundred thousand miles ago, plus there's water pump and fuel pump problems. Probably why it died. Hasn't it been running rough? I mean, there are other things too, like the car was probably only running on a couple of plugs. The other two are like welded into the crankcase. Then there's the brakes, which are down to nothing, and a couple more minor things—"

"Stop!"

"Actually, the two grand doesn't include new brakes, but you need them fixed pronto. I sure wouldn't let my wife or kids drive this thing until they was fixed, eh?"

I hyperventilated into the phone for a couple of beats.

"Or..."

"Or what?" I said.

"See, she's a Subaru and there's still value, but not enough to make fixin' worthwhile. At least not for *you*, what with the cost of labor and parts and all. But I got some kids from a program with the state that tries to keep teens out of trouble and give them some skills to boot with a summer job. I signed up for a batch of them kids, since I don't think there's enough mechanics these days. Plus, they pay minimum to the kids and cover supplies and I get paid some, too. I guess a car would be a supply. We can't have them boys—and I think a girl or two—working on paying customers' cars on account of liability and all. Your Subaru would be just the ticket."

"Any idea when I'd get paid?"

"Not sure. Of course maybe yous just want to donate—"

"Nope. I'm more interested in getting paid," I said. "How much do you think?"

"Well, for scrap she's worth a couple hundred. But given that it's not going to scrap, I think I'd tell the director of the program seven or eight hundred."

"Sold!"

"Alrighty," Mike said. "I'll get in touch with Mr. Leppaninen—he's the director—and see what we can work out. Yous'll need to sign over the title and whatnot. Make up a bill of sale."

"Happy to as soon as that nice, juicy check is in my hand."

We hung up and I felt strangely conflicted. My beloved Subaru—the car that had seen me through nearly a quarter of a million miles of blinding snowstorms, icy hills, muddy ruts, and washed out two-tracks—was going into the heartless care of a bunch of teenagers. On the other hand, committing it to scrap would have been unconscionable. And I had hoped that I might be able to get it fixed and have something for Aunt Lin to drive. However, since that wasn't going to happen, I already knew what I'd be spending the cash on. While Rusty and I seemed to have an amenable arrangement with me doing all the work and him loafing around, at some point I intended to ride the beast. For that I needed a saddle and bridle. Even used, a saddle could easily exceed the value of the Subaru. But I had found something promising on Craig's List from a person in Escanaba. The saddle was a Stübben hunter/jumper model, my size, and supposedly "like new." They'd throw in a bridle and saddle pad. Stübben saddles, new, run in the thousands. The seller on Craig's List indicated the price of $500, firm. I'd have to do a little research on how to authenticate a Stübben saddle.

The office phone rang and I heard Rose's clipped greeting, then: "Gerald! Where *are* you?" The remainder of the conversation was in urgent whispers. Very curious indeed.

At lunchtime, Rose asked if she could leave for the day. Claimed she wasn't feeling well. Seemed everyone was under the weather that day. Of course she had approximately twenty weeks of sick and vacation time accumulated, so naturally Dad agreed.

"You want me to catch the phone?" I asked.

"Tell you what," Dad said. "We'll get that flash stick and you can head home to start working on it. There's not a lot of privacy here."

"What about the phone?"

"Hey, you forget, there was a time when I didn't have any help. I guess I can answer the phone. Plus, your mother is coming in to do some work, so she'll help out. He pulled open a drawer and peered at a note stuck to one of the brackets. "I'll get the combination."

Just as I was clambering up into Uncle Phil's truck with my laptop and the flash stick in a leatherette carrying case, my cell whinnied. I glanced at it and saw it was Aunt Lin.

"'Lo?"

"Kat! They're here. They were out in the woods, so I didn't bother you. But now they're going through *my* stuff. How dare they!"

"Huh? Who's there?"

"The damn police. There's two of them and they're going through the *house*!"

"I'm on my way."

I hurried out of the office and clambered into the truck. "C'mon baby," I said, cranking the engine. "Let's see what you can do."

20

When I pulled into Wildwood, there were two state police cars parked in the lot. They had left their engines running and one of the vehicles had the overhead lights flashing. I left my office satchel and laptop in the truck and hurried over to Aunt Lin. She telegraphed all kinds of attitude from her stance on the stoop of the mod. She was wearing what most would describe as a muumuu made from a wild, floral shower curtain. Her hair was wrapped in a towel and her hands were on her hips.

"Are they inside?" I asked her.

"Were, but now are scrounging around somewhere else. They gave me this paper," she said, handing me the search warrant we had all been waiting for. "I've been trying to figure it out, but it's written in legal mumbo jumbo."

"Yeah, we'd need an attorney to decipher it," I said. "And of course we don't have one anyplace handy right now."

"They went through all my special herbs and oils. Then they went to the medicine cabinet and took my syringe I keep for insulin. They asked what it was for and I told them, and they went to the fridge and took my bottle of insulin I had stashed behind the condiments."

"I thought you were off the insulin."

"Well, I am. But according to my health coach *and* my doctor, I should keep it on hand. Actually, I am on pills for diabetes right now. I still monitor my blood glucose, you know. Since I've turned my life around with diet and meditation, I haven't had to use the injection form. But I do need to have it—just in case."

"Sorry," I said. "I guess I didn't know that. I should know, in case, well, I wouldn't know what to do if—"

"We can talk about it later," Aunt Lin said. "I'll have to get a new bottle of insulin, and it isn't cheap."

I looked around the grounds to locate the troopers. Rusty was showing great interest in one of the troopers who was petting him. I headed in that direction and even from the distance I could tell it was Sergeant Witz who was one of the responders when Scott Summers and I had our encounter.

"I'm the owner—Kathryn Wilde. That's Rusty," I said nodding my head toward the horse. "Mind if I ask what you're looking for?"

"Hello," she said. "I just stopped to pet your horse. He's a big boy. Anyway, I gave the search warrant to your sister—"

"Aunt," I said. "We met before. When Summers assaulted me."

"Yes ma'am," she said. "Are you doing okay now?"

"Yeah, pretty good. Knee twinges now and then, but I'm pretty much back to normal. You interviewed my, er, friend Nikko Olsen too."

"Yup," she said. "I get around. Anyway, glad to hear your injuries are healing. Now, as far as what we're looking for, we have authority via the search warrant to search all the buildings and items within those buildings, the grounds, vehicles, and equipment and remove items that may be construed as evidence."

Rusty bumped Witz with his nose. That was his command for more scratching.

"Cool it, Rusty," I said and turned to face Witz. "I'm sure you have the *authority,* but you took my aunt's insulin. It was prescribed to her and it could be a while before she can get a replacement."

"Oh, my apologies. The other trooper took it to take a photo, catalog some info. We'll certainly return it before we depart. Anything of significance that we do take we will provide a receipt."

"Over here!" came a shout from behind the barn.

Sergeant Witz and I hurried around the barn and back into the weedy field where I had created my farm dump pile. The second trooper, a youngish African American man, was squatting over the debris, picking through it. He wore blue gloves such as found in dispensers in the doctor's office.

"We noticed that you removed Scott Summers' property from his encampment," Witz said. "We're wondering why you did that."

"Because it was an eyesore and needed to go. The police have been through everything there a couple of times and I wanted to clear it out and get rid of it. Nobody told us not to. I would have thought you guys would be out at the place where Summers, ah, passed away. Anyway, it's all in that pile of stuff your partner is going through. What *are* you looking for?"

The other trooper stood and had a coffee can in his hands. He worked on prying the plastic lid off.

"I would be careful opening that—"

The top flipped off and liquid splashed the trooper in the face.

"Oh Christ," he said. "I hope it's not hazardous."

"I think it was his chamber pot," I said to Witz, who was trying not to laugh.

"Hey Iggy, she tried to tell you," Witz said.

"Iggy?" I said.

"Short for Ignatius," she said.

"Like the saint?" I said.

"Hardly," she said. "Trooper Ignatius Roberts is the full name. Hey, Iggy, this is the owner of the place, Kathryn Wilde."

"Don't call me Iggy in front of civilians," he mumbled. "Anyway, hello Ms. Wilde." He peered into the can then gingerly reached in and pulled out a black piece of plastic with his thumb and forefinger. "Got something in here. Some kind of gadget—maybe for a computer. We'll take this with us."

"Be my guest," I said. "You can take the whole pile of stuff. It's going to the dump as soon as I get a chance."

"We'd prefer you hold off on that," Sergeant Witz said. "We've been through the barn, but rather than break into that room in there, we'd like you to open it for us."

"Well, the key's hanging on a nail next to the door," I said. "I'm surprised you didn't see it."

"Guess we missed it," she said, giving Trooper Roberts a poisonous look.

"Right now there's nothing of great value in there," I said. "But horses have an uncanny ability to break into wherever the feed is stored, so we keep it locked."

We all went into the barn and headed toward the feed/tack room.

"Hey, will you look at this!" Roberts said.

He was standing at Rusty's stall; the door was slid open as I'd left it. Witz and I went over and peered in.

"Well, hello there," I said. The fawn—presumably Floppy's—lay in a pile of shavings. When we stepped in to look, it flattened itself as much as possible.

"It's a baby deer," Roberts said.

"It's called a fawn," I said. I explained the unusual birthing situation on the night of the snowstorm.

"But where's the mama deer?" Roberts said.

"Good question," I said. "I bet she's not far off. See, when does— that's a female deer—give birth, they often hide their fawns while they go off to forage. I guess Floppy thought this was a safe haven for her baby. Floppy's the name I gave the doe."

"For the record," Sergeant Witz said, "I do know that a female deer is a doe and a male deer is a buck. Trooper Roberts is from Detroit and got transferred up here a while back. Not a lot of deer in the hood."

"I lived in the suburbs," he said. "Not all brothers live in the hood."

I wasn't going to ask why he was transferred. Sometimes a transfer to the Upper Peninsula was likened to banishment to Siberia. While some transplants make the adjustment, even thrive, others find rural dwelling nothing less than cruel and unusual punishment.

I opened the feed room and flipped on the light.

The two officers looked around. I had spent a good deal of time spiffing up the room. Gone were the trails of mouse droppings and cobwebs that had previously infested the place. Even though there wasn't much by way of tack, Aunt Lin and I had straightened and reinforced the saddle racks, which marched along one wall in a neat row. Uncle Phil had used hooks to hang bridles, which could cause them to become scored at the headpiece. I had removed the hooks and replaced them with empty soup cans that I attached to a board and then to the wall. Not fancy, but functional and basically free. The window was cleaner than it had been in years and I had even hung a horsy-themed valance along a rod at the top. A couple of metal garbage cans were put into use to store the sweet feed I fed Rusty. In spite of all my hard work to sanitize things, the place still gave me an uneasy feeling.

"So this is where the woman was found," Witz said.

"Yup," I said. "In a feed bin. Police hauled it off."

"Trooper Roberts," Witz said, "do you want to go over this room?"

"Hmm," he said, lifting a lid off one of the garbage cans. "Smells sweet."

"Sweet feed. Horses love it, it has sorghum—like molasses. I'm almost out. I'll be stocking up later today—hopefully."

"A good place to hide something," Roberts said. He pulled a blue vinyl glove out of his pocket and snapped it on then reached into the feed and rummaged around a bit.

We watched Trooper Roberts do his sweet feed exam. Witz had a smirk on her face but didn't say anything.

"What would be hiding in there?"

"Can't say," Roberts said. "Just checking." He pulled his hand out and pulled off the glove and looked around then discarded it in a trash can in the corner. He bent over and peered in. "Empty, except now my glove. Okay, I'd like to take one more look out at the encampment."

Witz sighed. "Okey dokey, trooper. You drive this time. I think the exhaust system got jarred loose on my cruiser when we went last time."

"Mind if I tag along?" I said.

"No problem. But we can't let you ride in the police car, unless of course you're under arrest," Witz said.

"I'll take my truck," I said.

We went back to the vehicles. The cruisers were still running, one with the lightbar methodically strobing.

"Why did you leave your overheads on?" Witz asked.

"And your vehicles running?" I said. "Just asking."

"Habit," Roberts said. "Just to keep folks aware, you know, that police work is in progress." He seemed to consider this for a moment. "I mean, you do get people coming and going, don't you?"

"Sure," I said. "All the time."

Witz went to her cruiser and shut it off then climbed into the passenger side of Roberts' car. The lightbar went off and the car eased forward. We bumped down the two-track and pulled into the now defunct camp. It was good to see the ugly tent gone. We all piled out and looked around.

"You know," Roberts said, "I'm thinking we might have this all wrong."

"Yeah?" Witz said.

"I don't think the altercation with Summers started in the woods. I think he may have been attacked in the tent and either was dragged out into the woods or ran, trying to escape his assailant."

"Attacked?" I said.

Roberts looked at Witz. "There were a lot of tracks, but some of them were around the tent site. Maybe Summers went back to get something. How well did the lab guys go over the tent?"

"I think they went inside, looked around," Witz said. "Maybe bagged some things."

Roberts looked at me. "That coffee can, you say he used it to, um, urinate in?"

"I have no idea," I said. "I never looked inside; you did. I can't even say it was the coffee can that I saw in Summers' tent earlier. For all I know, used motor oil could have been in the one you found."

"No, it was pee alright," Roberts said. "and a piece of plastic. I'll have to look at it closer. Maybe just trash Summers threw in there. I'm wondering why the lab guys didn't find it and take it though."

"I think they were scouring the woods, looking for a needle in the haystack," Witz said.

"Yeah," Roberts said. "A needle—"

"Like a syringe?" I said. "Is that why you took my aunt's stuff—the insulin and the syringe?"

The two looked at each other, sensing they may have given me a tidbit of info I shouldn't have. Especially since I still lingered on the "person of interest" list. Of course I already knew that it looked as if Summers had been injected with some kind of drug, so naturally a syringe with traces of whatever substance he was injected with would be very helpful to the investigation. But insulin? I'd never heard of any evil-doer injecting his or her victim with insulin. Wasn't it supposed to be like sodium pentothal or fentanyl or some other nefarious potion?

"But if Summers went to his tent to get something," I said, "how did he get there—or here? I mean, there was a ton of snow that night. I had to walk along Horse Camp Road for a mile and thought I might not make it. If Summers had to come in the back way, even if he could find the two-track road, it would have been much too far to come on foot in a snowstorm."

Sergeant Witz smiled at me. "Perhaps he had a ride."

"If he did, they came in the back way. Nobody went through the parking area. We'd have heard them and seen some sort of tracks, even with the snow. And Nikko and I were looking around because we heard the engine noise off in the woods. Figured it was either snowmobiles or ORVs. Only somebody who was drunk would have chanced it."

"Or somebody who was already here," Roberts said looking at me.

I knew what he was implying. But he and Witz likely knew that things really didn't add up for Nikko and me to be the culprits because, number one, Nikko and I didn't have an ORV at our disposal. It would have been logistically impossible to borrow the DRN ORV, commit the crime and return the ORV, then get back to Wildwood. Especially since the only ORV available to Nikko was in Ontonagon, some 80 miles away. Number two, there were four or five sets of footprints all over the place back in the woods where Summers' body was found. If it had been Nikko and me, there would have only been his, mine, and Summers'. Also, why would Nikko and I try to kill someone, then try to revive him? For show? We sure wouldn't have called 911 if we were sensible murderers. We'd have hauled Summers' carcass off into the swamp to be consumed by Mother Nature's recycling program.

Nope, there were other folks doing the deed, whether it began in the tent or elsewhere.

We all went back to the parking area and Trooper Roberts provided me with a receipt for the items they took. They returned Aunt Lin's insulin and syringe, all neatly sealed in a plastic bag. I wondered if they would have kept it had we not made a stink.

In addition to the coffee can and its mysterious contents, the list of confiscated items included the cooking implements from the encampment, the tent, (good riddance), and some canned food items. Most everything else belonging to Summers had been previously confiscated.

"We do not need to notify you of things taken that have no value," Trooper Roberts said.

"But for the record," Sergeant Witz said, "it's items such as cigarette butts, food wrappers, bottle caps, fibers, hair. Do you have—"

"Syringes?" I said.

"—any questions?"

"I guess not."

21

I thought about calling Dad and letting him know what happened, but he'd be mad that I hadn't invited him along. It had occurred to me, but I knew that one Wilde on the scene was probably enough to annoy the police. Plus, I'd just thrown the whole thing in his lap about Uncle Phil's philanthropic endeavors. I'd fill him in later about the needle in the haystack search.

I got my laptop and work satchel out of the truck and headed into the mod. Technically I was still on the clock for Wilde Accounting. I went no farther than the kitchen where I set up my spanking-new laptop on the table.

"YOW!"

"He's been fed," Aunt Lin said walking into the kitchen. "How he can eat that stinky stuff is beyond me. Today it was some kind of chicken liver combo."

"Yow!"

"Nice try, buster," she said. "No more catnip either for a while. He chewed through the burlap and ate the stuff, then threw it up in the bathroom on the only existing rug in the place."

Aunt Lin had changed the brazen muumuu for a pair of stretchy pants and a hoodie. Her hair was out of the towel and fluffy dry. It was actually now a color that could be found in nature.

"Hair looks nice," I said as I pulled out the flash drive stick from a little pouch in the computer case.

"I thought it was time to go back to my original color," she said. "This is called Burnished Chestnut."

Well, it looked brown to me, but it was shiny and flowing. I still hadn't made an appointment to have my mop trimmed. So far I was a natural brunette with overly aggressive natural curl. Mom said she started to go gray in her twenties so I needed to be vigilant in conducting daily inspections. And furthermore, it did no good to pull out the gray hairs. They just grew back all wiry. Best to visit the hair color touchup section at the local Walmart.

I plugged the flash drive into a USB port. My laptop gave a bling that the thing was loaded and the files appeared on the E drive. I had expected a few Excel or QuickBooks files, but all I found were JPEGs.

Maybe in our haste, Dad and I had grabbed the wrong stick. JPEGs were usually photos or graphics of some kind. Maybe pictures of the office Christmas party or a design for a new office logo.

I double clicked on file number one and an image filled the screen. And it wasn't the Christmas party. Or at least not the usual Wilde Christmas party.

"Yow!"

"Whatcha got there?" Aunt Lin said, looking over my shoulder. "Porn? You and Nikko need a little, er, boost?"

"Oh. My. God." I said.

"Hey," Aunt Lin said. "They're both guys. Not my bag. You wouldn't believe how many women have made passes at me in my yoga class. Well, only two actually, but one was the instructor. Where did you get that—off the internet?"

"I only wish," I said as I stared at the screen. The two men entangled in the throes of sexual bliss made me squirm but somehow I couldn't stop staring.

Aunt Lin leaned in closer. "Wow! I always wondered how, you know, gay guys did it. I mean—hey, that guy looks familiar."

"He should," I said. "That's my Uncle Phil."

"Yow!"

I slammed the laptop closed while the room spun like a whirligig.

"Hey, Kat, you okay?" Aunt Lin said.

"No," I said. "Well, I'm not gonna pass out, but..."

"Yeah, I get it. Kind of a shock."

We sat quietly for a moment. Jupiter, sensing that the humans were not interested in his needs, took his leave.

"I wonder if Gary knows," Aunt Lin said. "I mean, your dad would not have broadcasted it, but, you know, being gay isn't a big deal these days. They have a whole holiday, maybe a complete month, and parade and whatnot just for gay people. The movement is huge."

"Yeah," I said, "If you're in San Francisco. In Peshekee, not so much."

We both stared at the closed laptop.

"There are more," I said.

Aunt Lin looked at me. "Ready when you are."

By photo number six—last but not least—I was numb. It was strange that only Uncle Phil's face showed up in all six photos. His so-called lover always had his head turned away. So, unless one was familiar with the idiosyncrasies of mystery guy's man-parts, there was no way to be sure who the dude was. The whole thing smelled of a setup.

"Hey, you know they can do a lot with photoshop these days," Aunt Lin said. "Maybe it's all fake."

"Well, we could have Raymond, our techie guru, check it out, but then he'd be in on the whole thing."

"Sure looks like blackmail."

"Why else have photos—and stashed in the office safe," I said.

"So who can get into the safe?"

"Supposedly only Rose and Dad. However, everyone knows Dad keeps the combination on a post-it note taped to the inside of his right-hand desk drawer. Probably even the cleaning crew know where it is. They sure found my stash of Snickers bars quick enough, and I had them well hidden under a box of tampons. Well, I can't prove it was the cleaners that took the Snickers, but obviously somebody pillages."

"So anyone working there could really get in the safe. But why put the computer stick thing in there? Why not take it home or put it in a safety deposit box or something?"

"Maybe it was a mistake," I said. "We thought it was the flash drive with Wildwood's spreadsheets and other business stuff for several years. Maybe it was supposed to be."

"Very curious," Aunt Lin said.

"How am I ever going to talk to Dad about this?"

"Do you really have to?"

I thought about the large sums of so-called donations to the most likely bogus Equine Rescue Foundation. Aunt Lin, of course, wasn't aware of that little nugget.

"Yeah. I gotta."

"Well, if you're heading into town, can I have a ride? Maybe borrow the truck to run some errands? Did I tell you I'm getting certified as a health coach? Big bucks coming my way."

I looked at her, amazed at how quickly her focus had changed.

"What? Hey, I'm sorry if this is a crummy time for you. I guess I never knew Phil all that well. Clara did try to fix us up once, and now that I think about it—"

"Okey dokey," I said. Mom would try to fix up a slathering wolf with Bambi if she had the chance. I sighed, dreading another downer meeting with Dad. "Let's hit the road."

* * *

Turns out Dad did *not* know, exactly. "Well, Phil never got married," he said.

"I'm not married either."

"Yeah. But with you, there's still hope. Phil didn't date much. Kind of maybe went through the motions. We all just figured he was shy."

"I wonder about his time in the Army," I said. "How'd he manage that?"

"The repeal of don't ask, don't tell. That said, obviously Phil wasn't open about his sexual preference. At least not with family. You have to understand that your Grandma and Grandpa Wilde were, shall we say, from the old school."

"I wish I had known them better," I said.

"Well, they did love Phil and me and wanted the best for us, but they put a new meaning on the word strict. There was no smoking, drinking, cussing, or disrespect in our upbringing. And the idea of premarital sex let *alone* a homosexual relationship would earn a person an eternity of damnation."

"You've never told me about that before. I always thought Grandma and Grandpa Wilde were just a sweet, loving pair. I remember Granny knitting me hats and mittens, and Gramps reading to me."

"They adored you and doted on you. You were a darn cute girl, what with your curly hair and batting those eyelashes."

"Oh stop." I sighed at their memory. "I was so sad to lose them—first Granny then Gramps when I was, what, five?"

"About that. Dad didn't want to go on after Mom passed away. They did mellow a bit as they aged, but were ironclad in their expectations when Phil and I were growing up. And him being the older brother—well, they came down hard on him. I'm pretty sure that even if Phil knew he was gay back in high school, he would have been terrified to tell anyone. Not even me, let alone Mom and Dad."

"Probably carried around a lot of baggage about it," I said.

Dad was quiet for a moment, as if reviewing an old video, looking for something he missed.

"Plus," I said, "what about the supposed relationship with Sasha Saari-Summers' mother? I mean, if Uncle Phil was the father, well, he'd have to be able to, you know..."

"Perform," Dad said. "And why would he if he didn't have the desire? I mean, what would he need to prove?"

Dad and I opened the safe again and rummaged around looking for another flash drive labeled for Wildwood Stables. The flash drive sticks for all Wilde Accounting's clients bore tiny labels with names and dates and were neatly stored in a box with individual compartments for each device. Unless the accounting flash drive for Wildwood was mislabeled, it was not in the storage box. Dad shut the safe door and spun the dial.

"It has to be someone in this office," he said, looking around. "And everyone seems to suddenly be sick or missing. What the hell?"

"Well, Gussy can't stay away forever," I said. "He's where I'd start."

"Yeah, and I'd like it to be away from Rose. But how?"

"Lunch," I guess. Tell him it's time for his review and maybe dangle the prospect of a promotion or something."

"Good plan."

"Can I come?"

He looked at me. "Sure, bring those spreadsheets with the expenditures and maybe download the photos on your phone so we can spring them on him. I don't think we want a laptop broadcasting your Uncle Phil and whoever all over Bill's Burgers."

"Oh goody!" I said. "We're going to Bill's Burgers. I'll have another Yooper Burger with the works."

* * *

Wednesday marked the day of the arrival of Shadow and Misty, Wildwood's first boarders. After that event, I was to meet Dad and Gussy at Bill's Burgers. Apparently, the so-called bug that everyone had the previous day had miraculously disappeared and most of Wilde Accounting's staff had reported for duty, except for Char and me. It was my day off, but mystery grew around Char's continued absence. I had downloaded the disgusting pictures on my phone to "shock" Gussy into some kind of confession to help us get to the bottom of things. I figured he would crumble like tissue paper on Christmas morning. I had to admit I had mixed feelings about ambushing Gussy. He seemed more like a victim than an instigator.

I spent the morning cleaning out Rusty's paddock while Aunt Lin, bless her heart, labored to install a mailbox at the end of our drive. Our address was officially associated with Little Mountain Road, which was the public road Horse Camp Road intersected with. Unfortunately, since the ground was the consistency of marshmallow cream, Aunt Lin resorted to planting the pole in a large barrel she had found next to the barn, which she filled with rocks and sand. The mailbox was a bit crooked, but serviceable. She even used decals she had purchased along with the mailbox to spell out Wildwood Stables, with our five-digit street number. Previously, next to the driveway, there had been a metal pole with a red sign bearing white reflective numbers, which was what we called our "fire number." Eventually fire numbers were converted to street addresses, but folks still called them fire numbers. Whatever you called it, we could now receive mail as we had an official USPS approved receptacle and Aunt Lin had notified the local post office.

Right on time a truck pulling a fancy horse trailer worked its way up Horse Camp Road.

"Here they come!" I said to Rusty, who watched the approach, ears swiveling.

The truck and trailer pulled into the lot and Al Koskinen and Susie got out and waved. I went over and looked at the trailer.

"Wow," I said. "Nice trailer."

"Yup," Al Koskinen said. "Shame to let it sit around and collect dust so I figured we could park it here—if that's okay—and if you need it, she's available. Comes in handy, eh?"

I glanced over at Uncle Phil's derelict trailer that we had parked back in the weeds, which had a rotted floor and rusty frame. "Fantastic! I'll take good care of it."

"Oh, and that loafing shed will be here later today. Got some guys I work with are bringing it. I promised them pizza and beer."

"I don't know how to thank you,"

"No problem," Al said. "Just take care of my Susie when she comes out."

"Oh Daddy," Susie said as she flipped through her phone. "Hey, here's a picture of me and Shadow winning a blue ribbon at the fair," she said, shoving the phone in my face.

It was a nice photo, with Susie decked out in her riding habit and her horse's dappled coat gleaming brightly in the sunlight. His mane was braided with precision along his arched neck and the tack shone with neatsfoot oil. A blue ribbon was attached to his bridle.

"Pretty nice," I said.

Rusty let out a high-pitched whinny. The two horses in the trailer returned the call.

"Guess we better get them out and let them look around," Al said.

We decided it was best to put the two newbies in the combo riding ring/paddock next to Rusty and let them sniff noses over the fence. Once turned loose in the enclosure, Shadow and Misty pranced around a bit while Rusty watched with, I swear, a smarmy expression. Soon the two new horses sniffed the ground, then dropped and rolled.

"Guess they feel right at home," I said.

"I just brushed them!" Susie said.

The horses got to their feet and shook off the dirt then explored the water trough and hay net. The mare, Misty, eventually went over to Rusty and let out a squeal. He nickered back.

"I think he likes her," I said.

Susie giggled. "Shadow will be jealous. I have my saddle and bridle and some other stuff. I brought along my sister's stuff too. She rides western. I also brought some buckets and brushes, and his favorite treats in case you need them."

"Sure, Susie, help yourself to a saddle rack—the key to the tack/feed room is hanging next to the door. Also, you can swap out whatever you want in your horses' stalls."

"Um, you can ride them," Susie said. "They're good horses. Don't tailgate Misty, though. She kicks. And use our tack. I don't think I'll be able to come out very much for a while and my sister probably never. Oh, and please give them treats."

"Of course, Susie. I'll take care of them like they were my own."

Susie's lip trembled and she nodded. After she unloaded her things, Al backed the trailer in a small gravel patch near the barn and unhitched it.

I watched Susie go over to Shadow and pet him, then slip him some kind of treat. She put her face against his head and her shoulders shook. Cripes, she was crying. Now I could feel a lump in my throat. I knew all too well what a difficult transition in life could do to a person.

"Okay, I'm ready," Susie said, wiping her eyes and climbing into the truck. Her horse watched her intently, his head hanging over the fence.

Susie and her dad swung around and headed out, beeping the horn on the truck a few times.

⚡ 22 ⚡

Dad and I arrived at Bill's Burgers ahead of Gussy. We wanted to make sure we had a few minutes to grow a game plan. Dad went to the counter go get us beverages while I grabbed a semi-secluded table.

"So, I talked to Ollie," Dad said. "He says the staties aren't bending over backward to keep him in the loop. But he still has his contact there." Dad chuckled. "Ollie said he had to give the guy information on his secret fishing spot to get more out of him. Ollie won't even tell *me* where his secret fishing spot is."

"You need some leverage," I said. "You know, tit for tat."

"Yeah, I'm working on that."

"So, what did Sheriff Olsen have to say?"

"Well, he said that Nikko talks about you," Dad said, grinning. "A lot."

Dad was getting as bad as Mom. "Besides that," I said, trying to suppress a smile.

"Two things. First there was a USB flash stick in that coffee can that the state police confiscated. I don't know if they've been able to look at what is on it, since it was immersed in some sort of liquid."

"Pee," I said.

Dad looked at me. "Go ahead, but hurry."

"No," I said. "I mean the can apparently had pee in it. Like Summers used it for a nighttime receptacle when he was camped out. It was one of the few things left behind after the second time the police went over his compound. Nikko and I threw it in the dump pile at the stable."

"Well, that certainly doesn't clear up a damn thing," Dad said.

"I bet Raymond could resurrect the data if need be," I said. "But of course the state police have it."

We were silent for a moment, trying to figure out the elusive significance of a flash drive in a can of urine.

"This thing with the computer gizmos—it's all got to be connected," Dad said.

"Maybe more photos?" I said.

"My God," Dad said.

"Did Sheriff Olsen say anything else?" I said, keeping my voice low. Bill's was starting to fill up with the lunch crowd.

"Yeah, the cause of death seems to be a bit murky," Dad whispered back. "So far I guess there was no sign of toxins or alcohol in the body. They think maybe something accidental."

"Accidental?" I said loud enough to draw the attention of nearby patrons. It was no secret in our rural little burg that there had been some misfortune at Wildwood, and I could see people leaning in to eavesdrop.

I lowered my voice. "How could they think that? I mean, something happened in the woods, and if it was an accident, why was Summers abandoned by whoever he was with? And who *was* he with? I never saw anybody at his encampment except him. How could he have injuries that Nikko and I didn't see? Nikko's trained in advanced first aid. Wouldn't he notice if Summers had a broken neck or something? And wouldn't the autopsy show it anyway?"

"I would think so. Though internal injuries are hard to spot. Maybe his spleen burst when he had some sort of traumatic impact. Ollie's going to try to get a copy of the autopsy. He should be able to; it's in his bailiwick. Apparently, however, collaborating police agencies sometimes get competitive and officious. Ollie is trying to keep it amicable. I suppose something could have happened and the person or persons Summers was with panicked and split."

"Or maybe they had part in the so-called *accident*," I said, making air quotes.

"Hello!" someone shouted across the room.

"Gussy's here," Dad said.

I waved at Gussy and he made his way to our table.

"Hope I'm not late," he said. "The parking lot was full."

"You're right on time," Dad said. "What kind of burger do you want?"

"Um, do they have a menu?"

"Sure," I said. "It's written on that blackboard next to the counter."

Gussy got up and went over to study the menu.

"He's never been here?" I said.

"Apparently not," Dad said.

"Wow."

Gussy made his way back to our table. "I guess they only have hamburgers. No salads or anything like that?"

"Nope," Dad said. "I recommend the Smokey Bear, if you like barbeque."

"The Yooper is to die for," I said, immediately regretting my choice of words.

"Well, okay, maybe the barbeque one. Mother makes barbeque chicken sometimes and I like that."

"Soft drink?" Dad asked.

"Oh, just water please."

"Smokey Bear with a side of water it is," Dad said and went to the counter to order.

I asked, "So, are you feeling better?"

"Huh?"

"I thought you, Rose, and Char had the crud on Tuesday. It was like a morgue in the office." Another poor choice of words.

"Oh, well, I guess we probably all had a twenty-four-hour bug," Gussy said, looking down at his lap. He pulled a napkin out of the spring-loaded dispenser and began shredding it. Gussy did not have a good poker face. "Or maybe it was something we all ate," he added with a tinge of hopefulness.

"Yeah," I said. "Food poisoning is a bummer."

"Oh, probably not poisoning exactly, just maybe a little, um—"

"Here's your water," Dad said to Gussy as he returned to the table. "Our food will be up in a minute."

"Thank you, Mr. Wilde."

"We're not in the office so please call me Gary."

Gussy nodded and pulled out another napkin to shred.

"So, Gerald, you've been with Wilde Accounting for how long?" Dad said.

"Um, three years. And you can call me Gussy Mr.—er, Gary. I don't care for Gerald."

I wondered if Gussy ever had the nerve to tell his mother that he did not *care for* the name Gerald.

"Okay, Gussy, then three years. Have I given you a raise?"

"Um, yes sir. We all get the raise each year after tax time is over. Plus the nice bonus at Christmas."

"Sure, sure. I mean a merit raise just for you—you know, for the job you do."

"No sir."

"Gary."

"Gary, sir."

This was painful. Gussy was about as at ease as a cat at the Westminster Dog Show.

"And when will you be done with your CPA coursework?" Dad said.

"Well, I've got one more semester of online classes, then a test. Probably within six months."

"Excellent," Dad said. "Well, at that time, we will take a very close look at your position in the office. Meanwhile, I am going to tell Clara—Mrs. Wilde—to incorporate a four percent raise into your salary."

Gussy brightened. "Thank you, Gary, sir. My mom will be happy to hear that."

Indeed she will, I thought. I had never known a person to be so tied to his mother's apron strings. More like strangled. Well, not that I had a lot of room to criticize, what with just having vacated my parents' basement for the mod, which Dad was financing.

Our food arrived and we all dug in.

"Wow!" Gussy said. "This is the best hamburger I've ever had. And the fries are good too."

"The coleslaw is homemade," I offered. "Secret recipe."

"Glad you like the lunch," Dad said. "I guess I should take my employees out more often."

"Well, Mother always says that restaurant food is not to be trusted, so I don't go out much. We used to get pizza when my father was still around. But not since."

My God, this poor guy. We had softened him up with an impromptu annual review, including a raise—something I could use, but no matter. I felt like the Gestapo. I looked at Dad. He squared his shoulders and plunged in.

"So Gussy, I think that Kat brought up some questions about my brother Phil's expenditures to a rather questionable charity."

Gussy struggled to swallow the mouthful of food he'd been chewing. His Adam's apple bobbed wildly for a moment. He took a drink of water and swallowed with a loud gulp.

"Yes, Kat did ask," Gussy said, wiping his mouth with a tattered napkin. "I thought she should talk to you. I mean, I did cut some checks and I kind of wondered about them."

"You never thought to ask me?" Dad said. "And who signed these checks?"

"Well, I thought you did."

Everyone knew that Dad's signature stamp was in Rose's desk, which she used to rubber stamp routine documents.

"Not that I recall," Dad said. "Aren't you usually the one who puts checks on my desk to be signed?"

"Usually," Gussy said taking a deep breath. "But sometimes if you're in a meeting or just have your door closed, I have Mother put them in the safe or if Char's working late, ask her to give them to you."

"Gussy, you're a smart guy," I said. "Didn't you wonder about almost ten-thousand dollars in donations to some place in California with a post office box? Why didn't you go to Dad and ask him about it?"

Gussy pulled another napkin out of the dispenser for shredding. "Well, I did talk to Char about it because she's the accountant. I'm just the bookkeeper. She's—well sometimes she likes to remind me of that and tells me to worry about my job, not hers."

"I see," Dad said.

I cleared my throat. "So you asked Char about all these checks going to some equine rescue place?"

"Right."

"And...?

"Well, Char just said that even though Phil Wilde was your brother, Gary, sir, there was the need to keep client confidentiality and all. That we had no right without Phil Wilde's permission to discuss his affairs with anybody, even his brother."

"Really?" Dad said. "Char said that?"

Dad had been Uncle Phil's conservator toward the end. Char was giving Gussy a line of bull.

"Something like that," Gussy said, pulling another napkin from the dispenser. This one he used to wipe the sweat off his forehead before he mangled it.

"Did you talk to your mother about it?" I asked.

More napkin abuse. "I might have. I'm not sure."

We all chewed thoughtfully for a moment.

Dad picked up his coffee cup and looked at me over the rim and nodded. Time to go in for the kill. I wasn't proud, but nonetheless pulled out my phone and brought up one of the disgusting photos of Uncle Phil and his mysterious homosexual partner.

I shoved it in Gussy's face just as he was taking a drink of water. His eyes bugged out and he sprayed the mouthful of water all over the table and Dad.

"Oh! I'm so sorry Mr. Wilde." Gussy began pulling napkins out of the dispenser and dabbing at the table and offering a handful to Dad.

Dad sighed. "It's okay. I trust you've never seen the photo, or one like it involving my brother before?"

"No sir," Gussy said. He looked up. "I wish I had told you about the checks. I didn't even ask Mother because I, you know, didn't want to break client confidentiality and all."

"But everyone has some access to the files." I pulled out the papers I had purloined from the to-be-shredded box and slid them over in front of Gussy.

"But where ...? Oh, cripes."

"Spill it, Gussy," I said.

"Huh?"

"Did you try to get rid of these documents?"

"No, Kat. I just know they disappeared."

"Who was looking for them?"

"Well, Mother for one when she, uh, well she was rotating out files you know, and noticed someone had rifled through the Wildwood Stables file. I think she figured it was you, Gary, sir, so didn't say anything."

Gussy reached for another napkin, but the dispenser was empty.

⩵ **23** ⩵

My phone dinged as I climbed into Uncle Phil's truck. It was a text from Nikko. I smiled and touched the dialog bubble.

Ready for adventure?

I responded with an emoji with a question mark over its head. *Maybe...*

Wear something fast drying. He included an emoji showing a drop of water.

Where are we going?

Surprise!

When?

Saturday, be ready at 9:00.

Curious!

Good! See ya.

Okay

Neither of us included anything lovey dovey. No heart emojis or XXXs and OOOs or even a "luv ya" sign-off.

I started the truck and sat there for a few minutes, wondering not only where Nikko was taking me on the Saturday adventure that required quick-dry clothing but also wondering about *where* Nikko and I were going, that is, our relationship. He talks about me. I think about him. I felt a flush creep up, remembering our night of the blizzard.

Of course, Mom and now apparently Dad were eager for me to find a man and act according to the traditional expectations of marriage, children, and a wholesome life that helped *them* sleep at night. But I was just getting my feet under me, trying to make a defunct horse stable come back to life, which had been Dad's idea, so where was he coming from? Then of course there was the gnawing distraction of two murders (accident, my patootie), the revelation of my Uncle Phil's sexual preference, which may well have been used for blackmail, and a lot of money had been funneled out of Uncle Phil's coffers to a bogus horse rescue foundation that reeked of fraud. *And* the situation that seemed to start the whole tangled mess: an apparent "love child," Sasha Saari-Summers, conceived sometime while Uncle Phil was in the service, even though Uncle Phil was gay. Maybe bisexual? I remembered that Sheriff Olsen said that multiple sums of money had gone in and out of a bank account that Sasha had downstate. He was trying to get more information on that.

After our meeting with Gussy, Dad and I felt no closer to fitting the puzzle pieces together in the Wildwood conundrum. My instincts told me that Gussy was a dupe. A momma's boy, a pathetic wimp, someone to push around and intimidate. Yet maybe this persona he put forth was a little too over the top. And there was speculation that Gussy was smitten with Char, who viewed him below the status of a worm. And Rose. She had access to everything. And I would bet the farm she would do anything to protect her Gerald who secretly hated his name.

Char was the next person to talk to, but she had texted Dad again requesting to work remotely, due to a "bug." Dad was a face-to-face person, so talking with Char wouldn't likely happen until she recovered from whatever malady had stricken her.

The big question was obviously where, exactly, did all of Uncle Phil's money go? It was possible only Uncle Phil and whoever got the bucks were the only ones who knew the answer. Still, something smelled fishy at the office of Wilde Accounting.

I realized I was still sitting in the parking lot of Bill's Burgers with the truck running. I put it in gear and headed out. I had a stop to make. I was going to meet up with Mike who owned the auto repair shop that had taken custody of my Subaru. He had sent me an email letting me know a check for the Subaru was ready to be picked up. It had apparently been overnighted. I had dug out the paperwork required for the transfer and was ready to get the exchange over with. *It's for the best*, I told myself. I needed that saddle and bridle. *Watch out Rusty ol' boy. Your leisurely days are coming to an end.*

After officially relinquishing the Subaru's future to a bunch of derelict teens, I debated heading into the office. Technically, it was my day off—interrogation of Gussy aside. I decided to just head to Wildwood. I was taking my office laptop back and forth with me now that I could get on the internet at the mod. Raymond had gotten us hooked up to Wi-Fi and some kind of streaming gizmo for the TV. I had already reactivated the landline at Wildwood, and Raymond also said he'd get it hooked into an answering machine. While people were abandoning landlines for cell phones, I was old school and felt that a business just seemed more professional with a landline that didn't echo, drop calls, and have annoying delays in transmission where everyone talked over each other. Of course, that didn't mean that me and my cell weren't attached at the hip. I had promised Raymond fifty bucks for his trouble. Any hopes of Aunt Lin chipping in were fruitless in that her current means of support was unemployment compensation (for being fired as a waitress because she slugged a "handsy" customer). She had to make believe she was looking for another job, which was a stretch in the rural high-unemployment expanses of the U.P.

The check from the State of Michigan was in the oddball amount of $734.84, which I would deposit with a hundred bucks cash back. Fifty would go to Raymond for his tech support and fifty to have my hair brought under control by Jeannie, my stylist. I had no idea why the check was such an odd amount, but apparently some bean counter in Lansing had calculated the Subaru's worth right down to the penny.

I moved up a car-length closer to the pneumatic tube that would carry my endorsed check and deposit slip to a teller ensconced somewhere within the building. I wondered when AI would be taking over the process. I got a bing on my cell. I smiled, thinking of Nikko, but this time it was another email from the 4Hoof Rescue—the place that had rooted me out from my online search of equine rescue foundations. Since the bank line was moving at glacial speed, I figured I might as well read the thing.

Hello and please don't delete us until you have checked out the 4Hoof Rescue. We mainly rescue abused and neglected horses along with some donkeys, mules, as well as cattle, pigs, and goats.

Cattle, pigs, and goats? What kind of outfit was this? Now my curiosity was piqued and I continued reading.

We are looking for places to foster our rescued animals. We are a Michigan-based legitimate 501(c)(3) foundation (check out our website at 4HR dot com) and pay our foster "parents" for the care of these animals. There are two auction places in Michigan where we regularly save horses from slaughter. These animals have served and worked for people and deserve better than to be dumped off for a hideous fate.

Yadda yadda yadda. Of course I agreed and all, but I was skeptical.

I moved up a bit in the bank line. The guy ahead of me must have been trying to reconcile his checkbook with the teller or possibly take out a car loan. Why didn't these people go inside? For that matter, why hadn't I?

I scrolled down to the end of the email and wished I hadn't because there was the most pathetic photo of a horse that I had ever seen. Rusty was no prize upon arrival at Wildwood, but he was the epitome of beauty by comparison. The animal in the photo was so weak that rescuers were holding him up with a sling. He was beyond emaciated and covered with scars and open wounds. His dull eyes were sunken into a bare skull.

This is one of the lucky ones. The caption said. I scrolled down a bit more. After medical care and a lot of TLC, Jubilee has a wonderful new life at his forever home.

The photo showed the horse—Jubilee—now ribs barely showing, and his chestnut coat gleaming. His head was perked up and a tween-aged girl was hugging him. Even the tiny photo on my phone worked its magic. I suppressed a sob. Oh, this outfit knew how to tug at the ol' heartstrings.

Bank business completed I headed to the mod. I noted with pleasure that the plank flooring was installed, the furniture in place, and the TV apparently functioning because it was on some daytime TV cooking show. I watched it for a moment and when they added a third ingredient that I had never heard of I picked up the remote and shut it off. I heard lyre plinking from Aunt Lin's bedroom, so let her be. After dumping my work satchel and laptop on the kitchen table, I changed into barn clothes and headed out to see how my charges were faring.

The day had turned warm and sunny. Rusty was still separated from the other two. He was not alone, however. Floppy and her fawn were in his paddock, with Floppy helping herself to the hay net contents. The fawn was curled up and sleeping under Rusty. The boarders, Misty and Shadow, were watching Rusty and his guests. I took out my phone and snapped a photo. This had to be the oddest stable in the universe. After a few barn chores, I went into the mod and found Aunt Lin in the kitchen making something.

"Hey," she said.

"Hey," I said. "What's cookin'?"

"You forgot good lookin'."

"Okay, what's cookin' good lookin'?"

"Vegan stew."

"I was afraid of that."

"Well, you can add some meat if you like. Here, taste."

Bland. But I was no fool. "Yum," I said. "But I'll put in some of that pre-cooked chicken in mine." Plus salt and pepper and whatever else I could think of.

"Suit yourself. I also have gluten-free corn muffins."

"Perfect," I lied.

After dinner, I went online and checked out the website for 4HR. It was very professional, but of course anybody could create a professional website. Didn't mean that the business was legit. Since I had the background in grant writing, I knew where to look to verify the legitimacy of 4HR. While working at the hospital, I'd used a website that had a directory of literally hundreds, if not thousands of charitable foundations, with info on how to apply, what was eligible, timelines and so on. The directory also rated the foundations using a multitude of factors. The 4Hoof Rescue had been approved for non-profit status seven years prior and had a high rating. Their goal was obvious and coincided with the email they sent me, i.e., that they rescued abused and neglected animals, fostered them into health, and found them forever homes. Those wishing to foster animals could fill out an application. Eventually someone would come in person and interview the applicant.

Next I read some testimonials. For the most part, they were positive, glowing actually. Those that weren't seemed to be applicants who didn't measure up. My heart did a little pitter patter when I saw that the organization would pay (pre-approved) medical and farrier costs along with a going rate for board. The foster stable was required to do a weekly report for the first few weeks, then it would be monthly. Once the animal reached its health and behavioral goals, potential adopters would be involved.

Okay, it was legit. I'd give it a think.

* * *

"So, how long has it been?" Jeannie, my stylist, asked.

"Since when?" I slipped into the chair. Jeannie snapped open a cape and attached it around my neck.

"You know what I mean, sweetie pie. You look like a cavewoman."

"Well, I've been busy..."

"So, what are we doing today, besides trimming it up? How about some auburn highlights and a new style. I mean there is no style right now."

"Um," I said.

"But I will admit, you've got some nice thick hair. We have to embrace the curl, yet control it."

"Well, I—"

"How are you?" Jeannie asked as she headed toward the back room where she kept her hair products. "I mean, you must be totally freaked and all."

"Yeah, it's been kind of crazy, but things are settling down now." A total lie, but I knew that Jeannie would repeat every word I said including words I never said, so I would need to tread lightly.

"How about this?" Jeannie said, holding up a board with swatches of fake hair on it. She pointed to a swatch that was a subdued reddish brown. "It's called Autumn Breeze. Subtle but will make you look a lot younger. Not that you are that old, but, well anyway, so this dude who died out there. They know why?"

"Under investigation, I guess," I said.

Apparently, the color Jeannie recommended was what we were going with.

"Well, I heard that somebody broke his neck!"

I didn't know what to say to that. I knew a fishing expedition when I saw one.

"I don't know," I said. "I hadn't heard that."

"Uh huh," Jeannie said as she began separating strands of hair and placing foil under them. Next she took a small, flat bristle device and began painting the Autumn Breeze on said swatches.

Jeannie sighed. "Well, it would take somebody very strong or well-trained to break a neck. Do you think the killer is lurking around town? I mean, I am always cautious and all, but sometimes I'm alone at the shop. I've started locking the doors and customers have to call me to get in."

"Smart," I said. "One can't be too careful."

"And you. All alone out there at that place with your auntie. I mean I went there in high school, ya know, to, like, make out. Back in that campground, when nobody was there. It was creepy, but hey, we were a bunch of kids and thought it was cool."

I didn't know what to say. My journeys to Wildwood were to see my uncle and ride horses. Then of course toward the end, just to see Uncle Phil and try to act chipper when my heart was breaking. I wouldn't have dreamed of sneaking out to the campground—presumably the back two-track road route—and make out. Besides that, nobody had invited me. Most boys were shorter than I was, except Nikko Olsen, and he was always dating a cheerleader or prom queen.

Jeannie had apparently finished with the Autumn Breeze and set a timer she kept on her vanity.

"Twenty-five minutes."

I picked up a magazine.

"I wonder if things had been different, you know, if it weren't for the horse camp hangout."

I looked at her.

"Well, I was just a kid and what did I know?"

Uh oh. I knew that Jeannie had gotten pregnant sometime during her senior year. She opted not to marry the guy, whoever he was. Claimed she didn't know. She graduated high school when eight months pregnant. It took a lot of nerve to walk across the stage, but she did it. Soon after, she had a baby girl. Her parents helped Jeannie get through beauty school and often babysat the grandchild. It would seem that maybe her life began its twists and turns out at the horse camp.

"Well, I wouldn't give up my Brianna for the world," she said with a sigh. "I can't believe she starts kindergarten next fall. So, anyway, am I making you beautiful for anything special?"

"Not really," I said. "I do kinda have a date."

"Kinda? Do tell."

I decided there wasn't any harm in letting the gossip mill start grinding. Depending on where our so-called adventure was taking place, it was possible Nikko and I would be seen together anyway. Speculation would run rampant.

"Yeah, Nikko Olsen and I are doing something this weekend."

I expected Jeannie to squeal or at least raise her eyebrows. "Nikko Olsen?" she said rather flatly. "I thought he was working in Ontonagon County."

"Yup. But he comes home to see his folks and all."

"Oh, sure."

"So, I don't know, I guess he's going to surprise me with some kind of outing."

"I bet," she mumbled.

"No big deal. I'm really just getting my hair done because I finally got some spare cash."

"Well, you will look smashing," Jeannie said, brightening with a smile.

I looked in the mirror. Smashing maybe as in a car wreck. An explosion of foil wraps stuck out every which way, giving me the appearance of a cross between Medusa and a space alien. I hadn't bothered to swipe on any makeup before coming and noted a few blemishes rearing their ugly heads.

I gave a derisive snort. "Well, Jeannie, you can only do so much," I said.

"I could do so much more!"

"Maybe next time."

"Okay Kat, let's rinse you out and get out the hedge clippers."

I swear there was a tinge of malice in her voice.

≈ 24 ≈

The party I was to purchase the Stübben saddle and bridle from lived in Wisconsin, but apparently had business in Marquette and offered to meet up somewhere in between. They wanted $500 cash for the whole shebang. We had decided to rendezvous at the Waterfront Park in L'Anse. It was easy to find and very public. For some reason I felt as if I were embarking upon some back-alley transaction. Counterfeit Stübben saddles were not unheard of, so I had done my homework online and knew what to look for. I hoped.

I had expected some rough and tumble ranch hand to meet up with me, climb out of his badass truck and say, "Psst, lady, wanna buy a Stübben?" Instead, I watched an older lady pull up in a Toyota with a bad muffler and climb painfully out. She stretched and looked out at the water. It was a sunny day and the bay sparkled like a turquoise jewel. She looked at me and smiled.

"Beautiful, isn't it?" she said. "I never get tired of looking at it."

"Uh huh. Sure is," I said.

"Are you the person who wants to buy my saddle?" she said.

"Yes ma'am," I said.

"Call me Bernice," she said. "It's Bernice Perry."

"Kat—Kat Wilde," I said, extending my hand.

We shook.

Bernice Perry sighed and popped the trunk on her car.

"I guess this marks the end of an era," she said. "I've hung onto this thing for years, hoping against hope that I'd be able to ride a horse again someday."

"Why not?"

"Bad hips, among other things. I'm headed to Marquette to have some surgery. I'll have a long recovery and I'm pushing eighty. Plus I live on Social Security. How can I afford a horse?"

I didn't know what to say, so I nodded.

"Well, here it is," she said pointing.

I leaned into the trunk and saw the Stübben. I inspected the nails, which according to my research should either have the Stübben logo on them or be blue. Also there would be Stübben medallions by the stirrup bar and the Stübben name stamped on the girth strap protectors under the flap. The nails were worn but showed remnants of the Stübben logo, meaning it was manufactured between 1970 and 1980. Almost an antique! The medallions were there along with the stamped name. The saddle was well soaped and oiled and the stitching looked to be in excellent shape. I took out a measuring tape I'd brought along and checked the size. I noted that Bernice was a pretty tall lady even though slightly hunched, and the saddle measured seventeen and a half inches, which is what I needed. The bridle and saddle pad were also clean and ready to go.

"Looks perfect," I said.

"I followed the hounds in this saddle," Bernice said. "And did a little eventing. Now that was exciting."

"Wow! I'm just getting back into the swing of things with horses. I've got a gelding I acquired as a kind of rescue, and a couple of boarders. Right now I just want to get my skill level back to at least a beginner."

"You'll do fine in the Stübben. I'm glad you aren't getting it so you can sell it online and turn a quick profit."

"No ma'am," I said. "I'll treasure it." I reached in my pocket and pulled out five crisp hundred-dollar bills and handed them to her.

"Thank you, dear," she said. "You don't know how much this will help me. God bless you."

I nodded and picked up the saddle and other tack and put them in the passenger side of the truck. No way was this saddle going into the bed of the truck. Ever.

"Well, I have a ways to go," she said. "Best of luck getting back in the saddle."

"And good luck to you, too."

We paused a moment. Bernice looked at the bay again. A slight ripple made the surface sparkle like diamonds.

"Nope, never get tired of it." She slowly climbed into her car.

"Hey!" I said. "When you pass through this way again, why don't you come out to Wildwood Stables for a visit?"

Bernice looked at me and smiled. "Well, dear, I might just do that."

"Do you have a cell?"

"Of course. I'm old but I'm hip," Bernice said, holding up a cell phone.

I gave her my number and email and she entered it in. She gave me her cell number as well.

"Give me a call," I said. "I'd love to have some help learning to ride again. I mean, if you think you could—"

"Well now, that sure gives me something to think about," Bernice said. You're making an old lady happy."

On an impulse we hugged through her open window and I stepped away. I watched her back slowly out of her spot and pull away.

* * *

When I got back to Wildwood, there was not time to do a test run with the new tack. I put the Stübben on one of the saddle racks and hung up the bridle. From this day forward, the key to the tack/feed room would *not* be conveniently hanging by the door for would-be thieves' convenience. I found a nail hidden behind a two by four and hung it there. I'd have to let Aunt Lin know. Of course, anyone could break down the cheesy door, which had the hinges on the outside and a dollar store lock. Maybe someday we'd be able to upgrade.

After putting things away, I took several flakes of hay out to the paddocks to feed my mini herd. I had not noticed when I drove in, but the wooden boards on the fence separating the two paddocks had been popped off and all three horses were hanging out together at the loafing shed. Apparently, any concern for pasture bullying and fights was unfounded, at least for the time being. I picked up the boards and carried them over to a miscellaneous pile of misfit lumber pieces and added them to the heap, nail side down.

Al Koskinen had donated a free-standing metal hay rack designed for outdoor use. In that all three horses were now sharing the same space, I could stop using hay nets and feed them in the rack. I tossed the hay in and my equine trio moseyed over and began munching. I checked the water trough and scooped some manure dotting the paddocks into a bucket and put it in my newly-purchased wheelbarrow. Chores done, I headed back to the mod to get ready for my great adventure. Clearly if Nikko had intended it to involve "romance," he would have suggested I wear something sexy not quick-dry, right?

* * *

I rummaged around in my closet until I found the expedition pants I had purchased in college. I had taken an outdoor exploration course, which involved hiking, canoeing, and, among other things, a terrifying afternoon of rock climbing. To my delight they still fit and, in fact, needed the stretchy belt cinched tighter. Perhaps life at Wildwood was getting me into shape. I dug out the top of my tankini bathing suit, which was quick drying, comfortable, and required no bra. In that it was about forty-five degrees out, I put a sweatshirt over it and pulled my camo-lined nylon jacket out of the closet. I didn't hunt, but camo was the tried-and-true style for the U.P. I had a Boonie hat with a string that would tighten around my chin. I pulled on wool socks and hiking boots to complete the ensemble.

I was clueless as to where Nikko was taking me to do what, but unless we were headed out on an Arctic expedition or a float down the Amazon, I was duly prepared.

I clomped into the kitchen and decided to whip up a hearty breakfast. I opened the fridge and pulled out eggs, bacon, juice, and salsa.

"Yow!"

Jupiter made his appearance and sauntered over to his empty food dish, which held the crusty remains of the previous meal.

"Yow!" he repeated and began to wind around my ankle.

"What, didn't Aunt Lin give you your yum, yums?"

"Yow!"

"Hey, good morning," Aunt Lin said as she staggered into the kitchen. "What the hell?" she said, looking me up and down. "G'day, mate. Headin' ta the Outback are ya?"

"Ha ha," I said.

"Well, your new hairdo looks great, anyway."

"Thanks," I said, reaching up to touch my hair. Jeannie had worked magic with a new cut. The Autumn Breeze highlights looked great, and she gave me a curl relaxer that converted my frizz into soft waves. "Nikko is taking me on a so-called adventure and told me to dress like this. Well, he said something quick-dry. That was all the info I have."

"YOW!"

"Okay, okay," Aunt Lin said, reaching down and picking up the empty cat bowl. She dropped it in the sink and turned on the tap to soak it, then pulled a clean dish from the kitty cupboard. Taking care of Jupiter had been passed off to Aunt Lin since she was living rent-free and was around all day to serve and obey.

"Want some breakfast?" I asked, knowing full well that she wouldn't want anything to do with consuming barnyard victims, as she called them.

"God no!" she said, plopping a fresh bowl of cat food down. Jupiter circled it one way, then the other. I swear he was pretending it was live prey. Finally he went in for the kill, breaking into his usual annoying humming. "It's bad enough I have to smell the cat food. Are the chores done?"

"Mostly," I said. "I didn't sweep yet."

"I'm on it," Aunt Lin said. She headed back to her bedroom.

I got out the skillet and started frying bacon.

Aunt Lin reappeared wearing jeans and a flannel shirt. "Oh God," she said. "I think I'm gonna throw up." She grabbed her coat and slammed the door behind her.

"What a diva," I muttered to Jupiter. He had gobbled down his stinky repast and wandered off in search of a sunny spot for his first nap of the day.

I sat on a rickety lawn chair on the tiny mod porch to wait for my Prince Charming to arrive. Toward the back of the mod, I could hear the rushing noise of the Peshekee as it carried the winter snowmelt out to Lake Superior. I had zipped up my coat and jammed my hands into the pockets. The sun did promise warmth, but it was still too early. I spotted a yellow patch at the edge of the parking lot. Daffodils. Uncle Phil had planted some spring bulbs; God love him. Eventually. I saw a car working its way up Horse Camp Road. Something indecipherable was sticking out of the hatchback of the vehicle.

Oh good Lord.

"I can't believe you've never been in a kayak," Nikko said.

"Nope," I said. "Aren't they dangerous? I mean, what if it tips over and I'm trapped upside-down?"

Nikko laughed.

"What's so funny?"

"We're not doing any Eskimo rolls today. Besides, if you tip over, you'll die of hypothermia, not drowning."

"Very comforting."

We had been bumping down a narrow dirt road up and down hills and around blind corners while dodging immense potholes and boulders partially submerged in the mud. I was clinging to the seatbelt, trying to keep it from locking up and crushing my boobs. Tobey had come along and was crammed next to me since the kayaks required the back seat to be folded down. He had a bad case of doggie breath and engaged in his nonstop panting/clicking noise. According to Nikko, Tobey's stiches had been removed and he was now released to resume normal activity.

We came to a large area of standing water. "Um…" I said.

"Hang on!" Nikko said, gunning it.

We bucked and bolted through the water, spraying mud everywhere. I looked back and miraculously the kayaks had survived.

"They're fine," Nikko said. "I bungeed them in."

"Bungeed?"

"Surely you know what a bungee cord is?"

"Of course. One of those stretchy things with hooks. We use one to hold the gate open."

"Almost there," Nikko said.

"Almost where?"

"Keewaydin Lake."

"That tells me nothing."

"Perfect for kayaking."

"Of course … LOOK OUT!" I screamed and instinctively grabbed Tobey.

A bear scurried across the road in front of us. Nikko slammed on the brakes. The kayaks shifted forward and one bashed into my headrest, which likely saved me from a concussion.

"Wow!" I said. "Did you see that? A bear!"

Okay, it was a stupid question.

"Here we are," Nikko said, pulling into a small gravel area off the side of the road.

Ahead I could see the sparkle of a lake. The sun was warming things up to a balmy fifty degrees or so. We unloaded the kayaks and pulled them to the rustic boat launch, which essentially was just a muddy path through the weeds.

"No motorboats allowed on this lake," Nikko said. "We'll probably have it all to ourselves."

"Good. Then nobody can hear my screams."

Nikko turned to look at me and waggled his eyebrows beguilingly.

"Oh, please," I said. "Most likely nobody in the history of the world has successfully had, well, done the hoochie coochie in a kayak."

"Always a first time," he muttered.

Nikko took a small cooler out of the Tahoe and secured it to his kayak. He stuffed a waterproof bag containing a blanket and some inflatable cushions into a cargo hold in the nose of his boat. We put on our life jackets and he snapped a doggie flotation device on Tobey. The pooch looked like a bloated sausage in a bun. We pulled the kayaks to the water's edge and Nikko put Tobey in the front of what he called the cockpit of his kayak.

"I'll help you," he said, pulling my boat almost all the way into the water and holding it steady. "You probably should be wearing rubber boots."

"Now he tells me," I muttered, wading into the frigid lake. My hiking boots made a gallant effort to slough off the frigid water, but eventually a gallon or so seeped over the tops and instantly numbed my feet. I stepped gingerly into the kayak, almost fell, and sat down heavily. I grabbed my paddle and Nikko gave me a push. I wobbled violently, then, thank God, the thing steadied.

Nikko got effortlessly into his kayak and scootched himself onto the lake. He dipped his paddle left and right and began moving. Tobey put his front paws topside and I swear to God a huge grin spread across his enormous pittie terrier mouth.

"Follow me," Nikko shouted.

I had to admit that once I got over the terror of capsizing and drowning, or more likely freezing to death, I began to enjoy the "adventure." I had to keep correcting course as apparently my right side was stronger than my left. Most likely Nikko was holding back so that I could keep up. Periodically he turned around to check on me, which was mildly comforting. Nikko had been right. Not another soul in sight. No visible houses or camps along the shore. No boat motors, no highway noise. Rocky islands with sprouts of trees dotted the lake. The silence was incredible. Then I heard a strange warbling cry.

"What the hell!" I said.

Nikko turned around so I could hear him. "Loons," he said. "They'll be nesting soon, and we shouldn't crowd or harass them."

Leave it to me to hang out with a conservation officer who found it necessary to spout off the rules and regs. I mean, like I would harass the wildlife. Off in the distance I saw the pair of loons glide onto the lake, sending a fine spray into the air. I quit paddling for a moment to watch them move steadily away from us.

"There," Nikko said, pointing to a tree-studded island. "We can land our kayaks."

This was good news to me because I needed a potty break. I was no stranger to the lack of amenities for ladies in the great out-of-doors and always carried a packet of tissues with me.

We glided onto a small, sandy beach and dragged our kayaks out of the water. Tobey clambered out and found the nearest shrub that needed his mark. Nikko grabbed the cooler and bag with blanket and cushions and headed up a path.

"Where are we going?" I asked, snapping a leash on Tobey.

"There's a rustic campsite up the hill."

The so-called hill seemed more like a mountain, its smooth rockfaces mottled with lichen. Tiny sprouts of weeds and wildflowers bravely poked through the cracks and crevices in the rock. Eventually we reached the top, which offered a spectacular view of the lake. It positively sparkled as if blessed by the angels. I could see why people felt the presence of something magnificent and spiritual when nature's bountiful beauty presented itself. We were in a small clearing that marked the campsite. A ring of stones served as a fire barrier for the campfire pit. Various stumps and logs for seats surrounded the fire ring. Off to the side of the campsite stood a picnic table, which looked strangely out of place.

"How the heck did they get a picnic table here?" I said, panting from the climb.

"Rowboat," Nikko said. "And a lot of muscle. By the way, there's a forest latrine up that path. It's really just a box with a hole in it and has a great view of the lake."

"Sounds good to me," I said. "How do you know about this place?"

"I come here sometimes," he said. "I'm a woods cop, remember?"

So he had taken me to his special place. I was feeling a little honored but also getting pretty desperate for the so-called forest latrine and headed up the path. Nikko was right. The latrine was a simple wooden box with a hole cut in the top. When sitting, one had a panoramic view of Keewaydin Lake. When I returned to the campsite, Nikko had put the blanket over the picnic table, inflated the cushions and placed them on the picnic table bench. He was in the process of laying out some food.

"We'll call it brunch," he said.

"Hey," I said. "You'll make somebody a great wife someday."

"Damn right."

We stuffed ourselves with crusty bread spread with a concoction of goat cheese and herbs. Nikko had made a fruit salad, which was coated with a honey-lemon dressing. We also had some deli meats smeared with cream cheese and wrapped into a tube around zesty dill pickles.

"I had to use what I could find in the fridge," Nikko said.

By fridge, I assumed he meant his parents'. Nonetheless, I was impressed and nodded my approval. Tobey was click/panting at my feet and I slipped him a chunk of bread, which he swallowed whole.

Nikko and I had carried water bottles, and we sipped our tepid water along with the meal. I noted that he had put a couple of mini bottles of wine in the cooler, but we decided it was best to keep our faculties for the long paddle back.

"I will admit that Ma made the dessert," Nikko said. "Her double fudge brownies."

We ate our brownies and stood to stretch our legs. Nikko put his arm around me.

"So, what do you think of the adventure so far," he said.

"I'm gobsmacked," I said.

"More fancy words," he said, turning to face me.

"It means—"

He cut me off with a kiss.

We pulled apart and he pushed my hair away from my chin. "What did you do to your hair?"

"Why?"

"Looks nice."

"Okay, well when you say what did I do—"

He kissed me again, longer, and tried to get his hand under my jacket.

"Hmm," he said. "That's a lot of layers."

"I wanted to be prepared for an adventure."

"Disappointing."

We pulled apart and I pulled my jacket back into place.

"Come sit around the campfire," Nikko said, grabbing the inflatable cushions.

"What campfire?"

"The one I'm gonna make."

We moved to the fire ring and plunked the cushions in front of an enormous log.

We sat and leaned back against the log. Nikko put his arm around me and pulled me close.

"I still don't see a fire—"

Nikko turned my face toward him and drew me into a kiss. We were melting into one another when Tobey put his paws up on my lap and nudged me.

I had to laugh, and that pretty much ended the moment.

"I think someone's jealous," I said.

"He's been very clingy since his, ah, transition surgery."

I pulled Tobey up onto my lap and put my arms around him. "Who's a good boy?"

"I'm a good boy," Nikko said.

"Hah!"

We sat for a moment, enjoying the twittering birds and hush of the breeze through the pine boughs.

"I like to come here and just forget about things for a while," Nikko said.

"I can see why," I said. "It's wonderful."

"However—" Nikko said.

"Uh oh."

"Maybe I should let you know that Dad and I met with Lieutenant Spiller yesterday."

"Yeah?" I said. "How did that go?"

"Well, I think that Spiller realizes that he needs to get Dad into the loop on things with the two suspicious deaths out at your place. Being the local sheriff, Dad is more likely to get the inside scoop from locals than state police brass. For example, your dad told my dad about the photos. They figure it puts a whole new spin on the case."

I felt my face flush. Before this thing was over, everyone would know about Uncle Phil. The stigma of being gay was a lot less prevalent these days, even in Peshekee, but having porn-like photos was humiliating. It was only a matter of time before the whole village would know about the photos and things would explode into ridiculous speculation.

"The good news is that you and I have moved from persons of interest to simple witnesses."

"Well, that is good news," I said. "I guess the sheriff told you that Dad and I got the USB flash stick out of the safe, thinking it would have the spreadsheets of Wildwood on it."

"Yup," Nikko said. "And now everyone knows that a similar device was found in a coffee can of pee in your dump pile. Apparently they were able to access the files on it, even though it had a less than ideal storage history."

"And?"

"Dad said that Spiller told him it just looked like ordinary business documents, except one thing. There's apparently a video recording but I don't think they were able to get it working."

"No JPEG photos though?" I asked.

"Nope," he said.

"So, maybe the flash sticks got switched somehow," I said. "I think Scott Summers *thought* he had the flash stick with the incriminating photos. I think he was in on blackmailing my uncle, but Summers was living in a tent, so I don't think he had gotten any of the money."

"Maybe a double cross, or he blew it," Nikko said.

"Like on drugs?"

"Well, according to Spiller, the autopsy didn't show anything indicating he was a doper. But it did come up with something weird."

I looked at Nikko. "Weird?"

"I guess the dude's blood sugar was in the toilet."

"Would that be from, like, starvation or alcohol or something?" I asked.

"Well, something. Such as an overdose of insulin," Nikko said.

"They can tell that?"

"I guess not very well. I did find out that there was no evidence of regular insulin injection, though. Just the one possible injection site at the back of his neck."

"When those two troopers came out with the search warrant, they tried to confiscate Aunt Lin's insulin and syringe, but when confronted, just took photos and returned it."

"Yeah. I guess they wanted to know if it was the same type of insulin. Like you and I pilfered your aunt's insulin supply, tackled Summers, and gave him an overdose. But they have no empty vial or used syringe conveniently left around Summers' body or anyplace in the search area to compare."

"Besides, there was the little issue of the ORV tracks and extra footprints back at the, ah, scene of the crime."

"Spiller said we could have still been involved, you know, in with whoever had the ORV."

"Yeah, but then there's the big-ass donations to that bogus horse rescue thing. It all ties in somehow—the photos, regular sums of money going to Sasha Saari-Summers and disappearing. Other money being sent to a bogus charity to some P.O. box in California. Thing that is so bad is that Dad and I are pretty sure someone in the office is involved. He's feeling very betrayed but we're clueless as to who it could be. Maybe all of them."

"Well, it's not you and it's not me," Nikko said. "I'm sorry I brought it up, but I thought you should know. Guess I spoiled the moment."

"Never did get that fire going," I said.

"Maybe a little ember left?"

"Maybe."

He pulled me closer into a kiss. The maneuver was awkward because Tobey thought we were playing. But we still managed to slide down the log and lie on our seat cushions. Nikko put his leg over me and pushed his hips against mine. We kissed again, tangling legs around one another. This was apparently a signal to Tobey that action was required by him. He barked madly, growled, and began pawing frantically at us.

We rolled apart and burst into laughter.

"Who needs a chaperone when you have a guard dog," I said.

"Damn dog," Nikko said.

"He's my hero."

"Saved from the brute, eh?"

"For the moment," I said. "Guess we should head back. I have some things to do at Wildwood."

Nikko sighed and stood. He reached down and pulled me to my feet. In spite our few moments of heated interaction, the day seemed to be cooling off and a witchy wind had begun to blow.

"Clouding over," Nikko said. "They said sunshine all day. And only a little breeze."

"Well, the weatherman has been known to be wrong."

There was a rumble of thunder. Nikko looked out over the lake. "Ways off, maybe will go south. In any event, we should pack up."

Once we got on the lake it was obvious that the front was not "going south" but creeping ominously toward us.

"We'll never make it back to the car in time," he shouted. "I have an idea. Follow me."

⚞ 26 ⚟

We did not make it anywhere in time. While we paddled frantically toward shore to some elusive spot Nikko had in mind, the sky turned an ugly steel gray and the heavens opened up, dumping rain in biblical proportions. A crack of thunder shook the sky and lightning flashed a couple seconds later. The rain pounded the lake, roaring like a waterfall. I powered forward against a headwind. Left, right, left, right, pushing the paddle with my whole body until my arms burned and my shoulders ached. Water poured off my Boonie hat and ran down inside my coat. I was sitting in a puddle and my quick-dry pants were drenched. I could no longer wiggle my toes and was uncertain if they still counted as part of my anatomy. The rain continued to fall in torrents, and I was beyond caring about anything other than getting off the damn lake.

Nikko turned to look at me and pointed to a tiny opening in the trees on shore. I got the signal and pushed toward it. We slid onshore, dragged our boats well away from the water, and flipped them over. Nikko grabbed the cooler and blanket bag and handed them to me. He picked up Tobey and nodded toward the woods. "This way," he said.

Once in the woods the rain wasn't quite so intense, though the trees had become saturated and occasionally spilled a collected pool of water down our necks. The path we were following had turned into a rushing stream. Through the trees I spotted something white. As we got closer it shaped up to be a round plastic tent of some sort.

"It's a yurt," Nikko said.

I'd heard of yurts. They were something the nomadic folks in cold, frigid climates used because they were portable and easy to assemble. But weren't they made out of animal skins? This one looked like heavy-duty vinyl.

The yurt had a conventional door, which was secured with a padlock. Nikko unzipped a pants pocket and pulled out his keys. He slipped one into the padlock and snapped it open.

"What the heck?" I said.

"I told you, I'm a woods cop. I have a master key to all the DNR yurts and cabins."

We stepped inside. Of course there was no light to flip on and the outside flaps had been secured over the screen windows. Nikko set Tobey down and dug out his phone and turned on the flashlight. I did the same with my phone. Rain pounded on the plastic roof of the yurt, but the wind didn't seem to have any effect. I shone my flashlight around and saw that the structure was supported by a lattice-like frame along the walls and roof supports that reminded me of the underside of a giant umbrella. Two sets of bunk beds, a table and four chairs, a dresser, and a woodstove with a pile of firewood next to it were the sum total of accoutrements. The furniture was made of notched logs and knotty pine. The bunkbeds had mattresses that reminded me of the tumbling mats we used in school gym class. There was a stubby candle on the table and another on the dresser.

"Be it ever so humble," Nikko said, going over to the woodstove.

"What is this thing?" I said.

"A yurt," he said, motioning his arms out like a realtor at a showing.

"Well, yeah, I know. But why is it here?"

"To rent. The DNR rents out cabins and yurts. Luckily this one apparently isn't rented for the weekend."

"So we stay here for free?" I asked.

"These shelters can be used in an emergency. People have even broken into cabins from time to time when they've hugely underestimated the danger of hiking in flip flops and shorts. I'd say being caught in a rogue storm works as an emergency."

I sat at the table, shivering uncontrollably. Nikko put some newspaper and small pieces of wood into the woodstove. He checked a lever on the pipe going up to the roof and pulled a little metal cannister out of his pocket.

"My waterproof match carrier," he said. "I never leave home without it."

"La-lucky for me," I said, trying to suppress my shivering. I was probably slipping into hypothermia, and I hadn't even fallen into the lake.

A sliver of light flickered from the woodstove, which immediately started to warm things up. Next Nikko lit the two candles and dispelled the gloom a little. Tobey had put his front paws up on one of the lower bunks and looked at us. He was still wearing his life jacket. Nikko went over and removed the jacket and put Tobey up on the mattress. The dog was shivering, so Nikko took off his coat and made a nest, which Tobey curled into.

Even though the yurt was warming up, I couldn't quit trembling.

Nikko came behind me and put his arms around my shoulders. "Ya know, you'll never get warm unless we get you out of those wet clothes."

I answered with chattering teeth.

"I have a sure-fire method of quieting those teeth," he said, pulling me out of my chair and into a kiss.

My teeth quit clicking, but my chin quivered. Maybe not from the cold.

"Are ya-ya-you t-t-taking advantage uf m-m-me?"

"Certainly not," Nikko said. "I am administering first aid. The next step is to get your body core temp up. The wet clothes are wicking away all of your heat."

"Ca-can't have that," I stuttered.

"The blanket is dry," he said, digging it out of the bag. "You can wrap up in it."

"O-o-okay," I said.

"And of course sharing body heat is an excellent way to reverse hypothermia," Nikko said.

Leave it to a woods cop to have all the answers. But who was I to argue.

* * *

"Home sweet home!" Nikko said as we drove down Horse Camp Road toward Wildwood. Mud had made it all the way up onto the hood of the Tahoe and over the windshield. A smeary view had been created by the wipers and a few dozen squirts of washer fluid.

The rain had stopped while we were in the yurt sometime between our so-called survival warming event—known to most as fervent sex—and the consumption of the wine and leftover bread and goat cheese. Nikko had carried some armloads of firewood in from a woodshed adjacent to the yurt while I swept the floor and blew out the candles. Nikko clicked the padlock shut on the yurt door, and we exited our love nest and headed to the kayaks. I would have killed for an Uber. There's a hot business idea: Uber watercraft. A few snags to work out, though, since rarely was there cell service on the backcountry lakes and rivers, not to mention a lack of street signs and GPS global positioning availability.

The paddle back to the car was not nearly as magical as our paddle heading out. I was certain that we were somehow taking the long way back, perhaps even lost, and adding several nautical miles to the trip. All the islands and inlets looked the same to me, but Nikko seemed to be cocksure of our route. And of course, even if he were lost and a dozen other people were cruising the lake, being a typical male, he would never ask for directions.

After being soaked to the skin and battered by the mother of all storms, not to mention engaging in energetic warming techniques, Nikko still managed to look as if he had just completed a photo session for the centerfold of *Outdoor Man*. I, on the other hand, had not fared so well. I could not remember ever being so exhausted. A glance in the rearview mirror revealed a haggard woman who looked as if she had endured six weeks at boot camp. Furthermore, I was disappointed that the curl relaxer in my hair had failed to live up to its "holds, even in the rain" claim.

Tobey lay comatose on my lap as we pulled up to the mod. I wasn't sure I had the energy to open the car door. I didn't even want to think about the chores awaiting me. I could see all three horses staring my way. Dinnertime was upon us.

Nikko turned to me and smiled. "You are a plucky gal for sure. I can't think of anyone else I've ever dated that, well, anyway, thanks for one hell of—"

"Plucky?"

"You know, ya got Sisu, moxie, guts, fortitude and, um, I really enjoyed our survival experiment, if you get my drift."

"I get your drift, buster," I said. "Sex in a yurt. And a barn. Both coinciding with a freak weather event. Jesus. Do you think God is trying to tell me something?"

"Yes I do," Nikko said, "and I think you should listen." He pulled me into an embrace somewhat confounded by the center console, then planted a kiss on my chapped lips. Tobey stirred and grumbled.

"So," Nikko said, "I was thinking next time we go out we could maybe rent an ORV or jeep or something and—"

"Maybe we can find a porta-potty or haunted castle to hang out in next time, you know, during a tornado or locust infestation," I snapped.

"Oh, funny. Well you never know but I was thinking—"

"Are we ever going somewhere *normal*?"

"Normal?" he said.

"Yeah, normal. See barns and yurts are not normal places to, you know, mess around."

"No, I suppose not. So, a normal place is like the sleazy motel at the edge of town that rents by the hour?"

"First off, we don't have any such motels at the edge of town," I said. "They're all respectable mom and pop establishments and the owners would tell my parents about us before we even got in the door. Most couples whisk off far from their hometown to some luxury resort with a pool, live entertainment, fine dining, king pillow-top beds, jacuzzi tub, a view—"

"We can do that," Nikko said. "You didn't like this adventure?"

He seemed truly perplexed.

"Parts were okay, I guess."

Nikko smiled. "Maybe we could go to dinner or something next time."

"Sure."

I would not have been a Wilde if I didn't seek restitution, or some may say revenge. I mean, the guy nearly did me in. I smiled sweetly.

"Tell you what," I said, "I pick the next adventure. And beware. I shall have my revenge!"

Nikko looked at me. "Can't wait," he said.

27

"Well, Rusty ol' man, this is the moment of reckoning," I said as I ran a brush vigorously over his muddy coat. Powdery dust floated down along with large globs of his winter coat. Rusty was in full shedding mode, and I swear we could stuff a mattress with the hair I'd pulled off.

I had Rusty in the barn crossties and was cleaning him up in preparation for our first ride. He liked being brushed, which he demonstrated by sticking his nose out and curling his top lip.

"You are a goofball," I said, bending over to pick up a hoof. The farrier had worked hard to get his feet back into shape. We kept him shoeless, being that his life of Riley did not require any great wear and tear. I picked packed mud out of each hoof then stood back and inspected my work. Rusty eyed me, maybe wondering what the extra fuss was all about. He probably figured it out when I gently placed the pad and saddle on his back, adjusted it, and snugged the girth. I was pleased that the Stübben fit him well. I was almost as eager to try out the saddle as I was to ride the horse. Next I worked on getting him bridled. To my surprise, he lowered his head to make it easy. As a reward, I slipped him an apple-flavored treat.

"Good boy," I said. I was a little out of practice in tacking up a horse, but the lessons that Justin Wright and my uncle drilled into me were soon resurrected. I led Rusty out of the barn and maneuvered him next to an inverted galvanized washtub that would serve as a makeshift mounting block until I could get something more suitable. I checked the girth one last time, gathered the reins, and hoisted myself up onto Rusty's back. His head popped up and he snaked around to look at me.

"So, do you remember what it's all about?" I said, reaching forward to pat his neck.

I was asking myself more than the horse. I gave him a squeeze with my lower leg and he moved forward. Good start. We headed out into the parking area where we practiced a few basics such as stopping, turning, and easing him into a trot. In English one does something called "posting," or a rising trot. Rather than bouncing and banging on the horse's back, the rider uses the uplifting motion of the trot to rise in the saddle, then does a controlled return to the seat. In that most horses' trot is bone-jarring, the invention of posting has saved a lot of wear and tear on both the horse and rider over the years. All was well until we swung near the paddocks and Misty began neighing and running around like a lunatic. This stirred up Shadow, who joined in the fray. Rusty neighed back, his body vibrating with the effort. He also decided to bolt in an effort to be shed of me and join his friends. Miraculously I managed to stay on, though I lost my stirrups and the reins had slipped through my fingers.

"Oh no you don't," I said, reeling in the reins and fumbling for the stirrups.

Eventually I got his attention and managed to steer him away from his sweetie and head toward the two-track to the horse camp. Rusty balked stubbornly, but I gave him a firm squeeze with lower leg, adding heels, then pulled his head to the side. If a horse won't move forward, sometimes pulling the head around gets him moving. Rusty relented and plodded quietly down the road.

"That's a good boy," I said, reaching down to give him a pat. "Your girlfriend will be there when we get back."

We came upon the abandoned squatter camp, now really just a trampled spot on the ground where the weeds had been smashed down. I didn't fancy riding into the woods where Summers' body had been found, so steered Rusty toward the overgrown trail skirting the woods that would eventually lead back to the barn.

We don't always know why a horse spooks. It can be a piece of litter fluttering in the wind, a loud noise, a movement that only the horse sees. Or, perhaps, even a ghost. Rusty froze and I could feel him tense. His neck was arched and he let out a snort as he stared off into the woods.

This time the phantom horse was mostly white, like a mist. It flung its head up and down, mane flowing in slow motion. Rusty snorted again and did a 180 bolt that launched me out of the saddle and flung me into the weeds. I lay on my back for a moment, wheezing. After recovering my wind, I pulled up on one elbow and looked off into the woods. No spectral horse. I looked down the two-track and glimpsed Rusty's hindquarters hightailing it back to the stable.

Well, at least something else had finally seen the apparition besides me. While this proved to me that it was real, a horse wasn't the best eyewitness if I wanted to share my story.

I got up and brushed myself off and started the walk back to the stable. My knee was acting up a little, causing me to limp. But I wasn't done for the day. It was required in the equestrian world that after a fall, unless you were unconscious or in the emergency department with multiple fractures, you must get back on the horse.

* * *

Monday morning rolled around quickly as did 5:00 a.m. when my alarm went off. After dragging myself out of bed, I could barely move. The combo kayak/equestrian shenanigans had wreaked havoc on my body. My arms and legs felt as if I'd been drawn and quartered. Additionally, my previously bruised ribs and messed-up knee were barking at me. I soldiered through morning chores and managed to burst into the office about one minute before eight. Rose was at her post and presumably Gussy was in his cubicle crunching numbers along with a granola bar.

"Morning, Rose," I said.

"Good morning."

"Have a good weekend?"

Rose looked up as if I had asked about her sex life.

"I suppose," she said. She did not return the inquiry.

Too bad, because she would have had a stroke if I'd told her about mine. I tossed my satchel on the desk and pulled my laptop out of its case and plugged it in. I booted up the computer and checked my messages. Among a bunch of spam, I had another one from the 4Hoof Rescue. It was accompanied by some more heart-wrenching photos and a repeat invitation to apply as a foster care facility. I didn't delete it. I had actually created a file and saved it along with the other 4HR emails I'd gotten.

Dad came in and greeted everyone. "Char in yet?" he asked.

"No," Rose said.

"Have we heard from her?" Dad said.

"Not that I'm aware," Rose said.

Gussy's head popped up over his partition. "I think she's still, um, sick."

"Strange," Dad said, punching at his phone. "We'll see if she answers my text. If not, I think we should check on her."

"Oh!" Gussy said. "Oh, no, I don't think she'd like that."

Everyone, including Rose looked at Gussy.

"Gussy," Dad said. "Is something going on I need to know about?"

"Um, no, I mean, well, she might be contagious, is all."

Dad and I looked at each other and Rose answered the phone.

"Anyway," Dad said, "Ollie wants to meet with us sometime today."

"Sure," I said. "Do we know what Sheriff Olsen wants to talk about?"

"Same ol' thing," Dad said. "You know, murder and mayhem."

Gussy and Rose gasped simultaneously.

"Dad!"

"I told Ollie we'd bring lunch with us."

"Sure, sounds good."

*   *   *

Sheriff Olsen's office looked pretty much the same as before. In fact, it probably had looked the same as it had for the past ten years. However, somebody had emptied his wastebasket and the outdated calendar had been removed from the wall leaving a lighter, cleaner square spot on the painted cement blocks. There had been a time when people smoked in their offices, including sheriff departments, until it was banned in 2010. However, the previous decades of nicotine accumulation on the painted cement blocks had left a ghastly yellowish patina.

We stood at the door, Dad holding a large plastic bag that wafted out the enticing smell of Bill's Burgers and homemade fries. Ollie was on the phone but waved us in. We sat in the miserable plastic "guest" chairs and Dad divvied up the food. Ollie hung up and we all dug in.

"Nothing like a double Yooper to make my day," Sheriff Olsen said, taking a huge bite. "Frieda won't allow me to eat these things. She packed me a tuna sandwich on frickin' whole wheat along with carrot sticks and an apple. I put it in the breakroom fridge; maybe someone is desperate enough to steal it."

We ate for a while, wiping our hands repeatedly on a couple dozen napkins that were provided. Once we had all slowed down, Dad cleaned some barbeque sauce off his lips and cleared his throat.

"So, Ollie, now that you've suckered me into buying lunch, what gives?"

The sheriff took a swig of his jumbo soft drink to wash down his food. He looked at both of us and smiled.

"Well, you know we've been pretty caught up in the Scott Summers death, but I might remind everyone that the Sasha Saari-Summers' death is also not solved. In fact, I don't think the staties are making much progress on either. But I just found out something from our beloved Lieutenant Spiller about that hospice place—Yarrow—that your brother Phil used. Specifically, its former director."

"Former?" I said.

"Yup, she recently left Yarrow more or less in the dark of the night. No notice, didn't turn in anything or even put in for her final paycheck and unused vacation and sick time."

"Seems a bit suspicious," Dad said.

"Oh, yeah," Ollie said. "Hey, did you get any cookies?"

Dad looked at the Sheriff. "What do you think?"

"I think you better have, or no more info. I could catch some grief, you know. Spiller is such a tight ass." He looked at me, debating if he'd been too crude in my presence, then shrugged and took the giant chocolate chip cookie that Dad handed him.

"So, anyway," the sheriff said, "apparently this former director, one Melissa Swift, aka Melinda Smith, has a warrant out for her arrest."

"And?" I said.

The sheriff looked at me, then popped the last of his cookie into his mouth. He chewed slowly, as if trying to build drama.

"And?" Dad said.

The sheriff smiled. "Seems Melissa Swift had a scam going wherein she scrounged up people—typically desperate types similar to those that pimps and con artists tend to prey upon—and got them to go along with the plan."

"Plan?" Dad said.

"What? Are you my echo? Yes, plan. Swift did her homework—or had her minions do it for her—digging up background on the patients that Yarrow Hospice caregivers were assigned to. Some were probably squeaky clean and not good prospects, but others had something either in the past or present going on that could be used as leverage. If there wasn't anything definitive to work with, Swift would beef up or even manufacture something."

"Thus," I said, "the opportunity for blackmail."

"Smart girl.," the sheriff said. "The patients, or *friends* that place Yarrow called them, were encouraged to make payments to keep the misdeed, or alleged misdeed, under wraps. What the hell kind of name is Yarrow? Anyway, in the case of your brother, Phil, Sasha went there posing as his love child. The director of course knew that Phil had been in the service and that most military men—and women for that matter—get a thing called leave. They don't usually spend their leave time going to church or shopping for thoughtful gifts for their mothers. So, maybe Phil thought hey, I did have a couple of rolls in the hay with women. Maybe there is a kid out there of mine. Or maybe he even met someone special."

"Except as you now know, Phil was gay," Dad said.

"Ah, yes," Sheriff Olsen said. "But some gay people try to fit in with the norm, try to develop a heterosexual relationship."

I said, "Maybe the guys pressured him. I bet he gave it a go—heterosexually. He may have had relations with Sasha Saari-Summer's mother, making the story feasible. Maybe Sasha was actually his child, who knows. If Uncle Phil *knew* that there was no possibility of him producing a child—that is, he never had, ah, relations with a woman—there wouldn't have been any dirt to work with."

"And here's what I think," the sheriff said. "I think Swift had her associates in crime do a little digging around into the personal effects of their potential victims. Maybe Sasha found something that connected Phil to a woman in the past, that is, such as a letter or photo. Thus Swift and Sasha concocted the plan to pose Sasha as Phil's love child. It's my opinion that Sasha was no more related to Scott Summers' mother than to the King of England. They built the case around a totally bogus story."

"But why not just demand proof?" I asked.

"Oh, Swift had that covered. She conducted fake paternity and DNA tests and presented her victims with the so-called proof. Hell, you can buy these things online now, but of course Swift needed the results to be manipulated. Sometimes she claimed to have gotten the swab while the victim was sleeping. Told them it was routine or that they had agreed. In that many of the so-called friends using Yarrow Hospice were on heavy painkillers, it was pretty easy to manipulate them. Of course there was no actual test, just fake results. In some cases, her targets may have a checkered past so no proof was needed. I suspect that Phil was given a fake test."

The sheriff rummaged around on his desk. "Something called Generations Ancestry did the so-called paternity test. It's totally bogus. No lab, no technicians. Possibly operated overseas. You can buy the results you want. People can do such naughty stuff on the internet these days."

Dad and I sat without talking for a moment. Things weren't quite adding up.

"So, Sasha and this Swift woman were scamming Uncle Phil?" I said. "And Sasha's last name was fake, then?"

"My guess," the sheriff said. "Staties have run both Scott and Sasha's prints through AFIS—Automated Fingerprint Identification System—but so far nobody's shared anything with me. I think we can dig out Sasha's real name eventually from the Yarrow business records, but things are tied up right now in the lawsuits. I did find out that she was twenty-three years old *and* I did get to go through a few things when I stopped out at the now discredited Yarrow Hospice and Home Healthcare place. They let me take this—or I should say, they didn't try to stop me."

The sheriff held up a photo. Dad and I looked at it. It was a man and woman standing next to each other. She was smiling and holding his arm with one hand and a small bouquet of flowers in the other. The man was none other than the despicable Scott Summers. He looked bored and surly and had the unmistakable blotchy birthmark on his forehead. The woman was plump but pretty. She wore a sleeveless dress, which revealed the unicorn tattoo on her upper left arm. She looked radiant while he looked like he'd crawled out from under a rock. There was one thing for sure, I saw no family resemblance with Sasha and my uncle. Of course, she may have taken after her mother. But to further doubt any genetic connection, Sasha and Scott did not look like brother and sister, either. Granted, different fathers, but still...

"That would be Miss Sasha Saari-Summers and her supposed half-brother, Scott," the sheriff said.

I turned the photo over and penned in blue ink was the date July 11, 2022; a little over a year before Uncle Phil passed away.

I looked again at the photo. "Cripes, this is a wedding photo."

The sheriff snorted and snatched it back, giving it a look. "Married to her brother—or half-brother?" he said. "Incest?"

"I have a feeling that you were right earlier, that the brother/sister story is a lie," I said. "

"But why?" Dad said.

"Christ," Sheriff Olsen said. "He looks twice her age."

"I pegged him in early forties when we had our face-to-face at the campground," I said, "so yeah, robbing the cradle."

"If I took a wild guess, I'd say he married her thinking he could get his hands on some of her money from the con. Maybe Wildwood itself," the sheriff said.

"But where did he come from?" Dad said. "What's the connection?"

"That, dear friend, is the million-dollar question," The sheriff picked up his jumbo drink and finished it off with a slurp. "Unfortunately, hard to ask him, since he's dead and all."

"It seems so convoluted," I said. "And the idea of Sasha going through Uncle Phil's personal belongings and paperwork to try to find something to give substance to their plan seems awful risky and kind of a longshot to score any useful info."

"I agree," Dad said. "Hey, whatever happened to that box of papers that we scooped up from Phil's trailer before we had it razed?"

"I have it," I said. "I got it out of storage and stashed it in my closet." Before we had Uncle Phil's trailer dismantled, we had gone through the papers, photos, manuals and so on that Uncle Phil had randomly stored in a desk in the spare bedroom of his trailer. It would have been easy for Sasha to riffle through the stuff. Dad and I had been less than thorough when we collected up the items, tossing out things obviously no longer needed, such as outdated owners' manuals and yellowing newspaper clippings. We did save photos, greeting cards, and military memorabilia in a box to sort through some day. That day had come.

"I'm thinking Phil went along with the whole mess," the sheriff said, "in hopes to keep Sasha's paws off Wildwood, which she might have had a claim to as his kid. And as we know, Scott Summers came on the scene after Sasha's death making just such a claim and hoping he'd get something out of it."

"But why pose as her half-brother?" I said.

"If they were married, then he'd still have claim on her so-called estate," Dad said.

"Maybe so it was a more feasible explanation of his surfacing," I said. "You know, her semi-estranged brother coming to settle her affairs. Plus, I think the marriage was a way of manipulating Sasha to go along with the scheme. Eventually Scott got desperate trying to get something out of the deal, making a claim of entitlement for Wildwood. And, for the record, I sure didn't see Scott showing any evidence of grief for Sasha during our altercation at the horse camp. He should have been devastated over the death of his wife or even sister—if that was his ruse—and seeking revenge of the culprit. Mostly he just ranted about Wildwood being his."

"Our attorney says it wouldn't have flown, anyway," Dad said. "But maybe Scott Summers didn't figure it that way."

"I'm not sure when he got into the thick of things," Sheriff Olsen said. "The caregiver scams apparently didn't go on all that long. I agree that it was Scott Summers in conjunction with Melissa Swift, who put Sasha up to it all. Somehow, he knew Phil and where to find him. Whether he placed Sasha there or she was already there as a caregiver and he manipulated her—perhaps through Swift—is yet to be determined. Probably charmed Sasha, who was still young and vulnerable."

"Yuck," I said.

"Well, maybe he promised her great wealth," Dad said.

"Hah!" I said. "Chances are we'll never know, unless that Melissa Swift is caught and decides to fess up."

"Money was deposited and withdrawn on a regular basis from a downstate bank," the sheriff said. "I mentioned this before. Not a major fortune individually, but if you combine it with other Yarrow clientele being tapped, we could be talking about a tidy sum. The payoff money went into that bank account, which was held jointly by Sasha and Swift's alias, Melinda Smith. Swift probably had accounts all over the place. We're trying to track them down; it's a nightmare."

"House of cards coming down," Dad said.

"I hope so," the sheriff said. "As I mentioned, your brother wasn't the only victim of Swift's game. The place has been shut down and is tangled up in a major lawsuit now with some of the victims and their families. I bet Swift got greedy with the wrong person who blew the whistle on her. To top it off, they were treating their caregivers as independent contractors instead of employees, thus avoiding paying social security tax to the feds and saving bucks on unemployment insurance. Plus less bookkeeping by not having to collect and pay state and federal taxes, issuing W-2s, and so on. Likely a major violation of labor law, to say the least. But that is how they could get vulnerable people to do their bidding. People who may not have their credentials in line."

"So, no 1099s?" Dad said. "They have to account for the expenditure. That would tip off the feds and the state too, about taxable income to their alleged independent contractors."

"Not sure how that was handled," the sheriff said. "But probably it was up to the so-called independent contractor caregivers to deal with. But if there was fake information, it would backfire on Yarrow, which it may have. I heard that there was someone planted for a sting operation but haven't verified. Can't say for sure, but I suspect Swift did a double cross with Sasha. So, then, I bet Sasha was going to turn on Swift. Maybe both she and Scott were turning coat. Of course now she's dead and so is Scott."

"So," Dad said, "Swift is your number one suspect in Sasha's death?"

"Yes and no. I mean, we're not sure how a woman—unless she was a weightlifter—would be able to handle transporting the body from wherever the victim was shot then getting it into the feed bin. We've determined that Sasha wasn't shot in the feed bin itself or even the room that the feed bin was in. Moving a dead body is no easy feat. I mean, it would be hard for a fit man to do it alone."

"So, maybe Swift had an accomplice?" Dad said.

"Yeah, but who?" I said. "Scott Summers?"

"Maybe," the sheriff said. "He apparently didn't get any money out of the deal. And now we've figured out that he married her. I'm not liking him for one of the perps, though. See, she was his cash cow. Sasha died before she could make a claim for Wildwood, which was likely the plan. It was not helpful to Scott Summers to have her gone before the plan was carried out."

"He tried to pick up the pieces and still make the plan work," Dad said.

"Hey!" I said. "Remember the shoe? You know, Sasha's body only had the one shoe, and Tobey found the other at Scott Summer's encampment."

"Sure wish we knew where Summers found it," Sheriff Olsen said. "Even after all this time, there might be some valuable evidence at the place where Sasha was shot. I still think she was killed not far from where she ended up, you know, in that feed bin. Perp—or perps—probably had to drag her body from wherever she was killed and the shoe came off in the process."

"Maybe Summers was keeping it as insurance," Dad said. "Suppose he knew it was Sasha's shoe."

"Well, it didn't work out so hot as insurance," the sheriff said. "And another piece of info. The state police found an empty insulin vial along with a very large syringe between the rain fly and shell of Summers' tent. As we knew from before, there was a probable injection site in the back of Summers' neck. No evidence of him being an insulin user, such as lancets or other testing paraphernalia. No other obvious injection sites or packages of syringes or vials of insulin. Pretty sure a massive dose of insulin is what killed him."

"Nikko mentioned that Summers' blood sugar was *in the toilet*," I said.

"And what about the payments to the Equine Rescue place?" Dad said. "Where's that money now?"

"And the blackmail-worthy photos of Uncle Phil and that—that other guy?" I said. "Plus, those photos had to have been taken *before* Sasha came on the scene. Uncle Phil was clearly still fairly, um, vigorous. Once he had a caregiver, he barely had the strength to sit up, let alone…"

"Now that, Miss Wilde, is the *two*-million-dollar question. I think your poor Uncle Phil was the victim of two separate cases of extortion. If there's a connection between Melissa Swift and the Equine Rescue fraud and the whole *outing* of Phil being gay, I have no clue what it is."

"What are the odds of someone like Phil, who really didn't have much wealth, being the victim of *two* scams?" Dad said. "And right under my damn nose."

28

Dad had not gotten a text back from Char by the time we left the sheriff's office, so we decided to head over to her condo to check on her. In spite of Peshekee being a small, rural community, a developer had snuck in and bought up some land and slapped up an obnoxious eyesore of a condominium building called Riverside View just outside the village limits. The more expensive units had spectacular views of the Peshekee River. The cheaper units had a view of the parking lot and scrubby woods beyond. By the time the locals realized what was going up, the permits had been approved and construction was underway. There had been a lot of mumbling about payoffs.

Word was, however, that less than half the units had been sold. The idea was to sell them to Chicago people and other hoity toity folks who would flock in from big cities looking to get away from it all. That speculation didn't pan out, probably due to the lack of a Starbucks and strip malls to support the needs of those coming from upscale America. Char bragged that she had gotten one of the units, *with a view*, for about half of the original asking price.

We pulled into visitor parking at Riverside View and got out of Dad's car. He looked at his phone again.

"Something's not right," he said. "She's not even pretending to work remotely anymore."

I had to agree. It wasn't like Char to just not show up. In fact, it had never happened that I could recall. At the condo building, you entered a vestibule and were required to either punch in a code to open the door to the lobby, which was obviously what tenants would do, or you needed to push a button coinciding with whomever you were visiting so they could buzz you in. Dad repeatedly pushed the buzzer for C. Houle but got no answer.

"I don't like this," Dad said, frowning at the panel of buttons. One said "security;" he gave it a jab.

"May I help you?" came a polite, disembodied voice from a little speaker box.

"I'm concerned about one of your tenants," Dad said. "She works for me and hasn't shown up for work in a few days."

"Who is the tenant?"

"Char Houle. She's in unit 4B."

"Come on in."

The door buzzed and we stepped into the posh lobby. A gray-haired male security guard stepped out of a back room and walked up to us and asked, "So, what is it I can do for you?"

Dad explained the situation and asked if we could just check Char's condominium to see if she was ill, injured, or gone.

"Sorry folks," said the guard. "No can do. Unless there's an immediate emergency, like smelling smoke or gas, or someone pushed their emergency pendant, I'd need the police for a wellness check."

"I can arrange that," Dad said, pulling out his phone. He punched in a number and obviously was calling Sheriff Olsen.

"The sheriff said he'll send someone right over," Dad told the guard. "By the way, name's Gary Wilde and this is my daughter, Kathryn Wilde."

"Nate Leppanen," he said stretching his hand toward Dad. The two shook.

I've always wondered what the deal was. Guys hardly ever offered to shake my hand, and if I was introduced to a woman, a handshake was either limp or nonexistent.

About ten minutes later a patrol car pulled up in front and a deputy came into the vestibule. It was Sergeant Tori Haapala, Sheriff Olsen's best and brightest. The guard let her in and we all exchanged pleasantries, then headed over to the elevator. Leppanen pushed the up button and the doors swished open. He pushed the fourth-floor button and the elevator came to life, whirring smoothly, then gliding to a controlled stop.

"Here we are folks," said Leppanen.

We headed down the hall to 4B and the guard knocked loudly and shouted Char's name through the door. Next he used a passkey, swung the door open, and stuck his head inside.

"Miss Houle? Security," he bellowed.

No answer.

He opened the door for all of us to enter. We stepped into a small, tiled entryway and looked around. While the place smelled like places do when shut up for a while, nothing immediately appeared out of order. The curtains were drawn, making the place gloomy. Leppanen flicked on the light switch. The condo was nicely decorated. The drapes matched a scattering of decorator pillows on the creamy white couch. An expensive-looking Persian rug was spread under a gorgeous rose-colored coffee table. The dining area had a beautiful table—wood, not plastic—and matching chairs. A bouquet of dead flowers sat in the middle of the table, dried petals sprinkled across its gleaming surface. The kitchen had wonderful stainless-steel appliances. No dirty dishes sat in the sink, no food crumbs lay scattered on the countertop. Sergeant Haapala opened the refrigerator, which contained various containers of beverages along with a loaf of bread and some fruit. Haapala took out a container of milk, removed the top and gave it a sniff.

"It's getting to the end of its freshness date," she said, capping it and putting it back in the fridge.

Next we explored the bedroom and bath. Char's condo was a one-bedroom unit, which was likely more affordable, but by no means low-budget. The walls were perfect, the fixtures top notch, and the carpet so plush I wanted to take off my tennis shoes and dig my toes in. The bed was neatly made with a designer comforter and decorator pillows, both matching the curtains. Sergeant Haapala went into an enormous walk-in closet and poked around, then opened and closed dresser drawers. Next she explored the bathroom, opening cabinets and inspecting all the products that lined the vanity. The place was meticulously organized and immaculate.

"Something's definitely wrong here," Sergeant Haapala said.

"But nothing looks disturbed," Leppanen, said. "No sign of any problems."

"That's just it," Haapala said.

"It's as if she just evaporated into thin air," I said. "No globs of toothpaste or hair clumps in the sink. No used tissues in the wastebasket."

"Exactly," Haapala said.

"I think she has a cleaning lady in on Thursdays," Leppanen said. "Looks like nobody lived here since then."

"Good to know," Haapala said. "I'll need her name and contact info to confirm that."

"Sure, no problem," Leppanen said, pulling out his phone and tapping a few keys. "Here you go," he said, passing the phone to Haapala.

Dad looked around. "Maybe she met someone, you know, took off or something." He didn't sound convinced.

"Seriously doubt that," Sergeant Haapala said.

"I agree," I said.

"How can you tell?" Leppanen said.

"What woman would take off and not pack some things?" Haapala said.

"But she may have," Dad said. "I mean, maybe she has lots of clothes."

"It's not the clothes," I said. "It's the other stuff."

"Right," Haapala said. "Makeup, meds, skin products, curling iron, blow dryer, shampoo—all the essentials are still in the bathroom."

"Maybe she has separate things for travel," Dad said. "She does have to go on business trips sometimes for the office. She could have things pre-packed."

"Maybe," Haapala said. "But there are suitcases still in her closet—I unzipped them and found several all nested and stored. Plus there's also a tote sitting in there with toiletries in it along with a travel-size curling iron and blow dryer. And, at the risk of being indelicate, I noted a partially used dispenser with birth control pills in her bathroom medicine cabinet. Why leave behind birth control pills if one is heading out *willingly* for a romantic getaway—or any overnight outing for that matter?"

Everyone stared at their shoes for a moment. I noted mine were very scruffy and disgraceful and had no business walking on the pristine carpeting.

Sergeant Haapala looked at Dad, then at me. "Do you know if Char was seeing anyone? Had a boyfriend or even women she might hang out with?"

"Char was pretty vocal about her escapades," I said. "As far as I know she was a kind of love 'em and leave 'em woman. I know she dated, but I don't think she had anyone special. And truthfully, I don't believe she had a bunch of girlfriends she might meet up with."

Sergeant Haapala looked at the security guard. "Do you know if her vehicle is gone?"

"It's still here," Leppanen said. "Tenants have specific parking places. Miss Houle drives a white SUV and I'm positive it was still in its parking spot when I did my morning outdoor rounds. But there is something missing."

"Missing?" Haapala said.

"Yeah. Her ORV. She keeps it parked next to the maintenance building, So, like I said, when I was doing rounds, I noticed that the trailer was there but the ORV wasn't. I was going to ask her about it next time I saw her."

"How about yesterday?" Haapala said. "Do you remember if it was gone then?"

"I've been off a few days. We could check with Ralph. He covered my shift while I was gone. I suppose you want his information too." He pulled out his phone.

"That'be great," Haapala said. She entered the information into her phone. She looked at Dad. "Do you think Miss Houle would take off on some kind of outing on her ORV?"

"Well, maybe, but I think only for a few hours, and probably on the weekend. She's never gone on a multi-day outing that she mentioned." Dad looked at me.

"Me neither," I said. "She never talked to me much about it, but I can't imagine her just taking off for several overnights along the trail. How do I put it? Typically, here are no swanky motels or vacation rentals on ORV trails, just campgrounds. Char was very committed to her personal appearance. Several days without a shower and fresh makeup doesn't sound like her thing. Plus, why not clear the time off with the office? Remember, she called in sick for a few days and asked to work remotely."

"Well, I suppose she could have been playing hooky," Sergeant Haapala said. "You know, pretending to be sick and maybe taking off with a boyfriend."

"All she had to do was ask for the time off," Dad said. "Except at tax season crunch time, I am very flexible with my staff. She wouldn't have had to lie about it."

"Do you believe that she could have been involved in something illegal—embezzlement or fraud?" Haapala said. "Maybe she was part of the whole thing with the caregiver and when things started to unravel she hightailed it off somewhere? Perhaps planned to buy what she needed while on the lam?"

Dad shook his head. I wasn't sure if he was capitulating to the idea or rejecting it.

"But she didn't take her car," I said.

Haapala said, "Maybe someone picked her up,"

"Yeah, but then why is the ORV gone?"

"It doesn't add up for me either," Haapala said. "But we'll dig into her bank and charge accounts, see if she cleaned out her savings or maybe a charge card will show a plane ticket or something."

Dad was still shaking his head.

I said, "She just fell off the radar."

Sergeant Haapala sighed and looked around the empty condo. "Mr. Leppanen, are you able to give me a description of Miss Houle's ORV?"

"Sure. It's a black and red Polaris. It had a top and doors. Not sure of the year, but fairly new. It had a front and back seat. And if you come to the office, I probably have her trail sticker recorded. The condo association requires that everything with wheels must be licensed or have some kind of registration. They don't want some junky car on blocks sitting off in the weeds."

Sergeant Haapala nodded. "Okay, I'm putting out a BOLO on Ms. Houle. I don't like the smell of this."

29

"Kidnapped!" Aunt Lin shrieked, looking around the mod as if the boogeyman were going to jump out of the walls. "I'm getting a gun. I think we both need guns. And those zappy things. Teasers, or something."

"Tasers," I said, shaking my head. "We don't need guns or Tasers. Just calm down. We don't know for sure that Char was kidnapped, but I will admit that something weird is going on."

"Well, I'm here all day with no car. All alone when you go to the office!"

It was true. Aunt Lin was a bit of a sitting duck, should someone decide to go duck hunting.

"Maybe I should take you into town with me when I go to work. You know, at least until you get a car, and maybe we get a hired hand."

"I *am* your hired hand," she said with a snort.

It was true. Aunt Lin had stepped right up to the plate with the chores and such around the place. She kept the mod clean, cooked, tended to Jupiter's needs, helped with the horses, and she was always fixing something. I really couldn't have handled it alone.

"I don't like to be one of those helpless women, you know," she said, "but if there were a fella around—preferably one with *no* criminal record and who legally carried a gun, I'd not think it was a bad idea."

Even if we could find someone to bring on board, there were a couple of problems. One: people generally wanted to get paid. Two: where would this "fella" stay? In an extra stall? And who would want the job? Maybe a retired steel worker or logger would fill the bill. They always had a lot of muscle and of course any self-respecting man living in the Yoop had a couple of hunting firearms.

"Yow!"

Jupiter made his appearance and offered his opinion, which was generally derogatory unless it involved his needs. He bumped against my leg and went over to his empty food dish.

"Yow!"

"He's been fed," Aunt Lin said. "Go play with your crinkle." She looked at me. "I wadded up some foil and he batted it around for a while. I guess it's stuck under something. He also likes to shred newspaper. What a mess."

I nodded. Jupiter had the attention span of a goldfish. That was why I hadn't wasted any money on toys, kitty towers, hidey hole devices, or any of the other pricey feline entertainment creations being marketed. A wise cat owner found that an empty cardboard box or paper sack or a discarded grocery receipt were well received as acceptable playthings for their feline charges. A live mouse or two also sweetened the deal.

"I supposed I can post an ad at Pete's for some help," I said.

"Okay, but he can't stay in here, right?"

"True."

"Where did your uncle put his hired hands?"

"There was a bunkhouse way back in the woods. I think it had been a hunting cabin or something, and they fixed it up as a bunkhouse. It was off the grid and not particularly convenient, especially in the winter, so Uncle Phil rented a trailer for his hands that could be situated closer to the stable. I believe that he eventually rented the bunkhouse out to guests as a kind of rustic equine vacation rental. Then, of course, as things declined, there were no more guests. Boarders left and employees were let go. The trailer was disposed of and I have no idea if the bunkhouse still exists or if anyone would be willing to live with no electricity or running water."

"Well, it sounds feasible," Aunt Lin said. "Sort of. Maybe Gary—your dad—can help with paying someone until you get more income. And who knows, a rustic place might be perfect for the right person. Granted, we'd need to figure out some things, such as how they could shower and cook and watch television."

I laughed. "There's always the wash rack in the barn and maybe there's a woodburning stove in the bunkhouse. At some point we could even try to rig up a portable generator."

Then I got an idea. Actually, three ideas. Idea one involved creating some income by fostering abused and neglected horses. The second was to rummage through Uncle Phil's box of miscellaneous materials that represented bits and pieces of his life. The third and most titillating idea would involve my yurt partner, Nikko.

"Payback time," I mumbled.

"Huh?"

"Oh, just thinking of my next adventure."

* * *

"No time like the present," I muttered, dragging the dilapidated box of Uncle Phil's papers and whatnot from the back corner of my closet. I sat on my bedroom floor and began pulling things out of the box. I couldn't imagine that if Sasha had hit paydirt by finding something useful in his things, that it would still be there. However, it was worth a shot.

I immediately got caught on a trip down memory lane, mostly from the photos. An old photo album held black and white as well as faded color pictures, which dated back to when Uncle Phil and Dad were kids. Many of the photos had been held in place with tape. Over the years, the tape had lost its adhesive and the pictures tumbled out. I picked them up one by one, smiling at the assorted school pictures along with family photos. In one Dad and Uncle Phil stood next to each other, grinning at the camera. In front of each boy stood a bicycle, presumably new gifts, since they each bore giant bows. The back of the photo said simply "Merry Christmas boys!" There were photos of grandma and grandpa Wilde, now both gone, posing awkwardly for the camera and looking as if they were facing a firing squad. Other photos had all four doing things that families do. Vacation, new car, carving pumpkins, hunting for Easter eggs, dressed up for church where the boys looked miserable.

I found a mishmash of loose photos, which seemed to represent the years Uncle Phil was in the Army. He had joined shortly out of high school and had reupped a few times. I especially loved one photo of him astride a beautiful black horse. The back of the photo said "Eclipse." There were photos of him as he moved through the military ranks, ending up as a high-ranking sergeant. In that photo he was standing at attention, with a line of soldiers in the background. I didn't know much about the Army, but guessed the soldiers in the background were new recruits, maybe in basic training. They all looked terrified. The back of that photo said, "last inspection."

Then a photo caught my attention. It was of Uncle Phil with a woman. They were both in uniform, posing for the camera, with the woman turned toward my uncle. He was smiling and had his arm around her. I flipped over the picture and all it said was, *March to the beat of your own drum! Love, M.*

"Very curious," I said aloud. I looked through more pictures and found several more of Uncle Phil with horses, some with other soldiers, and one more with the woman "M." It looked like they were sitting at a table in the mess hall. The camera picked up a few soldiers—men and women—in the chow line and sitting around. I would have loved to go through all the photos with Uncle Phil, have him describe things. Tell me about "M." Was she the one? Mary Saari-Summers? A lot of women's names begin with M. I felt melancholy, thinking about Uncle Phil. I had loved him, but never took the time to really know him. I looked again at the two photos with Uncle Phil and "M." I couldn't help thinking that I was missing something. Obviously, there was no bundle of joy cradled in anybody's arms. And the two photos with "M" were far from incriminating. Yet there was something there.

I sorted through some miscellaneous papers and found a plain white envelope, which looked fairly new. I pulled out a single piece of paper and unfolded it. A lab report of some kind. At first I wondered if it had to do with the medical records relating to his illness, which were all in a thick expanding folder along with medical insurance paperwork and stashed in the Wilde home office. The top of the paper bore the name of the lab: Generations Ancestry.

"Aha!" I said to my empty room. "The game is afoot!" Silly, but satisfying.

Sheriff Olsen had been right on target about the fake paternity testing. And, wonder of wonders, upon reading the results, it was indicated that Uncle Phil was 99.9% likely the biological father of Miss Sasha Sari-Summers.

* * *

Gussy caved like a sandcastle at high tide. The investigation of two murders and a suspicious disappearance were in full swing and it was time to put the thumbscrews to Gerald Gustafson, who was born guilty. Sheriff Olsen decided that inviting Gussy to the department would just spook the boy and if Lieutenant Spiller got involved, Gussy would probably swallow his tongue. So, he sent Sergeant Haapala to the office to blindside our reluctant witness. Dad sent Rose on a contrived mission at the courthouse, citing the need for her expertise to get information that I, simpleton that I was, would likely screw up. We all gathered in Dad's upstairs office suite and sat around his conference table.

Gussy looked from Dad to me to Sergeant Haapala. His Adam's apple bobbed wildly and he blinked so much he was going to wear out his eyelids.

"They said they'd hurt her if I told," Gussy mumbled.

"Okay, Gerald—may I call you Gerald," Sergeant Haapala said.

"Gussy," he said.

"Okay, Gussy, let's start at the beginning. First off, you are not under arrest or in any way required to talk to me. And even though you are *not* under arrest, you are entitled to have an attorney present. Also, I'd like to record our talk here today if that's okay with you."

Gussy gulped madly, and reached for his water bottle and took a swig. "It's okay," he said. "I haven't done anything, well yeah, you can record. I wanna help Char. It's just..."

We were all quiet for a moment.

"Just what, Gussy?" Haapala said.

"But now I'm afraid that they'll hurt her."

"Who is *they*? Is it a man or a woman or several people?"

"I don't know," he said.

"How did they make the threat?"

"They sent a text."

"Okay, maybe we can track that," Haapala said. "You saved the texts, right?"

"Yeah," Gussy said, "but they said they had a burner phone and if anyone tried to find them, they'd—they'd kill Char!"

"Okay Gussy, let's go over what you know."

"Well, at first I thought we were doing the right thing, you know, keeping things quiet," Gussy said. He looked at Dad. "Mr. Phil—you know, your brother—asked us to just make the payments to the horse rescue place and that we were to not involve you, sir."

"Call me Gary."

"Gary, sir. Anyway, Char said we needed to respect Mr. Phil's wishes and she talked about client confidentiality and everything. She went out to the place, you know, Wildwood sometimes and had Mr. Phil sign the checks. Sometimes she just stamped the checks with the office signature stamp, you know, with Mr. Phil's permission. We kept track of everything on the spreadsheets. Char was on top of it and all. I guess she and the guy working there hit it off, so she didn't mind going out."

"What guy are we talking about?" Dad asked.

"That Wright guy, you know, the one with the English accent."

"Ah," I said. "I sure remember Mr. Just Right. He taught riding lessons, yours truly included. His actual name is Justin Wright."

"Do we know where this Mr. Wright is?" Haapala asked.

"Not anymore," Gussy said. "He left Mr. Phil's place after he passed. I don't know if Char and Mr. Wright were still seeing each other. She doesn't talk to me much about her personal life."

"So, when Wright left, did the payments to the horse charity stop?" Haapala said.

"Well, before that. Maybe around the time that Mr. Phil got terribly sick. It was a good thing, too, there wasn't much income anymore to cover them."

"And you never thought to talk to me?" Dad asked.

"Well, Mr. Phil still insisted that we don't. But then, well, we thought it was okay, and like I said, he got sick and they sent that woman to take care of him. Things got a little weird then."

"How so," Sergeant Haapala said.

"Mr. Phil didn't want any more money sent to the horse charity, but then he wanted to start some other payments."

"Other payments?" Dad said. He looked at Haapala and shrugged. "Cash, or did he have checks cut?"

"I don't know," Gussy said. "I think it was from Mr. Phil's personal checking account, not the business one. I guess Sasha took care of the personal account. Char didn't like the idea at all. I thought the amount was a lot, you know, for a caregiver. But Mr. Phil said the woman, Sasha, was his personal assistant and doing stuff other than the normal caregiving duties and kind of told us to stay out of it."

Dad and I looked at each other.

"Like what other stuff?" I knew it wasn't likely to be nookie in the broom closet.

"Char said she ran errands and did some correspondence and things. You know, like a secretary."

"I see," Haapala said. "So he paid her under the table, so to speak."

"Uh huh," Gussy said.

"And this went on until when?" Haapala said.

"I think until Mr. Phil died. Char would know for sure. Um, there's something else I should probably tell you."

"Okay, Gussy, go ahead," Haapala said.

"Char gave me one of those USB flash drive sticks and asked me to label it for Wildwood Stables and put it in the safe."

"Did you have Rose open up the safe for you?" Dad said.

Gussy looked down at the tabletop. "Char gave me the combination. She was in a hurry to go somewhere and asked me to do it."

"Did you look at what was on the flash drive?" I said.

A deep blush crept up Gussy's neck and spread into his cheeks.

"No. Well, okay, yeah. But just one of those—photos. I thought it was going to be Wildwood spreadsheets. Honest! Anyway, I locked it in the safe."

"So, let me get this straight," Haapala said. "There are *two* USB flash sticks. One contains blackmail photos, which ended up in the office safe and a second that ended up in a coffee can in Scott Summers' tent located at the campground at Wildwood."

Gussy shrugged.

"Sasha and Scott were partnering up," I said. "So Scott coming around after Sasha's body was found, threw us off. He had been around much longer, staying out of sight."

"It would seem so," Haapala said. "Maybe living with Sasha and then the old campground after she was eliminated. According to the state police, the flash stick that was recovered from Mr. Summers' coffee can that ended up in that dump pile at your place had some spreadsheets and a video or recording they can't open. It's protected and they're working with an expert to break the code."

I thought of Raymond and wondered if he was somehow involved.

"Be nice to know if there's anything significant with the video or recording," I said. "And how did Sasha get it to give to Scott?"

"Maybe they thought it had the blackmail photos," Haapala said.

"Or didn't know what it was," I said, "but snitched it from Char's purse or briefcase."

"Swift was in the mix by then," Haapala said. "She had Sasha extorting money with the claim of being his offspring."

"So Dad and I got the flash drive out of the safe that Gussy put there, thinking it was Wildwood records that might help us get to the bottom of all the so-called charitable donations but we were instead greeted with some lovely photos of Uncle Phil and some other guy."

"I—I didn't know what to do," Gussy said. "You know, those photos…"

"So, you didn't mention the photo you saw to anyone?" Dad said.

"No sir," Gussy said.

"What a cluster," Haapala muttered under her breath.

Interesting choice of words, I thought. And I had a strong suspicion of who the other guy was in the family photos.

"Justin Wright," I said.

Haapala looked at me.

"The man with Uncle Phil," I said. "Justin Wright."

Haapala nodded. "Blackmailer and creator of the bogus horse rescue cover for a place to funnel the payoffs," she said.

Gussy looked beyond terrified. Haapala must have decided it was time to wrap up before he fainted.

"One more question, Gussy," she said. "During the time all this was going on—before Phil Wilde died—do you know if anyone that might have been Scott Summers ever came around, looking for Sasha or asking questions?"

"Nope, but I didn't go out to Wildwood much—only a couple of times. It was usually Char. Maybe she knew him."

"I think Char is into something pretty deep," I said.

Haapala nodded and shut off the recorder on her phone. "And Gussy, I'd appreciate it if we kept this conversation between just us in this room for now."

"Yeah, okay," Gussy said. He lowered his chin and may have been holding back a sob. "I sure hope Char is okay."

I had a terrible feeling that Char was not okay.

30

"So tell me again why we can't just drive back to this place," Nikko said.

We were in the barn getting Rusty and Misty ready for a ride. I had decided that my payback adventure would involve some time in the saddle while at the same time Nikko and I could check out the old bunkhouse and see if it had any potential for a future ranch hand.

"Because," I said, "this is an adventure. You can ride Rusty. He's very steady. Since he is smitten with Misty, I'll ride her, which will make him happy. Plus, I'm not sure what shape the two-track road is in going back there. It could have some limbs or even trees down for all we know. Horses can get around and over stuff."

"Over?" Nikko said. He was making a try at brushing Rusty, who was the epitome of docility.

"Sure, they can jump over things. Don't worry, it'll be fun."

"Yeah, right. And this bunkhouse..." He waggled his eyebrows.

"Don't get any ideas," I said. "It's not the kind of adventure that will result in, ah, any desperate measures."

"Desperate? I was thinking of a different description of—"

"Just stop," I said. "Have you ever been on a horse?"

"Sure, well, you know, the pony rides at the fair where they are hooked up to some kind of thingamajig and they walk around in a circle."

"In other words, no," I said. "Okay, I'll give you some basics and we can head on down the trail."

"Can Tobey come?"

"It might be a little too far for him, and we can't just drape him over the saddle," I said. "Aunt Lin will doggie sit."

"What about that cat. Doesn't he hate Tobey?"

"Jupiter will enjoy tormenting Tobey. They'll be good for each other."

Nikko nodded and gave another swipe at Rusty with a brush. "How's that?"

"Good enough," I said, heading to the tack/feed room for saddles and bridles.

I helped Nikko saddle up Rusty. I used the western saddle the Koskinens had brought when they delivered their two horses. Rusty took the bit easily and got his apple-flavored horse treat as a reward. After a less than smooth mounting from my inverted wash tub, we were on our way, with Misty and me leading and the Rusty/Nikko combo following.

"Don't get too close," I said. "Misty might kick."

"Tell that to Rusty," Nikko said. He was slumped over and clung to the saddle horn with one hand while clutching the reins in the other.

"Don't hang onto the saddle horn," I said. "And put some slack in the reins."

"Isn't that what the horn thing's for?" he said.

"Nope, it's for lassoing cattle. You wrap the lariat around the horn and, oh never mind."

"You mean like in cowboy movies?"

"Sure. Exactly. We'll just start out at a walk, for crying out loud. Grab his mane if you need to."

"His main what?"

I gave up and let Nikko cling to whatever he wished. Eventually, he did relax a bit and almost seemed to be enjoying the ride.

I hadn't been to the bunkhouse in eons but knew that the two track that led through the old campground veered off into the woods, and if we could still find the road, ended up at the bunkhouse that sat on a small body of water we called Mosquito Pond. I knew that ORVers generally trespassed on the old road, even back when Uncle Phil was alive. Likely the ORV Nikko and I had heard back when Scott Summers died would have used the two-track, even though it might have been tough to find with the snow.

The first thing I spotted was the dull metal roof of the privy that went with the cabin.

"Hey, I think we found it!" I said.

"Found what?"

"The cabin. There's the outhouse."

"Ah, good to know."

We halted our horses in front of the old cabin. It was a basic log structure with an asphalt shingled roof and a stone chimney on one side. Most of the varnish or stain or whatever finish had been applied to the logs was peeling away. The roof was covered with moss and years of twig and pinecone accumulation. The outside stone chimney seemed intact. The windows were shuttered with bars over them and the door was barred closed as well. Two rickety steps led up to a small, rotted porch. There may have been a corral or hitching post at one time, but if so, they were long gone.

I dismounted and went over to Rusty and held his head. "Okay, swing your leg over and lean against the saddle, pull the other foot out of the stirrup and slide down his side."

Nikko tried but failed to get his second foot out of the stirrup in time, hung sideways for a moment then fell on his back. Fortunately, the trapped foot slid free.

"Oooof. Damn, I think I landed on my keys."

I stifled a laugh. Paybacks were glorious. I reached down to give him a hand up. He reached back, then pulled me off balance and down on top of him.

"What the...?"

"Can't resist me, eh?" Nikko said, wrapping his arms around me.

"That was a dirty trick," I said, although I didn't struggle to get away.

"It's those hoochie coochie pants you are wearing. They drive me mad!"

"They're riding britches. They're made to be non-binding and smart looking."

"And with those black S&M boots," he said.

"They're functional *riding* boots that let me to move with the horse and protect my legs as well."

"Hubba hubba!" Nikko said.

"Hubba hubba?" What are you, my grandfather? Now leggo. The horses are wandering off."

I had packed a couple of halters and lead ropes along with a piece of rope to fashion a picket line. We put the halters over the bridles, snapped on lead ropes, and tied them to the picket line.

"Why not just tie them with the reins?" Nikko said.

"You mean like on the TV westerns?"

"Yeah. They just wrap the reins around the ol' hitching post in front of the saloon."

"Great until something spooks them and they jerk away and break the reins or bridle. Very expensive."

"Oh."

We walked over to the cabin, which looked even worse up close.

"Hey, look," Nikko said, pointing at the ground. "Footprints."

He was right. There were several fairly fresh tracks in the mud around the steps of the cabin.

"Hmm," I said. "Somebody's been trespassing." But the barricade is over the door and it looks like the padlock is still there, so I suppose they either left or decided not to go in. I don't think the place has much to offer. Guess we go in and check it out."

"What's the barricade for?"

"Mainly to keep out bears," I said. "Some CO you are."

"Oh, right."

We gingerly stepped onto the creaking boards of the porch, took the barricade off the door, and looked at the padlock.

"Looks fairly new," Nikko said.

"That's weird!"

"New screws on the hasp plate," he said, "but rotten wood." He looked around and found a fire poker propped up against the cabin wall along with an axe head, well-worn broom, charcoal grill, and a rusty snow shovel.

"Stand back," he said. "Muscle at work."

"Oh, brother."

Nikko put the poker to the hasp and grunted a bit as he pried the screws out of the wood. Suddenly it let go with a crack and the whole thing came loose and clunked on the porch.

"And we're in!" he said.

"My hero," I said, with obvious sarcasm.

We stepped into the cabin, which was nearly pitch dark except for the light coming through the open door. I heard a snuffling noise.

"Did you hear that?" I whispered. "Something's living in here."

Nikko and I activated our phone flashlights and shone them around. The light danced off dust motes and cobwebs. I could make out some bunkbeds, a table and chairs, and a fireplace along one wall. A hump of something seemed to be moving in the corner. The muffled noise was coming from the hump and was joined by a clunk and a crinkling noise.

"See anything?" I said. Then my flashlight picked up a couple of eyes. "There in the corner!"

"MMMFFFF!!"

"OH GOD!" I shouted and ran toward the noise.

31

She was slumped in a chair partly covered by a tarp. Her arms were behind her and she had duct tape over their mouth.

"CHAR!" I yelled. "OH MY GOD, are you okay?"

"MMMFFF!!"

"I think she's trying to say mother fu—er, you know," Nikko said. "Don't blame her."

Nikko held his light on her face and I, as gently as possible, removed the duct tape from her mouth.

She gasped for a few seconds and shook her head angrily then spewed the most colorful string of explicative swear words ever spoken. The explosion of anger seemed to drain her and she slumped to the side.

"My hands..." she said. "Behind."

Her hands were duct taped behind the chair and her ankles were also taped together. She had managed to move the chair a bit by hopping, but any chance of escape was hopeless.

Once all the tape was removed, we helped her stand. Her arms hung limply at her sides.

"I can't move my arms," she mumbled. "Thirsty. So thirsty. I think I wet myself. Oh God!"

"Get some water out of the saddlebags," I said.

After a few swallows of water, Char seemed slightly revived. She could lift her arms a little. We walked her outside and she sat on the top step of the cabin. I pulled a granola bar out of my pocket and handed it to her. She wolfed it down.

"They brought food and water at first," she said, her voice gravelly. "Then nothing for, I don't know, a couple of days."

"Who did this to you?" I said.

"That fucking bastard," she said. "He said he loved me and we'd go off to England. What a pile of bullshit."

"Who?"

"Justin," she said. "Justin Wright."

"He locked you up in the cabin?"

"Yes, the sonofabitch. And that slut that was with him. She put the tape over my mouth."

Nikko and I looked at each other.

"The slut being?" I said.

"Melissa Swift," Char said. "She runs Yarrow—the hospice place."

"Or at least used to," I said. "Why?"

"You mean why lock me up, or why run off with the slut?"

"All of it."

"It's complicated," Char said with a sigh. "But I was on to him—Justin. He was screwing, er, having an affair with your uncle. I think he'd screw an elephant if there was money in it for him."

"I pretty much had that part figured out," I said. "I mean, not the elephant thing, but the homosexual, er, encounters, the photos, and the blackmail funds going to the bogus horse rescue place as a kind of legit cover."

"Yeah, and I fell for it," Char said. "At least for a while." She was quiet for a moment. "What photos?"

"Of the two of them, you know, having relations. Wright used them for the blackmail scam. Somehow they ended up in the safe at the office."

"Ah, right. The flash stick. Yeah, I had Gussy put it in the safe," she said, taking another swallow of water. "My throat feels like shit."

"You're dehydrated," Nikko said. "Just take your time."

Char nodded. "Somehow this had to do with something else, too. That girl, Sasha, and then her brother—or half-brother who came around after, well, you and your dad found the girl's body."

"Actually, it turns out that Sasha was Scott Summers' wife," I said. "The marriage apparently took place around the time Sasha came on board to care for Uncle Phil. But Scott stayed in the background until after Sasha died."

"Seriously?" Char said. "Married?"

"That's what it looks like," I said. "Police are verifying it."

"I was onto him—Wright—but I didn't want to let on," Char said. "Even after I figured him to be the main character in the murders, I had to try to find a way out. Didn't wanna be the next in line."

"I'm having trouble following all of this," Nikko said.

"Like I said, it's complicated," Char said. "God, I'm so hungry."

"Hey, I have some trail mix," Nikko said. "I'll get for you."

"Great. Anyway, I secretly recorded good ol' Justin on my phone, who was boasting about his brilliant scheme and how he and the slut hooked up. He acted like it was the heist of the Hope Diamond or something. I'm not sure which one or if both killed Sasha, but I know it was both of them with Scott Summers. It's all in the recording."

"The police couldn't get it to open up," I said.

"Right, well as I said, I recorded Wright on the sly using my phone. I knew I needed out and thought maybe the recording would be my ticket. I had Raymond transfer the recording from my phone to the Wildwood Stables flash drive stick. Just for the record, Raymond didn't know what he was transferring. I told him it was a confidential meeting with me, Gary, and a client. We recorded meetings sometimes. Anyway, I pretended to be onboard with the whole thing with Justin. I mean, we had, well, you know, been intimate. He said he loved me and that we'd go away. But then I realized all these so-called donations were obviously bogus, but your Uncle Phil was very clear that we *not* tell his brother. And when people died, well I knew I was in really deep and needed a way out but didn't know how to do it without being the next victim. So, like I said, I got the recording as collateral and carried the flash stick with me. It was really an audio recording. The video was of the inside of my purse. But the audio worked surprisingly well. Justin had the photos of him and Phil on another flash stick."

"We figured there were two flash sticks," I said, "but weren't sure what was on the second one with the Wildwood spreadsheets."

"Yeah, the confession," Char said.

"But the so-called confession flash stick with the Wildwood spreadsheets on it—why did you have that in the first place?" I said.

"I, ah, well, I had gotten that out of the safe a while back to— review the spreadsheets. Strictly at your uncle's direction."

"Review?" I said.

"Fudge them?" Nikko said. "Here's the trail mix."

Char sighed and stuffed some of the trail mix into her mouth. "Oh God, food never tasted so good! Anyway, yeah, to make some adjustments. Kind of cover up some tracks. I guess he was paying Sasha in a roundabout way with his personal checking account but had to keep transferring funds from the business to his personal account. Those transferred funds likely were payments directly to Sasha rather than Yarrow. I suspect that Swift was also in the loop. I was trying to make sense of it all and figure out if I was in deep doodoo with the sketchy bookkeeping methods."

"Sasha, and we think Swift under an alias, shared an account somewhere downstate," I said. "That's likely where those payments went. I think my uncle believed Sasha was who she said she was. He was basically bribing her to keep her mitts off Wildwood."

"How did Scott Summers end up with the stick from your phone recording?" Nikko asked.

"I think through Sasha. I was at Wildwood one day meeting with Phil and left my purse in the car with the flash stick that had the spreadsheets and the encrypted recording of Wright's confession. Very stupid of me. I bet Sasha riffled through my purse and snatched it. I didn't notice until later that the stick was missing. Thing is, I had by this time swiped the flash stick with the JPEGs of your uncle and Wright, which I had already given to Gussy to put in the office safe. I should have given both, but still, ah, needed to clean some things up with the spreadsheets. Regardless, they were on to me. But I still played along. That's how I got the JPEG flash stick in the first place. Justin and I were in a motel—he stayed in low-budget dives. Anyway, we were still, ah...well, I had the opportunity to swipe it. I wish I'd had a fake one to replace it with."

"So Wright and Swift knew it was missing and that you most likely had it," Nikko said.

"Yeah, he kept it in a special pouch with his phone," Char said. "Dumbass told me all about it back when he thought I was on his team."

"And thus had Sasha go through your purse," I said. "Bingo! There was a flash stick, which they assumed with the JPEG version."

"But it was the spreadsheet and recording stick," Nikko said.

"Exactly," Char said. "Probably once Wright discovered that the JPEG stick was missing, he had Swift direct Sasha to go through my stuff."

I said, "I noticed some of Wildwood's hard copies of spreadsheets for the last fiscal year were stuffed in a to-be-shredded box. I'm just wondering..."

Char sighed. "Yeah, I was hoping they'd just disappear during the regular course of events if I put them in line for shredding. Again, your uncle was wanting things covered up regarding payments to Wright. If I got rid of that stuff and fixed the flash stick, all would be okay. I didn't think I could smuggle the Wildwood paperwork out with the old battleaxe watching my every move. And I know she pokes through stuff in my office."

"The old battleaxe being Rose," I said.

Char nodded. "She's out to get me."

"Out to get all of us. So, anyway, Sasha gave the flash stick she stole from your purse to her husband like a good little wife. He probably made all kinds of promises to her."

"However, double-crossing Wright and Swift likely did not bode well for Sasha," Nikko said.

"And it wasn't even the right flash stick," Char reminded us. "Far as I know, nobody knew about the spreadsheet/recording version except me and Raymond. And like I said, he just transferred the recording from my phone to the stick—so really just me."

"And then Scott tried to extort money from Wright and Swift, knowing that *he* possessed an incriminating flash stick," Nikko said.

"Which eventually cost Scott his life as well," I said. "I imagine they didn't mean for him to die before he turned over the flash stick. It wasn't even the stick with the JPEGs that everyone was freaking over. In a way, another botched caper."

"But nonetheless, a very incriminating thing should it fall into the law's hands," Nikko said.

"And my days were numbered," Char said. "Wright and Swift stashed me in a sleazy motel room and had me text that I was working remotely. We were all three sharing the room and I had to listen to them screw."

"Jesus," Nikko said.

"It was a horror show," Char said. "I didn't know whether to be angry or terrified or hurt." She took a deep breath. "I think the motel owner was getting suspicious when Justin refused to let housekeeping in the room so it was time to find a better hiding place, thus this shithole," she said, jerking her head toward the cabin. "They needed my Polaris to get back here. Swift had a car, but I think it was hot and they ditched it somewhere after they got my ORV."

"Starting to add up, now," I said.

Char sighed. "God, what a mess I've gotten into."

"Well, Mr. Wright can be charming," I said. "I would have run off with him in a minute back in my more impressionable years."

Nikko looked at me. I smiled.

"I acted like a fool," Char said. "A dupe." She looked at Nikko. "Got any booze? I could really use a drink. God, I feel like crap."

"Sorry," he said. "Just water. I'll get another bottle."

"Thanks. Like I said, it's complicated. Everyone double-crossing each other. Then he and the slut partnered up—"

"Right, Melissa Swift," I said. "By the way, there's a warrant out for her arrest."

"Good!" Char said as she chewed a mouthful of trail mix. "I think Justin and the *slut* were going to move on with something new and improved after your Uncle Phil passed and was no longer of use to them. And of course Sasha was no longer of use, either."

"Who's the slut?" Nikko said, handing Char a fresh bottle of water.

"That's Char's pet name for the former director of Yarrow Hospice, Melissa Swift," I said, aka Melinda Smith."

"Oh, that slut," Nikko said.

"AND MY NEXT NAME WILL BE EVEN BETTER!"

We all snapped our heads around to see a woman stepping around the corner of the cabin. She held a gun.

"The slut has arrived," Char said.

"Takes one to know one," the woman said.

There is a saying that originated in the horse world: Rode hard and put away wet. When applied to a horse, it means they were not properly cooled down and cared for after a major exertion, such as a horse race or gallop across the prairie. When applied to a person, like the one who stepped out from behind the cabin, it means she is rough looking, as if she has been spending her time with a horny biker gang.

Char snorted.

Nikko stood and started to move toward the woman. She held up the gun and shook her head. I wondered if Nikko was armed. I had no idea if he carried when off duty.

"Melissa Swift?" I asked.

"Formerly," she said. "Now I'm partial to the name Melony. You know, like that first lady."

"That's Melonia," came another voice. "President Trump's wife." Justin Wright also stepped around the side of the cabin and stood next to Swift.

Wright had aged a bit since I'd last seen him—probably the life of extortion taking its toll—but still spoke with his beguiling English accent and was one of those men who kept a full head of hair along with timeless good looks.

"No it isn't," Swift said. "It's Melony. That's what's on my new passport, so I'm sticking with it."

"Whatever," Wright said, turning his attention to the three of us. "Bloody hell. We seem to have a situation here."

"Where's my Polaris?" Char asked.

"That's the least of your worries, luv," Wright said, "but it's safe and sound waiting for Melony here and me to head on out—"

"Not all the way to Minnesota," Swift said. "We're—"

"For God's sake, Melissa—," Wright said.

"Melony—"

"Whatever your name is, shut the fuck up."

"You're taking the Polaris to Minnesota?" Char asked.

"Best you shut up, too," Wright said. He looked at me. "My, but Miss Kathryn has grown into quite a lovely thing. Too bad there isn't more time to—get acquainted."

"You're a filthy pig," I said. "And you and my uncle—God! And blackmailing him. There is a special place in hell—"

"Oh, please, save me from all the righteous indignation," Wright said. "I think Phil was more than happy to pay for my services. He was finally free to be who he was."

I wanted to spit on him, but my mouth was bone dry.

"My Polaris," Char said again.

"You won't be needing it," Swift said.

"Obviously they didn't want to drive up to the cabin—too noisy— so they stashed Char's machine somewhere," Nikko said. "I'm thinking you knew we were here and that the jig was up?"

"The jig is hardly up, at least for me," Wright said. "But you are pretty astute for a woods cop, ol chap."

"You left me here to die!" Char said. "You—you bastard."

"What's the matter, *slut?*" Swift said. "You don't like this place? Maybe you shouldn't be stealing things like, oh I don't know, flash sticks. Hey, guess what? Scott didn't care for it here either."

"You had Scott Summers, ah, locked up here?" I said.

"Oh, Melissa—"

"Melony!"

"Melony, you just love to spill it out, don't you?" Wright said. "But no matter. Yes, we put Mr. Summers here to give him time to think about the error of his ways. He claimed to have some sort of incriminating evidence—"

"Would that be a USB flash stick?" I said.

"Asshole said he had photos," Swift said. "Justin here is, ah, very versatile."

I wasn't inclined to let the Wright/Swift duo know about the second flash stick and hoped that Char would do the same.

"Well," Wright said, "I was really not visible in the photos, but nonetheless, it wouldn't take a genius to figure things out. Obviously, since Miss Wilde here did just that. Yes, we took Summers back to his camp where he promised to give it to us."

"But he tried to get cute," Swift said. "Tried to screw us out of our hard-earned money. What had he done to earn it, huh? Marry that fat dingbat?"

"So we gave him a little surprise in the back of the neck," Wright said. "Told him we had an antidote we could use after he turned over the flash stick. Of course there was no official antidote. A candy bar or spoonful of sugar would have turned him around. He tried to run, which was very annoying. We hadn't planned on just letting him go on his merry way, of course, but wanted the so-called damning evidence, just in case something delayed our departure."

"It was in the coffee can he kept in the tent," I said. "Which he apparently also used as a rustic commode."

"Very clever hiding place," Wright said.

"Well, the police have it now," I said.

"Well actually, no, they have the—" Char began.

I looked at Char and gave a tiny shake of my head.

"I mean, there are a bunch of duplicates now," Char said, "and the original, ah..."

"No worries," Wright said. "It seems we are keeping on schedule with our plans. And Char, rest assured that the Polaris is still very much alive and well. You may even get it back some day. Oh wait, I don't think so. Maybe your next of kin."

I didn't like the sound of that. Maybe keep the "old boy" talking until we had some kind of epiphany on how to turn things around.

"Just curious how you knew we'd be here," I said.

"Oh, why not chat for a while longer," Wright said. "Sometimes I do enjoy the drama of people trying to delay their demise. Well, your auntie was so very helpful. See I called and pretended I was a person wanting to board a horse and she said you had gone horseback riding with your hottie—that's what she called Mr. DNR here—hottie. She even told us where you were headed, which of course was worrisome. Back in the days of my employment with Wildwood, I stayed in this bloody bunkhouse for a while and it *seemed* an ideal place to stash Miss Houle. Let her just ferment away."

"You mean like Sasha Summers?" I said. "In the feed bin."

"He was supposed to bury her!" Swift said. "Lazy—"

"My, but your mouth does run on. News flash: by the time I had the *opportunity* to move Miss Summers from her temporary resting place, the bloody ground was frozen and hard as cement. A bit of miscalculation."

"Now who's the blabbermouth?"

"Touché." Wright sighed and looked at us. "While I've enjoyed our bantering, it really is time to leave. We'll have to borrow your horses as going on foot is so tedious. We need to put some distance in before the fire brigade gets here."

"Fire brigade?" Swift said. "And what do you mean borrow the horses? I'd rather walk! It's only a mile."

"I really don't want to have to tell you again, *Melony*, to shut up," Wright said. "I have no idea why I let you tag along."

"Tag along!" Swift said. "If it weren't for me, this thing would have blown sky high. It was me, *Justin*, who got the insulin—"

Wright sighed. "I really do wish you'd just—"

"It almost worked, too. Making it look like an accident," Swift said.

"You are an idiot," Wright said. "Though I do appreciate the arsenal of drugs that you pinched from that place you ran. Sure quieted down Sasha, but of course not permanently." He patted his waist. "Sometimes it just takes a bullet, so long as nobody is within earshot. The drugs did come in handy, including the insulin. But the fact that Summers ran around like a rabbit on steroids means it didn't work so great, now did it?"

"How was I to know how much to give?" Swift said. "Plus the jerk was supposed to be found sleeping in his tent, not out in the fucking woods. But it worked. Eventually."

"Is that why you needed my ORV a while back? To ambush Scott Summers?" Char said.

"Well, an ORV is perfect for sneaking in the back way to things," Wright said. "And I object to the implication that we ambushed Summers. He came willingly enough at first, thinking he'd get a chunk of change from us, what with the so-called 'insurance policy' he claimed to have in his tent."

"We pretended to go along with it," Swift said. "Then took him for a nice ride to this lovely cabin."

"Why did you call Wildwood looking for us?" I said. "The police–"

"Oh, you know, just trying to keep an eye on you. We knew Scott Summers and you, Miss Wilde, had *words*. I had no way of knowing what exactly he told you. Plus, of course, Nikko here is the son of the sheriff. I just didn't feel comfortable with you two sniffing around."

"We were waiting for my passport," Swift said.

"Well, as my nitwit partner here has said, we had a bit of a time crunch. Needed to stay ahead of the game until we could make our departure. Then Miss Houle turned on me. I could tell, even though she played along. She worked at your daddy's place and we had a feeling we might be running out of time. It was easy to shut that chap up that works there, Gussy I think he's called. He apparently has quite a thing for Miss Houle here. I of course knew it wouldn't be possible to keep you two from poking your nose in things. Thought about tucking you away somewhere."

"Pig!" Char said.

"I am weary of name-calling. And truthfully, pigs are noble creatures. Char, luv, you had such lovely names for me when we were an item."

"*Fucking* pig," Char reiterated.

Nikko tried to inch toward Wright, who pulled a gun out of his belt. "I wouldn't try anything if I were you," he said.

Nikko held up his hands and backed off.

32

"How much duct tape can one person use?" I said. "Talk about overkill."

Char, Nikko, and I had been forced back into the derelict cabin and told to sit on the floor with our backs to one another. Then Wright held a gun on us while Swift wrapped an entire roll of duct tape around all three of us. She taped our hands together at the wrists and our feet at the ankles. When the roll finally reached its end, she stood back to examine her handiwork.

"A few well-placed bullets would be so much more efficient," Wright said. "But guns make such a racket, and we really aren't tucked away quite enough to not draw attention. So, we think our plan B will be sufficient. Splendid job, Melany, except forgot to tape their mouths shut."

"Oh shit," Swift said. She looked at the empty tape roll. "Well, they can shout until they go hoarse, but nobody's gonna hear them."

"Time to skedaddle," Wright said. "Ta, all of you losers."

"Yeah, we gotta make the airport, what two hours ahead of—"

"Again, luv, shut up," Wright said.

"But they'll be—"

Wright looked at Swift. Not that it was helpful to us, but I had a feeling that she was not going to be his partner much longer. Clearly a liability and likely to cave under interrogation, should it come to that. Her scheme with the home health care place obviously went awry, likely due to a lack of visionary planning.

The door to the cabin shut behind them and plunged us into near darkness. We heard the barricade being placed across the door.

"We'll get out of here eventually," Nikko said. "As Wright said, your Aunt Lin knows where we are. Meanwhile, start working on getting your hands loose. Once someone does that, we can work on the other thousands of yards of tape."

The shutters on one of the windows had sagged out of square over the years, allowing a sliver of light to penetrate along the edges. A small wisp of fresh air trickled through, perhaps a pane was broken or cracked. With the air came a strange odor.

"Do you smell something?" I said.

"Like what?" Nikko said. "Did someone, you know, lose control?"

"Not recently," Char said. "It's not that kind of smell. This is, ah, like the stuff you squirt on charcoal."

"Lighter fluid," Nikko said. "There was a can next to the grill on the porch. They've sprayed something with lighter fluid?"

"Thus the mention of the fire brigade," I said.

"I smell smoke!" Char said.

"It won't be as easy as one might think to start an old place like this on fire," Nikko said. "Wood is spongy. Anybody making progress at getting her hands free? If you bend over and start chewing, that might work."

We could not bend forward, at least not far enough to gnaw on our wrist bindings, since we were tightly wrapped together at our torsos.

"I hear some crackling!" Char said.

"It could just be some leaves and twigs burning," Nikko said. "Should go out soon."

Within three minutes we could see flames flickering through the slits of the window shutters.

"Or, perhaps the shutters caught," Nikko said.

"I'm thinking that old varnish may be flammable," I said.

"We should scooch toward the door and try to kick it open," Char said.

"Nothing to lose there," Nikko said. "Okay, on the count of three!"

We managed to get a rhythm going, scooching a few inches at a time toward the door. It had been time consuming and the snap, crackle, pop of the fire increased. The frame around one of the windows gave way, and flames reached in and licked at the interior. We scootched more vigorously and eventually reached the door.

"Okay, brace yourselves and give me some support," Nikko said.

We did and he kicked mightily with both legs. The door gave a hearty thud and held firm.

"Again!" Nikko said.

And so on, until Nikko was exhausted and thought he may have injured one of his big toes. The flames reached aggressively through the window, searching for more fuel. The shutters had fallen askew and the window glass shattered, allowing lots of oxygen to feed the flames.

"Son of a bitch!" Char said, coughing. "This smoke is killing me. I have asthma."

"If any of you are good at praying, now would be a great time," Nikko said.

We were all silent for a moment. I began my silent prayer asking God's forgiveness for only checking in with Him at a time of need. However, I vowed to do better in the future, should He see fit to send a miracle our way. I have no idea what my fellow captives said to Him, but I assumed it was similar. God probably heard such pleas regularly and thought, *Oh, sure,* now *you believe in me. Well, better late than never...*

"What's that rumbling noise?" I said, gasping. "Fire trucks? They can't get back here."

"It's not a vehicle," Nikko said.

"Thunder?" Char said.

We all swiveled our heads trying to look at each other, you know, wondering if God really did answer our prayers.

"It's getting closer," I said. "Can't breathe..."

The next clap of thunder shook the entire cabin and a flash of lightning shone through the window.

The next sound was the muffled pounding of a downpour on the mossy roof and against the sides of the cabin.

We listened in silence.

"Ohmygod!" Char said. "God sent us rain to put out the fire!"

"I checked the weather at three places before we headed out today," I croaked, "and it was less than five percent chance of rain."

"Well, thank God for answered prayers," Nikko said.

The flames that had snaked inside the broken window began to retreat, like Satan shrinking away from an exorcist. We heard some hissing and billows of smoke poured through the window, but it was smoke from an extinguished fire, not an active one. Eventually the smoke subsided and fresh air poured in.

Just as quickly as it started, the rain quit and sunlight poked through the window.

Again, we were silent for a moment, mentally counting our blessings.

Nikko turned his head toward me. "Well, Miss Wilde, I will say one thing, besides being plucky, you sure know how to show a guy a good time. I bow to you, oh exalted mistress of adventure."

"Plucky?" Char said.

"Yeah," I said. "That's me."

* * *

"The two horses came galloping into the parking area, all lathered up," Aunt Lin said. "I thought to myself that you two had been thrown, and would come walking back, royally pissed off. I caught Misty and unsaddled her and put her out with Shadow. When I tried to do the same with Rusty, he would have no part of it."

We were sitting in the mod at my tiny table, smelling heavily of smoke, BO, and probably beer since we were all on our second one. Except Aunt Lin, who sipped her yucky tea. She did make some sandwiches for everyone, including a meat-eater's selection. We wolfed them down.

Char had borrowed some clothes from me, as hers were soiled from two days without access to a powder room. She vowed to burn them, even though they included her favorite pair of jeans and most flattering sweater.

Tobey lay at Nikko's feet and Jupiter stood coyly at the door, his tail lashing to and fro. We were waiting for the police to arrive along with Mom and Dad. I had no idea where everyone would sit. I made a mental note to look for some folding chairs at the thrift store.

"Well, anyway," Aunt Lin said. "Rusty wouldn't cooperate at all. Another beer anyone?"

"Actually," I said. "I'll make a pot of coffee. We don't want to be blotto when the cops get here."

"Good idea," Nikko said, finishing the last dregs of his beer.

"I'm so relieved that the horses found their way back," I said. "Wright said that he and Swift were going to take them to ride wherever they had the ORV stashed. I'm hoping Rusty dumped his ass and Misty followed his lead. In any event, they got loose or were set free and hightailed it back to the barn."

"He pawed the ground and tossed his head, then took off toward the horse camp," Aunt Lin said. "But he stopped, turned back, and looked at me. Well, it reminded me of those old episodes of *Lassie*, you know, where that collie wanted people to follow her because Timmy had fallen down a well."

We were all getting a bit bleary-eyed with Aunt Lin's digressions from the main talking point, being our incarceration and attempted murders. And then one couldn't forget God sending rain and maybe Aunt Lin, presumably, to wrap up our rescue. Aunt Lin was wound up and I wondered exactly what kind of tea she was drinking.

"Tobey was barking like crazy too. I mean do horses and dogs communicate? I think they do. Yeah, I'm sure. Anyway, I managed to get on Rusty—he was dancing around like a marionette—using that stupid wash tub to hoist myself up into the saddle. And before I got my other foot in the stirrup—oh, I think someone is here!"

I rose to my feet, stiff from the duct-tape experience, and peered out the kitchen window. It looked like Sheriff Olsen was the first to arrive. I opened the door and let him in. He took off his hat and looked at Nikko whose face was still smudged with soot and filth. My God, the sheriff was crying. He rushed over to Nikko who rose and the two embraced, thumping each other on the back. I started to feel a little choked up myself.

"You okay, Corndog?" the sheriff muttered to Nikko.

Corndog?

"Anyone got a tissue?" Char said, wiping her nose on the sleeve of my good sweatshirt she had borrowed.

"So, anyway, the rest is history," Aunt Lin said. "Ol' Rusty took off at a gallop, well, trot anyway, with that pooch at his heels and headed down the trail. I just flippin' hung on for dear life. Then I saw the smoke! Oh my God, I asked Rusty to hurry and boy, did he ever. That horse took me full speed right to the cabin. Tobey kept up, too. Looked like there had been a fire. I guess that bizarre rainstorm put it out, but still, there you all were tied up—or taped up. Sorry if I ripped off anyone's skin."

I stood and gave Aunt Lin a hug. "I forgot to thank you," I said. "You are beyond wonderful and I'm so lucky to have you here, lyre and all."

Our voices got a little warbly as we hugged and muttered our mutual love for each other.

The sheriff and Nikko broke their embrace and Aunt Lin and I did the same. We all took a deep breath.

"What's wrong with my lyre?" Aunt Lin said. "By the way, you need a shower."

That broke the emotional tension and we all burst out laughing.

"Okay, so here's the deal," Sheriff Olsen said. "State police are looking for the two. They have an APB out to the Minneapolis-Saint Paul Airport. We're banking on them heading there, since the woman let slip that they were headed to Minneapolis. Anyway, they'll look for and apprehend if they find a Melony someone—probably last name starts with an S since that's been her MO— along with Justin Wright or whatever alias he may be using. Authorities have both their photos. Ain't technology great? I'm thinking that since there aren't a lot of women named Melony, they might just find her on a flight roster. And the mention of a passport probably means international. Maybe Wright's homeland of England, or maybe some place less obvious. But they'll nab them. The FBI is involved as well. Oh yeah, those two are going down."

The coffee was done gurgling and I poured everyone a cup. I put the cream and sugar on the table along with my traditional plate of Oreo cookies.

"So that horse is a hero," Aunt Lin said, reaching for an Oreo. I wasn't about to tell her that Oreos might not be "kosher" to vegans. "When I got there, you know at the cabin, darned if Rusty didn't go to the door and pound on it with his hoof."

"That's my guy," I said.

"And the dog was barking like crazy!"

"Good boy!" Nikko said, reaching down to scratch behind Tobey's ears.

"And there you all were, trussed up like Thanksgiving turkeys."

"Well, we had worked loose a little," Nikko said.

Truthfully, it would have been hours getting the miles of duct tape off. We all had inhaled a lot of smoke and were exhausted. I was never so glad to see anyone as I was when Aunt Lin opened the cabin door and Tobey rushed in and leapt onto Nikko. Rusty stuck his head in the door and whinnied. Seriously.

Our captors had not bothered to search Nikko for weapons. While he didn't have a gun with him, he did have his Leatherman tool in a carrier on his belt. Aunt Lin got it out and sawed us out of our duct tape prison. I rode Rusty back to the stable, put him in his paddock, and got Uncle Phil's truck then drove back to the cabin to get everyone. The two-track was a challenge and I added a few "Yooper racing stripes" to the oxidized paint job of the truck but made it through. We all crammed into the cab, including Tobey, and rode back to Wildwood. Nikko used his phone to start the ball rolling with the police.

I gave Rusty a good rubdown and a few treats along with fresh water and hay. "Best horse in the world," I had told him, hugging his neck. "My superhero."

Floppy and her fawn appeared from behind the barn and walked cautiously toward Rusty and me. He perked up and nickered. The deer's timing was uncanny. I believed Aunt Lin was right about interspecies communication. Floppy was coming to be with her friend after his ordeal. I was sure of it.

"Anyone mind if I go lie down?" Char said. "I'm not feeling so great."

"I think she should be checked out," Aunt Lin said. "She might be shocky."

"I agree," Nikko said.

"I'll call an ambulance," Sheriff Olsen said, unclipping his shoulder mic.

I escorted Char to the couch in the living room and she flopped down. I covered her with a throw I kept on the back of the couch.

"Just-so-tired," Char said. "Are they gonna lock me up? Am I fired?"

"No, of course not," I said. Actually, I had no idea how things would play out for Char.

"Your folks are here," Nikko said from the kitchen.

I rushed to the kitchen door, flung it open, and raced into the parking lot. We collided into a three-way embrace. Sometimes even a grown-up girl needs a family hug.

"I told your father that your staying here wasn't a good idea," Mom said sniffing loudly. "My baby!"

"I'm fine," I said, looking at Dad.

He smiled and shrugged his shoulders. "Hey, our Kat can take care of herself."

"Sure can," I said.

Dad turned to look up Horse Camp Road. "Looks like the state police are here."

* * *

Sheriff Olsen had rushed out of the mod after hearing a call from Sergeant Haapala requesting backup. Just Nikko, Mom, and I were left sitting around the table as the minutes crawled past. Dad had offered to drive the state police out to the bunkhouse in his truck. Aunt Lin was meditating in her room.

"Wright and Swift," I said.

Nikko nodded. We were both thinking the same thing. The fugitives were armed and desperate. Nothing could be more dangerous for a police officer.

Mom got up and started puttering around the kitchen. She opened and closed the cupboards as if looking for some purpose. Next she washed some dishes by hand, even though I had a dishwasher. Tobey slept at Nikko's feet and Jupiter stared off into space. We heard Aunt Lin's lyre plunking away.

"That is one thing I don't miss," Mom said, putting the clean dishes into the cupboard. "I wonder if I should try to get in touch with Frieda."

"Mom has been through this many times," Nikko said. "We both have. Dad'll be fine, so long as he doesn't drive like a maniac and end up hitting a deer."

That brought a few chuckles.

The kitchen clock ticked loudly, its secondhand jerking around one increment at a time. It reminded me of a time bomb.

Nikko's cell phone rang.

"Nikko," he barked. "Yeah?" A smile spread across his face. "They got 'em."

⚞ 34 ⚟

Nikko and I sat basking in the warm sun on the tiny porch of the mod. Not a cloud in the sky and the birds were tweeting. The sun felt glorious on my face. The river was still running strong, and the rushing noise almost lulled me to sleep.

"Where did you get these chairs?" Nikko asked, "the village dump?"

"Hey, these were Uncle Phil's lawn chairs. Have a little respect."

"So, Wright and Swift got some 'splanin' to do, eh?"

"Oh, yeah," I said. "I heard their attorney was trying to get a deal for manslaughter instead of murder one. Don't think the DA will go for it."

"Sure, the gun just accidentally went off and killed Sasha, right?" Nikko said. "Then her body was stuffed in a feed bin. Yeah, those two are going bye bye for a long time. Just as we thought, Sasha Saari-Summers wanted a bigger piece of the action, so her so-called boss, Swift, decided she must be eliminated."

"I suspect Justin had a hand in it,"

"And the insulin strategy with Scott Summers was, well, kind of original."

"Supposed to look like he died of natural causes, I guess," I said. "It was their footprints with ours out in the woods by the horse camp. And Char's ORV, which apparently lover boy basically stole from her."

"Too bad we didn't get there sooner," Nikko said. "Summers died of cardiac arrest, apparently caused by severe hypoglycemia."

"Yeah, well you tried to revive him."

We were quiet for a moment, recalling the scene.

"Hey, keeping the so-called incriminating flash stick in his pee can was very creative on his part," I said.

"I'm kind of wondering about Char. Is she in the soup?" Nikko asked.

"Well, right now she's in a care facility. She kind of had a breakdown at the hospital when she went to be checked out."

"The looney bin?"

"We don't call it that," I said. "It's strictly voluntary on her part. She is getting some counseling. She has a lawyer—a good one. I think she'll get off, especially since she got that recording of Wright basically telling it all. Plus, I don't think Dad will press charges."

"How did they get that thing to open?" Nikko said.

"Raymond, who else?" I said. "He's the one that encrypted it and the police had him get it open."

We sat in companionable silence for a few moments. Nikko reached over and ran his hand down my bare arm. Things tingled.

"So," Nikko said. "Time to think about our next adventure."

I turned and gave him what I hoped was a withering look.

"Now, hear me out." He pulled out his phone. "I found something, ah, a little less rustic than our last adventures." He handed me the phone.

"Hmm," I said. "Surfside Resort. Luxury retreat for romance and adventure." I looked at him. "Are you making this up? Where is this place?"

"Check it out," he said. "It's in St. Ignace."

"Looks posh," I said. "Since when is St. Ignace posh?"

I flipped through the photo gallery and list of amenities. Of course there were plush king beds, fireplaces, beachside patios, indoor and outdoor pool, hot tub, sauna, massages, two dining rooms, music, bonfires, kayaks, a dinner cruise (extra fee) and ziplines.

"Ziplines?" I said.

"Sure. Why not?"

"Why not? How about me zipping to my death? Did you take out an insurance policy on me or something?"

"I put a deposit down," he said. "Not on an insurance policy! On Surfside. We have a date over Memorial Weekend. Surprise!"

I gave him another look. He waggled his eyebrows. "Adventure time! Of course we could do some more interim dating."

"*More?*" I said. "Have we ever actually had a date, *Corndog*?"

"I was wondering when you'd bring up the corndog thing.'

"Yes, well, do tell."

"I liked corndogs when I was a kid. Got them mostly at the fair. Dad said I'd turn into a corndog, and sometimes called me that. Corndog. Again, when I was a *kid*. Dad and I had a retro moment there after the bunkhouse debacle."

"And now?"

"Now what?"

"Do you still like corndogs?"

"Matter of fact, I do."

We turned our attention to a vehicle making its way down Horse Camp Road.

"Hey! Here they come."

"Who?" Nikko said.

"The 4Hoof Rescue people with my first foster horse," I said. "I *told* you about it."

Nikko shaded his eyes with his hand and we both stood and watched a truck and large stock trailer approach.

"Right, the foster horse thing, but I thought there was a lot of prep and all."

"Well, we did an interview by Zoom a while back. The physical inspection involved me taking a video of the place. I passed muster and they are delivering a horse they rescued from a meat auction."

"What kind of horse?" Nikko said.

"Don't know. His name is Big Mac, you know, like the hamburger."

"Perfect name for a meat auction," Nikko muttered.

The truck and trailer pulled around into the Wildwood parking area and stopped. A woman got out and stretched her back. I walked up and we shook hands. Finally, a woman with a decent handshake.

"Welcome to Wildwood Stables," I said. "I'm Kat Wilde and this is my friend, Nikko Olsen."

"Pleased to meet you both. I'm Marjorie VanderVeen. Boy, it's a long way up here, and I have to say your road is, well, challenging."

"Yeah," I said. "It's due for a good grading. On my to-do list."

I heard some thudding from the trailer.

"Big Mac is a sweetie," Marjorie said. "But he's been cooped up for a long time. Where are you thinking of putting him?"

"Well, I have a nice stall, or we can put him in a separate paddock from the other three horses. I have rigged—well my Aunt Lin actually fixed it so we can keep our new boy separate."

"Good idea. We don't want him to be tormented. He's been through hell. Please don't be upset when you see him. Believe me, he is doing much better. And been quarantined and vet checked."

Marjorie went to the back of the trailer and opened the ramp. She disappeared inside. There was some thudding and finally she came down the ramp leading the most enormous horse I had ever laid eyes on.

"A Belgian draft horse," Marjorie said. "Dumped at auction when he couldn't work anymore. Has arthritis. We figure he's about 20 or so."

I walked over to the horse and petted him. Big Mac was massive, in spite of being thin. He was honey colored with a cream mane and tail, as was typical for his breed. He had ugly scars on his chest and rump, but his hooves were recently trimmed and his coat was clean and held a sheen. Big Mac arched his neck and had a look around the place, ears swiveling.

"Hello big fella," I said taking the lead rope from Majorie. I led Big Mac over to the paddock and he followed me in. I gave him an apple flavored treat, which he mouthed a bit. Probably never had a treat in his life. Eventually the treat passed muster and he chewed and swallowed. I removed the lead rope and petted him. "Welcome home."

Marjorie handed me a packet of papers, which included a nice fat check.

"The goal is to find him a forever home," Marjorie said. "I'll contact you with any appointments that need to be set up for interested parties. You cannot sell or dispose of the horse yourself."

"Of course not."

"But who would want a used-up work horse?" Nikko said.

"Not the easiest one to place, but you'd be surprised how great these gentle giants are with kids. Well, gotta scoot. Please call me if you have *any* questions or concerns."

We all looked over at Big Mac. He was rolling gleefully in the mud. Rusty and the other two horses watched him then also dropped and rolled.

Marjorie laughed. "Monkey see, monkey do."

35

I was running hopelessly late when I stumbled into the office on Monday morning. Now I had *four* horses to tend to. While the paddocks worked out to a degree, they were not ideal at feeding time. My small herd of horses ranged from a dainty Arab to giant Belgian. Plus, Rusty was always pushing Shadow away from the hay rack. Thus, I had been putting the horses in their stalls at evening feeding time and leaving them there through morning chow. Rusty had capitulated to being stabled so long as the other horses were in their stalls as well. Once they finished eating, there was the tedious process of leading them out to their paddocks. And at some point the stalls needed cleaning, water buckets needed filling, and the aisle needed sweeping. Even with Aunt Lin's help and getting up at 5:00 a.m., the routine, followed by a quick shower and breakfast then a long commute, was incredibly time consuming. Plus the truck was being temperamental and refused to start until I lifted the hood and jiggled the battery cables. I felt as if I'd already put in a day's work by the time I *got* to work.

"Morning, Rose," I said as I tossed my satchel and laptop on my desk. "Sorry I'm—WOW!"

I caught a look at Gussy who was wearing a classic three-piece suit, complete with a yellow power tie and polished shoes. He had a new haircut, too. Very professional. Normally Rose butchered his hair every so often by, I swear, using a bowl and pruning shears.

"You look great!" I said to Gussy.

Rose was positively glowing. She hadn't even bothered to pull out her Nasty List drawer to notate my tardiness.

"Thanks!" Gussy said, reaching up to tug at the tie knot. "Ma got it on Amazon. She had to alter it some."

"Very nice," I said. "You look dashing!"

The reason for Gussy's new look was because he had been promoted by Dad from flunkie to assistant. He had been given Char's old office and a pay bump. I was offered his former cubicle but saw no great advantage in moving closer to Rose. Dad would need a new flunkie before the next tax season anyway. The rise in Gussy's status had Rose in a rare good mood. She even brought in a cake to celebrate his promotion.

Char Houle was on temporary leave from the office. How temporary, we weren't sure. She had been tightly wound all the time I had known her. The bunkhouse imprisonment, attempted murder, and of course being jilted by someone she was madly in love with sprung the intense coil of her being, and as the song says, she came undone. Dad had contemplated letting her go but then, as he said, "Love makes people crazy." He was saved from an immediate decision when Char decided to move back to Lower Michigan and live with her parents for a while. Her brother and his "woman" ran a cannabis store and Char was thinking of changing careers from bean counter to weed dispenser.

"Well, time to start the next newsletter," I said to nobody in particular.

Rose went back to frowning at her computer and Gussy pranced into his new office to attack some spreadsheets.

"Morning all," Dad said as he came in the door. "Beautiful day."

We muttered agreement.

Dad went up to his second story lair and we all put our noses to the grindstone. The blandness was palpable. I had to admit that it wasn't the same without Char.

*   *   *

When I arrived home, the parking area in front of the mod was lined with cars. I recognized Raymond's jeep with its tribal plates. Had no idea what he was doing there. A dark gray Subaru, which looked something like my old one, sat next to a big kickass truck, which may have been Al Koskinen's.

I was right about the truck. Susie Koskinen came out of the barn and waved at me. I waved back and walked over to her.

"Hi Kat," she said.

"Hi Susie. Nice to see you."

"I came for a ride. Hey, what kind of horse is *that?*" she said, nodding toward Big Mac.

"He's a Belgian draft horse. I'm fostering him," I said.

"He's *huge!*"

"And he does pack away the grub," I said. "Your dad bring you?"

"Nope. He let me drive the truck. I can barely see over the steering wheel. I don't have any classes for a while. Daddy decided that I can come out here without him now that the, um, murders are solved. And

I have a check for June and July. Daddy wants to pay early because he and Mom are taking off for a while. I have Shadow in the crossties. He looks great! Thank you."

"My pleasure," I said. "Hey, I'll go for a ride with you, but gotta go change. Feeding time is in about an hour. For the horses that is."

"Sure, I'm just spending time with Shadow. And maybe you can ride Misty?"

"You bet." I said, heading toward the mod. Al Koskinen had not only paid board in advance, but earlier had also donated some things to Wildwood, including several rolls of high-tensile wire for pasture fencing.

When I went in the mod, I found Aunt Lin and Raymond in her bedroom. No worries, he was apparently hooking up a television,

"Hi niece!" she said. "I got this TV like for nothing at Walmart. It was a display and Raymond is setting things up for me. I'm going to buy him a Bill's Burger later."

"Hey," Raymond said, poking his head out from behind the TV.

"Hey back."

"But how did you get to Walmart?" I said to Aunt Lin.

"My new car! Didn't you see it? The Subaru."

Aunt Lin's unemployment had run out a while ago and I was paying her a paltry wage. Of course she lived in the mod for free, but I couldn't imagine any dealership managing a car loan for her.

"Doesn't that Subaru look a little familiar to you?" she said.

"Sure, looks like my old one, only, well, in a lot better shape."

"It *is* your old one!"

"But how—"

"I won it in a raffle. Cost me twenty bucks for a ticket. The kids that fixed up your old Subaru raffled it off to raise money for the program."

"Wow!" I shook my head. Some people fell on their butt and some landed on their feet.

* * *

"There's a campground somewhere, isn't there?" Susie asked as she easily mounted Shadow from the ground. She didn't need the inverted washtub but just stretched one slender leg up into the stirrup and sprung into the saddle with ease.

"Yeah," I said clambering up the washtub and maneuvering my leg over my beloved Stübben saddle. "The old horse campground. Why?"

I settled my feet into the stirrups and wondered how the lady who sold me the saddle—Bernice—was doing. It was sad, having to give up something you love. Too much of that going around.

"Well, I was wondering about something. Can we go see it?"

"Sure."

We headed down the two-track toward the campground, riding side by side. I hadn't been out that way since the bunkhouse ordeal. The campground made the hairs on the back of my neck bristle. Nothing good had happened there, at least to me.

"Like, you know that I'm getting certified in equine therapy," Susie said.

"That's right. How's that going?" I gave Misty a little squeeze with my legs. She tended to want to dilly dally when heading away from the barn.

"Really well. Thing is, there isn't anything at all in Upper Michigan for equine therapy. And when I look for a job I want to work up here. The director of my program said there is a need, but, like, no money for it."

"Money is always a bump in the road."

"But she said that she could work on a grant, if we had a place, like a horse camp. It would be for special needs kids. I love working with them. They get so excited, riding a horse. Some of them have spent their whole lives in a wheelchair. Imagine for once looking *down* on someone instead of having to look up."

"I never thought of it," I had a feeling that I knew where this was going.

"Well, I guess I thought there was a campground here that maybe could be, like, fixed up and stuff."

"It would take a lot," I said. "The old campground is pretty much kaput. And if you had kids in wheelchairs, how would that work?"

"They make things accessible. Even the outhouses. They make cabin tents, with ramps and hard floors. Not all the kids with physical disabilities are in wheelchairs. And some are, like, emotionally disabled."

"Well, Susie, you certainly are an ambitious young woman. It's just up ahead."

"Yeah, just like you, Kat. I mean, this place gets better all the time."

"Thanks. It's been quite a lot of work."

We dismounted and Susie surveyed the weedy campground with its falling-down corrals and rusty fire rings.

"This doesn't look so bad," she said, looking around. "It's real peaceful. There could be campfire cooking and toasted marshmallows and trail rides and counting the stars in the sky. Can I have the director of the program call you?"

"Sure, I guess."

I felt the hair bristle again at the back of my neck. I wasn't able to envision the campground as anything but a reminder of things I'd just as soon forget. But I had to admire Susie's youthful enthusiasm.

I held the horses while she poked around. She got out her phone and started taking pictures. Then something spooked the horses and they nearly jerked free.

"What the..." I said, looking around for a skittering squirrel or chipmunk.

This time the phantom horse was a misty green. It tossed its head, causing the mane to ripple and wave in slow motion. The image pawed the ground and reared, its head disappearing into the foliage. I heard Susie yelp. The spectral horse faded and disappeared. Misty and Shadow were still tensed, staring at where the image had shown itself.

"What was that!" she yelled. "Did you see that? Did you?" A ghost, it was like a ghost. Ohmygod!"

At last someone else, besides another horse, saw it. And she had taken pictures.

* * *

We rode back to the barn at a brisk trot—fast enough to get away from the campground, but not so fast as to get the horses too hot. After untacking and putting them into their paddock, we headed to the mod.

Aunt Lin and Raymond were sitting on the couch. Raymond had an arm draped across Aunt Lin's shoulders and held a beer in the other hand. Aunt Lin was plunking out a tune on her lyre. Raymond seemed to be enjoying it. Jupiter sat staunchly on Raymond's lap, staring at Aunt Lin. It was close to his feeding time.

Susie looked at me as if to comment on the strangeness of things at Wildwood. I shrugged.

"Hey guys," Aunt Lin said. "How was your ride?"

"Well," Susie said. "It was, like, weird."

"Weird?" And Lin said. The plunking stopped and Raymond swiveled his head to look at us. He took the last swig of his beer and put the bottle on the coffee table. This freed up his hand to scratch Jupiter, who hunched against his touch.

"Yes, well—show them the picture, Susie," I said.

Susie took out her phone and scrolled through her photos until she came to one of the phantom horse. She showed it to Aunt Lin and Raymond.

"Hey, nice hologram," Raymond said. "Something for a class you're taking?"

Susie shook her head.

"This is an image that I've been seeing back in the old horse camp," I said.

Raymond just stared at me. "I saw it for the first time way back when we found Sasha's body. I thought it was a real horse. I told the police and they thought I was a nut case, so I never mentioned any more sightings."

"We *both* saw it today," Susie said. "The horses spooked."

Raymond nodded and took Susie's phone. He studied the photo and thumbed through a few more.

"Looks like it's from the hologram show I set up for Phil back when the horse camp was being used. There were a lot of different images. I used a special propeller and projector that worked outdoors on solar power."

"Seriously?" I said. "I never heard anything—"

"It was all for fun. A mystery event, you know, the haunted campground and all. Great family adventure. None of the images were scary. Friendly animals."

"So, why didn't you dismantle the, ah, hologram contraption when people quit camping?" I asked.

"I did."

Aunt Lin plunked out a tune on her lyre that mimicked the theme song from the early 60s TV series, *The Twilight Zone.*

* * *

Maybe it was hearing the lyre that triggered something in my brain and connected some dots. I hustled to my bedroom and pulled the photos I had set aside from my search through Uncle Phil's memorabilia. I looked again at him on the horse, Eclipse. Then the "final inspection" and the two when he was with "M," who I was pretty sure was the reason Uncle Phil bought into the whole idea of Sasha being his offspring. But how did Sasha find Uncle Phil? I could find no evidence that my uncle and "M" had any after-service contact, let alone their so-called offspring.

I looked closer at a few of the photos I had skimmed through. Then I found the clincher—actually two of them. The first was a photo of Uncle Phil and another soldier standing at a table doing some sort of project. There was a saddle on the table and what appeared to be a disassembled bridle. Both men wore Army fatigues. I was almost positive I knew who it was. There was something about the smirk and the jutted chin that seemed familiar. He was much younger in the photo, but the telltale birthmark confirmed it as Scott Summers. A second photo was stuck to the back. When I pried them apart, I was delighted to find a nice picture of "M" and Scott Summers. She had her arm around him and was smiling for the camera. He looked mighty glum. The inscription on the back probably explained why. It simply said: *My baby shipping out.*

I wondered if Uncle Phil took that photo of mother and son. If "M" was indeed Mary Saari-Summers. Of course she was. And obviously, if Uncle Phil had developed a special relationship with her, then likely he knew about her son, Scott. Thus, perhaps took the young man under his wing, as shown in the first photo.

So, Scott Summers certainly knew that there was *something* going on between his mother and Uncle Phil. One can only guess why Scott Summers pursued such a twisted, downright evil plan. Jealous? Angry? Post traumatic stress?

36

"I think you're going to have two black eyes," Nikko said as he pulled the cold compress off my face. "Nose is a little red, but the eyes—"

I snatched the compress—a plastic storage bag full of ice wrapped in a towel— away from Nikko and returned it to my face. I wasn't speaking to him for the moment, though it really was a freak accident.

The romantic getaway had started out splendidly. It was a glorious day to begin the Memorial Day weekend. We had a lovely drive—we borrowed Aunt Lin's Subaru—and arrived at the swanky Surfside Resort in time for a mid-afternoon cocktail and late lunch. We checked into a plush king room with luxurious bathroom and jacuzzi tub. There was a balcony overlooking the harbor and a separate little area in the room with a couch and coffee table. Another nook held a small round table and chairs. As promised, Surfside was a dream, with a fancy restaurant, pub, pool, and all the other upscale amenities. In an attempt to stand above all the rest, the resort featured semi-extreme activities such as off-roading, kayaking, and, of course, ziplining.

I knew it was a bad idea from the get-go, but was darned if I'd be taunted by Nikko, perhaps for all eternity, if I didn't give it a try. I'll admit, the first fifteen seconds or so were thrilling, zipping past the newly minted green leaves of the forest, feeling the rush of wind on my cheeks. And then something just swooped down and bashed into my face. I was to later learn that it was an eagle. While the thing did lose a couple of feathers, a fellow resort guest with binoculars said that it flew away, seemingly unharmed, and landed in the top of a very tall pine tree. In my short walk back to the room (I refused medical attention, except for an ice pack), people pointed and said things like, "There she goes! It's the eagle girl." And, "Wow! Did you hear that woman scream?" And so on.

"Good thing the eagle was okay," Nikko said. "They're protected, you know. I might have to lock you up!"

I took the compress off my face and glared at him.

He held up his hands. "Just kidding. Okay, after the bunkhouse and duct tape situation, maybe not the best thing to say. Anyway, the guy at the zipline said he's had people throw up, pass out, soil themselves, and occasionally twist an ankle but never—"

"So glad to make history. Maybe they'll put me in Ripley's."

"If it makes you feel any better, they shut the zipline down."

"Why would I feel better?" I snapped. "I feel like an idiot. Everyone will know it was me that wrecked their fun. I mean, I can't exactly cover up two black eyes and a gash on my cheek. I'll stand out in the crowd."

"Not really a gash. A pretty good scrape, though. Good thing you had on a helmet, or you might have been scalped by eagle talons. You wouldn't be the same without your crazy curly hair."

I reached up and felt my hair, which had been twisted into a nest of snarls.

"Anyway," Nikko said, "I told the zipline attendant that the eagle was probably nesting nearby and thought it was protecting its territory. You invaded its territory, see, and it was just trying to drive you off."

"Oh, it drove me off alright," I said. "I won't be zipping there again. Ever. You and your adventures!"

"Actually," Nikko said, "the bunkhouse was technically your adventure."

I glared at him. "Calling two murders, a kidnapping, and three attempted homicides an adventure is probably the understatement of the century."

"Fortunately, Wright and Swift are locked up with no bail," Nikko said. "I think it's hilarious that they got Char's Polaris stuck. They had the thing in two-wheel drive. If they'd switched to four-wheel, they'd have driven right out of there. According to Dad, the two of them fought like a couple of wolverines and had to be taken to the station in separate cruisers. I think the feds are working on tracking down the funds those two stashed away. More victims are coming out of the woodwork. Purloined money is likely in an overseas account. But maybe it will get sorted out and who knows, your dad could get something someday on behalf of your uncle."

"I know Uncle Phil and Mary Saari-Summers had either a friendship or something more during his time in the service," I said. "But it was Scott, not Sasha and probably not Melissa Swift, who initiated scamming Uncle Phil with the love child ploy. Obviously, Scott and Uncle Phil knew each other in the service. Maybe my uncle even took him under his wing. I'm not sure when Mary Saari-Summers passed away, but it was after she was discharged and into civilian life.

Summers was close enough to Uncle Phil in the Army to know where he'd be headed after he mustered out."

"Mustered out," Nikko said. "Wow, since when did you get so—military?"

"Hey, listen and learn. Summers perceived that his mother and my uncle were intimate. I guess they must have been, though obviously Uncle Phil eventually turned out to be gay."

"Gay people sometimes try to live the life expected of them," Nikko said. "Or sometimes people are attracted to both sexes."

"Hmm," I said. "You seem quite knowledgeable."

"All part of the training we have crammed—er we're exposed to."

"I think it was Scott who planted the idea with Swift at Yarrow to extort from their clientele," I said. "And, as you probably know, Sasha was not Scott's half-sister, but rather his wife, though it was a very short marriage when death did part them."

"Yeah," Nikko said. "A pretty, young, and foolish wife who likely went along with her husband's scheme. Scott couldn't come around when Phil was alive because he would have been recognized, so he needed someone on the inside. Dad said that the state police have been digging around and found that Sasha may have been a runaway back when she was a minor. Might have a fingerprint match. Her real last name was Polish—I think Sarna—something like that. They're trying to track down her parents in Hamtramck. Give them some closure. That is, if they're still alive."

"And if they care," I said. "Sadly, Scott and Sasha's grand ideas and greed cost them both their lives. I feel as if Sasha was just a patsy. Scott was still looking for a payoff, even after his wife was murdered."

"Yeah," Nikko said. "Nice guy. A real bottom-feeder."

"And Uncle Phil is not around to shed more light on all of this."

"I had a feeling all along that Swift didn't get the idea herself. She was, well, not too swift. I mean everyone knows Trump's wife's name is Melania *not* Melony."

"Sure."

"I bet Swift will, as they say, sing like a canary," Nikko said. "They recovered Wright and Swift's guns. Likely something will match with the bullet that killed Sasha."

"I wonder how long this will take to untangle," I said. "Dad's still a little unnerved that this was all going on right under his nose. I mean, he hasn't quite been himself. Worries me."

"Well, maybe my plucky girlfriend can turn that around, you know, get Wildwood Stables back into a new heyday."

"There you go with the plucky," I said. "Makes me think of a chicken."

"Nope—you soar like an eagle!"

I took a swipe at him with the compress and ice flew all over.

"Well, that broke the ice!" he said. "Literally."

I rolled my eyes but felt a smile tug at my lips.

"How about a glass of wine from the mini bar?" he said.

"They'll gouge you if you use anything out of the fridge."

"Hey, cost is no object if it will make you happy. And if you don't want to go out into public, we can order room service."

"Okay, I'll take a glass of whatever is in there. But I'm not hungry."

We both sipped our wine. I was getting over things a little. The knotted mess of the past few weeks seemed to be loosening up. But I was still steamed that not one, but two people took advantage of my Uncle Phil, especially when he was in the final stretch of his life.

"Penny for your thoughts," Nikko said, putting his arm around me.

"Just thinking about how greedy people are, I guess."

"Well, a couple of them are dead and a couple more in jail."

"Yeah, there is that. I want to kill them all. But of course, then I'd be in jail."

"Well, as my father likes to say, 'Let God sort them out.'"

"We'll probably be called as a witnesses at some point, along with Char, and Gussy. Probably Dad, too."

Nikko shrugged. "Maybe. Since Wright and Swift's ill-gotten gains are currently inaccessible and the two don't have much on-hand cash, they have court-appointed counsel. I'm thinking plea bargaining, which means no trial."

I didn't like the thought. "They better not get off."

"Nope, not with that recording and the papers from your office, not to mention a large collection of first-hand witnesses and, oh, let's not forget the confiscated guns. Wright's was a semi-automatic Glock, locked and loaded. Swift had an older Colt revolver on her, empty. And they were headed to the airport, so must have had a plan to ditch the weapons at some point. Fortunately, that hadn't happened yet. I'm betting that Wright's gun was the one used to kill Sasha. The evidence has piled up pretty high against both of them."

I was starting to feel mellow from the wine and the aftereffects of my fading zipline adrenaline rush, so asked him, "Do you believe in the supernatural?"

"Where did that come from?"

"Oh, someday I'll share my experience with you," I said, smiling.

"I'm intrigued."

"Good."

I had not been back to the horse camp since riding there with Susie when we saw the misty green vision of the horse. Raymond, who was a man of few words and also held a strong belief in the spiritual aspects of nature, just shrugged and advised me to accept that some things remain unknown. We should respect what we don't know and not try to destroy it. No wonder he and Aunt Lin had hit it off. Part of me wanted to believe that Raymond was being deep and metaphysical and part of me cautioned that I was being hoaxed.

Nikko reached up and ran a finger softly across the so-called scrape, which I think was a disfiguring gash from the eagle's talon—and then traced the same finger down my cheek, to the neck.

"Does it hurt?" he asked

"My neck doesn't. You can forget the lips, though. I think they're swelling."

He bent down and kissed my neck.

"I'm still mad at you," I said. "I get to plan the next adventure." Whatever it was going to be, it would involve riding horses and maybe herding cattle or foxhunting. The options were many, yet costly.

"Um huh," he said, moving to my earlobe. "What can I do to make it better?"

"I did not give you permission to nibble my earlobe," I said.

"Oh? Sorry," he said, pulling away.

"I didn't say you should stop."

We set our empty wine glasses on the coffee table.

"Okay, just say *uncle* if you want me to stop," he mumbled as he moved to the back of my neck, making me shiver. We had somehow shifted from sitting to lying down.

"Oh, I never cry uncle," I whispered.

Sneak Preview for
Kat's Next Adventure
STRAW HORSE

⚡ 1 ⚡

"Are you okay?"

I heard the words but couldn't answer.

"Susie, call 911!" Nikko said.

911?

"How will they get her out of here?" Susie asked.

"They'll need to know we're on the trail about a half mile from Big Lake Road, and they'll wanna bring a portable stretcher. Kat, can you hear me?"

"I got no bars," Susie said.

"Mine's satellite. Use it."

Big Mac!

"She blinked! She's trying to say something."

This observation came from Nikko Olsen, whose face was strangely out of focus. Nikko was my sort-of boyfriend and a Michigan Department of Natural Resources (DNR) conservation officer, or CO for short. He was assigned a couple of counties away, but his roots were in Peshekee (Pah-Shee-Key) where I happened to live.

"Big Mac!" I shouted. At least I thought I had shouted it.

"She's mumbling something," Nikko said. "Where the hell is the ambulance?"

"It's only been, like, two minutes since I called. I think she was asking about Big Mac."

This last string of words sounded like someone talking underwater, but I still recognized the voice as Susie Koskinen's. Susie is a college girl with a lot of ambition.

"It's been more than two minutes," Nikko said. "Kat! Can you hear me?"

I nodded. The entire county could likely hear him. Maybe the ambulance could follow the bellowing. Kat is short for Kathryn. My last name is Wilde. People love to tinker with my name. Very annoying people.

"Big Mac!" I said.

"She's wondering about Big Mac," Susie said.

Big Mac was the Belgian draft horse I had been riding. Susie, Nikko, and I had been cantering through the woods when something caused my horse to bolt. Mac is a rescue horse I have been fostering through an equine rescue nonprofit called Four Hoof Rescue, or 4HR. He's a big fella, but generally solid as a rock. Susie was the reason I had been out riding Big Mac. We were testing him out for his suitability for special needs children to ride. Susie was studying to become an equine therapist and had wrangled me into her plans.

"I expect he's headed back to the barn," Nikko said.

"Nope," Susie said. "He's right over there. Got no bridle."

"Huh?" I said, running my hand over my face. When I took my hand away, there was blood. Nikko had pulled my helmet off and was dabbing at my face.

Great. Just call me Scarface. Another gash on my face. It would be added to the talon slash across my cheek, delivered by a territorial eagle during my zipline escapade, which had been Nikko's idea of an adventure. The current disaster was my doing and had been meant to be a simple ride in the Crystal Lake Wilderness, which abutted my land.

Branches snapped. Voices.

Some might call me accident-prone. But it wasn't until I "inherited" my uncle's horse operation, Wildwood Stables, that my physical wellbeing had seemed to be in constant peril. Since taking ownership, I have suffered a torn meniscus (knee injury), been nearly defaced by the aforementioned eagle, endured an apocalyptic storm during a kayak adventure, barely escaped a live cremation (courtesy of a couple of baddies who had been blackmailing my uncle), and now find myself seeing stars and apparently bleeding to boot. Well, life isn't dull.

"Over here!" Nikko shouted.

Next thing I knew, I had a bandage slapped on my face, a contraption put around my neck, and then, they carefully lifted me onto a stretcher. Someone put a blanket over me and secured their handiwork with several straps.

"Is he okay?" I asked.

"I'm fine," Nikko said.

"She means Big Mac," Susie said. "I got him. He's fine, but the bridle is toast. Don't worry, Kat; he'll follow Shadow and Rusty back to the barn."

Shadow and Rusty were Susie and Nikko's mounts.

On the count of three, the first responders hoisted the stretcher.

"I swear to God," one of them muttered. "I'm getting too old for this."

Nikko leaned over me. "I'll get to the hospital as soon as we get the horses back to the barn."

* * *

The person who pulled the curtain back was the same incredibly handsome doc who had treated me during my last visit to the emergency department at Peshekee Memorial. His ID badge featured a name that was long and complicated. He smiled.

"Hello. I'm Dr. Zahid Sulaimankhel," he said with a trace of a Middle Eastern accent.

"Me again," I said. "Nice to see you Dr. ah...."

"Call me Dr. Zee. I remember you. You're the horse person!"

"Uh huh."

"My wife has *three* Arabians now. I will never be able to retire."

This made me smile. It was true. Horses were a money pit. My late Uncle Phil, from whom I had indirectly inherited Wildwood Stables, had been deeply in the red before he passed away from cancer. So far I wasn't doing a whole lot better financially than Uncle Phil and still had to keep my part-time pity job at Wilde Accounting, which was owned and operated by my father, Gary Wilde. My mother handled payroll and benefits.

"So, you had a fall. Laceration on your left cheek." He looked at it. "No sutures needed. It will heal well with the butterfly bandages we put on. X-rays came back okay. I understand you were wearing a helmet, but the EMTs indicate you were dazed."

"Uh huh."

"How are you feeling now?"

"Ridiculous," I said, sitting up. "I'm fine."

It was a lie. The room took a spin, and I grabbed the handrails of the bed.

"Perhaps a mild concussion, in spite of the helmet," he said. "No other apparent injuries."

Someone said, "Thank you, nurse." The curtain swished open, and my mother, the one and only Clara Wilde, bustled into our cramped space.

"Kathryn Wilde!" she bleated. "What on earth—oh, hello, doctor, er...."

"Dr. Zee," I said. "Same one who saw me when I messed up my knee."

The knee injury had occurred during a tussle with the now deceased Scott Summers, who had claimed ownership of Wildwood Stables. His twisted scheme involved a secret marriage to Uncle Phil's caregiver, Sasha, who posed as my uncle's love child from his military days. Sasha had been the first dead body found at Wildwood Stables. Scott Summers had been the second. Both were homicides. We're trying to live it down.

Dr. Zee shook Mom's hand and gave a 100-watt smile. "Your daughter will be fine. I do have to ask, however, was she accident-prone as a child?"

"Let's just say she didn't have tea parties and play with dolls," Mom replied.

"Hey, Mom," I snapped. I wasn't keen on my mother recounting my unorthodox childhood. Mom found my preference for "boys' toys" over girlie things troublesome.

"Hello, darling," she said, bending over to give me a peck on the cheek. "How are you?"

"I'm okay, and Nikko will be here soon to take me home," I said, giving Dr. Zee a hopeful look.

"Nikko called me, dear. I'm here to take you home. He said he's having the vet out to look at some horse—Max? Apparently a cut on his leg."

"Oh no!" I said. "Mac, not Max. I've got to get out of here. Can someone put this rail down? Where are my clothes?"

Dr. Zee placed a hand on my shoulder, blocking my futile attempts to push down the bedrail.

"Now Miss Wilde, no need to worry. I'm sure your horse will be fine. In any event, I intend to discharge you so long as you don't drive for at least forty-eight hours, and you cannot be alone tonight. Also, no horseback riding for a few days. I don't want your brain bounced around right now, and we need you to watch for symptoms of a concussion. The nurse will give you instructions, and if your condition worsens, which I don't expect, please give your regular doctor a call or come back to the emergency department." He turned to a laptop attached to a rolling apparatus and began briskly typing.

"Oh dear," Mom said. "I can take her home, but her father and I are leaving tonight for a conference."

"Nikko…" I said.

Mother gave me a penetrating look. Nikko staying with me overnight was clearly not an option.

"I mean for a while," I said. "Aunt Lin will be around tonight. I'll be okay so long as she doesn't try to poison me with one of her tea concoctions."

The click of computer keys halted and Dr. Zee looked up from his laptop.

"Kidding," I said. Aunt Lin is what some would call eccentric. I call her a lifesaver for the help she is at Wildwood Stables, and all for a paltry wage. Plus, she can cook, though mainly vegan, and keeps our cat, Jupiter, mellow on catnip. Aunt Lin is my only and thus favorite aunt. She is Mom's much younger sister and more like an older sister than an aunt to me. She lives with me in a modular home—the mod—at Wildwood Stables along with Jupiter, who I swear is part raccoon or ocelot or both. Aunt Lin is beyond eccentric, and I love her, in spite of her determination to play the lyre and push strange herbal tea on everyone.

"Well, I suppose Lindsey will have to do, though I'd rather have you home."

Lindsey was Aunt Lin's full first name. To Mom, the mod was where I lived and home was where I grew up.

"Well, then, that will do fine," Dr. Zee said, snapping his laptop shut. "The nurse will be in shortly."

* * *

Mom dropped me off at the mod with strict instructions to "take it easy." Fortunately, she was in a hurry to go home to do some laundry and pack for her and my father's trip to Chicago for some kind of accountants convention. While the CPAs would be inundated with deadly PowerPoint presentations and handouts featuring esoteric bullet points and colorful Venn diagrams, Mom would be hitting the shopping district in the Loop. Neither activity remotely appealed to me.

Wildwood Stables is located at the end of Horse Camp Road, a rutted, washed-out dirt monstrosity that keeps out the riffraff and gives welcome visitors second thoughts about coming. Aunt Lin's Subaru was not parked at the mod, so I wouldn't be facing any questions or medicinal tea from her. I had to admit it rankled me a bit that Aunt Lin's Subaru used to be *my* Subaru. The vehicle betrayed me and developed a multitude of expensive problems. I sold it to Mike's Auto to be sacrificed to a bunch of teenagers enrolled in a program to learn by "doing" under the mentorship of a supervisor. Once the Subaru was in tip-top shape, it was raffled off. Aunt Lin purchased the winning raffle ticket for $25. Some people just had all the luck.

My aunt had many things on her plate, including a meditation class, vegan cooking, and music lessons on the lyre. For the latter, she was mainly self-taught via YouTube since there weren't many local opportunities for professional lessons on ancient Greek musical instruments.

I slipped just inside the door and watched Mom pull away. The moment she moved out of view, I hustled to the barn to check on Big Mac. When I got there, the vet had already left and Mac was quietly munching hay in his double-size stall. Susie and Nikko were giving Rusty and Shadow their post-ride rubdowns.

"How is he?" I asked, rushing over to Mac's stall and sliding the door open.

"He's fine," Nikko said, coming over to me. "How are you? Hey, sorry. I couldn't come to get you. What's the word from the doc?" He pushed my hair away from my face and looked at the crusty cut on my cheek, then gave me a chaste kiss on my cracked lips.

My hair, on a good day, could best be described as an overgrown shrub. On a bad day, it had a zip code of its own. My mother claimed it was our Hungarian blood. That, combined with the Irish side of the family—being Dad's—caused my hair to somehow get caught in a deranged genetic battle. Having Hungarian hair combined with my 5'9" height made me a bit of an outcast during my high school years. While being tall was handy when assigned a top locker, it tended to be intimidating to boys who had not yet reached their final growth spurt.

"I'm fine," I said. "Just have to take it easy for a day or two. Can't ride or skydive. I can go to work tomorrow, though. Yippee. What about Mac?"

Susie came over to join us. "His leg was cut from the brush you guys got into. I mean, it was a bramble bush. Dr. Jukkila did some stitches in his hind leg and gave us this ointment to put on the other cuts. There's, like, a million of them."

I went into Mac's stall, looked at the damage, and petted his neck. Mac, being a cold-blooded horse, was generally calm and steady. The term cold blood to describe a horse has nothing to do with the actual blood but relates to the earlier breeds coming from arctic regions. Draft horses are generally referred to as cold bloods for their steady work ethic and quiet, dependable temperaments, in contrast to the hot bloods, such as Arabians and Thoroughbreds. Mac looked over at me and stopped chewing his hay.

"What was that all about?" I asked him. It just wasn't like Mac to spook and bolt as he had in the Crystal Lake Wilderness. He had run blindly into the bramble thicket, somehow losing his bridle and throwing me into Br'er Rabbit's habitat.

"He seems calm now," I said. "But something sure set him off out there."

"Maybe a deer?" Nikko said.

"Are you kidding?" I said. "Deer are all over the place here, and he never bats an eye."

"Maybe something blew across the trail," Susie said.

"Yeah, but there wasn't a breath of wind," I said.

"Do you think he smelled a bear or maybe a moose?" Nikko asked. "A moose would spook anything. They're beyond weird looking."

"Shadow didn't spook," Susie said. "Wouldn't he and Rusty have smelled or seen something too? And Shadow will freak at a gum wrapper on the trail."

"Could be poachers," Nikko said. "Not my district, but I can still check it out."

CO Nikko Olsen: always on duty.

Mac gave me a benevolent look, sighed, and shook his head as if to tell us we were on the wrong trail.

About the Author

Gift Horse is Terri Martin's second full length mystery, and the beginning of the Kat Wilde mystery series. Martin also has three anthologies of humorous short stories, which were previously published in UP Magazine. In addition, she has two middle-grade novels, with *The Home Wind* being the recipient of the U.P. Notable Book award. She started her writing career as a regular contributor to several Midwest publications and has authored seven books of fiction. Her stories often reflect the culture and characters she has encountered during her 25 years of living in Upper Michigan. Terri and her husband enjoy watching the menagerie of freeloading wildlife from their home on the Silver River. While the winters are harsh, the soul never tires of the beauty of the Northwoods.

Martin has a master's degree in English and has taught college success courses, tutored English at the college level, and served as an aide for college composition classes.

Visit Terri's website at www.terrilynnmartin.com or e-mail her at gnarlywoodspub@gmail.com

This witty and suspenseful romantic mystery is set in Michigan's Upper Peninsula, where life for Kathryn "Kat" Wilde is anything but tranquil. Though only in her mid-twenties, Kat finds herself juggling the many demands of a struggling horse operation, Wildwood Stables, while navigating a perplexing romance with her "sort-of" boyfriend, DNR officer, Nikko Olsen. A pleasant trail ride on her rescue horse, Big Mac, turns harrowing when her horse bolts and throws her for no apparent reason. The mishap begins a chain of events, starting with the discovery of two bodies deep in the wilderness. Kat soon launches her own investigation, which circles back to something very rare and valuable on Wildwood land. Bad things happen and sabotage is suspected, but by whom or what? The arrival of dodgy characters intensifies Kat's suspicion that someone or something is targeting her beloved Wildwood Stables, and she needs to find out why. Rich in humor, heart, and intrigue, *Straw Horse* blends romance and suspense with unforgettable characters and a setting as wild and unpredictable as the heroine herself.

"*Straw Horse* is everything a great mystery is made of—loveable characters, mysterious strangers, a whack job or two, a little romance, some family secrets, and plenty of action. Terri Martin has created the beginnings of a soon-to-be favorite UP series with this second installment of Kat Wilde's anything-but-dull life as she handles horses, investigates murder and mayhem, and gets to know better the man in her life."
— Tyler R. Tichelaar, PhD and award-winning author of *The Mysteries of Marquette*

"The Kat comes back in *Straw Horse*, author Terri Martin's second installment in a hopefully long run of U.P. mysteries, starring stable owner/sleuth Kat Wilde.Martin's humor and endearing cast of supporting characters, ranging from a cow-eyed accountant to a lyre-playing hippie aunt, help Kat cinch the deal in *Straw Horse*, a true pleasure to read."
—Nancy Besonen, author of *Off The Hook* and *Off The Hook*

A suspicious death in a game processing meat locker is just the beginning of bizarre events happening in the Upper Michigan village of Moose Willow. It all starts when a mysterious woman appears at the Methodist church during choir practice. Janese Trout and her best friend, State Trooper Bertie Vaara, team up to connect the woman to a growing number of disturbing occurrences around town includeing the disappearance of Janese's eccentric lover, George LeFleur, and an undeniable increase in Bigfoot sightings. Meanwhile, Janese faces a multitude of personal challenges as she grapples with a sagging career at the Copper County Community College, an elusive pregnancy test, and a controlling mother who inserts herself into every hiding place of Janese's life.

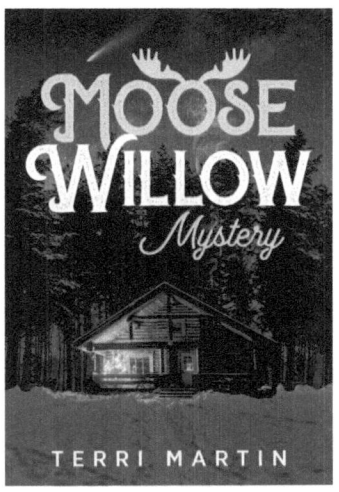

"*Moose Willow Mystery*, by Terri Martin, lets cozy mystery fans know they are about to experience something wildly different with edgy characters, a big dose of humor, and an insider's look at America's best-kept secret the mysterious Upper Peninsula of Michigan."
—Carolyn Howard-Johnson, award-winning writer of fiction, poetry, and the HowToDoItFrugally Series of books for writers

"Terri Martin manages to present the ordinary, the bizarre (of which there is a steady stream), and even the violent in a way that will open a hilarious glimpse into the world of a small town. With brilliant characterization, she takes the reader on a wild ride of murder and mayhem, so let me warn you. Don't start reading until you have the time to keep going."
—Bob Rich, PhD, author of *Sleeper, Awake!*

Take a mini-vacation and read this delightful mystery! Laugh away the problems of the world (and cry a few times) along with the remarkable, talented characters in *Moose Willow Mystery*. A refreshing whodunit with plenty of mystery to keep the reader unable to put the book down."
—Carolyn Wilhelm, M.A., *Midwest Book Review*

Learn more at www.TerriLynnMartin.com

Featuring Yooper Woodswoman Nettie Bramble!

Nettie Bramble lives with her ma in Upper Michigan in a cabin that's slightly off the grid. She claims to "subsist" off the land and prefers to do so without the benefit of hunting or fishing licenses. Nettie is bound to have a clash or two with the local woods cop, CO Will Ketchum, and the chronically cranky Judge Nightshade. Most places that Nettie goes, her "citified" nephews, Wanton and Wiley, tag along to muddle up her plans. Nettie will meet up with Church Lady Bea Righteous, as well as Tami and Evi Maki (thrice-removed cousins) in an erratic road rally with a cash prize that brings out the worst in everyone. No spoiler alert for the surprise ending in this collection of short stories featuring a strong dose of the Yooper way.

"Terri Martin writes fast-paced little tales peppered with humorous disasters following one after another... If you live in the U.P., you'll have heard plenty of fish tales and hunting sagas from your outdoor friends. Some of them may be whoppers, but none as big as the ones Nettie Bramble tells."

—Jon C. Stott, author of *Yooper Ale Trails*

"Roadkill Justice has to be among the funniest books I have ever read. Our heroine's ongoing battle with the law, the clever use of malapropisms and the caricature of a now-gone culture had me laughing several times on every page."

—Bob Rich, author of *Hit and Run*

"Roadkill Justice's" unlikely heroine, Nettie Bramble, is rough-edged but 'big-hearted, with 'sisu' to spare. Author Terri Martin does a fantastic job of capturing the spirit and the spunk of the Northwoods character in a plot that sweeps her reader along, like a fast-running trout stream, on a delightful ride filled with twists, turns, laughter and the occasional explosion."

—Nancy Besonen, author of *Off the Hook*

Learn more at www.TerriLynnMartin.com

Join Iris and the Voodoo Shack gang as they investigate a mysterious death and an unsolved crime!

When 11-year-old Iris Weston discovers a ramshackle hunting cabin deep in Hazard Swamp, she and her friends decide it's perfect for a secret clubhouse. The gang dubs it the Voodoo Shack and meets there to swap stories and play card games. Ol' Man Hazard, the former owner, died under mysterious circumstances, and the kids speculate whether it was an accident, suicide or maybe even murder! The gang believes that cash from an unsolved crime  may have been stashed within feet of the cabin. Even as things go badly awry, feisty Iris learns how to use her wit and independence to put things right, discovering what family really means in this adventurous and often humorous coming-of-age story set in rural Michigan in 1962.

"Set in the early 1960s, Martin's novel traces a girl's journey toward understanding the true meaning of love, family and friendship. Iris is an appealing character whose relationships with friends and family are realistically portrayed as she struggles to find her place."
—*School Library Journal*

"Martin has drawn on her childhood memories to create an engaging, feisty heroine, lively supporting characters and an easy-to-visualize early 1960s rural Michigan setting. And, although Iris doesn't solve all her mysteries, she finds the answers to the most important ones in this fast-paced story." —*ALA Booklist*

"Readers fond of lightweight mysteries solved by spunky heroines will take to this fiction debut, though a heavy ballast of tragedy and near-tragedy keeps it low to the ground. Some of the dialogue and set pieces show a promising authorial gift for comedy. (Fiction. 10-12)"
—*Kirkus Reviews*

Learn more at www.TerriLynnMartin.com

Jamie Kangas struggles with turbulent emotions caused by the death of his father, who perished in a logging accident—an accident for which Jamie blames himself. While his mother works as cook in a logging camp, Jamie is run ragged as chore boy. The grinding dreariness fades when Jamie meets a Native American boy, Gray Feather, who carries a burden of his own. The two boys become close friends as they face the challenges of a harsh environment and prejudiced world. And as trees fall to the lumberjack's blade, Jamie hears the ghostly words of his father, warning of future catastrophe.

The Home Wind is a middle-grade children's novel (ages 9 and up), which takes place during the 1870s in a Michigan logging camp. Quality paperback, 198 pages plus discussion guide.

"*The Home Wind* is a beautiful novel for both middle grade readers and a wonderful a read for adults, too. Steeped in carefully researched historical events in Michigan's Upper Peninsula, *The Home Wind* is a delight. Martin's characters captured my heart and made the story come alive--two boys struggling to understand the world around them. This is also an important book for anyone interested in the history of Michigan's logging industry and in the Native peoples of Michigan. I highly recommend *The Home Wind*, and if you are looking for a gift for your middle reader, it's perfect!"

—Sue Harrison, author of *The Midwife's Touch*

"Martin's descriptions of the scenes and action make a reader feel as if they are right there in the middle of it all. Readers can't miss the symbolism found throughout the book and a wonderful way to learn about the past at the same time. This book should go far, and not just with young audiences."

—Deborah K. Frontiera, *U.P. Book Review*

Learn more at www.TerriLynnMartin.com